Best of the Best:

2024 Literary Review

Best of the Best:
2024 Literary Review

California Writers Club

Best of the Best: 2024 Literary Review
compiled by:
California Writers Club, High Desert Branch

ISBN: 978-1-7356372-3-5

Library of Congress Control Number: 2024911622

COPY EDIT: Elisabeth Tuck

BOOK DESIGN: Jenny Margotta, High Desert Branch

BRANCH DIVIDER GRAPHICS: Joyce Krieg

ORIGINAL WATERCOLOR COVER ART: (Morro Bay, CA)
Richard Zone, High Desert Branch

PRINTED IN THE UNITED STATES
PRINT DATE: 7-30-2024

DEDICATION

Robert Douglas Isbill

August 6, 1934 – June 21, 2024

This book is dedicated to the memory of our dear friend, Bob Isbill.

Bob was a unstoppable force, a whirlwind of vision, dedication, and energy. He was an incredibly devoted husband and friend, and in many ways, the heart and soul of our club.

We will all miss him.

TABLE OF CONTENTS

THE CALIFORNIA WRITERS CLUB STORY

The California Writers Club is a 501(c)(3) educational nonprofit corporation founded in 1909 out of the lively literary scene in San Francisco's East Bay region that flourished in the first decade of the 20th century. The CWC incorporated in 1913 and has held meetings for over 100 years.

Today, the CWC has nearly 2,000 members in 22 branches throughout the state and remains one of the oldest organizations for writers in continuous operation in the nation.

The CWC's mission is to educate members and the public in the craft and business of writing and opens membership to writers of all interests, levels, and genres. Our website, calwriters.org, has specific information about membership and links to the individual branches.

2023-2024 OFFICERS

President – Roger Lubeck, Redwood Writers
Vice-President – Geri Spieler, SF-Peninsula
Secretary – Elisabeth Tuck, Mt. Diablo
Treasurer – Constance Hanstedt, Tri-Valley Writers
Member at Large – Sandy Moffett, Writers of Kern

PRESIDENT'S NOTE

The *Literary Review* was instituted as a way to recognize the best writing from our members. In the *Best of the Best: 2024 Literary Review* we have a strong sample of the best writing from our members. These stories and poems were chosen at the branch level. Some pieces have already appeared in other publications many are original unpublished works. For example, Linda Stamps' memoir "Ashes to Ashes" comes from the Redwood Writers Anthology *Sunset Sunrise*. I believe that a such powerful story like Linda's deserve to be read over and over. Much of the poetry was new to me. For example, Sally Carter's "Finding the Littoral" struck a chord in me. As did Lenore Hirsch's "January Rain" and Jordan Bernal's "Writing at Zero Dark Thirty." From the opening poem by Joan Goodreau, the novel excerpt by Ginny Rorby, and the two closing stories by Kevin Corfield and Mary Camarillo, I believe you will find this edition of the CWC *Literary Review* a joy to read and share.

Finally, I want to add my thanks to Mike Apodaca, Jenny Margotta, Elisabeth Tuck, Joyce Krieg, Richard Zone, and all the others in our branches who made this 2024 *Literary Review* possible.

INTRODUCTION

I was born and raised in California. I cherish its geographic diversity. California seems to have an unending array of eye-pleasing geographic wonders. In one day I can body surf at the beach, hike amidst towering pines in the mountains, and enjoy a breathtaking sunset in the desert. It's also a fun state to fly over. From your small, oval window you observe cities, mountains, and the patchwork of farms filling our central plains.

California has a unique history. It began with Native Americans forming tribes throughout the state, adjusting their lives to each of its biomes. Then the Spaniards came up from Mexico and staked out ranchos, some stretching hundreds of miles. Afterwards, the white folks came, homesteading on the Spanish land, and, ultimately declaring this territory the forty-eighth state of the United States of America. And it wasn't long before people were declaring, "There's gold in them thar hills!" A terrific book beautifully illustrating the clash of cultures in early California is *Ramona*, by Helen Hunt Jackson. (You can also see the story reenacted annually at the Ramona Festival in Hemet, California).

California has been a magnet for immigration. From the Chinese who came to build the railroads to the many foreign students who seek out California for its excellent universities, California is a perfect illustration of what America was created to be, and what it is becoming.

Being raised in California, I never saw race, politics, or religion as a barrier to warm relationships. Rather, differences always made people more interesting, just like the multiple California landscapes. I've always had friends of different races, religions, political parties, and sexual persuasions. I cut my teeth on debates with people with different views and lifestyles from my own. Showing respect and appreciating differences while holding firm to your own beliefs makes life fascinating.

You have before you a book produced with the many flavors of California. There are offerings here from young and less young, from every shade of color and belief. Submissions came from all parts of the state. The California Writers Club has 22 branches spread throughout the state from north to south.

This is a uniquely California book. There are multiple genres, as each writer must choose the best way to express themselves.

So welcome to the best of the California Writers Club for 2024. May you enjoy its many varied flavors.

~~Mike Apodaca, President
High Desert Branch
California Writers Club

◊ ◊ ◊

You turn the pages of the book,
sip your coffee quietly, duet
you love. Whatever else our reading means,
it's this: a body balanced, mind refreshed;
    voices rising from the page,
    close companions as we age.

Kate Adams

San Francisco Peninsula
2023

NORTH STATE

"Today Decides Tomorrow."
—*Motto of Chico State University*

North State Writers

Photos on the Wall

Joan Goodreau
North State Writers

Pressed together between
the glass and picture frames
we brothers keep ourselves
in memory.

Side by side
in front of our house that held us
we stand together stiff and still.

A foot apart
in front of Grandpa's grave
we look our separate ways
into the distance.

My arm around you
we sit in matching jackets
with tight grins on the couch
battered from our years of
bouncing up and down.

Now when we see each other
I call your name and
ask you who am I and
you exhale my name in
soft breaths back to me.

In the spaces from each other
that speed by, he does not forget
because we are sealed in frames of time
held deep in each other's mind.

Joan Goodreau's recent books are *Strangers Together: How My Son's Autism Changed My Life, Another Secret Shared,* and *Where to Next?* Her latest reading of her poems from her interviews with families of autistic children, *Covid Cloud,* is now on YouTube. Her plays have been produced in Northern California theaters. A Pushcart nominee and Hedgebrook Residency Alumna, Joan Goodreau has published numerous poems, articles, and short stories in anthologies, journals, and reviews. Her experience as a teacher, Program Specialist and parent has given her insight into the challenges of families with children on the autism spectrum.

MENDOCINO

"Talk to me of Mendocino."
—*Kate & Anna McGarrigle*

Excerpt from the novel[1]

A Following Sea

Ginny Rorby
Writers of Mendocino Coast

1

Daniel

March 2012

At school on Friday, after the final, loud bell stops ringing, I take my fingers out of my ears and dash to get my bike. I walk it past the row of cars where mothers, and a few fathers, wait to pick up their kids. My mother works and can't come for me, and my dad's gone. Gone for good.

I stay close to the cars because it's safer. Kids, except for Todd, don't pick on me in front of adults. If I don't run out of cars, I can get all the way to Little Lake, the main road into town, without being called names, or knocked down and having my bike snatched.

I hear laughter and glance around to see Todd running to catch up. He's in eighth grade with me, but is two inches shorter, but fifty pounds heavier. He skips sideways along the walk parallel to me, flapping his arms and cawing. He's already breathing too hard to run any faster. I steer between two cars, jump on my bike, and pedal toward the road. He laughs when I look back and gives me his middle finger.

My name is Daniel Scully. I like animals better than people. I like being alone. I like having a routine. Every day after school, I ride my bike across Highway One, through the village of Mendocino, and down the long steep hill to the ocean. There's not much traffic on Little Lake, but Highway One has lots of cars and trucks with really loud engines. I stand at the crosswalk with my fingers in my ears until the light changes.

According to the three-and-a-half-ounce piece of junk of a

---

[1] Previously published in the 2024 Writers of the Mendocino Coast Anthology, *Transitions*.

watch my father sent me for Christmas, it's 3:14 and I'm crossing Lansing, the main north-south street through town, when the fire station siren goes off.

No. No. I don't like that. Loud noises feel like electricity through my head. The sound starts low but will get really loud before it goes down then up again three more times. I stop my bike and start to rock with my eyes squeezed shut. Before it reaches its first high pitch, I cover my ears with my arms crossed over my head, and groan. Next will come the honking, and the rolling scream of the fire engine leaving the station. Before my head explodes, I push off and race my bike down the hill.

Three cars are parked with their bumpers against the huge logs meant to keep cars from rolling off the cliff into the ocean. I'm concentrating on escaping the noise and don't see the high school boys sitting on the ground with their backs against the logs. They hang out here to drink beer and smoke pot. Troy, Todd's brother, hears my brakes squeal, stands up, and hollers, "Look who's here—Assbooger."

He's short, fat, and mean like Todd.

I turn my bike around.

"Hey, Assbooger, kiss this." Troy unzips his pants, turns, drops his jeans, and wiggles his bare butt.

He's done it before. When I told Mom, she said someone did that to her once. She told him that he had the fattest, whitest ass she'd ever seen, and asked why he showed it to anybody. I thought that was good, so I wrote it down and practiced it, but I don't think I should say *ass*.

I shout over my shoulder, "That's the fattest, whitest butt I've ever seen, Troy. Why would you show it to anybody?"

"The retard's right," one of his friends says, and they laugh.

"Hey, Assbooger, catch this." Troy throws his beer bottle at me.

I'm riding away as fast as I can and it misses. I glance back and nearly tip over as it shatters in a spray of brown glass and foam on the road a few feet behind me.

The road makes a loop back to Lansing, so I don't have to ride past them to get home. I know because there are maps in the front of our phone book, not because I've ever ridden all the way around before. I like to go the same way every day.

Ahead, where the road curves back up to Lansing, I see a light flash on the next point of land to the north. It's the Point Cabrillo Lighthouse. I went there with my fifth-grade class when we still lived in Fort Bragg. I remember wishing I lived there in some olden time. I didn't know it was this close.

I straddled my bike, put my hand up under my sweater, and begin to pat my stomach. I see the light flash again and count, "One-one thousand. Two-one thousand. Three-one thousand." The light flashes before I get to six. I start again. Nine seconds between flashes. I like knowing stuff like that.

Behind me, I see Troy and his buddies getting into one of the cars. Heart pounding, I pull my hand out from under my sweater and pedal my bike toward a dense stand of cypress trees. Hidden by those trees is a public bathroom. I ride to it, roll my bike into the Men's side, and lock the door. A minute later I heard their loud muffler. They slow and Troy shouts, "Where'd you go, Assbooger?" They all laugh, gun the engine, and drive away. I wait until I hear them leave the stop sign on the corner and turn right onto Lansing, headed back into town. To get home, I have to ride that way. I don't want to run into them again. I look at my watch. Three-thirty-seven. Plenty of time to ride to the lighthouse and still get home before Mom does.

◊ ◊ ◊

The sign on the fence says the Light Station is open from sunrise to sunset, but there's no gate or anything to keep people out. I remember from my trip here in the fifth grade that the lighthouse is only one part of the Light Station. There are three lightkeepers' cottages: a head keeper's and two assistant houses. One was restored and is a museum with old-fashioned furniture and kitchen appliances. There are three old garages where they used to store coal. The one behind the museum has bathrooms for visitors.

I ride through the opening in the fence and stop to read the sign in the parking lot listing all the things I'm not allowed to do while I'm here. The sign is confusing and the list is so long I get mixed up. The therapist I had before Dad left and Mom couldn't afford her anymore, showed me how to hold my hand across my eyes and look through the crack between my fingers at one line at a time. That helps.

While I'm reading the *Don'ts*, a car pulls into the parking lot. A man gets out.

My stomach knots. I look away when he nods at me. He takes the walkway to the bathroom that's been added to the side of the old Pine Grove farmhouse, which has been restored and looks brand new.

I steer my bike out of the parking lot through hedges onto the paved road. There's a long steep hill before the road flattens out. The eastern-most lightkeeper's house blocks my view of the lighthouse itself. I glance back at the farmhouse and see the man get back in his car. He starts his engine, revs it, and squeals out of the parking space. The Dos and Don'ts sign said no cars Beyond this Point, but he may not be a law-abiding citizen. I watch from behind one of the bushes and am relieved when he drives out of the parking lot and turns south on Point Cabrillo Drive.

For a moment, I stand at the top of hill before launching myself down the steep incline. I watch the speedometer climb to 22.5 mph. I tilt my chin up and laugh out loud, which is not at all like me.

I'm nearly at the bottom of the hill when I sail through a soupy layer of air. For a second my vision blurs like it did the time I tried on Mom's reading glasses, then I feel a bump and realize the pavement ended. From here to the houses the road is crushed shells and gravel. It was paved all the way three years ago. Maybe they spent so much money fixing up the farmhouse and adding bathrooms, they couldn't afford to repave it.

It's warmer, too. At the top of the hill, it was windy and the ocean was deep blue with whitecaps. Now it's calm with a cloud layer on the horizon. From the top to the bottom of the hill feels like whole different day. A whole different scene. I see a water tower with a windmill across the road from the first house, and beyond that, another building that looks like a barn. Mendocino has lots of old water towers, but none still have their windmills to pump the water up to the storage tank. Most have been turned into places for tourists to sleep.

I have an excellent memory. Neither of those two buildings were here before. They must have been doing a lot of construction in the last three years, fixing up it to look like it did when it was a real, working Light Station. I like it, but they really need to fill the potholes in the road. I'm afraid I'm going to hit one and be pitched off into the ditch. Mom says better to be safe than sorry, so I get off and walk my bike the rest of the way to where the road dog-legs left, turns right, and runs straight to the lighthouse.

Dog-leg is a golfing term. My father tried to teach me to play golf. He thought something less athletic than soccer, football, or baseball would be easier for me to learn. He only took me once. I'm not good at any sports, even ones like golf where you mostly stand still, except when you are walking around looking for your ball.

The lighthouse resembles a little church if you count the lantern room as the steeple. I'm disappointed. A curtain blocks my view of the lens from the road. Seems strange that I could see it flash from Mendocino but can't from this side.

Opposite the first house, the windmill blades clack and bang. I don't like that noise.

The first house is the museum and was restored to 1934—the year electricity came to the Light Station. I'd like to have been alive then, except I'd miss my computer. I think people were nicer in the olden days, like my grandmother. She was always patient and didn't mind when I did obsessive stuff, like making sure all her bridge cards were in numerical order. Both decks. All eight kings together, all the queens, etcetera. I like the word etcetera.

I chain my bike to the gate in the white picket fence and go up the front steps of the first house. The door is locked. There's no sign listing their visiting hours. It's 4:02. Maybe they close at four. I walk around to the back. There is an axe sharpener on the deck. It looks like a rusty stationary bike. I sit on it and try the pedals, which turn the big gritty wheel. Attached to it is a cup for water to keep the blades from sparking. My grandmother had one in her garage. I used to pretend it was a bicycle when I was trying to learn to ride.

I get off, walk over to back door, press my forehead to the wood, and close my eyes. I put my hands against the wood, which feels warm even though the day is cold. There are no rough spots or bubbles in the paint.

I hear a sound, and look up. A curtain flutters out a small upstairs window. I go down the steps, gaze up, and see it get sucked back in like what happens when a door opens, changing the pressure in a room. Someone's up there for me to ask why the curtain is closed in the lantern room. I try the door. It's unlocked. I open it and peek inside. There are twin washtubs on the porch with a hand-crank wringer to squeeze the water out of the clothes. The shelf above holds a box of Lux laundry soap, and something called bluing.

The kitchen is on my left. There's a wood-burning stove, and by the sink are utensils, an open recipe book, and a mixing bowl, like someone's getting ready to cook. I imagine I smell bacon.

I tiptoe through the kitchen to the dining room. On the mantel above the fireplace, beside an old clock, are two pictures in old-fashioned frames. One is of a pretty blonde girl. She's got a huge, silly-looking ribbon in her hair. Another is the same girl standing on the front porch with her family: a mom, a dad, and a brother. Her dad is standing behind her with his hands on her shoulders. They look nice even though they aren't smiling.

I'm not usually interested in faces. Their expressions are hard to read. I look at a nose or an ear or a forehead, but not the whole face. This girl is different and not just because she's pretty. The girls at my school wear too much makeup and their faces confuse me. I can't tell smiles from sneers. This girl's face looks kind, like pictures of my grandmother when she was my age.

I take down the one of the girl by herself. In it, she's sitting in the same rocking chair that's now by the front window, instead of to the right of the fireplace like in the photo. I go and sit in the chair.

This would be a good place for me to live. The house is neat, clean, and orderly. I close my eyes and imagine myself here when this picture was taken. I start to rock, and am rocking pretty fast when I feel a draft of cold air, like a door's been opened.

Go away. I squeeze my eyes shut and rock faster.

I don't hear anyone come in, and when I open my eyes, the room is still empty. A moment later, I think I hear footsteps of someone walking around upstairs. I don't want whoever it is to come down and find me touching stuff. I get up and put the picture back on the mantel.

A short hall connects the dining room to the living room. I stop first to look out onto the front porch. The coat rack in the corner by the door has a pair of paint-stained overalls hanging on one hook and a raincoat on another. There's a puddle on the floor beneath the raincoat as if someone hung it up wet not long ago. I wonder how they made that puddle look so real.

There's an old, black Remington typewriter on the desk next to a pair of binoculars, a sextant, and a little telescope. I'd love to have a sextant to measure longitude and how high a star is above the horizon. I put my head against the window glass and imagine what it must have been like to be a lightkeeper back then.

There's a huge record player in the living room. It's as tall as a jukebox, but narrow. It has a handle you turn to make the record go round. I look in the back for a plug, but there isn't one. Inside the cabinet are big records like my grandmother had of boring old-timey music. Across the room, by the fireplace, a book has slipped off the chair and lies open on the floor. There's a pipe on the table beside the chair. I pick it up and sniff the bowl. It smells nice, like cherries. The book is a Nancy Drew mystery, *The Sign of the Twisted Candles*. I close it and put it next to the pipe.

An old-fashioned phone is mounted on the wall by the stairs. It has a handle you have to crank, maybe to get an operator's attention. The part you speak into is sticking out of the wooden body. The part you have to hold to your ear has a cord and hangs in a cradle on the side. I pick it up to see if I can hear a dial-tone, and turn the handle. It makes a sound like bells ringing, then a woman's voice says, "Good morning." Startled, I drop the receiver. It swings and hits the wall with a loud whack. I should run. If someone's upstairs this will make them mad. They might throw me out and never allow me back. I grab the receiver and try to hang it up, miss, and have to try again.

I dodge into the living room and lean against the wall to catch my breath. The floor above my head creaks. I close my eyes and wait for someone to shout at me, or at least come down to see what's going on. Nothing happens, so I lean around and glance up the stairs. The girl from the photograph is looking down at me. She's a little older than in that picture, and she isn't wearing that ugly ribbon.

Ginny Rorby is the author of six MG/YA novels: *How to Speak Dolphin; Lost in the River of Grass;* 2013 winner of the Sunshine State Young Readers Award, *Hurt Go Happy*; 2008 winner of the Schneider Family Book Award, *The Outside of a Horse; Dolphin Sky;* and *Freeing Finch 2019. Freeing Finch* is the inspiring story of a transgender girl and a stray dog who overcome adversity to find love and a place to belong. *Like Dust, I Rise* (Dec 2021) is a coming-of-age novel set in Dalhart, Texas, the epicenter of the Dust Bowl. Her novel, *Girl Under Glass,* will be published in May 2024.

Coming to Dust[2]

Maureen Eppstein
Writers of the Mendocino Coast

Paintings of yellow leaves hang
on a wall of the artist's studio
where the poet reads.
Fragments of fallen leaves found
in the woods around the house
and wound with fine wire
flower into sculptural forms
that tremble on another wall.

Perched on a stool,
the poet looks as if the wind
could catch and toss her until
she folds in on herself
like the Japanese maple leaf she keeps
for company at her desk. Her poems
are full of the falling of leaves
and the silences that build
into big questions.

Outside the room a silver
sheen to the darkening day
foreshadows fog tomorrow,
when the poet will pack and go
and the leaves so lovingly gathered
will crack and crumble into a dust
that sifts unseen over notebooks
fertilizing her words.

---

[2] Previously published in the 2024 Writers of the Mendocino Coast Anthology, *Transitions*.

Maureen Eppstein's most recent poetry collection is *Horizon Line* (Main Street Rag 2020). Finishing Line Press published her chapbook *Earthward* in 2014, and will publish a new chapbook, *Daughter,* in 2024. Her work has appeared in numerous journals and anthologies, including *Fire and Rain: Ecopoetry of California* (Scarlet Tanager Books, 2018), and has been nominated for a Pushcart Prize.

Crossing the boundary between the arts and the sciences, her poems have been included in a textbook on geometric modeling, a university geology course, and a National Audubon Society report. A former executive director of the Mendocino Coast Writers Conference, she has run a poetry reading series in the Bay Area and taught poetry at the college level. Originally from Aotearoa, New Zealand, she lives in Mendocino, California.

Finding the Littoral[3]

Sally Carter
Writers of the Mendocino Coast

I was coughed out of the Rust Belt
Like a frazzled hairball
From a childhood swum along a river
That would catch fire
The yellowed chemical smell of
Burning rubber etched in memories
Alongside temperate forests
Glowing autumns
Frigid frost patterns on the corners
Of my heart.

Spit out onto the highways an
Internal magneto drove me west
In a one way migration
Gassing out before hitting
The trifecta of tectonic plates
I languished in the inertia of self-doubt
Forged in soils from a crucible of wildfires
And chemical agriculture deep
In the great California valley
Lulled by mountain creeks trickling
Ever westward still
to the sea.

To finally arrive-
Silver haired and traumatized
Brittle but not broke
To the edge
Where the giant trees grow
Ferns and fungi unfurling
primeval spores

[3] Previously published in the 2024 Writers of the Mendocino Coast Anthology, *Transitions*

Oceanic breeze and mist caress
This shelf of broke off land as if
It's too special to let it go.

My spirit becomes Of incinerated ethereal
Lungs cough out the dregs
Of incinerated lives
And slowly deepen in
Maritime swells and forest oxygen,
A green tinge lightens my eyes
My spine clatters over vertebra by vertebra
As my gnarled fingers sink into this sweet earth and ask permission
To finally grow
Home.

Sally Carter is a newly published author and artist who currently resides in Fort Bragg, California. She was raised in Northeast Ohio and attended Kent State University as an English major but graduated from California State University Chico with a Bachelor of Science. Her love of nature and the outdoors figures prominently in both her visual and written creative works.

Blue Women[4]

Sallie Reynolds
Writers of the Mendocino Coast

Crack! Thunder shudders the walls of Azalee's little house, doors and windows rattle. Rain thrums on the roof and soaks the curtains before I can get the window shut.

"Azalee?"

Her bed is empty. She used to crawl under it during storms, but now her old knees won't let her.

In the dining room, an oil lamp spreads a yellow pool of light on the tabletop. Azalee has unplugged everything electrical, drawn the blinds, sits in her flannel nightgown, clutching—a pistol? "Az, what on earth are you doing with that thing?"

Her face is a mask. Hair, ink-black with dye and shining with oil, fans out behind her head like a feather crown. *"Baad folks*, Sugar. Sneaking in, steal you blind. I heard 'em over the storm." She says "stawm." What she calls her hokum talk deepens when she's afraid.

Another thunder roll swallows us. *"Hear that?"*

The rain hammers, the wind is a giant heart—thu-thud.

What is there to steal? Azalee's house is a museum of the tattered. Though the worthless objects have a kind of beauty, "good sides" facing you, chipped sides to the wall. And every one, she says, has two spirits, one from the maker, one from the person who couldn't love it broken. You've heard people say, "Oh, I can't bear to look at that thing another second." Well, Azalee will love it.

"Old man Thompson just now died, Sugar. Kids wrecking his place, scared him to death."

"Who did?"

"Kids crawling back from Yankeeland—Doodey and Stickpin and them, running wild." Doodey is her own nephew. Stickpin got his name from stabbing his brother with a nail.

"Nobody want 'em here, not even their own mamas. I feel sorry for 'em—give 'em food, offer 'em little jobs. But nothing stop 'em from stealing."

---

[4] Previously published in the 2024 Writers of the Mendocino Coast Anthology, *Transitions*.

Or scrabbling for some scrap of control over their lives, I bet. I felt like that when my parents uprooted me and moved us away. *Oh, you're a big girl, Willis.* (I was eleven.) *You don't need looking-after anymore. We let Azalee go.* And Azalee slipped right out of my hands—smash onto the floor.

When I was about a month old, Mother let me go, too. *Here, Azalee, take her.* And while Mother swam in the bourbon bottle and played Canasta with her lady-friends, I had Az's warmth and order. Eleven whole years.

Children blame themselves for everything, you know. They think they have to make up for all wounds—sacrifice something to the All-Powerful. When I heard we were leaving, I cried, and Daddy gave me a glass horse. A bribe, a be-good-don't-make-a-fuss horse. He had blue shimmering wings, he rode the wind right over me. *You'll have a real horse, at the new house,* Daddy said, and slipped that lie right past me on a tale of glass as miracle, half-liquid, half-solid, slowly flowing like a glacier. He was a doctor, I believed him, and for a minute, I wanted to rush to the new life and the beautiful real horse. The glass one I abandoned in a kitchen cabinet in the old house, kissing his nose for forgiveness.

Now here he is on Azalee's treasure shelf. If you hold him up, the lamplight pours through, like opening your eyes under water. Hooves dance in the air, icy mane ripples. He's perfect except for one little chip on his wing.

The sky flashes. Thunder rocks the walls. Rain sizzles on the window—a blank eye, dark, dark, dark—tears streaking down. Azalee and I stare at each other, hearts bitten through.

When I was four, she taught me how to survive the night. Before she left to go home, she'd hide a "promise" under my bed. If I got frightened, I was to turn on my little flashlight and hunt for it. A pink candy heart, with "love" in purple ink, or a heart scissored out of red paper. I'd stick my head over the edge and shine the light underneath. There it was! In that tight circle, with the magic heart, I was safe.

The house shudders and something outside goes smash. Azalee grips the pistol and I set the horse down so I won't snap a delicate leg. If ever-flowing glass is going to mend itself, it'll need more than my lifetime.

"Lawd! Something blow down on the roof." she mutters.

Bang bang!

"Az, that's somebody *knocking*. What time is it?"

We both turn to look at the clock. The little hand is on the 3.

Azalee slides her pistol under her napkin, balls up her fists in her lap.

In the yellow porch light, a wavery ogre peers through the glass panel. Azalee's house is built all in a line "shotgun" style, so anyone, like this huge male blob, can shoot one blast at the front and kill everybody. I flick on the hall light. A fat, White man, water cascading off his hat onto his uniform, lifts a fist to pound again. In his other hand, sure enough—a pistol.

"It's the Sheriff!" I say it loud enough for Az to hear. "Better come inside, Mr. Hodgkiss, before you drown. I do hope you're not thinking to fire upon us."

He steps in, holstering his gun. "You aw-right, Miz Willis? Got a call 'bout some prowlers."

He says "prar-lers." Was that what we heard? *Prar-lers?*

We're cooked if he sees her pistol. I sandwich myself mid-hall, trapping him in the doorway. "We haven't seen a soul, but there were noises outside. You're welcome to look around out there." Where the wind will blow the rain right up your snotty nose!

He's sneaking side glances at us, making me blush for my old rat-fur bathrobe and filthy feet, Azalee's patched nightgown. Two helpless women in a wet pig of a night.

My face goes hot. "You really think somebody's after *us?"* Oh, way too loud! "You're going to *shoot* them?" Azalee swears my temper is going to be the death of me one day.

He stares. "Miz Willis, we git a complaint, we got to . . ."

"Why are you talking to me? This's Miz Azalee Neal's house." His eyes glide right over her. "Is this so-called prowler armed? Who called you?"

The neighbors wouldn't, not if they were dying. He comes down to the Bottom and hauls people off to jail, doesn't matter who they are or what they've done. Az told me he found a rifle in somebody's house one time, and he shot the man. For *possession!*

But I didn't dream he'd come while I was here.

Prowler? And stepping in this house with his gun drawn?

I know who called him! The other day Miss Winnie Williams, my old second-grade teacher, stopped me on Main Street—eighty if she's a day, over-starched and filled with the hot breath of the Lawd. *We know how you feel about your Azalee, Willis*—that ugly Uptown voice—*but you don't belong down there.* Day-un-they-ah. She had snooted right past Az and me earlier, didn't even glance up.

"Goodness, Mr. Hodgkiss," I put on my alligator smile, "as you can see, we're fine—do reassure Miss Winnie. Just now, though, something came down on the roof. Would you care to check the attic?" I point at the trap-door, the pull-chain dangling right over him. I can just see him trying to get all his fat through that little hole!

He backs out onto the porch, belts and holsters creaking. He's dripped a puddle in the hall, too. "I'll be watchin'," he growls.

"Aren't you going to check the yard?"

He tramps down the porch steps. Next minute, his patrol lights are flashing, engine revving over the wind. He hits his siren and peels away, rooster-tailing waves of rainwater.

Three in the morning!

At the table, Azalee and I hold hands. The storm has locked Hodgkiss out and locked us in.

Lead, lead, lead in my heart—why on earth did I poke the snake? Trouble enough, just my staying with Az. Maybe I shouldn't come anymore. Or stay at the motel. Or not walk on Main Street. Or hide my car in the shed. I keep begging Azalee to come to New York, even just to visit. But she won't. *"Watching us!"*

"Troublemaker, Sugar. Him and his brother—the Hawgkiss boys. Mistah Lance come by to put in my hot-water heater, picked up my big brass candlestick, walked out with it, big as life."

The Hawg-kiss boys!

Don't even ask if she reported it.

If I'd been here, would he have taken her candlestick? What if I went to the mayor to complain about tonight's incident—stepping in here, gun drawn?

Oh, but *prowlers . . .*

God. That bastard loved every minute of our fear.

She's got her pistol out again. Not a roscoe like his, but no cheap bosom-gun, either.

Hell, a White *child* in this place can have a gun, but not Azalee, an old Black woman living alone. After we moved, our new neighbor, nice old veteran with one leg, taught me about guns. I was twelve. He said, "*If you need to shoot, girlie, shoot to kill. Drag the body all the way in the house. It's Virgin-ya law. If he's* in *the house, you're* in *your rights.*"

Oh that worthless Hawgkiss—lard-belly straining his shirt buttons. He could smash down the door—openly—nobody in this town would say beans. And Az, whipping out her pistol? *Ka-pow!* Over he goes. Caught inside, his gun cocked.

But he could half-kill her, and still I'd have to drive down here, wrestle the body into the car, dump him somewhere on the Jersey Turnpike. Mob style.

Listen to me! Knee deep in the hate pit.

Azalee's face is drawn and shiny. She looks just like Eddie. Eddie—her son, her precious boy—who died before he was 30. She used to say, "I get old, Eddie look after me."

I slip into the kitchen and light the gas under the pots on the stove.

What if I have to stop coming? Or change what we do? There's nobody else to help her. I get her to the doctor, balance her checkbook, take her shopping.

"Don't turn on a light, Sugar, else you call the storm down on us."

"I know. Just heating up the stew."

Oh! Another crash, yard and sky flicker like neon lights.

"That the Blue Woman coming," Az growls. She means her great-great-grandmother—the magic witch-woman from Africa. The first Blue Woman. More powerful than any Blue Pegasus. The Blue Woman, she says, got hit by lightning, skin burnt black, hair fried, nipples charred to black buttons. *But Sugar, didn't she grab that bolt in 'er bare hand, throw it right back up in the sky!*

"All our soft parts turn solid," she says now. "Us Blue Women just get up and go on."

Why blue? I asked one time, and she said how we—all of us—carry on all the time about color. White, black, brown, red, yellow. Green, for envy. *Blue Women gotta reach for the sky.*

The kettle sings. There's a whiff of propane and the Azalee mix of fatback, Clorox, sweet bath powder. I put a cup of coffee under her nose, sugared to death and bitter with chicory.

We're listening, listening. Skin crawling up our blue backs. She uses her free hand to pour coffee from cup to saucer. She used to do that for one of Mother's old dogs, a terrier named Rumpelstiltskin after the fairytale ogre who stole a human newborn. The mother had to guess his true name to get her baby back. Befuddled as my mother was, I used to think that maybe, deep down, this showed she was sorry for being drunk and mean. But really, she was only sorry for herself. And poor Rumpy didn't like any of us.

Whenever I'd mention an animal's emotions, Daddy would say, "*They don't feel things the way we do.*" Even if he'd just finished listing the similarities among us all: heart, lungs, four limbs, and so on. *They live harsh, unthinking lives.*

Once he used those exact words about Azalee. Her husband slashed her with a butcher knife and Daddy said those words: *harsh, unthinking lives.*

I'm ashamed how long it took me to really feel that lie.

When we moved, he gave his hunting dogs to good homes, got jobs for his secretary and nurse, but the woman who raised his child for eleven years, who was, as he and Mother said a million times, *almost a member of the family?* Dumped.

What would the Blue Woman do now?

Her gramama, another Blue Woman for sure, delivered Eddie and, 29 years later, helped bury him.

Fairytales. Magic shields. Saviors.

The wind is plucking us to bits. The wind is a herd of wild Hawgkiss. Sounds like a joke. Until you remember what they are.

Azalee pours her cold coffee back in the cup, sips, presses a finger to that spot in the middle of her chest. All her dresses have smudges there. *No,* she says, *not a pain.* The doctor keeps saying her heart is fine. But soothing words and a smudged dress can't conquer fear.

"Them folks," Az says, "soon as you get old, they set you out to die."

And that, *that* is worst of her nightcrawlers, the ax over her old head.

Az, nobody's going to put you out to die. I promise. It's on the tip of my tongue. But I'm not superhuman, and I'm nowhere near as good a liar as Daddy.

The leftovers are ready. Rich peppery stew, cornpones. The stew is best on the second or third day, but the pones dry out. Azalee covers her pistol with a napkin, breaks her pone into her stew. She cooks all our old favorites. Every dish, like one of her cherished objects, has a story, a good sauce. Some from her African great-great, that first Blue Woman. Tonight's stew, made with "wild meat," from the Indian one, born down on the Dan River.

The wind drops. Now we hear a rustling. Is Hawgkiss back? I slip over to the window, peek around the blind. There's a shadow, out of rhythm with the wind, moving between the alley and Azalee's old shed. Under the light on the back door, I see the garbage cans, all on their sides, guts spilling out.

Plink, zing, thud!

"Hah!" says Azalee. *"Hail."* She straightens, calmly bites into a stew-soaked pone, slurps warmth and spices from her spoon.

Now I'm the one holding the fear-bag.

"Az, what would be some *real* protection?"

"Honey, *pro-teck-shun* means right-here-right-now. My man, he cut me, but he didn't kill me. I got me my pistol next day."

The hail suddenly stops.

The clock goes click-click. One hour since Hawgkiss left.

"Eddie showed me how to shoot, down at the river," Az says. "Gave me this gun. Say he'll come back, look out for me." She laughs. "Honey, one time that bitch from the Bluejay Bar, you know the one, try to knock me to the wall. I pull out this gun, she scuttle off like a scalded cat."

Another little piece of her life—pearls strung one by one, on a string. Now she's the oyster, alone in her age, grit in her heart.

"You check my So-sa Se-cur-ity?"

Money. High up on her list. For 30 years of vital work, cooking and raising children, the government gives her a pittance. She's a brilliant cook—she could be a chef in a restaurant up where I live, old as she is. But she'll never leave. She barely ekes by catering for parties. I tried to have her payments increased or attached to her husband's account, but she doesn't have proof of marriage, no record of most of her work. And I can't offer her money without making her mad.

The house judders. The storm has circled behind us, picked up new things to rattle.

"Lord, Azalee, the roof!"

She pats my arm. "No hole up there, honey. I just now had the tin tarred and painted. Solid as the walls of Jericho."

The ones that came down in a blast of trumpets.

Az's finger is at her chest again. "Long time, I ain't had much work. This house is my *real* se-cur-ity."

That's another thing she gets me to check—the deed to the house, in her bank box. She has to see it, hold it in her hand, once a year. "Clifford," her husband the slasher, "he worked at that car dealership uptown. He bought this place." Then cut her to pieces and run off.

Everybody leaves everybody. When my parents took me away from here, I longed for her. Endless Sundays, Mother and Daddy hissing and drinking, smashing things. Me, hiding outdoors, up a tree. At 16 I shocked even myself, cutting out for good. Leaving everything. Azalee—I didn't write her or call. But I kept the Blue Woman in my heart.

"I never wanted to leave you." I'm not just talking about long ago. However much she needs me, it's hard, even dangerous to her, for me to stay.

Silence. No tap-tap of rain. No far-off growl. The storm is dead.

After a long minute, Azalee sighs and turns on the lights. She gets out a stack of cards—her "star readers." Royals from old decks. Whenever there's a problem, she arranges them in a cross, puts the Queen of Hearts in the middle, and turns over the others, one by one. She used to say, *Gotta cross the Blue Woman with real silver.* So I'd up-end my piggybank, wiggle a nail file in the slot till a dime fell out. Azalee would set it on that stern painted face. She never says what she sees. All I know is, the Queen of Spades is Death.

As Az flips her cards, I take the lid off a little pot on the sideboard, pick out a yellow button shaped like a duck. From a boy-baby's sunsuit. Then a tangle, a circle woven out of hair. "Azalee? Whose hair is this?"

"Eddie's. Gramama cut his first baby hair, make it in a bracelet to bind him to us—old folks' way."

Little fat infant wrist, tiny power-rope anchoring it.

Outside, the silence is wet and heavy. Small sounds come seeping in.

"Sugar, do me a favor."

"What?"

"Sign me a paper."

"A paper?"

"So nobody take my house."

Dear lord—she means a *legal* paper.

"Make it so everybody know they got to call you if I fall out, get sent to the hospital."

A medical power of attorney! Around here, when you get old and helpless, the County "assigns" a lawyer to you unless your family steps in. A lot of Azalee's folks have lost everything that way, house, savings—they wind up in a dirt-floor shack, alone and sick. Families gone or too poor to look out for them.

But—now I'll be here. Now I'll be *hers.*

"New lawyer up town, he know how to get around the problems."

A flush sweeps across the top of my head, my scalp pricks with sweat. "O-kay! Tomorrow first thing! Today, actually!"

Azalee gives a little "hah," gets up, brings over two glasses and a pint of Four Roses bourbon. We toast, clink!-clink! Little old walnut woman, carrying years of poverty, loneliness, hard work. No opportunities. A knifing. And me, a skinny peeled cucumber from the gardens of the enemy.

"That papah, Sugar! *Our* papah!"

The words skip across my brain, stones hopping on water, vanishing under the surface—Azalee's age and death open my brain and slip in.

I finish my whiskey, go to the kitchen window, raise the blind onto the night. Our paper. Little pink sugar heart under the bed. It could blow up in our faces. *You have no bidness down they-ah.* Or it could give weight to us, a kind of *definition.* Or it could do both. *Till death do us part.*

"Thank you, Sugar," Azalee says. "Thank you, too, Sweet Jesus." She bends forward—hands knotted. A sound escapes her. A slow sound, as if she's been holding her breath for a long time. Then she straightens, walks past me, outside into the dark.

Quick, I pick up the pistol, open the cylinder. No bullets. Has it been fired? I sniff the barrel. I wish I could throw it away. The enemy's weapon. Use it and die. Don't use it and die.

I set the gun back down, exactly the way she had it, follow her outside. My feet are instantly soaked and freezing.

The light from the kitchen door cuts stark silhouettes on the grass. Azalee is standing by her old picnic table, head cocked. Listening to the shadows. Bits of the setting moon, like balls of mercury, skitter through the branches of the elm tree, drip down into inky pools of rainwater. The earth exhales a sweet animal smell—a child's wet hair.

Tap-tap tap . . .

Something—some *one?* That bastard . . .

I stalk out toward the sound, those little flashes of light. Could be his cruiser! Why didn't I bring the pistol?

I move past her shed, into the alley.

Empty . . . or tail lights maybe, way down the hill.

What the hell am I *doing?* I don't think I actually yell, but my hands are shaking. In the shadows, I stumble smack into my car. A branch of Az's old willow tree is going tap-tap on the metal roof.

And that's it. Maybe. *This* time.

Azalee grips my arm, and pulls me back through the yard into the house. Is she *laughing?* She wipes her eyes with a Kleenex, hands me one. "Sugar, we the only ones now, you and me. The stars say, remember that."

Eddie and her gramama, her Blue Woman, are dead. Daddy died in his bed, didn't even leave a hole in the night. Mother? I pretended to be sick so I wouldn't have to go to her funeral.

But Azalee's death, the real prowler—tall, taller than I am, takes me into his cold steel arms.

Azalee pulls the blind back down. Puts the Star Cards in the drawer. Disappears the pistol.

She walks to the kitchen, turns the gas on under the kettle.

What a little everyday thing.

That's what we have now.

We have it as long as we have it.

Sallie Reynolds, eighty-five, lives back of beyond in Northern California with her painter-writer-mechanic husband, a grand dog, and two hawks. (She's a licensed falconer.) She has had to live a long time in order to become a decent, whole human being. Her stories are here and there; her two novels are available on Amazon.

SACRAMENTO

"Its true character remains the Valley character, its virtues the Valley virtues, its sadness the Valley sadness."
—*Joan Didion*

Sacramento

A Chance Encounter Near the Himalayas

Brina Patel
CWC Sacramento

". . . one has to wander through all the outer worlds to reach the innermost shrine at the end."

~ Rabindranath Tagore

August 31, 2016

Though not yet 10 a.m., the Zirakpur bus station had long come to life. Fellow patrons scurried along, scanning each of the rusty vehicles for the right ride. Others leisurely passed the time by sipping *chai* or scrolling through their phones.

I boarded my bus. Bounding up the steps, I took stock of my fellow travelers—largely families and couples who munched on finger foods or stared stoically out the scratched-up windows. My eyes scanned the rows of passengers, instinctually seeking someone with whom the 9-hour ride might seem slightly more bearable.

Near the front, a woman with shoulder-length black hair sat solemnly, her almond-shaped eyes fixated on a large brown book. She wore a black cardigan and indigo leggings, with a gray coat hanging on the seat behind her. Among those already inside the bus, she looked like the only person who might speak English. I approached her.

"Excuse me," I said, clearing my throat. "Is this seat taken?"

"No, no," she said with a slight Indian accent, smiling slightly as she shifted in her seat to give me space. "Please sit."

I squeezed in, putting my items below my seat. The woman continued reading. With East Asian features and skin slightly darker than mine, I wondered where she might be from. I considered starting a conversation and eventually asking, though after hearing the perplexed "Where are you from?" question countless times on this trip myself (my accented Hindi and western attire quickly gave me away), I decided against it.

I'd been in India nearly eight weeks now, on an indefinite gap year volunteering and backpacking trip that would ultimately last a little over nine months. The first few weeks had been a whirlwind of reunions and sightseeing, as my brother, two college friends, and I visited my family's ancestral village in Gujarat. We then traced India's Golden Triangle—New Delhi, Agra, and Jaipur, with a side trip to the holy city of Varanasi.

Upon my companions' departure, my solo journey began, first taking me to a volunteer project in the Rajasthani desert, and then onwards to the northern state of Punjab. I'd spent a few days in Chandigarh, considered one of the most orderly cities in India, and then Amritsar, home of the esteemed Golden Temple.

Due to a financial emergency, my journey unexpectedly took me to Zirakpur, close to Chandigarh. One of my aunt's relatives happened to live there with her husband, and they happily hosted me for the night. After many frantic calls back home, I resolved the money issue and had enough cash to carry me through the next several weeks. Sweet, sweet relief.

The kind auntie and uncle accompanied me to the nearest bus station in the morning, helping me find the right one to Manali, a high-altitude town in Punjab's neighboring Himachal Pradesh, where I'd be continuing onwards. We bid each other adieu, expressing as much as we could with the limited Hindi and English we had.

As I sat in my seat, a constant stream of emotions buzzed through my body. I felt overwhelming gratitude for all the kindness I'd experienced on the journey thus far. Like the Zirakpur couple, so many people I'd met extended unconditional care and took me in as their own. I realized that much of the messaging I'd previously encountered—which endlessly emphasized that the world was full of ill-intentioned individuals, waiting to pounce once you let your guard down—was immensely flawed.

However, despite having constantly been around people—it's unavoidable in a country with over 1.3 billion people—I felt lonely.

Many of the questions I'd encountered in the past year that had fueled my desire to delay entering the workforce—What career do you plan to pursue? When do you plan on settling down?—only echoed louder in my ears, almost to a deafening level. I needed space to think through it all, and to find someone who could relate.

◊ ◊ ◊

"I'm guessing this is your first time taking this trip?" my seatmate asked, breaking the silence between us. She set her book down.

"Yeah, it is," I said, taken by surprise. "How about you?"

"Oh, no," she said. "I'm a regular at this point. Probably take this route a couple times a month." She closed her book and sat back in her seat.

"I'm Suchita, by the way," she said, extending a hand. Shaking it, I introduced myself in return.

We spent the next couple of hours chatting, sharing our life stories, and discussing our interests—books, travel, dogs. Suchita was on her way home from Chandigarh, where she'd been wrapping up a work project. An accomplished architect, she lived with her family in Kalath, a small village not too far from Manali, a popular hub for those into adventure activities and Himalayan hikes. Suchita had completed her studies in New Delhi, and her line of work involved designing homes from mud.

Raised Buddhist, Suchita no longer identified with the religion, but mentioned how the faith influenced her affinity for the spiritual. At 28, she remained a clear outlier in her community. Her chosen lifestyle—unmarried, childfree, career-oriented—wasn't common among most Indian women her age.

Suchita frequently worked with impoverished populations, which played a major role in influencing her decisions. "It's saddening," she said. "I see so many of these women forced into marriage very young. Then they have kids they can barely care for and remain stuck in this cycle of poverty."

"That's why I don't plan on having kids," she continued. "And at this point, I'm not set on getting married, either. I've worked hard to build this life and I feel called to help other people break out of these generational patterns. There's a lot of untapped potential in India."

A mix of admiration and surprise gave way, as I hadn't ever encountered anyone—let alone a fellow South Asian woman—speak such statements aloud with unwavering confidence and conviction. I'd always believed marriage and children had to be a part of my own story; of every woman's story. *There was no other way, right?* And not only this, but like so many, I'd bought into the notion that these milestones had to happen at a particular time.

Suchita and I intermittently talked for the remainder of the ride.

As the hours ticked by, some of the heaviness within me

dissipated.

◊◊◊

The sun soon set, leaving orange hues in its wake before gradually blanketing the sky in complete darkness. Our bus emptied out as passengers exited at their respective cities and villages. I glanced at my phone to check the time. 8:00 p.m. *Had the ride really lasted that long?*

"My stop is coming up soon," Suchita said. "Please stay with me and my family tonight, and continue on to Manali tomorrow. It's getting quite late."

"Oh, that's so kind of you," I replied. "But it's okay, really, I'll be fine."

"No, don't be silly!" she said, waving her hand to emphasize her point. "I'd much rather you go to Manali during the day. It'll be easier to find your way around."

We went on like this for a little while, until Suchita convinced me to accept her invite. A mix of excitement and anxiety arose as I followed her off the bus when we reached Kalath. My legs, stiff from several hours of sitting, rejoiced at the prospect of movement.

The darkness washed over us, yet instead of inducing fear and trepidation, its presence carried a pleasant anticipation. Given the minimal light pollution in the area, the stars, which peered out behind wispy clouds, were visible. I hadn't been prepared for such a strong evening chill, having grown accustomed to the often unbearable heat of Rajasthan and Punjab. Zipping up my jacket, I shivered and embraced the sudden shift.

I trailed along next to Suchita, who used her phone screen to complement the faint light of the minimal streetlamps. After a couple of minutes, we reached her home. Lanterns cast a glow against the minimalist two-story white exterior, with warm lighting and red curtains peering out from the windows. A pebbled walkway led up to the front porch, and we followed it indoors, kicking off our shoes and setting down our bags after a long day on the road.

A black-and-white mixed-breed dog greeted us with a flapping tongue and wagging tail. Suchita's father, who looked to be in his late fifties, had been sitting with his back against the wall, deep in prayer. He hoisted himself up and approached us, first speaking to Suchita in their native dialect and then switching to Hindi to greet me. With his bald head, glasses, Tibetan features, and soft-spoken nature, he reminded me of the Dalai Lama.

Insisting I "take rest," Suchita prepared dinner while I settled in and freshened up. Shortly after, I joined her and her father downstairs, where we enjoyed a warm meal of rice, *dal*, sliced cucumbers, *achaar*, and cabbage *sabji*.

We ate mostly in silence, savoring the nourishment after a journey full of bumpy highways and light snacking. Once we'd cleaned our plates, we made our way upstairs. I welcomed the silence that enveloped us, and soon my eyelids grew heavier with sleep. Wrapped up in covers and blankets, I felt truly cozy for the first time in weeks. Warmth and fullness cocooned me. In a literal sense, these feelings had come from the meal we'd just eaten and the heated air. But I knew they went much deeper than this; that I'd found the comfort and companionship that renewed my spirit.

◊ ◊ ◊

September 1, 2016

The morning light peered through the beige curtains. Blinking my eyes, I felt momentarily disoriented, and it took a few moments to register my whereabouts.

Suchita had long been up and preparing to head out for the day.

I freshened up and met her downstairs. We sat where we had the night before, a spread of apples, biscuits, *chai*, and peanut butter before us. Sadness weighed my chest down as I acknowledged that our time together was coming to an abrupt close. This proved to be one of the aspects of travel I struggled with the most—of saying goodbye just as quickly as I met someone.

"You know you are always welcome here," Suchita said, looking my way as she took a sip of her chai. "If you need anything, please reach out."

"I don't even know how to begin to thank you," I said, my voice catching in my throat.

"No need," she said, nonchalantly as she patted my shoulder.

"I'm glad we got to meet."

"Likewise," I replied.

"Just keep doing what you're doing," she said. "And don't ever let anyone make you feel like you have to justify your life decisions."

I nodded, taking her words in.

"Well, I'll be leaving now," Suchita said, standing up to put her mug in the sink. "Please take as much time as you need before heading out. I've left a bag of apples for you. Oh, and before you go, do take in the view from our rooftop. If you look further ahead, you can see some of the Himalayan Mountains."

She winked and stood up to leave. We hugged and exchanged contact information, and she gave me instructions on how to catch the next bus to Manali. With that, Suchita walked out the door.

Following her instructions, I packed my belongings and took the stairs to the rooftop before departing. I gasped as I beheld the expansive view. A river flowed to the left, its waters roaring in the background, providing a steady soundtrack alongside cheerfully chirping birds. A hilly expanse full of evergreens dipped down to the sides, with the snow-capped Himalayas faintly visible in the distance. Fellow villagers' homes—a mix of beige cottage-like façades and pastel edifices made up the foreground. Tibetan prayer flags swayed gently in the breeze, adding to the sheer grandeur of the entire scene.

I sat with awe, sadness, and excitement as I reflected on all that had transpired the past twenty-four hours.

Suchita was the first of many remarkable women with whom I'd crossed paths on this India trip, women who changed my perspectives on what it meant to live a meaningful life. Like Suchita, these women challenged societal norms and charted their own paths, leaning into the pushback that often resulted. They embraced marriage and parenting on their own terms or forwent it altogether, shaped their career trajectories according to their passions, and spoke openly about injustices in a society that so often encourages women to keep quiet.

I realized how privileged a position I was in to make similar choices, to question longstanding traditions despite the discomfort, rather than comfortably follow along for fear of what might happen in the unknown.

It surprised me that in India, of all places, I found the representation I didn't know I'd always needed; that I so readily encountered other women who, in their own ways, redefined what it meant to be . . . *women.* In a part of the world where those born female still had little agency, and defying prewritten rules could be dangerous, I found their actions all the more respectable. I hoped that

I, too, could one day be the representation for young women who needed it.

I'd ultimately realized that travel isn't just about the places we visit. It's about the people we cross paths with, and the inner shifts we undergo as we witness new ways of thinking, living, and being.

Travel opens us up to chance encounters that can potentially change and challenge what we believe to be true about the world—for the better. It introduces us to people who take us in as their own and remind us that love is always accessible. And we walk away from these encounters feeling a bit lighter, freer, and better able to handle the myriad uncertainties of this human experience.

Brina Patel is a freelance content writer and copywriter. Her bylines have appeared in several outlets, including *Business Insider*, *Metro*, and *Well+Good*. Her creative nonfiction has also been published in *Heartwood Literary Magazine* and *LEVITATE Magazine*. Brina is passionate about using storytelling to connect, heal, and delve deeper into the more difficult questions in life. She enjoys mentoring fellow creatives so they can share their talents with the world and leave a legacy through their words. When she isn't writing, Brina enjoys getting lost in new cities, diving into page-turning memoirs, and spoiling her sassy Maltese. You can learn more about her at *www.brinapatelwriter.com*.

When I See You

Eric Wiesenthal
CWC – Sacramento Branch

Yesterday, Amir,
when you brought pomegranates and melon to share,
I greeted you quietly at our front door.

Our village has been at peace for such a long time
no one can remember when it wasn't.

On Saturday, hell rained down
on the nation our families built.

And after the warning sirens abated,
we emerged from our bomb shelters,
trying to comfort our friends and families.

Sunday and Monday
we learned of
the wanton slaughter,
the kidnappings,
and the destruction in Gaza.

Our grandparents,
our parents,
and our generation
have watched, worried, hoped, and prayed
about our native land.

In our town, we never walk around starry-eyed.
Together we have sweated, spilled blood, and struggled.
Our families have celebrated together and consoled one another.

We read the newspapers, listen to the news,
argue, and discuss and always wonder,
"What will happen next?"

But we must preserve what we have.

We live the Tent of Ibrahim (Abraham)
with its open sides and
eternal welcome to the stranger.

Always.

.آمين .الناس في جيد هو ما ونعرف الصداقة إلى دائمًا نسعى أن رجون

(May we always seek friendship
and know what is good within people.)

מי שעושה שלום בשמים הגבוהים
עשה שלום עלינו, לכל ישראל ולכל יושבי הארץ.

(May the One who makes peace in the high heavens
make peace for us, all Israel, and all who inhabit the earth.)

When the sound of guns and the terror of rockets have ceased
and the smoke begins to clear, we will re-open our shops.

When we do, Amir, you and I will go
to the café on our village square
to enjoy a mid-morning Turkish coffee.

Eric Wiesenthal is a native New Yorker and holds a bachelor's degree in print journalism from The American University in Washington, D.C.

He was a newspaper reporter for five years including a stint on Capitol Hill. In Sacramento, he served in the State Assembly as a legislative aide and press secretary to one of the Latino members.

He has been writing poetry and short stories for the last five years.

The Last Supper

JerilynRing
CWC Sacramento Branch

The siren sounded, thin and shrill, cutting into the eerie silence. The protesters, for and against capital punishment, marched on opposite sides of the road leading to San Quentin Prison. They marched up and down, waving their signs at approaching cars driving through the main gate. The angry faces, for and against capital punishment, stared at him as he drove past. The prison walls, looming ahead, gray and forbidding, mirrored the mood outside the giant fortress. An older woman, held her sign aloft, the words "Stop the Killing" written in bold black letters. Tears streamed down her face. Who was she? Certainly not a friend. He had none. All the legal papers in my possession consisted of legal correspondence chronicling a twelve-year battle to obtain a new trial.

All legal avenues had been exhausted. The final appeal had been filed. I wondered if he thought about my mother, dead these thirteen years, unable to appeal to a higher court. Did he think about the fourteen-year-old boy, now a man, left behind?

◊ ◊ ◊

I had started visiting him on my twenty-fourth birthday at the prompting of my therapist. This man, my father, tattooed from neck to waist, his teeth brown, his skin pale, barely resembled the man I remembered. His face lit up as I entered the small cubicle, taking a seat behind the plexiglass barrier. He had a disarming smile, despite the gap from a missing tooth. That smile always disarmed me until his eyes, empty and mysterious, met mine, sending a cold chill through me.

On all subsequent visits, I tried to avoid those eyes, and when I couldn't, they filled me with fear.

Growing up in a series of foster homes, I worried. Most foster parents ignored my past, but others, less sensitive, wondered if a killer resided within me and it was only a matter of time before the tainted gene exploded and violence erupted.

My fear was reinforced by the image of my mother, her features unrecognizable, lying in a pool of blood, my father, the murderer, standing over her.

Fear motivated me to visit him over a three-year period. My psychiatrist suggested I write a summary of each visit and my subsequent thoughts, so I bought a journal. The first visit was awkward.

"Hello, Danny. You're all grown up."

Obvious, I thought. *The world didn't stop when you went to prison.* I nodded, waiting for the next question, aware I was annoyed.

"Did you go to college like your mom wanted?"

He mentioned Mom but showed no remorse. What did he think? I had a college fund. I bussed tables, worked my ass off and . . . .

I wasn't annoyed anymore; I was irritated. "I got an engineering degree."

"Your mom would have been proud."

The M word again. My irritation changed to anger. Dr. Shapiro's warning came into my head. *Express yourself. Danny.* "If you hadn't killed her, you both could have attended my graduation." My anger subsided; I felt better for speaking my truth.

"You're right, Danny. If she were here."

He's calm. Not in denial. Now what?

"I'm glad you came."

He sounded sincere. If only I could remember our relationship, but the past, our life before Mom's death, died with her. The man sitting before me, a stranger, defeated, was not menacing at all. Something inside stirred pity. Dad's eyes were disturbing, reflections of pain and suffering, which made me uneasy. He was a broken man. He deserved to die. He took her from me. I lost everything. I had prayed for this ending.

My mind went into overdrive as I went over all the reasons for hating him. Try as I could, I couldn't conjure up any hatred. This was a complete reversal of my former attitude. Unbelievable. How did this happen?

We were sitting across from each other, talking on a two-way phone, the heat unbearable. I loosened my tie, my neck wet with perspiration. He stayed calm, his skin dry.

"Are you alright, Danny?"

The caring tone disturbed me. This man, a stranger really, a murderer. I didn't want him to care about me.

I made an excuse to leave and departed hastily. I ran to my car, panting uncontrollably and drove away erratically. I found my way to the gate and vowed never to return.

The nightmares increased, always the same. I walk into the room, my mother is lying there, covered with blood, he is standing over her. I can't see his face, his back is to me. I back up, he turns toward me, and I run.

I always regretted running away, not facing him, not saving my mother. I play the what-if game, tormenting myself with all the things I could have done. Dr. Shapiro says I need closure. Visiting my father will facilitate the process. Reluctantly, I returned.

During our visits, we didn't discuss Mom. It was as if he knew the emerging relationship could not take another hit. Something else occurred—the nightmares stopped. That was odd indeed. For the past eight years, at least twice a week, I awoke bathed in sweat and unable to breathe, haunted by the images of my mother dead in a pool of blood.

A new fear emerged. If the visits stopped, would my nightmares return? At some point, the decision to end the visits wouldn't be mine. Time was running out.

Dr. Shapiro suggested I bring up the topic of my mother. "Why?" I asked. "The nightmares are gone."

"There's something you're not facing. Once you face it, the nightmares won't return."

The next day, I received a phone call from Dad's attorney. The last appeal had been denied, the clock was ticking. He had forty-eight hours left.

I called in sick and went to see him.

"Hello, Danny, how you doing?"

Me? He's the one being put to death. "Um, I don't know."

He smiled. "I've been expecting you."

Every visit. Always in control and I'm not.

"You're at peace," I said, bewildered as usual.

"Why wouldn't I be?"

"Mom! Don't you remember?" The old hatred surfaced. I loosened my tie.

"I remember, Danny."

"You took her from me." My eyes were dry. A numbness crept

through me.

"Do you remember that night?" he asked.

I shot back. "Of course, I do." Doesn't anything shake this guy. I'm rocking back and forth, beside myself, and he's unruffled.

"Tell me what you remember."

My mouth went dry. I licked my lips. My hands were shaking.

"Danny, talk to me."

Strange. He cares. My voice sounded far away. I can barely hear it. "I gotta go."

When I got home, I called Dr. Shapiro, who was pleased. He encouraged me to return the next day, to continue the conversations. Time, he reminded me, was running out for both of us.

◊ ◊ ◊

The next day, I returned. The guard escorted me to the visiting area. My dad had been moved to a different cell block. As I waited for him to join me on the other side of the glass, I noticed my hands were trembling.

"Hi, Danny," he said, taking a seat across from me. "Since tonight's my last night, I can invite a guest for dinner. Will you join me?"

I swallowed hard. "Sure," I said. What else could I do?

"What do you like to eat? I can order anything I want."

It's his last meal, and he wants to know what *I* like. With a sudden clarity, I realized my problem. He had won me over. Little by little, pretending he cared, and now, I didn't hate him anymore.

That night we ate together. Fried chicken, corn on the cob, and mashed potatoes, which used to be my favorite meal. "Can I have the legs?" I asked.

"Sure, I prefer the breast," he said. "Do you remember the last time you ate chicken?"

I looked down at my plate, almost empty. The night Mom died. "Yes," I said, meeting Dad's eyes. The eyes that stared back at me had changed. He was holding something back.

"What do you remember about that night?"

This was my last chance. "Blood on the floor, blood on my hands, you're standing over Mom, touching her neck."

"Why is she dead, Danny?"

"You were angry. You wanted the leg. She said no. Beyond that, I can't remember."

"Danny, I like the breast."

A numbness came over me. I tried to speak, I wanted to protest, but I couldn't speak.

I tried to speak, I wanted to protest, but I couldn't speak.

"It's over, Danny."

I couldn't move. He stood over me. I stood up, and he hugged me.

◊◊◊

That evening, I visited Dr. Shapiro.

"Well how did it go?" Dr. Shapiro asked, taking a seat opposite me.

"Dad suggested that I killed my mother."

"Oh," Dr. Shapiro said, rubbing his chin."

"Even at the end, he couldn't admit it," I said, feeling uneasy.

"You tried. Visiting almost every week for what, three years."

"Yes."

"The nightmares?"

"Gone, I said, standing up. "I won't be coming back."

"Are you sure?"

"Absolutely."

I shook his hand and strode out of his office, feeling a freedom that I had not known until this moment. My earlier anxiety had disappeared.

All these years, after Mom's death, I had been filled with fear. Now I knew why.

A lot of folks believed Dad was innocent, but the police didn't buy the intruder theory. It had too many holes. Yet, Dad had continued to insist an intruder killed Mom. An investigator from the DA's office believed Dad was covering for someone. He visited him several times, but Dad repeated the same story. The investigator discounted a stranger. The ferocity of the attack indicated the killer knew his victim. The number of stab wounds indicated an attack fueled by rage of a personal nature.

The migraines had kept me from remembering. Once I faced the truth, realized I was safe, and the only other person who knew would be dead by morning, I was free.

The next morning the phone woke me. The caller ID identified Dad's lawyer, Dave. Reluctantly, I answered. "Hello, Dave," I said, ready to tell him he had done all he could to save Dad, and I was grateful to him.

"Hi, Danny, I got good news. Your dad's sentence has been commuted to life."

I squeezed my eyes shut, recognizing the start of another migraine. In the background I could hear Dave asking, "Are you there, Danny?"

Jerilyn Ring was born and raised in San Francisco, later relocating to Orangevale, California. She obtained a Masters in Nursing and enjoyed working in different specialties, discovering that hospice, mental health, and chemical dependency were the most rewarding. She has drawn from her experience in these specialties to develop characters with depth and thought-provoking stories.

While she has enjoyed a career in nursing, writing has always been her primary passion, while reading is her past time.

Daddy's Girl

I. D. Kapur
CWC – Sacramento Branch

Your bright smile, dimpled chin
Eyes a warm gold brown,
Oh yes, my sweet, you're Daddy's
girl, his princess with a crown
Hold his picture close my love
Come sit here next to me,
We'll sing his favorite hymns today,
We'll make him proud, you'll see
Guns are pointed to the sky
An honor few receive. Remember him
With arms held wide, oh, you're too
Young to grieve
Everyone's so caring, people
Are too kind, hands are reaching out
To me, but I've gone somehow blind
Daddy rests beneath the stone
In perfect rank and file,
Now take the flag and thank the man,
There's no need to smile.

I.D. Kapur majored in journalism and is a speech writer and short story author whose debut book, *In Any Given Room*, was published in 2022. Kapur's second book, *A Year Without Men,* was published in 2023. Her prize-winning poetry and other works are featured in the anthologies *Ink Spots* and *One Universe to The Left*. She began traveling at seventeen to Europe and has visited over twenty-two countries. She lives in Northern California, where she and her husband, Gopal, manage their scholarship program, Light One Candle, for underserved students in Northern India.

The Writer

Jackie Alcalde Marr
CWC – Sacramento Branch

When the stars wink in the cold night
They come dripping from the pen
Black ribbons
Supple curves and stiff lines
Slivers, splinters
Fragments wavering in a sleep
A word floating until it drifts up into consciousness

Indigo, lavender, then the apricot sky
And the steam of the French roast
Coaxing the thought
That falls on the page when the morning is still

Wet ink drying as the thought unfolds
A note on the parchment, then another
A melody, faint and soft on a breeze
Attracting a harmony that compels a smile
A memory, an idea, a dream

The story dawns
And grows warmer, bold and fierce, and vivid blue
It spills from the pen in a torrent, landing in place, moving time forward

Until shadows grow long and longer
Then left for sleep
When the stars wink in the cold night

Jackie Marr loves wine, nurturing old friendships, all things Spain, and the lessons found in history. After a long corporate career as an organization development leader, Jackie created Evolutions Consulting Group to help individuals and groups achieve their goals.

She is a consultant, trainer, and leadership/life coach, and is currently being certified as a book coach. She's been an adjunct faculty member at the University of San Francisco, Drexel University, University of the Pacific, and California State University, Sacramento.

Jackie co-authored *Social Media At Work: How Networking Tools Propel Organizational Performance* (Jossey-Bass). She has published several short stories and poems in a variety of anthologies and has been published in the *Sacramento Business* magazine and the *Organization Development Journal*. She's currently writing a novel based on her family's immigration from Spain to Hawaii to California. Jackie lives in Folsom, California, with her husband, Jeff, and their aging dog, Quincy Noodlebutt.

Appah

Lally Pia, MD
CWC – Sacramento Branch

I've had to pronounce death twice in my life.

The first time I was a third-year medical student at UC Davis, decades back. Then I had to do it again, yesterday. For my father.

The morning began with a frantic call from my mom. My father wasn't waking up, she said.

I drove to their home faster than you can say home hospice.

His cheek was warm to the touch, but his mouth hung open. His eyes were closed. I felt his forehead with the back of my hand. He was warm. Too warm. He couldn't be . . . I couldn't even say the word . . .

I leaned forward over the bed railing and put my ear to his mouth to listen. I choked up.

He wasn't breathing!

I felt for a pulse, wishing I'd brought my stethoscope. Still nothing. Dread made my heart gallop. Switching to doctor, I tried to recall the pain protocol. I had to squeeze the skin between the toes. The thought of doing that to my hypersensitive dad made me squirm. Appah is the world's biggest crybaby. Only yesterday he'd bellowed, "Cold, too cold!" when I rubbed Vaseline on his dry toes. I didn't want to hurt him anymore.

I hesitated. The family depended on me, the *doctor,* to tell them if he really had passed away. Taking a deep breath to summon the remnants of my vaporizing courage, I leaned over the foot of the bed and gently lifted the blankets covering his feet. Heaving a deep breath, I dug my nails into the soft tissue next to his big toe, my squinted eyes glued to his face.

Surely, he'd shriek and leap up in agony.

He didn't twitch.

Please! I silently mouthed. Please, Appah!

It was then that full realization percolated into my stunned brain—the truth I'd tried to steer away from my logical mind. The first hot tears tracked silently down the side of my face as I set aside my protective medical filter to become his daughter again. I allowed the pain of this loss to fully grip me as cold tendrils of constriction snaked around my heart.

Appah was gone. He was really gone.

Fragments of thoughts tumbled out in disarray. This man who'd shown the world so much passion for 94 years could no longer feel a thing. This was no patient, this was my proud father, an emotional man, who would choke up and cry when he gave a heartfelt speech to the family at Thanksgiving. His still-open mouth would never utter another word. I dragged my gaze to dry lips that would never make us laugh again, never share his famous tall tales.

This beloved man had helped my mother provide us with the most cherished childhood that four children could imagine. He'd instilled in us that we could do anything we wanted. He was right. The four of us had thrived under that philosophy, both in Kumasi, and then later in California. We'd made him proud with our achievements. You could see that in the glowing way he spoke about us to anyone who would listen, as we rolled our eyes. He hailed every accomplishment as if we'd won the Nobel Prize. He never failed to attend events of even the smallest significance, from my piano performance to a lecture to medical students which he proudly attended. When I left my first husband, my father took the place of their father to my two toddlers. He loved nothing more than to make them laugh as he held them close.

The silence from the other room was deafening. My mom. I had to go tell my mom.

Not yet; not yet. I wanted to prolong this final communion with my father.

Appah was the heart of our family's engine. The charisma and magnetism he exuded drew people in at every party we hosted in Ghana. He'd shared that Sri Lankan fortune teller's prophecy with anyone in the universe who gave him the time of day. Brushing aside my skepticism, he steadfastly and obstinately clung to his conviction for forty-one years, then shed tears of joy that fateful day when I walked onto the stage to pick up my Doctor of Medicine diploma.

My wonderful, incomparable father. I stared at him with reverence. His feet were still uncovered. Knowing it was illogical, I gently tucked the sheet back over him. He'd always exuded a warm cocoon of support that blanketed us whenever it was needed. When we encountered hardships or mishaps, he was always, unfailingly, philosophical. If we were stressed because we were running late to school, he'd cheerfully chant, "It's better to *be* late, Mr. X, than *the* late Mr. X." I smiled through my tears. Now *he* was *the* late Mr. X.

A pack of cards lay on his desk shelf behind me. We would miss him so much at our traditional Sri Lankan 304 card game. It is a game requiring significant memorization and calculation, but he rocked it. He was a chess champion at Nottingham University. He'd then played duplicate bridge in Kumasi for decades, which honed his brain into a sharp instrument all the way to the end. Dramatic and flamboyant bids turned each game into an adrenaline-infused spectacle. Many a time his temper would rise so fast that he'd storm out of the room, requiring cajoling to return and keep playing. My sister Viji and I inherited that same temper. Once, tensions ran high during a driving lesson. After an unforgettable explosion, my sister and I abandoned his car, then had to walk for miles to get home.

My dad had lived in Sri Lanka, England, and Ghana, but when political instability took hold and our lives in Ghana deteriorated, he recognized the potential and promise of America. It became his unwavering mission to move us to California where his sister and mother had already settled. When he later became a naturalized citizen, he always professed his pride in all the gifts America had given to us. I remember his patriotism as he donned his finest clothes to head to the park every year to serve as an election officer.

Trying to keep myself busy and distracted, I walked into his bedroom to empty boxes of pills from his drawers, sad that pills could no longer help him. As I did so, I came across a card I'd made for his 90th birthday. He'd treasured that creation for four years. It was too much. Tears flooded my cheeks. Even after death my father was showing me how much he loved me. I set the card down as if it were hot and slammed the drawer shut.

I called for body pickup. As I waited, I recalled the day my father took a tour of my workplace, the UC Davis Donated Body Program. He'd never so much as blanched as we toured the morgue, or when I discussed the process of body donation. On the contrary, he'd been *excited* to learn that preserved body parts might instruct medical students as long as thirty years after a person's death. The experience moved him so much that he told me he wanted to become a donor to the program. I told him he'd have to wait till after I quit—

I sure didn't want to flip open the morgue cooler and see my father wrapped in a white linen sheet on the rack! He'd waited three more years, then signed up.

They came to pick him up four hours later. The two men, dressed in black, were somber and respectful. They left me space to cry for a few seconds. My mom walked in from the living room. I knew how hard this must be for her. She'd always been squeamish about anything death related. I had to support her frail body the last couple of feet to my dad's side. She flinched as she held his hand.

"Goodbye, Maha," she murmured simply, but her face was crumpled up in anguish. She bestowed a look of utter love on him that only someone who's loved a man from 19 to 93 can express. Then she pulled away and collapsed into a chair.

"This is how I'd like to go too," one of the men said to me, clearly trying to cheer me up. "Make it to my nineties and go one day in my sleep."

I nodded. "I ran this program for years. It's . . . er . . . different when it's your dad."

The men stepped aside. This time, when I reached out tremulously to touch my father's face, I fought the instinct to recoil in horror. He'd become an icicle.

I'd seen and handled hundreds of dead bodies. However, when they began to remove his covers, I wanted to scream for them to stop. My dad *loved* warmth. Even when he donned multiple layers of clothes, he always declared that it was too cold. At home he baked in tropical heat with the thermostat cranked to 82.

As they removed his remaining clothes my hardest final task was to remove his wristwatch. My father's simple gold watch had an equally unpretentious metal strap. Treasured. Revered. My hands shook as I undid the strap and my vision blurred. Where he was going, he would no longer be a slave to the demands of time.

As the men busily transferred my father to the gurney and placed a blue tarp over him, I reflected on the events of the last few weeks. After his hospitalization, my ninety-four-year-old father had lost his ability to walk. He'd strongly rejected a transfer to a nursing home, electing to die at home, surrounded by family. the people he loved. We'd honored his wishes. One by one, all his children, grandchildren, and even great-grandchildren had paid their respects.

My father wanted to call the shots about his final exit and die with grace, not lie helplessly in a sterile setting as the life force slowly drained out of him while monstrous machines bleated out their alarms, and tubes sprouted from every orifice. He had a sound mind, and we'd accepted his terms, his autonomy. He chose home hospice with our support. It was the least we could do for a man who asked for so little but gave us so much.

Despite strong beliefs in the Hindu faith, he'd made it clear that there should be no fuss to serenade this final transition. In a final act of selflessness his body was to be gifted, and he made it clear that he did not want to saddle us with cremation or funeral costs. As an architect in Kumasi my father designed his buildings using locally procured materials in order to avoid wasting natural resources. His body was a natural resource.

I had never been prouder of my beloved father.

"Appah," I whispered, as I caressed the blue tarpaulin one precious, final time before they wheeled him away. "Appah, I love you."

Lally Pia, MD, is an author and a child and adolescent psychiatrist. Her award winning memoir, *The Fortune Teller's Prophecy: a Memoir of an Unlikely Doctor,* is currently available as an audiobook. The memoir will be published April 30, 2024, by She Writes Press. She is a member of the California Writers Club (Sacramento), the Elk Grove Writers Guild, and the Fremont Area Writers Group. Her video, *Day in the Life of a Psychiatrist*, has received over 65,000 online views. She was a finalist in the nationwide talent search for *America's Next Great Author* in October 2022. Her commentary about her stroke was published in *The Davis Enterprise* in May 2023. She has been featured in multiple podcasts and is a semifinalist for the Chanticleer Hearten Book Awards. She lives with her husband in Davis, California.

Noodling

Susan Dlugach
CWC – Sacramento Branch

Fishing this morning . . .
fingers noodle this cold keyboard
but bait's bad,
nothing's biting

The only ripple
in this river
is this continual
casting
and pulling back
casting
and pulling back

I throw the line again and again,
Watch it sink
settle
See only
stillness
stillness
stillness

I pull it up
see the untouched morsel
pull it off
sushi it onto the barb
toss again
watch the water ripple
as the line sinks

Ripples glisten like halos
in the slanted whispering sun
stark silver circles
on the water's dark surface

which my inner eye
cannot break through
today

Susan Dlugach is a former journalist and educator who taught English to non-English speakers and reluctant readers as well as New Age beatniks. She now finds time in retirement to write stories, poetry, and articles of local interest. Her work has been published in *Visions, California Update, More Than Enough,* and the California Writers Club *Literary Review.*

The Three Tenors

Tim Schooley
CWC – Sacramento Branch

"My Dear Colleagues,

It is with profound sorrow (and joy!) that I announce my retirement effective the end of this month. Through these many years, I have enjoyed working with each and every one of you (more or less, and you know who you are.) If you ever find yourself up Crater Lake, drift on by.

Yours,
Edward Lumbkin"

◊ ◊ ◊

Colin dropped his head onto his desk. Lumbkin's retirement memo stuck to one of his cheeks. He tried to slow his breathing. The end of this month, dear God. It was the fifteenth already. That meant Lumbkin would be gone in two weeks. How long did that give him? A month maybe, month-and-a-half at the most, before he was out on the street, collecting unemployment.

During his long career with the state, Colin had mastered one essential skill: brown-nosing. He'd put that skill to work to gain the directorship of the Division of Aesthetic Arts, which ran arts centers for the state's foster youth. Pretty good for a guy who couldn't tell his abstract from a Holbein on the wall. Upon achieving that lofty position, Colin embraced a new skill: delegating. His subordinates delighted in the trust he placed in them, and Colin delighted that his newly coined free time improved his golf game to an eight handicap.

But Colin's scheme unraveled when a new governor closed the arts centers. And, soon after, Colin found his division assigned to a department with two directors, Lumbkin and Keaney, who loathed each other so fiercely that they never spoke to one another.

Colin spotted an opportunity. He told Keaney that Lumbkin had retained him to perform special projects. He told Lumbkin that Keaney had hired him as a personal assistant. Colin thought his artifice might buy him a little time to hunt for a new state job but never imagined how well his plan would succeed. As week turned to month, and month to year, Colin decreased his profile until he all but disappeared. He kept his corner office, but he astutely removed his title from the door. He also kept his salary, a box of business cards, and, until she retired, his secretary. Fifteen years had now passed, and during that time Colin had performed not one jot of work.

Colin peeled Lumbkin's retirement memo from his cheek. His hands continued to tremble, but his heart had stopped pounding. What he needed more than anything was a stiff drink. Lumbkin would be gone at the end of the month. It would be only a matter of weeks, perhaps days, before Keaney discovered Colin's artifice and handed him his hat. That gave him precious little time to prepare for his own retirement. Or to come up with a new plan. Colin checked his wallet before heading across the street to the state capitol building.

To Colin, proximity to the Capitol, an architectural throwback to the Roman Empire, meant only one thing: access to special services that legislators had hidden within. Colin could get his clothing dry cleaned at one out-of-the-way office in the Capitol, his car registered at another, his shoes shined, his eyeglasses ordered, his prescriptions filled, his teeth cleaned, a suit tailored, his hair cut, and, lately, even his hair implanted if he had wanted it. Some of the services were intended for "members only," but Colin's graying temples and well-tailored suits allowed him to pass without challenge. On this day, his only thoughts were of the ATM machine in the basement followed by the members' bar on the fourth floor.

Colin entered the Capitol by leaning his bulk against the building's twenty-foot oak door. He pushed through hordes of school children and senior citizens, all favoring the same style in shorts and T-shirts. A Capitol tour guide stood facing a group of seniors in front of a statue of Columbus holding a globe while kneeling before Queen Isabella. Colin tuned in to the tour guide's spiel while he shifted from foot to foot, trying to negotiate his way around the group.

"Here we have Prunella, first queen of this territory, prior to statehood," the tour guide said. "As you can see, the sculptor depicts Queen Prunella at the very moment she relinquished the orb of power to the state's first governor, Pip Pirrip."

Colin stopped laughing when he realized the tourists were taking the guide at her word. Colin appraised the tour guide's high cheek bones and soft blue eyes. Difficult to see her figure in her getup, a state-issued sack-like blue apron covering a fluffy white blouse.

The tour guide gestured to the rotunda above the group's heads, a soaring structure lined to the ceiling with pink, flocked wallpaper.

"As you can see," the tour guide said. "The Capitol rotunda served as the very model for every wedding cake baked during the past century. One hundred years ago, wedding cakes were as flat as pancakes. Hence the custom in the 1800s of giving the bride a frying pan on the wedding night. Sociologists have shown that the rise of the rotunda led to an end of the wedding pan custom, and a very commensurate drop off in spousal abuse. One more example of your tax dollars at work to lessen violence."

The tour guide moved down the hall, leading her glassy-eyed gaggle. Colin trailed behind. The tour guide turned to an ancient portrait, painted in shades of gray and black, depicting one of the state's early governors.

"Please focus your attention on this painting of one of our first executives, Governor Pompadompa, inventor of the curling iron."

Colin wondered why no one else in the crowd seemed to notice the caption, "Governor Chapman," at the bottom of the painting. He caught the eye of the tour guide, who shifted her look and seemed suddenly uncomfortable. Colin no longer felt offense when young women failed to hold his gaze—he was fat, wrinkled, and gray, and unless a woman mistook his leer for a fatherly grin, he expected her to look away.

The tour guide announced the next stop on the program—the old print shop—and led her willing captives off toward the northern basement stairway. Colin continued his journey to the southern stairway and the waiting ATM machine. After extracting several twenties from the ATM, Colin turned and bumped head-on into the tour guide, knocking her to the floor. Colin apologized profusely while lifting her to her feet.

"I am *so* sorry. I should have watched where I was going."

"I'm all right. Don't worry. Anyway, I expect I deserved that for the things I was saying to that group."

"Are you serious? That was the funniest thing I've heard all week." Colin tried to brush the tour guide's apron, dusty from her spill, but she stepped back.

"Thanks, but I was a little off script," the tour guide said. "I suppose you could fire me."

"I could fire you? Why?"

"Don't you work for the Capitol tour service?"

"Whatever gave you that idea?"

"I just started a couple of weeks ago. They told me there'd be monitors. Spies is what they meant. And you were following me, dressed in a suit. Two and two."

"My name's Colin." Colin reached for her hand. "I work across the street. I'm the director of the state's Division of Aesthetic Arts."

"I'm Toni Ball." Toni retrieved her hand from Colin's grasp. "That's a new one on me. I had no idea the state had a division of aesthetic arts."

Colin reached into his wallet and fished around until he found a business card that wasn't too dog-eared.

"Division of Aesthetic Arts," Toni said, turning the card over in her hand. "I was an Arts major in college. You hiring?"

Colin started to say no, but an idea came to him. He smiled slowly. "We're always looking for bright, imaginative young people. Why don't you stop by my office tomorrow with your résumé?"

"I'll be there," Toni said. "Say, 8:00 a.m.?"

Colin almost choked. "Better make it noon."

"You're on." Toni looked over her shoulder. "I see my group emerging from the anesthesia administered them in the historical print shop. I'd better get back there. See you tomorrow."

Colin forgot about the members only bar. He practically skipped back to his office, his mind sorting the DNA of an embryonic plan. He found Edward Lumbkin in his office, placing his personal belongings into a cardboard box. Colin hadn't spoken to Lumbkin in almost two years.

"Hello, Ed," Colin said. "Came by to wish you the best."

"Thanks, Colin. Haven't seen you lately. The old prick must be keeping you busy."

"Funny you should mention it. Keaney's been running me ragged. I don't mean to sound disloyal, but I expect you've noticed he's a bit of a tightwad."

Lumbkin snorted in approval.

"I've been asking him to allow me to hire an assistant for some time now. But he keeps begging off, blaming it on the budget crisis.

Jeez, we haven't had a budget crisis in years. Far as I know, the state's flush."

"Flush enough for me to ride out of here on the back of a porcine pension."

"Good for you, Ed. If I don't get some relief soon, I may have to follow you, just to keep my sanity."

Lumbkin looked up from his cardboard box. "Hey? Anything I can do to help?"

Colin fought to maintain his poker face. He had him.

"I don't think so. Although. No, it would probably just blow up in my face."

"What?"

"I just had a thought. No, it would be too big an imposition. And I know you're trying to get out of here."

"No, really. What?"

"Well. I don't suppose you'd be willing to process the paperwork for me to hire an assistant before you leave?"

Lumbkin's eyes practically sparkled with the realization he'd just been handed an opportunity to undercut Keaney's authority one last time before his retirement.

"What do you think, Colin? Bring your assistant in at an Admin. Analyst level?"

Colin was surprised. He was thinking Secretary I, at best. This would help his plan along. After thanking Lumbkin, Colin hurried to the personnel office to get the paperwork moving.

His work for the day—actually the decade—completed, Colin retreated to his own office. Ever since his secretary retired five years before, other employees had stored surplus junk in her workspace, an antechamber to Colin's out-of-the-way corner office. Defunct computers and printers, cardboard boxes of indistinct content, and assorted bric-a-brac now so littered the area that Colin's door was all but concealed. Colin made his first effort in years to organize the clutter. After several minutes of huffing, he managed to clear a larger path to his door and then gave up, figuring that if he hired Toni Ball, her first order of business would be to clean up the mess.

Toni Ball showed up the next day promptly at noon.

"We've been so darn busy, we haven't even unpacked properly," Colin said, gesturing at the boxes outside his office door.

"Come in, come in. You've approached the division at a good time, Toni."

Colin heaved his bulk around the desk and settled into his chair. "A time of opportunity. One of our department directors, Ed Lumbkin, has just announced his retirement, and his co-director, Richard Keaney, will be taking over. I'm certain the Division of Aesthetic Arts will be called on to justify its programs, perhaps its very existence. Quite frankly, Toni, we need an infusion of new blood, someone creative enough to step up to the plate and run the ball into the goal. I think you may have what the division needs at this historical moment."

"This is so cool. You sound like you're ready to hire me, and you haven't even seen my résumé yet."

Colin noticed for the first time that Toni wore a gold post in her right nostril.

"Did you have that thing in your nose at the Capitol yesterday?"

"No, I take it out during the tours. But I thought, this being an arts division, there might be a hipper attitude about personal appearances."

"Oh, hardly. Let me tell you about pay and benefits, and then you can tell me how important it is to wear that third nostril plug."

As Colin described the compensation, health coverage, and pension eligibility of an administrative analyst, Toni reached into her right nostril, plucked out the stud, and placed it into her pocket.

"All right, then. I guess I should check out that résumé."

"Looks to be in order," he said. "Phi Beta Kappa. Very impressive." He noticed her internship with something called the American Anarchists League and tried not to lose his composure.

"This seems fine," he said, sliding the resume under a pile of papers that had been gathering dust in his out box for several years. "From anarchist to tour guide. Interesting career choices. Let's just say I was to give you this job, tell me some of your ideas for reenergizing this division."

Toni sat in uncomfortable silence for a moment. "That's an interesting question, Colin, and one I find a bit difficult to answer because I have no idea what your division does."

"Of course not. Good point. I seem to have skipped ahead a bit. Let's see. Historically, the Division of Aesthetic Arts was chartered to create arts centers for the state's foster children. You may be too young to remember." Colin was improvising. "But, with the closure of the centers, the division's mission had to evolve."

Toni looked lost.

"Basically, I've been doing special projects for the past few years. Trying to, well, trying to encourage arts education for foster children. Mostly small potatoes stuff. What I'm looking for is someone with a grander vision. Someone who can think outside the box, who can create opportunities for foster families throughout the state to nurture their appreciation for the arts. What I really want is one tremendous project to jump-start this division and get us back on track."

"Like a benefit or something."

"Exactly." Colin smiled expectantly.

"A benefit concert . . . for the foster children of the state," Toni said.

"That's the idea."

"Like, maybe, the Beastie Boys."

Colin frowned.

"The, um, the Rolling Stones."

Colin's frown deepened.

"The Three Tenors?"

Colin sat up in his seat. "That's it! That's just the kind of thing we're looking for."

Colin's plan was only half formed, but it involved convincing Keaney that all of the division's problems were the fault of Toni Ball. This would be a challenge given that Toni had only just been hired. But one big, spectacular failure by Toni could distract attention from Colin and give him more time to insinuate himself into Keaney's good graces.

A week went by as Toni careened about the office, dancing around Colin's flanks like a dolphin chasing a banana steamer. It took Toni only part of a day to clean out Colin's antechamber and claim it as her own. By the end of the first week, she had reorganized the office filing system, purchased her own business cards, and fired off a stream of emails to God only knows whom about what. Toni had to have figured out that she and Colin comprised the entire sum of the Division of Aesthetic Arts, but she kept that thought to herself.

His plan in place, Colin called Keaney's secretary, only to learn Keaney had suffered a heart attack and would be off work for at least six months. In the meantime, a management team had formed to carry on in the director's absence. Colin felt vaguely sorry for Keaney, finally prevailing in his years-long turf war with Lumbkin only to have victory snatched away by clogged arteries. Still, the interim managers would be so busy jockeying for power that they would have no time to bother with Colin. He chuckled at the thought that Keaney's ticker bought him another six months of retirement credits. And another six months to perfect the Toni Ball plan.

After giving Toni full rein, Colin reverted to form, the golf course. He checked in with Toni once in a while, and over time absorbed the details of her industry. Toni had set a date for the concert for early the next year, reserved a performance arena, arranged for the attendance of hundreds of foster families, lined up buses to transport the attendees, obtained volunteer musicians for the orchestra, signed up corporate sponsors, organized pre-concert entertainment, launched a massive advertising campaign, and printed and distributed thousands of flyers. The only bump in Toni's road was her inability to book The Tenors.

Colin counseled Toni to press ahead with her plans. The Tenors would sign on, would have to sign on, Colin insisted, once they realized the scope of the plan and the goodwill it would engender. Toni regularly phoned The Tenors' agents. Pavarotti was booked three years in advance. Domingo two years. And Carreras might have been available but was already over-committed with charity work. So, Toni organized a letter-writing campaign: hundreds of foster families wrote to The Tenors, begging their attendance. After that, The Tenors' booking agents stopped taking Toni's phone calls.

January rode into town on the back of a freezing ice storm, heralding the new millennium with shattered trees, frozen power lines, and impassable roadways. Colin felt elated. Keaney was due back in a week. Toni's benefit concert was scheduled for the week after that. And the event was destined to be a resounding fiasco.

Colin found Toni slumped at her desk.

"Hey, cheer up! There's still time for them to commit."

"Are you off your nut, Colin? Pavarotti's in Italy, Domingo's in Spain, and God knows where Carreras is holed up. They're not coming."

"Maybe it would help if I made a few phone calls."

"Yeah, right."

"What's that supposed to mean?"

"I just find it a little preposterous for you to offer to help when I haven't even seen you in weeks, and you haven't lifted a hand to help me with this project in over six months."

"Well. Toni. It *is* your project after all. I've got my own work to do."

"Yeah, right."

"Don't forget you're on a one-year probation, young lady. If I snap my fingers, you'll be back across the street, regaling the tourists with outlandish lies."

"Go ahead and snap. My life ends a week from next Friday anyway."

Colin made sure he was front and center at Keaney's back-to-work reception, and that Toni's name had been left off the reception invitation list. At an opportune moment, Colin sidled over to Keaney to tell him about the upcoming benefit concert, the single-handed project of his assistant, Toni Ball.

"You mean to say she's actually booked The Three Tenors?" Keaney said. "I'm a huge fan. Huge!"

"In that case, I insist that you and your wife join me, front row center, at the concert Friday night."

Colin feared Keaney might seize again, he turned so red in his enthusiasm. The final piece of the Toni Ball puzzle slipped into place. He prepared to offer Toni false sympathy as the week progressed, but Toni's mood had shifted from panic to a serenity induced by hopelessness.

The big night finally arrived. The airways screeched with the news of the small capital town's amazing coup. The Three Tenors. The greatest assemblage of vocal cords in the history of the world, performing, for free, in a benefit for foster kids. Toni Ball ran the operations center like a field marshal. Vendors were situated. Buses unloaded. Musicians arranged. Lights focused. Sound systemed. And, a limousine dispatched to the airport, just in case one of The Tenors actually appeared.

Colin caught an occasional glimpse of Toni issuing orders into a walkie-talkie. He felt a sudden pang of remorse, and at one point approached her, but turned away when he saw her mascara was streaked from crying. Toni was shrieking into the walkie-talkie, "I'm flying into a hurricane here, and you just killed my starboard motor."

Colin retreated to the arena's main entrance to meet and greet comrades from the department. Herds of foster families streamed past him into the arena. When Colin found Keaney and his wife, he led them to their seats of honor in the front row. The concert started late, with Toni's all-volunteer symphony orchestra launching into a medley of pops hits. Eventually the conductor ascended the stage and announced he'd just been informed that The Tenors were having transportation problems, but he begged the audience to bear with him and meantime the band would play on.

Keaney shot Colin an anxious look. After another fifteen minutes, Keaney leaned toward Colin.

"You sure The Tenors are actually booked?"

"Absolutely," Colin lied. "Toni Ball assured me this very afternoon they left together on a flight from London."

Another thirty minutes passed and the crowd grew noticeably restless. Keaney fidgeted in his seat, occasionally glancing irritably in Colin's direction. The orchestra began playing "The Star-Spangled Banner." Some in the audience stood up immediately, while others rose slowly, unsure whether to remain standing. Colin looked back over the crowd and thought people in the back were beginning to leave.

The orchestra stopped playing, and the conductor climbed to the stage again.

"I'm very sorry," he said. "I've just been informed that there's been a problem with a connecting flight."

The audience moaned. Keaney stood up.

"I've got a busy schedule tomorrow," Keaney told Colin. "I guess we'll be off. Have Toni Ball come see me in my office, first thing in the morning."

Just then the conductor looked back over his shoulder. "One minute, folks," he said before walking to the wings. He returned to the stage, a smile across his face, and descended into the orchestra pit. After a pause, the violin section eased into a slow, sweeping Puccini tune. The flutes responded trippingly, challenging the violins for control of the melody.

"Uh oh," Colin said out loud.

The audience reacted in confusion. Some began to applaud. Others stood, staring at the stage. In a moment, the audience erupted into a screaming, cheering, applauding mass. A large, balding man with a messy black beard strolled onto the stage, crooning "*recondita armonia*," already mopping at his brow with a handkerchief.

"Di bellezze diverse!
E' bruna Floria,
l'ardente amante mia."

The crowd screamed so loudly Colin could barely hear Pavarotti. This was impossible. He had checked the tenors' performance schedules on the internet that very morning. Pavarotti was at the Venice Opera; one of the Spaniards was in Madrid, the other in Belgrade of all places. Colin peered hard at the singer, thinking he was a little too fat, and too short maybe, to be the real tenor.

"Tu azzurro hai l'occhio,
Tosca ha l'occhio nero."

Keaney jumped up and down next to Colin. Pavarotti had moved to the apron of the stage, an arm's length from Colin. He came to the song's final verse. Just as he hit the high note, elongating "*Tosca*" into twenty piercing, reverberating syllables, his Spanish sidekicks strolled onto the stage behind him. Colin, a stranger to rock concerts, had never witnessed such pandemonium. The audience rose to its feet, screaming in adulation. Colin slumped into his chair, glancing from tenor to tenor. Maybe, just maybe, that was really Domingo, but no way that was Carreras, and anyone could tell the Pavarotti was an impersonator.

The concert, brilliant but brief, ended suddenly when Domingo explained that, unfortunately, he and his comrades must hurry to make their flight. As the lights rose, and the crowd began to file out, Toni Ball appeared. Colin mouthed, "What the hell?" but Toni just shrugged and smiled. A weight on his heart, Colin introduced her to Keaney, who actually hugged her. Colin's head swum. He felt a sudden shortness of breath. As he stooped to find his seat, he heard Keaney telling Toni, "And make sure you have Colin bring his files with him tomorrow. I'm positively dazzled by your work, Toni, but

I'd like to see what Colin's been up to lately."

Tim Schooley is the author of the novel *The Wool Translator* and the forthcoming novel *The Circus of the Vanishing Elephant*. He is the Treasurer of CWC Sacramento Branch, and lives with his wife in Fair Oaks, California. See more at *timschooley.com*.

CALIFORNIA WRITERS CLUB
SAIL ON!

REDWOOD

“The chosen spot of all the earth.”
—*Luther Burbank*

REDWOOD WRITERS

Hope You Like Fire[5]

Anne Keck
Redwood Writers

The police said his death was an accident, caused by a busted gas line, but that ain't true. I should know 'cause I'm the one who did it. I tell you, I killed him and I'd do it again given half a chance.

Grant Cleveland's obituary was a bunch a horseshit. Said he was an upstanding and righteous man, loved and mourned by all. Fact is, he was the company man who ran the town and everyone in it with an iron fist. Everyone loathed him. Grant Cleveland made for damn sure nothing grew in that town that weren't as black as the coal they pulled from the ground. As vile as his soul.

Me and my husband Earl weren't under his fist when he died, no sirree. Years ago I told Earl, if we didn't leave, if he didn't swallow his pride and join my momma's family on the homestead, I was going to abandon him, and he was going to die the ugly lung death all alone. He saw reason, which is why he's still by my side today.

I cain't say life at the homestead was easy, 'cause it weren't. But we did all right. Built us a nice house, had a green garden, good cow and a couple of goats, some chickens. Weren't much. Turned out, not enough to keep my youngest, my Tommy, away from that foul town.

He runned away when he was only fifteen. Too young for sense. Too young to leave home looking to impress the pretty girl who turned his head. Too young to go into that hell-hole of a town looking for work. Tommy weren't that smart, but he knew what power looked like, that it looked and smelled like money. So, he run right into Grant Cleveland.

Turns out, Grant Cleveland was not at all happy about me and Earl leaving, and he held a grudge. Earl was a good worker, a born leader with a knack for preventing accidents in the mines before they happened. For my part, I helped the womenfolk. Helped them pick the right kinds of herbs in the woods, mix the good brews, birth their babies, bury their dead. Everyone knew I had the gift and I gave it

[5] Previously published in *On fire*, Cynthia Gregory, ed. Santa Rosa: Redwood Writers Press 2022

freely.

What's my gift? I'm a caster. What you'd call a witch. One who does good, helps others.

Me and all the women on my momma's side of the family, we're all casters. Each of us is born with a different type of gift that makes us real good at something. Momma said I was born under the fire planet, so fire just comes naturally to me. I'm good at anything that needs to be boiled, smoked, scalded, or burned. When we lived in town, 'most everyone came by my hearth to seek my counsel, ask for my help.

As I heard tell, after me and Earl left that sorry-ass town, life there got even worse. And Grant Cleveland blamed us.

'Course Tommy didn't know about any of that the day he walked into Grant Cleveland's office asking for work. Grant Cleveland knew who he was the moment he saw him 'cause Tommy looks just like Earl, with his broad shoulders, square jaw, and sky-blue eyes. Grant Cleveland hired Tommy on the spot and sent him down the shaft the very next day. Worked him solid for three weeks, dual shifts, no breaks. Worked him so much that when the time came, Tommy didn't have it in him to fight. The fight had been plumb worked outta him.

Tommy didn't see it coming, then couldn't stop it from happening. See, Grant Cleveland was a bully with power, a master of violence. If he turned his eye on you, didn't matter if you were man or woman, young or old. He took what he wanted through sheer force, without asking and without remorse. No honey-coated words can describe what Grant Cleveland did to Tommy: he kept Tommy starved and imprisoned, and used him.

Heavens bless Maybell Drake, Grant Cleveland's housekeeper. She couldn't ignore what was happening, and her conscience couldn't let it go on any longer without saying something. I'd helped her out a time or two, and I figure she thought she owed me. She asked for leave to see her family, then came to my house first, dragging her tale of nightmares along with her carpet bag.

Maybell said Tommy was being held in the jail during the day and then taken to the Big House at night. But Grant Cleveland had just left to visit his cronies in Richmond, so Tommy was now spending all his time in jail.

When Maybell left, I got angry. A hungry beast made of flames and fury grew behind my ribs and quickly spread out, running through my veins. I couldn't have stopped it if I wanted, and I didn't want to. I could feel the rage engulfing me, changing me, making my blood boil and my aura turn a burning orange with wrath. Fire came quick to my hands, almost setting my own house alight. I needed to focus, to get control, so I concentrated on the most important task: getting Tommy outta there.

Earl was setting to rally his brothers, grab their guns, and break Tommy outta jail, but that was a fool's errand. There's no way in hell they would have made it to the town's jail before getting themselves shot dead. I told Earl I'd take care of it. He weren't happy, no sirree. But he agreed.

The sheriff happens to be my cousin Garret, so I paid him a visit. He's not a company man—not sure how he got the job, but I hanker a guess no one else wanted it. Tommy's was a hard story for me to tell him, but after hearing it, he got Tommy outta that jail and into my arms faster than a hawk can snatch a mouse.

Tommy's in bad shape, that's for sure. He's going to take a good long time to purge the demons plaguing him. But I know my Tommy. He'll work at it like he does with everything else—with single-minded determination. He'll be okay. And I got my boy back—scarred, but whole.

Tommy wasn't Grant Cleveland's first victim, but I was damned if I wasn't going to make sure Tommy was his last. I didn't know whether I could do anything to him while he was in Richmond, as long-distance casting is tricky, but the flames licking my innards wouldn't let me wait any longer to at least give it a try. Maybell had given me the address where Grant Cleveland was staying, so I decided to track him down that night.

At midnight, I slipped outta bed, grabbed my things, and headed out to the creek behind our house. There's a flat rock at the bend in it, perfect for sitting on and casting spells. Plus, I always aim to be near water when I cast, in case I have to put out a fire in a hurry. I set down on the rock and placed a small piece of wood in the clay fire bowl I put in front of me. After gazing at the clear star-filled sky to calm my breathing, I was ready to begin.

Us casters, we can see the threads of energy, of power, all

around us. The threads are the force that weaves through all beings and things, binding us together. Like a ball of yarn made of lightning bolts, the threads run round and round, connecting everything to everything else, all through the universe. Casters use those threads, that lightening energy, when we cast.

To start a casting, we pick an energy thread near at hand and push a piece of our consciousness into it. Mind you, we can still feel and control our body on the ground, but we can also feel the thrumming energy of the thread and sense everything around it. It's like being in two places at one time. Once we are mentally present in the threads, we can travel along them just like trains along tracks. When we arrive at our destination, we use our materials at hand, the energy from the threads, and the strength of our desires to cast our spells.

I started my casting by lighting up the wood in my fire bowl as a catalyst. While I can make a flame using my gift, I can't sustain it long without giving it fuel. For this casting to work, I had to use fire from my clay bowl and also find some proper fuel around Grant Cleveland. I reached out to the threads of the universe and let the angry beast in my breast loose along one of them. It followed a thread leading straight to where Grant Cleveland was sleeping in a bedroom inside a three-story mansion.

When I looked around the place, lo and behold, what did I find? Gas. Made by burning coal, gas was running under the houses, into kitchens, within walls, and into rooms to light wall lamps. Well, this was a stroke of luck! Gas was fuel for my fire, and it was in pipes that ran everywhere, even into Grant Cleveland's bedroom.

Problem is, with a gaseous fuel, I had to concentrate it around Grant Cleveland to prevent blowing up the whole house and everyone in it. Yanking a hair outta my head, I made a loop in it using a slip knot, and used a spell to weave the threads of energy around Grant Cleveland on his bed, just like the shape of the hair in my hand. I urged the threads to make an invisible bubble around him that would contain the gas. I then siphoned off gas from the wall lamp, making it stay within the bubble. Kept going until the bubble stretched and strained with the pressure, and then I lit up the gas. Took only a small spark from my fire bowl sent through the threads, sent with all my angst and anger, and Grant Cleveland became a one-man flaming inferno. He was a big man, almost as big as President Taft, and he let out a roar like a bear before I could pull the hair loop closed to put an end to him.

But something stopped me cold.

A tug on the string of hair in the other direction exhorted me to slow down. "He deserves this pain, earned it, it is righteous justice," whispered a voice. Another hissed, "Giving him a quick death would be letting him off too easy. He should be made to suffer longer for what he did to Tommy, Tommy and others." I'd never had a brush with Chaos and Destruction before, but I sure knew it was happening now.

I ignored their siren call and yanked the hair loop closed. Grant Cleveland's fire became so hot it turned white, melting him into his bed. Then the oddest thing happened.

Usually when a person dies, their spirit leaves their body and floats away into the universe. Whether to heaven or hell or some other place, all depends on who you ask. But Grant Cleveland's spirit, it just stuck there. Stuck to the melted mess on his bed like a fly caught in molasses. I figured I just saw firsthand the making of a ghost. Hope it's worse for him than purgatory.

I blew on the hair in my hand to extinguish the flames, just as someone finally opened the bedroom door after banging on it for a while. Next came the most god-awful scream. Since my work was done I stayed no longer, following the threads back to my casting rock, all the while trying to make a bargain with the universe.

Casting to create something or help someone requires nothing but the will of the caster and her tools. But casting to destroy something always has a cost, requires a payment, a sacrifice. I knew this from the start, but I thought I could bargain with the universe to let Tommy's pain serve as the sacrifice. As always, the universe had something else in mind.

Just before my casting came back to me through the threads, something held me up. Something kept part of my consciousness in the threads, suspending me in them. The siren songs of Chaos and Destruction then called to me again, stronger this time.

"That was a nice piece of work, fire witch," whispered Chaos. "Incinerated the monster without causing collateral damage. Takes talent that does."

Destruction purred, "Used the dark side of the power for that, you did. 'Course, the dark and the light are just flip sides of the same coin. There is no life without death, and no death without life. Both are necessary for the scales to balance."

Chaos crooned, "When humans tip the scales out of balance, we do what is necessary to put them aright. Great injustices now rage across this land, unbalancing the scales, even after your work tonight. Though it was a start."

"Appears you have a penchant for justice, though show more mercy than we usually prefer," Destruction sighed.

"Appears you have the will and know the ways of the threads, and have the gumption to use them," Chaos agreed.

I admit, I was curious. "What do you want of me?"

"We want you to help put the scales back into balance. We want you to seek out the monsters in the night, the destroyers of dreams, the ravagers of flesh, the makers of nightmares, and we want you to end them. We want you to use your powers in the service of justice."

Now, my momma didn't raise a fool. You don't make a deal with Chaos and Destruction without knowing the consequences. Knowing the price. "Tell me, what would it cost me and mine to dispense your brand of justice, hmm?"

The universe itself seemed to pause while they consulted, then the threads resonated with the certainty of a decision. "The price is your promise to answer our call each and every time. Answer the call and use your powers to balance the scales. If you fail to answer the call, if you refuse to do what we ask, you will lose your powers forever."

Now, I wasn't thrilled about being compelled to do Chaos and Destruction's bidding on pain of losing my gift, but the idea of slaying predators, torching abusers, avenging the wrongs of the rich and powerful who thought they could take and take and take from the rest of us, well, it made me smile. So, I made the deal.

Oh, you think I was wrong to do so? You think I made a deal with the devil and nothing good will ever come of it? Well, certainly not for you, because you are next on my call list. Hope you like fire.

Anne Keck writes speculative fiction and is published in several Redwood Writers' anthologies. Anne believes in ocean swimming, live music, public libraries, climate action, feminism, inclusivity, and cooking as an expression of love. Originally from Sonoma County, California, she and her husband now call Maui home. Find Anne at www.annekeck.com.

Star Chatter[6]

Betty Les
Redwood Writers

when earth's face
turns away from the sun
and in the darkness
we can see the stars shining
listen
for they are talking too

find a dark silent place
lie down under a sky
full of stars
feel them draw close
cover you with a blanket
of the softest bird down
then listen again
for the star chatter

their various observations
wars, acts of kindness
exquisite beauty, terrible grief
what they make of our travails
what they hope we will do
or not do to save ourselves

Betty Les writes about science, nature, and the human condition. Favorite themes are birds and insects, the deep presence of rivers and trees, and the consciousness of rocks. Betty was chosen as a Redwood Writers Award of Merit Poet in 2018 and nominated for the Pushcart Prize in 2023. She is a member of the Blue Moon Poetry Collective. Her chapbook *Just Enough to See* was published in 2023 by Finishing Line Press. Her second chapbook, *Touring the Stars*, is scheduled for release in spring 2025.

---

[6]Previously published Phases: Redwood Writers 2023 Poetry Anthology, ed(s). Les Bernstein and Fran Holland-Claggett. Santa Rosa: Redwood Writers Press 2023

Visiting Author[7]

Cami Rumble
San Joaquin Valley Writers

We put her in a jar
and tap on the glass—
How do you get your ideas?
What is your reading life like?
Notepads poised, observing diligently,
watching the merest flutter to determine pattern and behavior.
What is your editing process like?
How do you know when a work is finished?
We dissect her with eager hope.

She is the first specimen to fall into our grasp:
A creature submits to the microscope
and we gingerly prod its protected parts
in the name of artistic knowledge.
When during the day do you write?
How did you find your agent?
At last she is released, back to the
nebulous creative wild from whence she came,
leaving a glow of inspiration that will last
until we catch the next one.

Cami Rumble is a writer and stay-at-home mom who graduated from California State University Stanislaus with a degree in English. Her poetry has appeared or is forthcoming in *Teach. Write.*, Oprelle Publications, *Levitate*, and *Poetry Breakfast*, as well as Redwood Writers' Poetry Anthology *Phases*. Cami lives in California's Central Valley.

[7] Previously published in *Phases: Redwood Writers 2023 Poetry Anthology*, ed(s). Les Bernstein and Fran Holland-Claggett. Santa Rosa: Redwood Writers Press 2023.

Main Character Energy[8]

Crissi Langwell
Redwood Writers

The sun is setting on the golden horizon, ending another August night in the heart of Beachcomber Cove. We stand on the edge of a cliff, the same cliff we'd met on five weeks ago when we were set up on a blind date. I'd thought it was a strange place for a first meeting back then. But now, I find it comforting, romantic even. Especially with the way the waves are crashing against the rocks below, like my heart is crashing against my chest.

The breeze flirts with my hair, soft tendrils tickling my face. I start to lift my hand, but he's there first. Always ready to take care of my needs without me having to say a word. His hand goes for my hair as his gaze lowers, then rests on my lips.

"You look like someone waiting to be kissed," he purrs. He pulls me in closer, his arms wrapping tightly around me, his breathing intensifying as he lowers his mouth to —"

"STOP."

I tear myself away from Lorenzo, who stumbles backward.

"Violet, what the heck?" He tries to get his footing, but never quite makes it, and I brace myself as he teeters toward the cliff.

"Lorenzo!"

But it's too late. He's gone over, his feet the last things I see as he disappears over the edge. I suck in a sympathetic breath, glancing at the spot where he was standing. Then I peer down. His body is contorted unnaturally on the sand below, completely still.

"Oops," I wince, then turn back to where I was facing, calling out beyond the pages of this romance novel I live in. "Hey. Are you paying attention?"

I wait for Chloe Lambert, the author of this godawful novel, to acknowledge me. But there's no answer. Instead, a few romantic clichés stream across the skyline.

"I let out a breath I didn't know I was holding."

[8] Previously published in *One Universe to the Left: Stories of Speculative Fiction*, ed. Mara Lynn Johnstone. Santa Rosa: Redwood Writers Press 2023.

"The silence is deafening."

"Our eyes lock across the room."

"He is a vision for sore eyes."

"His kiss becomes the air I breathe."

"Spare me," I mutter. Obviously I'm going to have to get her attention before she fills this whole damn novel with dreadfully overused phrases. She already saddled me with that joke of a love interest.

Think, think, think.

I see the words appear in the blank sky above me. Big, bold THINK, times three. I realize my thoughts are being transcribed, that I have somehow manifested a shift in power. I start to cheer, but the cursor is blinking and I realize anything I say is going to end up on the page. So I clear my mind and then speak pointedly into the emptiness.

"Chloe Lambert, Violet Skye needs to talk with you."

Then I wait, watching the cursor blink a few more times above me. And then . . .

"Hello?"

I grin. It worked. I finally got through to the author. That's when I get busy.

"So, I accidentally offed Lorenzo, but it's okay because he was absolutely terrible. You really need to watch more romance movies or something, because that guy was one huge red flag, starting with his misogynistic vibes. Oh, and he was kind of a stalker. Did you know he sat outside my work for five days straight, and I hadn't even told him where I worked yet? Of course you knew. You wrote it. But seriously, if I didn't know better, I'd think I was in a suspense thriller and inches away from being filleted, and not in a romantic beach read. Also, can you please have my next love interest brush his teeth? Or maybe have him lay off the raw onions?"

I force a pause, catching my breath as I watch the typed words on the page catch up with everything I said. Then I wait as the cursor goes back to blinking. I study my nails, realizing they are in desperate need of a polish change. I'm going to have to get Chloe to write that in the story, too. Maybe a whole makeover, while I'm at it, starting with my long, red hair. I read somewhere that only 2% of the world's population has red hair, and yet romance novels make it seem like this is the norm. I've been a redhead in the past five novels, and I'm getting kind of tired of maintaining these lengthy locks. I'm practically Rapunzel when I'd rather be a dramatic brunette with a pixie cut. Maybe she can make me sporty, too. I mean, I'm already slender with a beautifully toned body, despite the fact that my diet consists of huge cheeseburgers and sushi gorge fests, plus multiple cocktails every night. She might as well give me athletic ability to at least make my perfect body a bit more realistic.

"Who is this?"

The cursor blinks after the words, and I pause for a second, wondering if she's for real. I mean, who else would be talking to her through the computer?

And then I realize how strange this must be for her, and that she's probably freaking out right now.

"This is Violet Skye, your main character. And I may have accidentally deleted your whole story because I'm sitting here in a blank document. But it's okay because your story suc—"

I pause, wondering how to say the next part without hurting her feelings.

"I have some ideas on how to improve the story and was hoping you'd let me help you."

The cursor then blinks a bit longer than it should and I know Chloe Lambert is currently going through a crisis of reality. So I know I need to act quick. I just hope this works.

"Chloe, type these words: The author Chloe Lambert finds herself inside a romance novel with her laptop."

I wait, and then, ever so slowly, those same words appear under my own typed text.

And just like that, she's here.

She's different than I imagined. A little chubby, but pleasantly so. Freckles all over her face. Coffee stains on her gray sweatshirt, and it's possible she hasn't washed her hair in a week. The dark circles under her eyes give away her late writing nights, and her pale skin tells me she sees more screen glow than actual sunshine.

"What the—" She slowly turns around, taking in the nothingness that surrounds us. Then her eyes land on me. "It's really you," she breathes. "Violet Skye. You're real."

"Well, kind of," I say. "I mean, I'm as real as your

imagination."

"You're gorgeous," she says, her eyes like saucers. I laugh.

"Well, I'd say thank you, but I can't take credit. You created me."

"I suppose I did," she murmurs. Then she looks around us again. "It's almost blinding in here. All this white. Is there a way to fix it?"

"Yeah," I say, pointing at her computer. "You have to write it."

"Oh." Chloe glances at the laptop. "Like this?" She sits cross-legged and opens the screen. After a moment of thinking, she starts to type:

"The gentle shush of ocean waves fills the salty air in Beachcomber Cove. It's the kind of day poets write about, with the pleading cries of seagulls floating on wandering winds and a blue sky that stretches beyond the horizon, not a cloud in sight."

The stark whiteness of our surroundings takes on color once again, from the creamy sands that extend for miles and an ocean that seems to go on forever. And Chloe and I are back on the cliff. Thankfully, Lorenzo is not.

"That's much better," I say. "The surroundings, and what you've written. I bet this second stab at the novel will go much better."

"I don't know what happened," she says. "One minute I was writing, and the next, my computer just kind of blipped." The expression on her face falls as realization takes over. "Oh God, you're right. I have to rewrite everything. All that work. It's . . . gone."

"Yeah, about that." She obviously didn't understand the first time, so I don't want to tell her again that it's probably my fault somehow. But she needs to know how bad it was. "It just wasn't working," I say. "It's not like your past works, with the amazing chemistry and super gorgeous scenery. I'll never forget that one romance that took place in a Paris café. I wanted to live in that one forever."

She looks at me curiously. "You were there?"

"I'm always there. I'm the main character. This time, I'm Violet Skye, living in beautiful Beachcomber Cove, meeting the man who is supposed to be the love of my life. Except, here's the thing." I scrunch my face, then shake my head. "Lorenzo was awful. And, well, I kind of killed him off accidentally."

"You what?"

"Well, it was an accident, but if I'd been given enough time, I probably would have done it on purpose. You know, that man cut me off every single time I started to talk. Whenever I'd start to say something, he'd get so excited about his own ideas that he'd just run over the top of me and I'd never get to finish what I was saying."

"He was a conversationalist," Chloe says.

"Not a very patient one. Or thoughtful. Like the time I said I wanted ice cream and he thought that was such a good idea, he got a cone for just himself." I raise an eyebrow in her direction.

"Uh, he knew how much you valued equality, including who paid for the dates."

"Well, that's convenient. I paid for the last date at that steakhouse, and he couldn't even buy me an ice cream cone."

"Hold on," Chloe says, then tilts her head as if trying to find the thought. "What about the time he took you out for an exquisite dinner at that rotating restaurant that overlooked the city, then treated you to a weekend in that fancy hotel suite?"

Admittedly, the restaurant was a major step up from our usual cheap ass dates. And the food was orgasmic. But that was the only orgasm that happened for me that weekend.

"Lorenzo stared at my tits the whole time —"

"That dress was killer," Chloe cuts in.

"And he was rude to the waiter when he thought the guy was flirting with me. Then schooled me on etiquette as if he thought I was raised in a barn. But that's not even the worst. He basically made it clear that a dinner like that meant a happy ending for him."

Chloe winces. "I was trying to make him more Alpha-like."

"There's Alpha, and then there's Alpha-hole, and Lorenzo was not the good kind."

"But there was that steamy scene in the shower."

I shoot her a look. "Have you ever done it in a shower?" I ask.

She bites her lip, then shakes her head.

"Let's just say that it's less than ideal in the best of circumstances. But in this one, Lorenzo got his, and I finally got to sleep. By the way, kudos on the ritzy hotel room. More of that, please."

"I just don't get it," Chloe says. "If you couldn't stand him, why were you with him?"

"Are you being serious?" I ask. Her nod confirms it. "Because you *wrote* it. I don't get to pick who I want to be with or make my own choices or do anything that isn't inside your will. What you write is what happens. And in this case, you wrote me a bad romance."

Chloe runs her hand over the keyboard, as if a story will magically appear. But so far, all we have is this cliff that overlooks gorgeous Beachcombers Cove.

"So what do I do?" she finally asks.

I grin. This is the moment I have dreamed of since the beginning. To be fair, Chloe has given me some pretty epic adventures. There was that one time I met this sweet guy at a park who ended up being a very charming prince. Then there was Chloe's fantasy phase, when I fell in love with the faerie prince who transformed me into a beautiful fae princess. And I'll never forget that dystopian adventure when she gave me kickass fighting skills, and let me save the guy, and then the world.

But sometimes her storytelling takes a weird turn, especially when it seemed she was trying new things. Like this whole Alpha thing. Don't get me wrong. The Alpha trope can be hot. It just has to be done right. The guy can be strong, broodish, even an asshole. But he also puts his lady above all things. He might be possessive, but it's all for her protection. He'll burn the whole world down, just for her.

As for Lorenzo, that jackass would have run from a fire and left me to burn with it.

"You'll really let me write my own story?" I ask. She nods, and I can already picture it. My brother's best friend—a hot, dangerous guy I'm absolutely forbidden from dating. But then he saves me from a Lorenzo-type tool, swinging me on the back of his motorcycle before peeling away from the restaurant. A love affair we have to keep secret from my brother who will absolutely kill us both.

"I have a few ideas," I say. "Get ready to start writing."

Crissi Langwell is the author of fourteen published books, with genres that include romance, young adult, and women's fiction. Her latest novel is *Naked Coffee Guy*, the second book in her Sunset Bay romance series. Crissi is the vice president and web editor of Redwood Writers, and she is the Communications Director for Oakmont Village Association. She lives in Petaluma, California, with her fellow writerly husband and a sassy Maine Coon cat.

Silver Spoons[9]

Inga Aksamit
Redwood Writers

I stood at the kitchen sink polishing Mom's silver spoons. Searing afternoon sun streamed through the window, catching the glint of the shiny metal. It was one hundred degrees—perfect weather for iced tea in Mom's tall, slender glasses etched with bamboo leaves. Mom always paired them with the special silver spoons. Or were they straws? They were both. The long, hollow straw was crafted to look like segmented bamboo with a small, cupped spoon joined to the end. At the highest segment dangled a petite charm. At first, I tried to race through the task quickly, removing just enough tarnish to make the spoons acceptable. As I polished, I felt the smoothness of the cool silver and the bump of the bamboo nodes. I haphazardly polished four spoons and put the other eight back in the drawer. *Good enough*, I thought.

The next morning, I looked at the half-polished silver and thought, *nope, not good enough*. Mom's been gone two years now, but she might as well be standing beside me saying, "You can do better." Mom would certainly have sent those back to the servants in the old days, when we were overseas. I sighed and got the polish out again. There was no big party to prepare for but I felt vaguely guilty for using the tarnished spoons the day before when two friends dropped by.

"Oh, look, how wonderful. I was dying for iced tea in this heat and here it is in these beautiful glasses. And the silver spoons are so lovely," one friend exclaimed, not noticing or being too polite to mention the deplorable state of the silver.

It felt odd to have the energy and motivation to do this kind of mundane, optional household chore. For the year after Mom died, I felt like I was walking through molasses every day, groping through endless lists.

"Inga, we need to go through what needs to be done," said Dad, sitting at the kitchen table the day after Mom died, and again the week

---

[9] Previously published in *Remember When: Fiction & Memoir Tales of Memories and Times Past*, ed(s). Shawn Langwell and Crissi Langwell. Santa Rosa: Redwood

after, the month after, and at regular intervals in between. Even at ninety-five, with his body failing him, his mind raced on, ticking off all the things we (I) needed to complete. I trudged through meetings with lawyers, paperwork, the will, cremation, and memorial planning and all the while, every day, I made sure that Dad, frail and now without his beloved wife, was cared for. I made certain that meals were on the table, doctor's appointments were made, errands were run, and caregivers organized when I couldn't be there. The lists filled an entire spiral-bound notebook, spilling over to a second one as "completed" check marks accumulated. Every morning, I tried to find one or two things to check off the list, my normally efficient brain feeling leaden and slow. New lists evolved as the months piled up.

"Dad, we need to think about what you want to do. It's been six months."

"I know. You can't be here forever," said Dad after a long pause.

"No, but you can. We can get more help to stay with you night and day or—" I trailed off, not wanting to mention other options. I underestimated his always-practical nature.

"I think I might be better off in a facility," he said. It felt like a knife to my heart, but it was a necessary step. I moved on to the search for an Assisted Living facility, boxed up the house, found a renter, and executed the move. Just as the mental fog started to lift, and I cautiously welcomed the first feeble sparks of energy, Covid-19 hit. A new fog descended. At least everyone was in this latest fog with me as I slid into the thick, paralyzing molasses again.

Another year passed. This flicker of interest in taking care of something as humdrum, not to mention entirely unnecessary, as polishing silver was a breakthrough in 2021. I embraced it and put my current to-do list aside.

I went to work on the first four half-polished spoons, then the next four. They were shinier but still had stubborn discoloration. I left the worst of the bunch, four spoons almost entirely blackened with tarnish, in the drawer. These were the ones that had lost their charms along the way after too many moves and too many decades. *Maybe I should toss those out,* a throwback to the molasses times when I often looked for the quickest solution. *But no, they are silver. That's silly. I can't throw silver away.*

A few hours later, I passed by the eight polished spoons, but the four remaining tarnished ones tugged at me. *I wonder if I can save those black ones*. I did a little research and next thing I knew, I was standing in front of the stove doing a chemistry experiment. A big pot of boiling water foamed angrily as I dumped the box of baking soda in it, seething and spewing like a volcano. When the soda water settled down to a whimpering mass, I poured it over the black spoons laid out on a sheet of aluminum foil in a glass baking dish. Small bubbles formed and dissolved, the soda reacting with the aluminum to slowly erase the black bits of tarnish. I felt my spirits rise with each bubble. It was magical. With energy surging, I plunked all the spoons in. Using tongs, I removed one of the charmless spoons. It still had some tarnish on it. I got the pot of silver polish, dipped the round sponge in water, and scooped out a bit of the white paste. The remaining tarnish had loosened in the hot soda bath and with a little polish, the spoons soon gleamed.

As I polished the silver spoon, I felt all the nodes, my memories racing back in time, skipping over the cocktail parties in Indonesia, happy hours in Peru and shindigs in Bangladesh. I zoomed all the way back to Pakistan in 1963 when I was four years old. We had moved there from California for my father's job as an irrigation engineer. This was the first of several overseas assignments that took us to scattered parts of the world. The glasses and spoons, acquired in Pakistan, somehow survived mostly intact through all the moves. The silver was hand carried round and round the world in a heavy blue Pan Am bag with the rest of the silver flatware. Dad carried it when he went overseas to find housing and get settled in before we arrived. When we were evacuated in two separate wars, it fell to Mom to carry the weighty bag because they evacuated only women and children. When we left Pakistan in the India-Pakistan war of 1965, Mom and I were evacuated by a U.S. Army cargo plane to Tehran with the heavy Pan Am bag. A month later, Dad realized there were no planes coming for the men. He pieced together a complicated patchwork of trains and cars to weave his way through Pakistan and Afghanistan before lining up a flight from Kabul back to the States.

For this round of polishing, I wasn't rushed or exasperated the way I had been after Mom passed away and Dad's care fell in my lap. I fell into a reverie as I picked up each spoon. I noticed how my thumb just fit in the cup of the spoon and ran my fingers up the straw, feeling the bumps. The memories rushed in.

"Mom, can I go outside?" shouted four-year-old me.

"Sure, but don't bother the servants. They're busy," said Mom. I slipped out the back door and squatted on the back porch the way the Pakistani men did, knees practically up to my chin, watching the action. The maid and the cook gossiped next to the *charpoy* string bed, surrounded by white cotton cloths and pots of polish, rubbing the silver to a bright sheen. They lounged around on the bed in the heat of the day when everyone wilted and work came to a halt, using it like a sofa. It was common to see *charpoy* beds under the shade of mango trees outside of shops or homes.

I picked up the first polished charm and couldn't figure out what the boxy shape was. I turned it over a few times. Oh, it was a *charpoy* bed. I tried unsuccessfully to polish the delicate legs of the bed. But the flat sole of an upturned *mojari* slipper shined like a luminous silver mirror, as did the surface of the flip-flops. With some work with a Q-Tip, I got the sail on the boat gleaming. The genie tea pot was intricate with a long, curved handle and spout, but I burnished it as much as I could as memories of tea parties in Pakistan floated up.

I sat quietly on the sofa in my "going out" clothes, a frilly dress with black patent leather shoes, a four-year-old absorbing the vocabulary and cadence of adult conversation. Mom, dressed in a slim pencil skirt and high heels, held her dainty tea cup up to Chip's mom for a refill.

"You should go down to the school and get Inga enrolled," said Chip's mom, pouring tea into Mom's cup from the tall, ornate tea pot. Chip, who always sported a blond buzz cut, was a grade ahead of me so he was already in school and was my best friend. I kept quiet. *School? Could I really be a Big Girl already?*

The woman looked at me and said, "You'd like to go to school, right?"

"Yes, of course," I said, without having the slightest idea if I'd like it or not. I would have been too young in the States, but somehow I was admitted to kindergarten at the Lahore American School the following week. I guess I was a Big Girl already and Mom was relieved to get some time to herself.

The elephant was the smallest of the charms and had many fine lines that retained the tarnish, providing a contrast with the shiny edges. I used the Q-Tip and dipped the cotton end in polish. Rubbing it on the elephant conjured up a memory of a traveling fair that came to Lahore one year with camels, elephants, dancing bears, a pigeon that pulled a cart holding a green parrot, and trained monkeys clothed in long dresses. One of the missing charms was a camel. The elephant stood in for my camel memories.

"Dad, look at the camel. Can I ride the camel with Lisa?" I asked at the fair. Lisa was one of my classmates at the Lahore American School, and the double saddle was perfect for the two of us.

"Okay, I'll lift you up," he said, hoisting me into the front seat atop the kneeling camel. As soon as Lisa's father lifted her up, the camel-wallah called out a command. The camel lunged forward violently, lurched backward and we were up. Up so high that I squealed with surprise, then giggled at our bird's-eye view of the fair, towering over everyone. We rocked wildly from side to side, and my legs, encased in white tights under my party dress, gripped the saddle tightly. My Mary Janes hung over each side with no stirrups to gain purchase. I was glad when Dad lifted me off and put me on solid ground.

The flower charm took me back to one of my favorite memories, slipping through lotus blossoms on Dal Lake in Kashmir on a narrow, wooden *shikara* gondola with pointed ends and a simple canopy to protect us from the sun. It was in Dal Lake that I caught my first fish and made Dad so proud. The intertwined hearts were for Mom and Dad, their love enduring many decades and tumultuous moves and only truly separated in death. A kaleidoscope of memories of this happy time in our lives exploded in my head.

The silver flashed as it caught the sunlight from the window, the tarnish driven away by my polishing and Mom's admonishments. It would please her to see me cutting the lengths of soft blue felt impregnated with minerals that would banish the dark smudges. I wrapped the spoons in three bundles.

The next day, I served iced tea with a sprig of mint in the tall glasses with the shiny silver spoons to some other friends who dropped by. As I prepared the tea, I shared a secret moment with Mom and Dad. I chose the *charpoy* bed charm for myself, knowing no one else would recognize it. It was my special connection to a unique time in my life. I realized that, finally, I could remember Mom and Dad with gladness in my heart instead of grief.

Inga Aksamit grew up in Pakistan, Peru, Bangladesh, and California as part of an expat family. She had a corporate career in healthcare but is now an award-winning author who is working on a memoir of her childhood adventures. You can follow her at IngasAdventures.com.

Open[10]

Jo Ann Smith
Redwood Writers

consider things that open
jars windows
lights roads
faucets awnings
elevators wounds
anemones

clouds open for rain
fall on open flowers
doors to neighbors, strangers
and trick or treaters
minds to wisdom
hearts to love

revelations of truth and myth
written on walls, hidden in shadow
behind closed blinds
reveal pathways to
courageous conversion
when they open

contemplate the pill bug
a roly-poly creature
its back crinkled like a lobster tail
touch it and afraid, it rolls into a ball
undaunted and curious, it opens
like an unclenched fist

---

10 Previously published in Phases: Redwood Writers 2023 Poetry Anthology, ed(s). Les Bernstein and Fran Holland-Claggett. Santa Rosa: Redwood Writers Press 2023.

Jo Ann Smith's career in public education culminated as a high school superintendent. In that capacity, her writing relied on the orderly left side of her brain. She now finds herself drawn to the reading and writing of poetry—a creative journey that continues to be challenging, revealing, and liberating.

Poet's Cramp[11]

Lawrence Sherman Cohn
Redwood Writers

Not exactly a block
But an emotional emergency.
And those damned percussive bells
Ringing in the numbness
More like a concussion than a KO.
First a catch in the lungs
The light headaches thinly pounding out
The consumptive drought.
Then, a mawkish vow of silence.
A simple retreat from the truth.

One foolish month it started up again
During an April thaw.
The ideas dangled like gold trinkets,
But every try was an unruly verse.
The voice rambled on eating its words.
How cruel the muse when with a flurry
It inspired everything everywhere.
Even the textures were chaotic.
Every cross out a genetic disorder
A rogue thought for every erasure.

Later the din ceased with veritable vibes.
No longer devilishly lost in subjunctives.
No longer time to treat my scars.
Poems flowed through with radiance.
Rhythms, Rhymes, and iambics
Sweet words tapped together like chimes.
Belated truths became ripened fruit.

Motifs, similes, and metaphors,

[11] Previously published in *Phases: Redwood Writers 2023 Poetry Anthology*, ed(s). Les Bernstein and Fran Holland-Claggett. Santa Rosa: Redwood Writers Press 2023.

Fashioned molds to cast images
The mystical onslaught - a reclaiming of privileges.

Lawrence Sherman Cohn started his career in poetry when he was first published in *Littack Magazine* (William Oxley, Ed.) as part of the Vitalist Poetry genre in Oxford, England, as well as in various college journals. His recent poetry publications in 2023 can be found in *Phases*, Clarendon House Poetica 13 & 14, and the *Fault Zone*.

Lawrence is a dual member of Redwood Writers and the San Francisco Peninsula branches.

Ashes to Ashes[12]

Linda Stamps
Redwood Writers

My brother's bones lay scattered in the New Mexico desert and the Florida Keys. He died when lung cancer, complicated by pneumonia, forced his last breath. His life was spent in and out of jails and institutions for mostly minor mishaps, wrong-place, wrong-time kind of stuff. He was schizophrenic and neither society nor the family knew what to do with him. After years of cleaning up after his "escapades" we mostly ignored him. It's not that we didn't love him. We simply didn't know how to wrap our arms around him without falling into the black hole of his existence.

Gene lived on the streets of Lorain, Ohio, our hometown, where he panhandled and heard the voices of hell in his beautiful head. My siblings and I lived in other parts of the country, home only for holidays and an occasional visit. I would sometimes see him and most times not.

His diagnosis and demise spanned six weeks. He knew he was dying, took it in as best he could. He lived in a dirty, rat-infested house for those on public assistance. He wanted to come home to die. Dad said no. He had spent the last ten years caring for our bed-bound mother. "I just can't do it anymore," he said.

My brother begged me to help, between coughing fits and pain, as he struggled to breathe in the back seat of my rental car. Our father had a live-in girlfriend, a retired nurse's aide, who, after hours of cajoling, agreed to care for Gene until he died. "Couldn't be more than a couple of weeks," she said. Dad did as he was told. My brother returned home to die.

The family held a backyard picnic in his honor. Friends, cousins, aunts all came like a collective amnesia had been lifted. He enjoyed, and struggled with, all the attention, his isolation and loneliness suspended for the afternoon. Except for his voices, or so we thought, he lived his life unconnected to anyone or anything except his monthly injection.

[12] Previously published in *Sunset Sunrise: A collection of endings and beginnings*, ed. Crissi Langwell. Santa Rosa: Redwood Writers Press 2020.

He didn't much care for it. Said it made him feel dull and lost in fog. Oftentimes, Gene skipped his clinic appointment. His case worker might find him in an alley, sleeping, or laughing like a wild man, chattering at the wind, freezing in the cold, blustery winters on the shores of Lake Erie.

He died in July sprawled out in a hospital bed in the living room. But before he did, I'd be amazed at what death resurrected, restored, and reopened. The great dot connector unearthed a barrage of images clear and true, some painful, others so simple that gratitude flooded my heart.

About a week before his death, we drove along the lake, Carlos Santana blaring on the CD player. He loved the acoustic boys: Hendrix, Clapton, Mick Fleetwood. We grooved together as Carlos wailed, "Black Magic Woman."

The moment weakened him. He grew tired. But, during that brief respite, we returned to a space we shared as kids, just the two of us perched in our own willow trees in the backyard. He'd find a spot up in the branches of his and I in mine. We'd sit in silence and look out across the yard or the neighborhood. Other times we would talk about whatever kids talk about, not quite shouting across the distance. Big sister and little brother born seventeen months apart.

I'd forgotten what it was like to be with him, be connected, calibrated, all that shared DNA tuned up, humming. I remembered how much I felt for him, not his disease or distress. I recalled the boy who held my hand when he got scared or looked to me for comfort when he needed it.

The memory faded. Stopped at a red light, I glanced at him as he was dozing off. He started to lay his head in my lap and pulled back. Perhaps the position became too awkward for his 6'2" frame. I like to think that was why he chose to lean against the door instead.

Several days later, too weak to get up, he drifted off into unconsciousness, his breathing so labored the bed rattled and shook like an endless earthquake. My sister and I sat with him day and night and watched his spirit struggle to release itself from his body. At times, he would gesture, move his hands back and forth, as though he wanted to stress a point.

Other family members visited while the hospice crew provided the foundation for his journey. A few hours before he died, we heard a knock on the door. A brother and sister team arrived from a local church. They sat by his bedside, prayed, cried, and told us how he helped them with a building project, how he'd hang out at the church and just be. The stories offered by these two friends of my brother shaped visions that pierced my scattered view of his troubled life. In that momentary community, perhaps peace silenced the voices in his head and breached his solitary confinement.

His friends left. The visit seemed to agitate him. His body temperature rose. He appeared restless. Some of us decided to go to the grocery store to buy food for dinner. By the time we returned, Gene was dead. I called the mortuary. We each kissed him good-bye and watched as the mortician and his assistant lifted him onto a gurney. As they slid his body into the van, my sister's grief overwhelmed her. Her legs and arms thrashed with sorrow and loss. I kept my arm around her. She, younger than he, had lost an ally in navigating the family dynamics.

Before Gene died, he made two things known. He wanted to be cremated and he wanted his ashes scattered in a warm place. Cremation came up as we were driving around one day. I asked him if that's what he wanted. He nodded. I told him I wanted to take care of it. "No," he said. "Dad will." I asked him to please let me do this. He took my hand and kissed it. He agreed. I wept. All that sweetness for a *mea culpa*, the last-minute effort to do something for all those do nothings.

Later, he raised concerns about cremation. I told him that's what he'd chosen. He said, "What do I know, I'm crazy," reminding me of a time I described him that way to a friend in his presence.

The cremation played like a grade B horror film. My sisters and I met the funeral director at the mortuary. The loaded van stood ready in the parking lot. The tiny procession wound its way past my brother's place and crossed some railroad tracks. We pulled up to an abandoned warehouse. The structure stood empty except for a room that contained a large, green incinerator.

Gene's body rested in a cardboard box. Someone had drawn an arrow and written "Head" on one end of it. We followed the gurney to where the cremator stood anchored to the cement floor. The attendant slid the container, headfirst, into the chamber.

He bolted the door closed. My sister knelt and bowed. The

funeral director, not understanding the gesture, assumed she fainted. My other sister and I assured him that she hadn't. We left before they flipped what appeared to be a light-switch. We'd been advised of the sound and smell.

We drove along the lake as the CD player blasted Carlos Santana. We moaned and wailed, sobbed and wept about the things we held dear and the legacy of neglect. It was clear he wouldn't be cold anymore.

I shipped the ashes to our brother Michael in Florida, who scouted the warmth of the Keys. He chose Islamorada where the temperatures rise to 99 degrees and never drop below 69. Later, each of us would receive a videotape of the event. Michael, standing in the ocean, a bucket of ashes in hand, making the sign of the cross, and then gently pouring them into the warm waters off the Florida coast.

Before I sent the ashes, my sister and I removed small pieces of bone fragment. We kept them until we let go. Our other sister released the shards in the high desert of New Mexico near two extinct volcanoes. Lots of sun and warmth. Gene's cremains received more care and concern than his living, mortal self. How easy it is to make a wish come true when the end is in sight.

Several months later we organized a private memorial service. It was Thanksgiving. We gathered at a local hotel for dinner. The service, held in one of the meeting rooms, accommodated the group of nine mourners. On a linen-covered table we placed his brogans, the shoes he wore when he walked all over the county, mostly for relief, not exercise. We displayed some of his paintings and drawings, his Cleveland Indians baseball shirt. I wrote a blessing for his next life wishing him all the things he never had in this one. I remember looking out the window before the service knowing, but for his death, he would not be among us to celebrate the holiday.

The thought was colder than the wind portending another frigid, Lake Erie winter. I understood my brother's desire for warmth, the heat of the sun, the affection of family and friends, memories of good times, the touch of a lover. The shocking news that someone you love is dying jarred me out of my aversion, avoidance, and anger at what his life had become. The expanse between the boy in the willow tree and the man living on the streets, drugged and haunted, corrupted my memories of him. While he was alive, I did not know how to reach across the expanse, to take his hand, pull him closer. Yet, Gene's death leveled that distance and resurrected our time together among the branches of those willow trees, if only for a moment.

When I look out across the high desert of New Mexico to those extinct volcanos, I shiver a little from the cold truth of all that warmth never given, never offered, so easily ignored. When I die, I too want to be cremated, ashes strewn. I haven't decided where yet. Maybe then the chill of love lost and withheld will come to rest. Gene is not forgotten. He is remembered with remorse and sadness. Not an easy legacy.

It has been eighteen years since my brother's death. Here's what I know to be true. Always seek the warmth, find it everywhere while you live. Give it freely, don't wait, hold back, or be timid. Because in the end, it's the only thing that frees the living from the dead. My brother is long-over his mortal torment. I still seek forgiveness, release, the warm [illegible]

Linda Stamps established careers in law, journalism, and higher education. She worked on staff at the *Mendocino Beacon* and the *Fort Bragg Advocate News*. She wrote for the Time Warner publication, *Out in All Directions*, an LGBTQ history and almanac. Her writing has been published in a number of anthologies. She is an award-winning flash fiction author.

Who I Was[13]

Mara Lynn Johnstone
Redwood Writers

I met up with Ethan in the waiting room. He was upbeat as ever while our two sets of parents exchanged pleasantries. His whole family was there: both parents, three younger siblings, one older, an uncle and a grandmother. I just had my parents.

"I can't decide if I want to be famous, or just cool," Ethan told me. "I mean, it would be a blast to have been the inventor of the hover engine, or some space pioneer or something, but I bet that kind of attention gets old. Still." He struck a snooty pose. "I daresay we can still be chums once the world finds out how amazing my past life was."

I laughed along, trying not to be nervous. It was easy to let Ethan do all the talking, like usual. I hadn't seen him in the last few weeks since graduation, but I'd known the guy for years. Some things never change.

But some do, I thought. Hoping to get my mind off my nerves, I picked up a magazine and flipped the pages. It was one of those "good news" ones, meant to put people at ease. It didn't really work, but I took some comfort in the highlights. Rainforests being restored, gorilla resort getting new teaching supplies, life support systems for the newest spacecraft getting upgraded for more adventurous trips.

Ethan didn't pause for breath. "I've always thought my birthmark meant I died of a broken neck," he said, turning to point at the small brown line just above his collar. "But maybe I was assassinated! I could have been somebody big! They don't tell you the truth about how the real celebrities die, you know. Any official story is a lie to weed out people pretending to be them eighteen years later."

I just nodded, fingering the birthmark hidden in my own hair. There was another along my ribs on the same side. Unusual to have two. Must have been a painful accident.

I really didn't want to be here. If I could have put off my birthday, turned eighteen another time when no one was keeping

[13] Previously published in *Sunset Sunrise: A collection of endings and beginnings,* ed. Crissi Langwell. Santa Rosa: Redwood Writers Press 2020.

track, I would have done it in an instant. But there was no way around this. All I could do was hope for the best and get it over with. At least they said the memory machine was gentle. The experience shouldn't be as intense as real life; more like watching a movie. I hoped it was true.

An attendant came for us much too soon. I stood up with my heart in my mouth while Ethan jumped to his feet among his family's applause. My parents stood too, to give me a group hug.

"You'll be great," Mom told me, holding tight.

"We love you forever, and we'll be here when you come out," Dad said.

I nodded with a lump in my throat. Trying to be brave, I left their arms and followed Ethan through the door that the attendant held open.

We might have been born on the same day, but we really couldn't be more different.

"I'll be sure to remember you when I'm famous," Ethan was saying to the attendant with a cheeky grin. "What's your name?"

The hallway was too short for much of a conversation. We were led into a small room full of cushy chairs and a video wall. I did my best to be patient through an extremely basic orientation video that I could swear we watched in second grade. Ethan whispered commentary throughout it.

Then it was over, and back into the hall we went.

This time we were separated, each following a different white-coated professional into a private room. Ethan waved a cheery goodbye. I gave him the best smile I could manage.

There was The Chair, like I'd seen in pictures. It was firm but comfortable. The attendant did *not* strap me down, despite what the older kids had always teased. There was a helmet. There was darkness.

Then I was looking out of someone else's eyes.

I felt my emotions drifting, like this was a dream of little consequence. I appreciated that. Jumping right into the memories should have been a shock, but it was instead only a mild curiosity. I turned my lazy attention to what I was seeing.

The sounds were muffled. I got the impression that I could learn to make them stronger, the more I practiced, but I wasn't interested just now. It was intriguing enough to wonder how tall my past body had been, given that I was looking up at someone now.

He was a clean-cut man with no memorable features. He smiled politely as we ambled along. There was a wall behind him. Pictures. Nature scenes. A window with bright sunlight.

Then I tripped, and the memory slowed down. I caught a glimpse of the man's panicked face and the way he reached for me, but it wasn't enough. I hit hard.

On my left side, with a distant pain in my ribs and my head. My vision blurred and faded away. The last thing I saw was my own arm, splayed on the floor in front of my face.

The floor was gray tile. My sleeve was pale yellow. My hand was dark, and there was something odd about it that I couldn't quite make out before the memory ended.

End of last memory, said a voice. Beginning happiest memories.

I sat through the highlight reel of my previous life with artificial calm. After the first two, the machine allowed me to skip forward and backward as I chose. I knew that no time was passing in the waking world. I was glad of it. This was a life I wanted to explore in detail. There might be a significant wait before I got the chance to come back and watch more.

It only took two memories to figure out who I had been. When I woke to see the polite attendant's face, I kept some of that unnatural calm.

Clung to it, truth be told.

"I'll want to talk to my family in private, please," I said. "Then someone official."

The attendant agreed and helped me up, then out into the hall. My legs were a little unsteady. The air conditioner seemed loud.

Ethan was louder.

"Hey!" he said when he joined me. Both attendants waited for us to talk, no rushing. "I was somebody awesome! Not famous, but badass at extreme sports! I think I've heard of her before, too: she died in the most epic wingsuit crash that she almost pulled out of. Won a bunch of awards. So a little famous, I guess. How about you?"

I thought back to the magazine in the waiting room. An ironic choice. My old face had been in it.

"I was famous," I said, my own voice sounding distant. At

Ethan's urging, I said the big part: "Grand Mattie. The gorilla."

"What??" Ethan shrieked. "No one's been a gorilla!"

"I have," I said. Emotions were starting to come back, now that I'd said it. I smiled. "And I can tell you that the push to treat them like proper citizens was the right choice. She was amazing."

"What?" Ethan said again, grabbing my hand and towing me toward the waiting room. "I've got to tell my family about mine, but you go first! I get to tell everybody I knew you when!"

"Yeah." The smile grew. I wasn't afraid anymore, even of the media attention that was likely to come. I had all the dignity and wisdom of my previous life to call on.

Mara Lynn Johnstone grew up in a house on a hill, of which the top floor was built first. With a lifelong interest in fiction, she has published several books and many short stories. She can be found up trees, in bookstores, lost in thought, and at MaraLynnJohnstone.com.

In this Bend of Time[14]

Margaret Rooney
Redwood Writers

from its perch the yellow bird
summons dawn note by note
like a T'ang lute player

day-blind stars
fade from the window
morning arrives thin as worn fabric

in soft lit air
your breath sounds like
the whisper of sea in a shell

mist moves in willows like smoke,
across the valley there is a suggestion
of rain in low blue-bellied clouds

the world with its ruptures and raptures
its dissolutions and resolutions
calls me into this moment

alive for now
in this curve of time
no longer edgewise to earth

your thigh
beneath my palm
warm as hot sand

in all possible

[14] Previously published in *Phases: Redwood Writers 2023 Poetry Anthology*, ed(s). Les Bernstein and Fran Holland-Claggett. Santa Rosa: Redwood Writers Press 2023.

multiverses
this is the iteration I love:

you curled beside me
casting a spell of home

Margaret Rooney is published in several journals and anthologies.

A poem of hers won first prize in the 2022 Redwood Writers Poetry Contest, and two poems were nominated for the 2021 Pushcart prize.

Her chapbook *A Wild Rain* is scheduled to be published on March 1, 2024.

January Rain

Lenore Hirsch
Napa Valley Writers

Manzanita's wet red twisted trunk
shines like something new
live oak leaves glimmer, free of summer dust
emerald blanket creeps up hillsides
separates dark rows in vineyards
even cracks in the road sprout green

subtle drips and trickles, roar of creek fill the air
hummer wings buzz in search of sweetness
wrens chirp among squawking crows
scent of grape compost wafts over vines

and the vines, the mighty vines:
bare and brown
they cling to guide wires
shunt moisture to the ground
suck energy from mud
and wait

wait for sunshine
wait for buds
to break through
wait for leaves and fruit
wait for spring

Lenore Hirsch is a retired educator who lives in Napa Valley. She writes in many genres, including short stories, poetry, memoir, humor, and travel. Her books include her dog's memoir, *My Leash on Life: Foxy's View of the World from a Foot Off the Ground;* a poetry collection, *Leavings;* humorous essays, *Laugh and Live: Advice for Aging Boomers;* a novel, *Schooled: Confessions of a Rookie Vice Principal*; and *Connection: Stories*.

Almost Peter Pan

Paul Moser
Napa Valley Writers

In kindergarten, I made endless crayon drawings of an island. It was always the same island with the same aerial view, mostly dark green, with brown Indian teepees at one end and tiny mermaids in a pale blue lagoon at the other. There was a black sailing ship anchored in a cove.

Each time I finished a drawing, my teacher, a rosy-cheeked young woman who wore her blonde hair in self-conscious, long tresses to cover her large ears, would ask me the name of the island, and each time I would avoid her eyes, give a little shrug and say, "It's just an island." Both of us knew that in fact the island was Neverland, the magical home of Peter Pan and a cast of other remarkable characters, but I would never admit it to my teacher or to anyone else. I was unwilling to expose to criticism the character—and the story--I revered most in the world.

I had been introduced to Peter Pan when my parents took me to see the animated Disney movie in the summer of 1954, and was instantly captivated. The saturated colors of Neverland, the glow of pixie dust, the agility of Peter in flight, his brilliance, his cocky smile, and his fearlessness, all served to enchant me. I began imitating some of Peter's vocal mannerisms. I nagged my mother to buy me the movie sound track, which I memorized. For the next few Halloweens, I dressed as Peter, complete with little suede boots, green tights and jerkin, and a green felt cap pierced with a red feather. Some days, when I felt the urge, I wore the costume everywhere I went. Though it never got past the planning stages, more than once I thought about getting up onto the roof of the house to see if I could fly.

My sister, two years older, thought I was an idiot. From her prestige position in the second grade, she mocked my Peter Pan obsession, often looking at me coolly and voicing some version of, "You're just making yourself look stupid, you know." I'd stick my tongue out at her, or sometimes even stab her with the little rubber dagger I kept in my belt. I thought she was a snot, with her pigtails, her big-shot second-grade friends, and the white bucks she wore with the houndstooth pleated skirt and white blouse required at St. Agnes

School.

In the spring of 1955, my mother held a birthday party for this horrible creature I had to call my sister. Because her birthday was in April, the party had an Easter theme, with lots of glittery pink and yellow Easter Bunny cardboard cutouts, little boxes of jelly beans, and chocolate eggs for each of the ten friends who were invited. To me, it was the worst possible display of girly stuff. I wore my Peter Pan outfit that day, a protest against all the frilly, pastel-colored decorations.

In the kitchen, my mother was frazzled, stacking dirty dishes, realizing she had not taken the ice cream out of the freezer to let it soften. "You promised to be a helper," she said, "and not just stand around moping. Why don't you go out and see if anybody would like more Coke or 7-Up?" I slouched my way through the swinging door that led to the dining room.

The girls were seated around the table in their party dresses, happily chattering away. Three girls who had been to the house before and knew me, were the first to exclaim, "Look who's here!" and "Oooh, it's the little brother!" The other girls turned their faces toward me for a moment before looking at my sister in wonderment. "Is that your little brother? Honest?"

"Yeah, it is," she said glumly.

One of them, a redhead with galaxies of freckles on her face and enormous front teeth looked at me challengingly. "What are you doin' in that elf outfit?"

"This is not an elf outfit," I said. "I'm Peter Pan. So there."

A thin, pale girl with close-set, dark eyes and long curly black hair said, "You look awful small to be Peter Pan." She laughed. "You need to grow up a little first!" The girls all giggled.

"I'm plenty old enough to be Peter Pan," I said. "My mom wants to know if anybody wants more Coke or 7-Up. Do you, or not?"

Ignoring my question, the girls rolled their eyes, snickered, and exchanged glances. My sister said, "Why don't you just go away? We don't need anything. You're bothering us." Sitting next to her, a husky girl with short blonde hair and glasses with pink frames piped up in a screechy voice. "You can't be Peter Pan anyway, 'cause I watched Peter Pan on TV a couple weeks ago, and Peter was played by a woman!" Most of the girls nodded, saying "Yeah!" and "I saw that, too!" They were starting to enjoy this game, goading the little brother.

"I know what you're talking about, 'cause we watched it, too, but that's not the real Peter Pan. Some girl with a wire hooked up to her back, up in the air, swinging back and forth over a stage? That's a joke. And Tinker Bell looked like somebody shined a flashlight on a wall. So dumb!"

The girl with the pink glasses sounded bossy now. "We don't have to listen to you talking stupid. We know Peter Pan was a girl, we saw it!" She looked at me with a sneering smile. "Maybe you're a girl, too. Are you?"

She was getting to me. "I told you, I'm Peter Pan, and Peter Pan is a boy. And that's that!"

The girls laughed some more, nudging each other. "Peter Pan was a girl! It's true, it's true!" The girl with the pink glasses was triumphant. "So what about you?" she said in a sing-song, mocking voice.

I stood for a moment, frozen with rage. Ridiculing Peter Pan was a criminal act. But what to do about it? What would Peter do? In retrospect, I realized it was not the most Peter Pan-like response, but before I could think about it, in one single motion I pulled down my tights and underwear, giving them all full view of my equipment. The rubber dagger slipped from my belt to the floor. I shook my hips for maximum effect. As I wiggled back and forth, I wore an exaggerated expression of horror--bulging eyes, gaping mouth.

The shrieks and whoops of the girls brought my mother running from the kitchen. Just as she pushed through the door, I tugged my tights back up and tried my best to look innocent. It was a lost cause. I saw my sister looking disgusted, rolling her eyes to the ceiling as she said to our mother over the din of the girls' screams, "I can't believe him! What a little creep!"

Even before my mother could gather exactly what had happened, she ordered me to my room. I was happy to comply. I picked up my rubber dagger and made for the door, relieved to escape the fallout of my imitation of Peter Pan's audacity and daring.

At Saint Agnes School the following week, the story didn't take long to reach the rest of the second grade. It spread among the students in the rest of the school only a bit more slowly. It was a sensation, a punch-line that no student could resist passing along to classmates. Eventually even the nuns heard some version of it, though in the telling it had moved into a fantasy/legend category that bore little resemblance to the truth. Some versions had me singing a song like the Disney film, "Think of a wonderful thought, any merry little thought," as I waggled my privates. Others said I was bare-bottomed and hobbled by tights gathered around my knees as my mother chased me around the dining room. One version even insisted I had threatened to pee on the girl with the pink glasses.

Some first graders at St. Agnes were branded early on because of embarrassing incidents in their first month of school, such as the girl who wet her pants on her first day in class, or the boy who vomited on the shoes of the nun who was his first-grade teacher. But because I didn't start first grade at Saint Agnes until that fall, five months after the Peter Pan incident, I managed to best all of these infamous kids by having a reputation even before I arrived at school. I would never be anonymous. I would always be Peter Pan—but maybe not in the way I had hoped.

Paul Moser is the author of four books, three of them reflecting a flagrant, indefensible obsession with satire and parody: *The New Revised Catechlysm, T-Bull and the Lost Men,* and *Inside the Flavor League,* and the memoir, *Seeking.*

Lightning Bugs

Rick Deragon
Napa Valley Writers

"Crickets," Jack said.

"What?" his mother asked from the kitchen as she arranged a pork chop on a plate.

"Crickets. I said, crickets. They're really loud tonight," he said.

"You can go listen to your crickets when you finish your dinner," she said, bringing a plate for her husband and a bowl of extra potatoes.

"Got your note about Cindy and her scout troop's overnight," Jack's father said, taking his seat. He unfurled his cloth napkin, placed it on his lap, and bowed his head.

Jack watched his lips move silently.

"How've you been, Jackie-boy?" his father said.

"I caught a mouse. Trapped it against a fence. He was tryin' to run away, but I stepped on his tail, then caught him."

"A mouse? A big mouse?" his father said.

"John, don't encourage him."

"Not really. Jus' a l'il one—like this," Jack said, cupping his hand to hold the imaginary mouse.

"That's mouse size, alright," his father said.

"Jackie, that's terrible. Those things are so dirty. He could bite you. John, talk some sense to him."

"He wasn't gonna bite me. He was hurt."

"You're always getting into such mischief, worrying me to death," his mother said.

"Hurt?" his father said.

"He was bleedin'. His foot. I carried him in my sweatshirt pouch all day."

"Oh, John," his mother said.

"What did you end up doing with him, Jackie?"

"Let 'im go after a while. Well, really, he just got away."

"Oh, the idea of carrying a rabies-infected creature all day. In your pocket. John, talk to him."

Jack's father studied his son's face. Jack ate a piece of carrot and cut a piece of the pork chop, but stopped after raising his fork just off the plate.

"He was probably scared, Jack, and he might have bitten you. They really don't like to be handled. After all, they are wild."

"Wasn't gonna hurt 'im."

"Go-ING," his mother said.

"Okay, go-ing. I wasn't go-ing to hurt him. Just wanted to feel how warm he was, his heartbeat."

"Jack, next time, let the little fells stay free," Jack's father said, taking another bite. "By the way, there are a few things I need to get after dinner. Want to come along?"

"Yeah—well, no. I was gonna go play. There's a lotta crickets tonight. An' lightning bugs."

"Go-ING," his mother said. Go-ING."

"Okay, go-ing."

"I saw a sale on baseball gloves at Anderson's. Think we can make it before they close. Want a baseball glove? It's the season. But you'll have to try it on first. Come along?" Jack's father said.

His mother hovered over them with a plate of cookies. Jack reached for them, but she pulled the plate away and nodded at the remaining carrots. Jack forced the tines of his fork into a sliced carrot. He moved to eat it, but stopped short of his mouth, returning his fork to the plate where he impaled the remaining slices. This mass of pulp he gulped at once, filling both cheeks like a squirrel.

"Dear God," his mother said.

His father looked down to hide his smile.

Jack gulped it down, snatched a cookie off the plate, and pushed away from the table in a flash of movement. "Bye."

He bounded off the back porch into a world that was as wide as the sea and as high as the highest cloud and twinkling star. The screen door slammed after him.

This world of possibilities that he roamed had dark night as its keeper and sunlight as its guardian. Twilight was its heart, dawn its soul. Into this world—his neighborhood—he entered and the realm of precious noises and sights revealed: of crickets chittering and frogs croaking, of boys yelling and dogs yipping, of rain pattering on the asphalt driveway and the startling magic of the thunderclap.

To his left in the distance, Jack saw the houses of the neighborhood fading in the evening light. White, beige, gray, blue, yellow, or green, the houses stood in rows. Two-storied, wood-shingled, with brick and wooden siding, the houses formed a theme and variations—front picture windows on the right or left, front doors on the left or right, light colors accented dark houses, dark trim outlined light colored houses. Wrought ironwork or lathe-turned posts appeared on every other house's porch, and every façade had a full beard of shrubbery running from ear to ear. Personal touches punctuated each house—a picket fence, a half-buried wagon wheel, a miniature wishing well.

The swelling twilight enveloped his neighborhood, and all these houses lost their details to the night, changed into dark shapes, evolved into pirate ships on the high seas, ominous castle keeps, cavalry forts on the hill, or enemy villages full of sharpshooters and evil.

Jack crossed the threshold of this dark and sultry twilight. He ran across backyards as fast as he could. He felt the humid air beneath his shirt, and his heart racing after three backyards. He heard the wind rushing over his ears, and his sneakers making soft thumps on the lawns. When he stopped, the night had triumphed, and it was dark. In between his deep breaths, he heard the crickets calling back and forth.

Dark maple trees surrounded his friend's house, and Jack could see no window light between the limbs. He didn't even try tossing pebbles to the bedroom window, or even knocking on the front door.

Two streets over a shallow ravine separated properties, and trees and underbrush grew thick along its banks. A trickle of water always crossed its way, and Jack knew he would find frogs there, and crickets, and lightning bugs. He ran.

Jack crawled under the lowest rail of a fence and looked back at the house on the hill. Standing stately against the sky, its second story windows peered down at him like two big eyes. A jack-o'-lantern, Jack thought. He jumped to his feet, ran across the last part of the hill, and flew into the trees along the ravine. He smelled the sweat of the creek bed, the perfume of honeysuckle, and the musk of milkweeds and wildflowers. Fine twigs and branches slapped his face as he slid to a halt next to the water.

There, Jack listened to the crickets chirping. He was sure they were assessing the danger he posed—his friendly presence against his potential for destruction. Then the frogs started up. They announced his arrival, too, and probably boasted of secret hiding places. Above, he watched the moon rise over the treetops to begin its march across the starry sky. Then he lowered his gaze and saw the lightning bugs.

His mouth opened in awe, and he felt a lightness bordering on flight. Like twinkling stars in a velvet sky, lightning bugs appeared and disappeared into the great silhouette of his neighborhood or the bulging profiles of trees. Mesmerizing, they floated through the darkness in shots of yellow and white, flashing here then there, shimmering as the highlights on a wonderful, unseen crown.

They were light, pure light, unconnected to the things of this world, the experience of light, of sight, captured in the simple darkness of this night.

Jack left the ravine and walked into a cloud of lightning bugs on the hillside. Holding out his hand, he cupped one after another, examining them as they crawled on his hand and up his arm. Some, alighted, some lingered and flashed.

He knew just what to do. When a lightning bug flashed, he pinched it in half. The fleck of phosphorescent light, sticky and long, he placed on his knuckles as diamonds. He decided to put them inside jars when he returned home to have them as lanterns.

Jack wandered over the hillside collecting them. From ravine to jack-o'-lantern house, he caught more of the flying insects. He pinched them as they flashed, and after thirty minutes, he had filled his hands with the flecks of a diamond's luster. He sat in the grass studying the smears of glitter and shots of light in his palm. One by one, he picked them out and placed them in a line across his forehead and down his arms. *My crown of jewels*, he thought, *my shining cloak. I am the king of the ravine, the prince of the water, the duke of the hillside*. He stood up and marched across the hill looking left and right for his afterglow.

Then he remembered the hall mirror and yearned to see himself like this—lights out, sparkles on. So, he crawled under the fence and walked through the yards of the neighborhood—carefully, so he wouldn't be seen as an errant king or prowler. He crossed lots and streets, passed between shrubbery and trees. He thought of the dinner and his father's invitation to Anderson's. Maybe it wasn't too late.

Jack picked up his pace, recalling a time the previous summer when he sat with his father under the moon. The man explained the distance of the moon from the earth, but it was too far for Jack to fathom. His father then told him about frogs, how they begin as fish-like swimmers, then lose their tails to become frogs. At that moment, the lightning bugs had appeared against the dark shapes of the neighborhood. Framed by trees and roof lines, the flashing insects appeared here and there, twinkling like signals from far away. They lit up with gentle, slow-blinking gold and white, and cast a spell across the yard. Their twinkling in thick and thin clusters gave the heavy cloak of nightfall a majestic air. Enchanted shadows everywhere glittered with gold.

Jack's father stood up and disappeared into that darkness. He walked back almost immediately and sat down next to his son. He held out his hand. Two lightning bugs crawled across his palm, flapping tiny wings, flashing their delicate lights.

"Watch, Jack."

His father picked up one, and when it glowed brightly, he pinched it. Jack heard a faint crunch. His father took the glowing tip and placed it on Jack's knuckle.

"There, you now have a fancy ring."

Jack then looked at his diamond-studded hands and arms, felt the sticky glue of the crown across his forehead. *I have to show him my costume*, he thought.

He trotted faster across the yards, watching his arms with their phosphorescent highlights swinging at his sides. He broke into a run.

Jack had to show his costume, tell his father about the frogs, and their language that Jack believed he understood. He wanted to tell his father about the crickets, and how the crickets had talked to him. He wanted to show his father the kingly crown and cloak and how he glittered in the night.

Jack's father stood next to the black sedan and looked around. He called out Jack's name, but not loud enough to bother the neighbors. The disc of the moon rose over the dark trees. The man heard crickets and smelled the damp and fertile night descend upon the houses up and down the street. He sat down on the padded bench seat. He turned the key and the car squealed and roared then settled into a mechanical drone. He put the car in reverse and backed down the driveway.

Jack ran as fast as he could, spurred by the expectation of

showing off his costume and the excitement of joining his father on the trip to the store.

He ran through a side yard and skidded on the grass as he made the last turn onto his street. A welling sense of desperation took hold of him. He worried that the lights on his crown and cloak might fade, that his father would not see them. He ran harder and faster, counting the houses remaining—six, five, four. Jack heard his father's voice, "There are a few things I need to get after dinner. Want to come along?" And he heard himself say, "No."

Confusion and desperation sickened him as he panted and ran. He wished he had said "yes" because he did want to go, but he had to go outside, too, for the crickets were so loud and so many, and the lightning bugs were enchantment itself.

Jack's father sat in the car at the foot of the driveway. He stuck his head out of the car window and called, "Jackie" in the voice he used at the baseball games they organized in the corner field. It wasn't the calling of a name as much as a cry, a thick-throated bark that shot into the night like a tribal incantation.

Jack knew the jewels on his crown and cloak would keep their glow long enough. *But will Dad be able to see them?* He hurled himself around the curve of the street, and as he came to their next-door neighbor's house, he saw his father's car down the street. The red taillights of the Plymouth sedan glowed, and the right one blinked, and the bulky mass turned right and disappeared into the night.

Rick Deragon earned a BA and a MA in Art, and a MA in Art History, all from CSU Chico. He wrote a weekly column of art criticism for the *Monterey Herald* and had art features published in assorted national art and craft magazines. He has been a high school art and English teacher, university lecturer, and adjunct professor in studio art and art history at Notre Dame de Namur University, as well as the curator of the Monterey Museum of Art and the director of the Napa Valley Museum. He self-published a historical novel, *Fire in the Year of Four Emperors*, which received good reviews. He is currently editing two new novels and a compilation of short stories. He lives in Napa with his wife and son.

SAN JOAQUIN VALLEY

"The valley of the San Joaquin
is the floweriest piece of world
I have ever walked."
—*John Muir*

Baba's Accordion[15]

Pamela Pan
San Joaquin Valley Writers

As if the setting sun knew it was the eve of the Lunar New Year, it cast brilliant hues of violet, ochre, and gold on the trees, fields, and houses near my childhood home in Zhejiang Province in Eastern China. Everything glowed.

The year was 1973, and I was four.

Standing on the porch near the door, I watched Mama prepare the special dinner. Her red sweater splashed with apricot blossoms made her particularly pretty. Her famous ginger chicken steamed in an iron pot, its aroma saturating the air. The *suh-suh-suh* as she cut the lotus root on the board, the sizzling and splattering as she dropped the slices into hot oil, and the *thunk-thunk* of her spatula against the pan made my stomach growl and my heart dance with expectation.

Mama glanced at me. "Has Baba come?"

"Not yet."

The lane nearest our home passed the two houses in front of us and extended far to the right, distantly connecting to a major road. As I stared, a dot appeared at the intersection, silhouetted against the sun. It gradually became a tiny figure. Then the houses blocked my view of him.

I waited in suspense, my chin resting on my palms.

The figure reappeared—medium height, dark hair in a crew cut, blue bag strapped across his shoulders, white collared shirt tucked into gray trousers. It could only be my father, who taught music at a high school in a town fourteen miles away, too far and too hilly to walk or bike there every day. The first bus going there departed at eleven, too late for his classes, so he stayed at school during the week and came home by bus on weekends. The fall semester had ended, but he remained at the school for an extra week to help students rehearse for their concert to be held after the New Year.

"Baba!" I raced toward him, too excited to tell Mama first. I must have presented quite a sight, small legs pumping, arms swaying,

---

[15] Previously published in Great Valley Stories by San Joaquin Valley Writers in 2023.

the red ribbons Mama had tied on my braids bouncing. When I reached him, I grabbed his pant leg.

"*Baobei*!" he called.

My hand dug into his trouser pocket, which I knew hid secret treasures. He chuckled, handing me a candy with a grinning tiger on the wrapper—my favorite kind. I put the wrapper in my shirt pocket and let the cinnamon-tinged sweetness tickle my tongue. Baba hoisted me up, kissed my cheek, and sat me on his shoulders. The sun followed us, casting a long shadow.

"How's your cold? Are you feeling better?" he asked.

"I'm fine now. I didn't like the bitter cough syrup you gave me though."

He laughed. "The herbs in the syrup helped you recover."

"Did you bring picture books?"

"I have three in the bag. I can read them to you during the holiday."

I bounced "Yay! Thank you!"

His hands held me tight. "Don't wiggle. You may fall!"

We met my nine-year-old brother at the door. He had come home from his friend's house.

Inside, Mama announced, "Dinner will be ready soon."

Baba strapped on the accordion he had carried home. His right hand stroked the black and white keys. His left pulled and collapsed the bellows. Sound emerged from the instrument. He swung left and right and bobbed his head up and down as if the music held an invisible string over his head. In my eyes, he was easily the most handsome man in the universe.

His music filled the air like Mama's cooking. Brother danced to the rhythm, tapping his foot, gliding across the floor. I whirled, clapped, and jumped up and down.

Baba sang his improvised song, his deep baritone voice penetrating every corner.

Mama is cooking,
The most delectable meal in the making.
My darling children are dancing.
The stars twinkle, twinkling.
What a happy family we are.

Mama laughed. "You're as silly as the kids. Dinner's ready.

First, let's thank our ancestors for protecting us."

Incense sticks in our hands, we bowed to the ancestors whose spirits watched us, and we prayed. After sitting down, Baba poured rice wine for Mama and put meat in our bowls. He raised his cup. "Thank you, my beautiful and capable wife. Thank you, my lovely children. What a lucky guy I am. Happy New Year!"

"Happy New Year!" we echoed.

"What do you wish for in the New Year?" Mama asked.

"I hope to join the chorus group in school," Brother said.

"I want crackers that are shaped like rabbits, the kind Baba brought back last time," I answered.

For the first two days of the New Year, while Mama stayed home receiving visiting kin, Baba, Brother, and I called on relatives, bearing gifts and New Year's wishes.

On the third morning, Baba installed a tuner and a speaker so we could hear news and music from the local radio station. After some static, the familiar melody of "Sailing in the Ocean Depends on the Captain" flooded the living room.

Mama clapped her hands. "You're a genius and our captain."

During lunch, three students from Baba's high school arrived on their bikes. "Sorry to disturb your vacation, but we need you to conduct our performance tonight. Mr. Huang is sick."

They ate lunch with us and left afterward. Baba departed later, taking his bike this time. He put his accordion in its blue bag and fastened it to the carrier rack—he took it with him wherever he went.

I followed him. "Please don't go. You promised to take me to the market."

"Let's go there tomorrow. I'll be back for lunch," he said.

He carried his bike from the porch and placed it on the ground below. Holding the handlebars, he set his left foot on the pedal, tapped his right, and propelled the bike forward. With one graceful swoop, he sat on his seat. "*Zaijian*! I'll see you tomorrow!"

Mama waved. "Be careful when you ride!"

"I will!" he pedaled away. I ran after him, watching him disappear around the bend and reappear farther down the road, growing smaller and smaller.

The next day, Mama set lunch on the table. "Could you check if Baba's coming?"

I scanned the road. Nothing, no dot, no figure.

One hour, two hours later, still no Baba.

"Maybe something delayed him," Mama said. "Are you hungry? Let's eat."

We were in the middle of the meal when a neighbor, Auntie Fei, burst in, her mouth open, her eyes wild. "Oh, you won't believe what I heard!"

Mama put down her rice bowl. "What did you hear?"

"I went to the hospital because my little one had a fever. The nurse said someone from our town had just been rushed in because of an accident, a teacher from a high school."

Mama grasped her arm. "Watch my kids."

She untied her apron, flung it on the chair, grabbed her purse, and ran out the door.

Mama staggered home past six. She waved a feeble hand toward us. "Fei, could you take care of my kids tonight? I need to lie down. Kids, listen to Auntie Fei."

Mama looked like a different person. Her face had morphed from a glowing blossom to a haggard willow leaf, dry, brittle, lifeless. Her bedroom door shut with a thud. Muffled sounds reached my ears, low, moaning, as if an animal was wounded to the core, with no light, no hope, only despair coursing through its veins.

Auntie Fei cooked dinner. Brother and I spooned food from every plate into a bowl, topped it with rice, and put it in front of Mama's room. "Mama, food is here," Brother said. "Eat. You must be hungry."

Auntie Fei tucked us in and stayed that night. The next morning, she walked Brother and me to the hospital a mile away.

"What is the Eternal Peace Room?" Brother asked.

Auntie Fei put her finger on her lips. I peeked in from the threshold. A man lay on a bed near the wall, far from us. A white sheet covered his entire body, except his head. I could only see the silhouette of his profile. A straight nose, and an enormous bump on his chin, near his lips.

What are we doing here? Who's this man? I looked up at Auntie Fei for answers, but she only shook her head and sighed. I stepped into the room, wanting to see who this man was and smooth away the enormous bump that must be uncomfortable.

"No, you can't go in!" Auntie Fei dragged me back by the hem of my jacket, picked me up, and took us away.

I turned my head and looked over her shoulder at the man's enormous bump. Why couldn't we see him? Why did we come here? Questions bubbled up in my mind like fish balls in a hot pot with nowhere to go except to sink back down.

And where was Baba? He had promised to take me to the market. Two days had passed, and he hadn't returned.

On the third day, Grandma entered our house. I ran to her and buried my face in her blouse. "I want my Baba. Where is he?"

Grandma hugged me close. "Poor child. Baba's not coming back. He passed away." Grandma pointed toward the western sky. "He's there now."

Baba had read me a book about someone who died and went to the sky. I stared at Grandma. Scattered images snapped into place like pieces in a puzzle—Mama's pale blotched skin and bloodshot eyes, the man in the Eternal Peace Room with the enormous bump. Was that Baba? All the fears I had pushed away, all the suspicions gnawing my insides since Auntie Fei barged into our home came crashing back.

My baba had died! But how could he? He'd just played accordion and danced with us. He installed the speaker. We were going to the market to taste roasted chestnuts and minced-pork cakes. He loved us and his music. How could he leave us like this?

"Baba!" I shouted toward the western sky. Only a line of sparrows echoed my call.

During lunch, the speaker came alive, bringing news and music. The song "Sailing in the Ocean Depends on the Captain" pierced my chest like sharp bamboo sticks. Our captain was gone.

The next day, Uncle Chun, Mama's elder brother, arrived. A few days later, Grandma dressed Brother and me all in white, with a black band on our elbows. We walked with hundreds of people. Some distance ahead, six men—three of them the students who had come to our house, three our neighbors—carried a long dark-red, wooden box on their shoulders.

With a start, I recalled the term for the box from Baba's reading: a coffin.

The procession stopped near a large grave site. The men slowly lowered the coffin into the grave. A man dug his shovel into the ground and lifted it holding dark soil.

Someone jumped on top of the coffin. Mama! Her hair had loosened from the braids, half covering her face. "Ma! Brother! Take care of my kids!" she shouted.

She lay on her stomach on the lid, spreading her arms over it, hugging it. "Bury me with my husband. Let me die with him!"

Shocked murmurs swept through the gathering. Uncle Chun also jumped on top of the coffin.

"Baba!" I screamed, leaning over the edge, ready to leap as well. I wanted to bring Baba back. If I shouted loud enough, he would awaken and come home with us.

Grandma grabbed me. I struggled, but her arms were strong.

Uncle Chun pried Mama's hands from the lid and enclosed her in his arms. She kicked, slid from his arms, and remained on her stomach on the lid. Uncle whispered to her, pulled her up, held her in his arms. She put her head on his shoulder and wailed.

Women around me sobbed. Men sniffled. A few neighbors cried out with tears running down their faces.

"Think about your kids!"

"Be strong. We're here for you!"

"You still have a life to live."

Uncle Chun lifted Mama and turned to us. She kicked but couldn't loosen his grip. Grandma, weeping, held out her arms. Others joined her. They pulled Mama up. She fought. They didn't let her go. Mama kept wailing, Grandma kept weeping, and Brother and I kept crying, "Mama! Baba!"

Shovel after shovel of soil thumped onto the coffin. Soon, only a patch of the lid showed, glinting in the afternoon sun. I searched my shirt pocket and found the tiger wrapper from the candy Baba had given me. I threw it toward the coffin. It fluttered in the wind but landed on the lid. Soon it was covered by soil. It comforted me to think my tiger lay in the grave with Baba, keeping him company.

After the funeral, Uncle took out something from the blue bag the hospital had given us. Baba's accordion, some keys missing, some twisted, the bellow stuck and couldn't be pulled out. It was severely damaged, like our family.

A few days later, the three students visited us, their faces gaunt.

One of them tried to hold me. I wiggled out of his arms and glared at him. These young men had taken away my baba. *How dare they enter our home again!*

They knelt in front of us. "If we had known a bus would hit his bike, we would never have asked him to conduct the concert. The concert was outstanding because of him. But we've made Auntie a widow, the kids fatherless. We've deprived our school of the best teacher we've ever had. We should have died instead of him! Hate us. Hit us."

Mama covered her face and ran to her room. Uncle shook his head, told them to get up, and said it wasn't their fault.

To my relief, Grandma moved in with us. I could see our family floundering. Baba had left us. Mama wasn't herself anymore. We would sink into the deepest valley on the ocean floor, among the wrecked ships of past centuries. With Grandma here, at least we could cook meals and not go hungry.

Uncle stayed for three weeks. Every night, when Mama sobbed in her room, he sat with her. He left early in the morning and came home late for dinner.

"What is Uncle doing?" I asked Grandma.

"Searching for a job for Mama. We don't have an income in the house anymore."

Mama was sick and stayed in bed. Grandma prepared soups and noodles with longans and goji berries, urging her to eat. "Be strong, my child. You're the captain now. The kids depend on you."

Mama nodded but ate little.

Two months after the funeral, Brother asked Grandma to take the accordion to a shop to fix it.

"Why?" Grandma glanced at Mama's room. "Our savings are running low. Soon we may not have enough to eat."

"Baba taught me how to play. I miss it," Brother implored. "Could I give you my New Year's money?"

I took out my small pouch from a drawer. "I'll give you mine too."

That day after dinner, Brother glided his fingers across the keys of the repaired accordion and sang.

> *Mama is cooking*
> *The most delectable meal in the making.*

My darling children are dancing.
The stars twinkle, twinkling.
What a happy family we are.

Tears rolled down my cheeks as I watched him. But I couldn't help smiling, recalling Baba's funny manners when he delivered this song. He was a happy man lighting up any occasion with music. He would have liked us to enjoy life, even though he wasn't around to share it.

The door opened behind us. I turned to see Mama standing there, pale, dazed. I froze—was she angry? She opened her arms and scooped me and Brother into her arms. "We'll still be a happy family, I promise."

Three weeks later, Mama started her first teaching job—she had all the needed credentials but had never taught. She transformed into a true dragon—her birth-animal sign—and became strong and brave. Instead of letting us descend to the ocean valley, she sailed us through storms.

As time passed, I began to grasp the full impact of Baba's passing. Sometimes anger surged through me like fire. Why did the gods take Baba? He was only thirty-five, a man in his prime, a loving husband and father, a talented musician, a dedicated teacher. Whenever I saw fathers visiting their children in school, a jolt of pain punched me in the gut, forcing me to avert my eyes.

In 1985, on the third day of the Lunar New Year, Mama, Brother, and I went to Baba's grave. It was the twelfth anniversary of his passing. I would start college in the fall.

We brought ginger chicken, tofu, lotus, cabbage, and rice—all Baba's favorites. After burning paper money, Brother, now a tall, strong young man, dug a hole next to Baba's grave. I wrapped Baba's accordion in its blue bag, covered by a layer of oilcloth to prevent moisture damage. I lowered the accordion into the hole. It had accompanied us for more than a decade, brought us joy, witnessed Mama's transformation, and watched Brother and me grow into young adults. It embodied the essence of the three of us. Now that Brother and I would both be away from home, we wanted the accordion to become Baba's companion again, alongside my little tiger wrapper.

Shafts of sunlight penetrated the clouds and illuminated the package before Brother shoveled soil on top to cover it.

"Baba. Keep protecting us." I prayed, sticks of incense in my hands. I knew he had been and always would.

Pamela Pan is an English professor at San Joaquin Delta College where she teaches and does research on reading, writing, and literature. She has a PhD in Education from the University of California, Davis, a master's degree in Bilingual/ESL Studies from the University of Massachusetts, Boston, and a bachelor's degree in Engineering from Shanghai Jiao Tong University in China. She writes historical fiction, short stories, essays, and poems. Her work has been published in various magazines and anthologies. In her spare time, Pamela loves to listen to audiobooks, walk, do yoga, and spend time with her family.

91 Going On 99 Fahrenheit[16]

Charity Romstad
San Joaquin Valley Writers

Smoke sags on the horizon, circling and omnipresent.
Blue sky is straight above, but it's hard
to keep your head back to see it.
Unless you are waiting to die.
The pool is vacant and it's mid-Sunday, mid-season, mid-life.

Last week a kid was having a standoff with his weekend father,
And everyone, including his brother, watched in silence,
Until the spectacle left. And then came the comments:
"If I acted like that. . . my dad would have. . ."

But today the pool is peacefully free
of power struggles and bystanders.
The sun glimmers on soothing waters
beckoning to ease my back.
And I step in, halfway, letting myself adjust to the cool water:
Moving and stretching without thinking,
I am soon neck deep and alone.

My morning hours of work in the wrong position,
Or simply too many hours at work instead of living,
tug and bind my movements but yet I move:
swimming through bills,
political extremes,
and community side-eye.

A near perfect breaststroke with my right,
but with my left I am reminded
of trying to rotate a plastic arm of a doll.
Barbie-like, I glide peacefully for an hour.
Enter two small children and their adult:

---

[16] Previously published in *Going On 99 Fahrenheit* was first published in *Great Valley Stories* by SJVW in 2023.

The tiny girl says "talk quietly" to her companions
and then screams her directive
when the whispers can still be heard.

They are happy and there are no real standoffs,
but the emerging leader is clear.
Adult and sibling play along with her and splash. I too pretend,
and wish for control. The distraction is just a mirror:
The 10% rent increase. The attempt to buy the dream of stability.

Only 2.98% interest, only 3% down, plus closing costs,
And a thirty-year mortgage with the same payment every month.
I've done the math:
It means I'll pay nearly double the sticker cost;
Interest rates and irritable bowel syndrome clog my calculator.

Visions of security lure me, trick me into the American Dream.
And if it works I say goodbye:
to the pool, to the view of the sunset,
to no yard work for the sake of the Joneses.
All for the hope of not throwing my money away:
for the opportunity to build a shitload of debt.

Suddenly more children descend and jump in with a splash,
And a text message tells me bidding wars will ensue.
Without me.
As the sun strikes from above,
last week's ornery one arrives complacent
with the other parent: The system has some balance,
yet it's dangling us all between guardians and dreams.

As I get up to leave, I see a blue plastic action figure
floating in the pool, his limbs
akimbo unable to paddle himself to safety.
"Keep floating and you'll get there,
eventually" I say, because that is what I've been told
to say to myself.
But I know, we are all just one stroke away from drowning

Charity Romstad lives in California's San Joaquin Valley. She has lived on five continents, working as a teacher and taking note of humanity. She holds a BA in English from Pacific Union College and a certificate in creative writing from the University of California, San Diego Extension.

TRI-VALLEY

"Let us cherish the hope that the day is not far distant when we will be in the midst of this next adventure."
—*Ernest Lawrence*

Writing at Zero Dark Thirty[17]

Jordan Bernal
Tri-Valley Writers

Ideas ricochet in my head,
And draw me from my bed.
Searching for the elusive muse,
Lightning quick before I lose.

Cascading words in a hurry,
Like snowflakes in a spring flurry.
Take too long and they'll be gone,
Melting with the warming dawn.

Can't give up the bones of thought,
While in the antithesis of a drought.
Pen to paper I must write,
Fingers to keyboard, laughing in delight.

Zero dark thirty, the clock glows,
That agony every writer knows.
Ideas fading much too fast,
I struggle to free one final blast.

Jordan Bernal is the author of *The Keepers of Éire, a* dragon fantasy that encourages adult readers to let their imaginations take flight. Jordan's enduring love of dragons and her pursuit of her Celtic heritage inspired her to write and publish her debut novel in her Celtic Dragonriders series through her independent press, Dragon Wing Publishing. *The Keepers of Éire* is the 2104 Global eBook Gold Award Winner and the Bella Online Gold Award Winner. In 2017, Jordan released a YA edition of *The Keepers of Éire* and published her middle-grade, anti-bullying spin-off novel, *Reluctant Paladin. The*

[17] Previously published in *Voices of the Valley: Encore* in 2013.

Keepers of Alba, the second novel in her adult series, was released on September 1, 2020. She is currently working on the final book in the Celtic Dragonriders series. Jordan has been a member of the California Writers Club Tri-Valley Branch since 2010. For more information on Jordan's current projects, visit http://www.jordanbernal.com.

A Cheese Sandwich on Main Street[18]

Shannon Brown
Tri-Valley Writers

Marty kept nervously looking at the sandwich maker, then his watch, then the scary plug of the machine. Any sparks from it would no doubt set off sprinklers and a tragic fate for park history that would be 100 percent my fault. Still, I couldn't help smiling. I was really here. This was really happening.

Asking if I could have a sandwich was pushing it, I know, and I'm still amazed Marty agreed. I really did owe him everything. As the sandwich cooked, no sparks or flames erupted, but the smell of slightly burnt cheese permeated through the air. It's not the typical odor for a place that pumps pleasing aromas at you when you pass by.

"I will never be able to get this smell out," Marty said, as he gingerly unplugged the sandwich maker.

"Just think of how much cigarette smoke this place probably had to endure once. It can handle one little sandwich," I responded. *I knew I would never have this magical opportunity again. If I was going to make a secret pilgrimage to these sacred grounds, I may as well go all out.*

Plus, I wasn't worried about the odor. Marty was a wiz at getting rid of stains, smells and doing other restoration. It was no surprise that he'd gotten a job on Main Street. If he put his mind to it, Marty could restore a real turn of the century street into one as nice as the artificially crafted street we were now above.

I got up out of the green chair with the average size ottoman, where Lily sat in the magazine photo. I'd already tested the other chairs and both couches. It's true what they say; Victorians didn't seem to value comfort all that much.

I still couldn't believe I was actually inside. This was a real fan's dream come true. I wanted to run around or at least do a little dance, but those would be heard downstairs. Instead, I did a little twirl, followed by a pirouette, while Marty's back was turned.

My feet were bare, and it was fun to imagine them touching the same carpet as Walt. Only it clearly wasn't original. I remember the

---

[18] Previously published in *Voices of the Valley: Journeys* in 2018.

picture in the August 1963 issue of *National Geographic*. The carpet was solid cranberry; this one had a busy pattern of multicolor roses.

"How's it looking?" I asked, joining him in the cooking area. It was so small you couldn't even call it a kitchenette.

Marty frowned, "we should let it sit, for a minute or so."

I poked around the cabinets. Amongst all the Victorian era glassware was a set of pink saucepans. "Wonder how much chili was made in these," I said. Marty chuckled, and we walked to the other side of the apartment as the sandwich cooled. He saw me eying the pair of identical red couches.

"Don't make Walt's couch into a bed," he said.

"You're no fun. Can I see the Edison rolls?" Marty showed me a small cabinet full of wax cylinders with names like *Boston Commandery March*. I knew better than to ask to hear any, but I did brush my hand along the phonograph's horn.

I walked over to what Marty called the Regina music player and admired the mechanics inside. It was a wood and glass cabinet containing a set of huge metal plates with notches and gears. "I would love to hear this Victorian jukebox do its thing," I said.

"Try YouTube." Marty shrugged, and headed back towards the tiny kitchen area.

Since I couldn't partake of any of the entertainment options inside the apartment, I stood quietly and simply listened. Outside, I heard the train station announcement clashing with a roaring elephant from the jungle cruise. I imagined what it would be like with the windows open during the parade.

"What was that sound?" Marty said. His normal speaking voice shook me since he'd been whispering ever since we entered this secret place.

"What noise? Probably the elephant or headhunters. Or maybe the backside of water?"

"I thought I heard a step," Marty whispered. He left the sandwich unattended and walked down the small hall leading to the door. "Coast is clear," he said a minute later, walking back towards the kitchenette. "Can you keep an ear out?"

An ear out? "Sure thing," I said. Downstairs I heard a small child admiring the firehouse equipment. I slowly wandered around the apartment as Marty attended to the sandwich. Eventually I grew tired of looking and gingerly touching all the antiques, so I crept towards the famous window with the always-lit lamp perched on a wood table.

"Don't."

"I wasn't."

"You know the deal, no peeking out front."

"Fine." I wandered over to Marty and looked at the sandwich maker. It was a metal rectangle with a dangerous looking frayed woven cord attached. No wonder he was such a vigilant baby sitter.

"I thought it would be more of a sixties model, but this thing looks like it's from the thirties."

"I'm just glad it didn't spark," Marty said, grabbing the paper plates from the bag he was keeping hidden in the mop bucket. I felt a wave of gratitude for the cast member who called in sick, leaving Marty stuck with apartment maintenance. He was supposed to get it spick and span for a tour of VIPs coming in the next morning. They would no doubt be the jaded sort who received all the perks and didn't care. I imagined a group looking bored while the guide describes the little details like the plates, vases, and lamps discovered in Europe and small antique shops.

Marty gingerly pulled the sandwich off the machine and gave me half. "I have the feeling this sandwich is going to taste blah," he said.

"Of course, it's going to taste blah. We didn't use any butter. But who cares? We're *here*! I never could have imagined—"

The sandwich was as promised. A bland mix of American cheese and wonder bread, burnt on the sides and cold in the middle. I washed it down with tap water since Marty was paranoid about spills and stains.

"Wonder what's on the menu at Club 33, tonight?

"Probably the usual," Marty said. "Five courses full of fancy food. A mere 120 dollars for the meal, but 12,000 for the membership and the bragging rights. Honestly, I'd rather have this sandwich, and *these* bragging rights."

"I agree."

"Too bad we can't ever tell a soul," he said, taking another bite.

"I know," I said between my last couple of bites. "Hey, can you show me where the fire pole was?"

"Sure, but then you gotta go. I have to get rid of this burnt cheese smell."

"Good luck with that," I said after seeing the closet where the pole once held court. Marty made sure the coast was clear before handing me back my phone. He worried about me sneaking pictures. I wouldn't have, believe me. I owe Marty big time for this.

Maybe someday many years from now I will tell the story on an online message board. Anonymously of course. Ninety percent of readers will not believe me, but maybe one or two will. Enough to repeat the story, enough to create a legend, or perhaps just an urban legend. I could picture the conversations now:

"You know that cheese sandwich maker, up in Walt's secret apartment?"

"That apartment's hardly secret; everyone knows about it. I saw a video on YouTube."

"Yeah, well my friend's cousin's neighbor snuck into that apartment once."

"Yeah right."

"I swear. They got in, hung out, and even made a sandwich. That grilled cheese sandwich maker still works. I heard it tasted even better than the Monte Cristo they serve at The Blue Bayou."

"Uh huh. Your cousin is so full of it."

I smiled at the thought, then slipped out the back, down the stairs, and through an alcove back to Main Street proper. No one was around. Marty had worked his magic, indeed.

As I wandered through the Emporium my stomach growled. A churro was in order. Even though my cheese sandwich hadn't hit the spot, it was still the most memorable meal I'd ever eaten.

Shannon Brown is the author of several books including the *Rock'N'Roll in Locker Seventeen* trilogy, a series of humorous novels about a teen who discovers what happened to a missing rock star. She also designs funny T-shirts and gift products. Her other interests include digital photography, reading, graphic design, listening to music, watching movies, and playing video and board games. Shannon lives in the Bay Area. Her website is www.locker17.com.

Nature Doesn't Seem to Know or Care

Kate McCarroll Moore
Tri-Valley Writers

The azaleas are in riotous bloom
a profusion of pinks and reds
their wind-driven petals scattered
across the walkway
to our front door
a floral carpet no one will cross

Out back the roses are showing off
their first shy buds opening
yellow and peach and red
oblivious to the fact
that there will be
no garden party here this spring

Meanwhile, two neighborhood cats
are perched upon the fence
facing each other
tails swishing slowly
shaking loose the wisteria blossoms
onto the playground behind our house
the stage is set for a catfight
that the schoolchildren will not hear

Between the press conferences
and the daily news
silently we wait
while the rain falls
and the flowers bloom

Kate McCarroll Moore is a lifelong educator and the former Poet Laureate for the City of San Ramon, California. She is the author of two novels for children, *Elinormal* and *New Girl: The Further Adventures of Elinormal*. Her debut picture book, *Chelsea Skye, Nature Spy,* was recently published. Kate also has published poetry collections for adults; her most recent collection is *Alphapoetica: A Poetry Primer for the Everyday Poet*.

She holds a Doctorate in Educational Leadership for Social Justice, and she continues to promote poetry as a tool of transformation and healing. She never grows tired of peoplewatching and eavesdropping, using her writer's imagination to turn ordinary events into unique characters with interesting stories to tell. She lives with her family in Northern California.

Search and Rescue[19]

Violet Carr Moore
Tri-Valley Writers

Tri-Valley Writers is honored to share Violet Carr Moore's short story in memory of our friend and fellow member.

The hawk circled above Emily. Seeing it away from the protection of the covered patio brought a feeling of helplessness. She shifted her weight from her right leg, injured when she lost her balance and tumbled down the hillside. She panicked until she freed herself from a thicket of brambles that raked her skin. Emily dragged herself to the creek, out of the hawk's view, where trees overshadowed the rocks. She drank, lifting her head in swift movements. Up to the sky. Down to the water. Cool water trickled over her legs, cleansing wounds where thorns had pricked her skin. She whimpered when she slipped on the wet rocks. No one but the hawk heard. Emily struggled to the creek bank where she sank down on last winter's leaves mingled with soft dirt beneath the trees.

Emily's stomach growled. It had been a long time since breakfast. Glancing around, she saw berries entwined in brambles nearby. Emily ate until her hunger pains subsided. She retraced her steps to the stream for more water, then back to the trees where she retreated to the leaves again.

After a brief rest, Emily tried to climb the hill, but she wasn't built for climbing. Hereditary weight restricted her to level surfaces. She looked up from where she had fallen. No way to reach the top of the hill alone. Emily squinted into the westward sun hovering over the tree tops. Was the hawk still watching? Darkness, another fear, made her forget the hawk for a moment and cry out again. How she wished for someone to hear her. Afraid to see the hawk, Emily closed her puffy eyes. Exhausted, she fell asleep.

◊ ◊ ◊

"Here, give me a hand with this food and party decorations, will you?" Mitzi said. "Where's Emily?" she asked when she saw Rick

---

[19] Previously published in Voices of the Valley: First Press in 2011.

was alone.

"Don't know," Rick replied. He grabbed overflowing cloth bags in each hand and slammed the door shut with a left-footed back kick. "She was on the patio watching me trim the yard. Right after that, she left for her daily walk. Maybe she went too far. Better yet, maybe she's at Jed's. Still, she should have been home by now. She doesn't like walking in the dark."

Rick inhaled the scent of fresh-mowed grass as he crossed the back lawn toward the pasture, now boasting an alfalfa crop. He took great pride working his five-acre plot subdivided from the large farm where he and his brother Jed spent their childhood. Rick quickened his pace, his lanky body casting an elongated shadow in the late afternoon sun. He approached the old barn doors, checked the lock, and scanned the surrounding area. Once housing a hub of human and animal activity, the barn now stored his grandfather's ancient John Deere tractor, old rusty tools handed down from his great-grandfather and mismatched family furniture.

Rick hurried toward the hedgerow that divided the two farms. He traced the pasture with his eyes, hesitating where the new metal barn roof gleamed in the afternoon sun atop traditional red clapboard siding. He glanced to the south toward the McCafferty's split rail fence, then back to the modern faux-wood surrounding the front of the Everton's farm. Rick noticed a hawk circling near the stream as he made another quick ground search. No Emily.

"Haven't seen Emily since yesterday," Jed replied when Rick reached Jed on his cell phone. "I'm in the barn. Can't see anything from here. Lenora's gone—ran over to Bagley's Bakery to pick up my birthday cake for this evening. She should've dropped it off at your house by now. If she stops back here first, I'll ask her about Emily. We'll be over early to help you set up the patio, probably a little after dark. See you then."

Rick punched another speed dial number on his phone. "Mrs. McCafferty, have you seen Emily today? No? Well, thanks anyway. I'll keep looking. Yes, I'll let you know if I don't find her. Bye."

"Charlie, glad I caught you at home," Rick said to Charles Everton. "Just checking to see if Emily's been over there this afternoon. Not today? Okay. Thanks. What's that? She was home until mid-afternoon, but I can't find her now. Yes, it could be too soon to worry. I'm just overly cautious, I suppose. Talk to you later."

Rick trotted around the curve in the graveled road. He doubled back and reached home as Jenny and Mark turned into the driveway from the opposite direction, their new Lexus covered with dust. Lenora trailed them in Jed's battered old Ford pickup. She drove around the SUV and parked near the patio. With a cake box in one hand and strings from a half dozen helium-filled balloons wrapped around the palm of her other hand, she eased the cake onto the patio table. Lenora tied the strings to the honoree's chair. As though longing for freedom, the balloons stretched until they touched the patio cover.

◊ ◊ ◊

Rick inhaled the familiar aroma of grilled steaks as he moved them to the side, away from the hot coals. He wiped his hands on a chef's apron and motioned Jed to step outside. "I'm afraid I'm going to be a wet blanket on your birthday celebration if Emily doesn't get home soon," Rick said. A furrowed brow and a deep frown attested to the concern.

Jed placed a sympathetic hand on Rick's shoulder. "I know. It's not like her to be gone after dark. My steak can wait. I'll help you take a second look. Let's go tell the others to eat without us."

"I know this is Jed's over-the-hill birthday celebration. The steaks are ready," Rick said to the guests, "but he's volunteered to help me look for Emily. She hasn't lived here long, and I'm concerned that she might not find her way home in the dark. We'll be back soon. Go ahead and chow down without us. Emily loves cake, so save it 'til we can get back and celebrate together."

"Wait. I'll go with you," Mark said. "Jenny's turned me into a vegetarian—well almost. I'll skip the steak right now and pair up with one of you for the search."

"I'll go, too," Jenny said. "Mark and I will hold the lights."

"Let's split up in the trucks and follow the trail above the creek, then circle back this way," Rick said as he grabbed a couple of high-powered flashlights.

◊ ◊ ◊

"Emily! Emily!" Mark's deep voice boomed out as he stood near the truck, not venturing away from the headlights. "Where . . .

are . . . you . . . Emily?"

"Em-e! Em-e! Em-e-e-e!" Jenny yelled in singsong rhythm, shining her flashlight into the dark shadows behind the truck.

Sounds from above drifting down the creek bank roused Emily from sleep. She struggled to her feet. She heard her name, but shivered at the strange voices.

Jed saw movement in the distant beam of his high-powered portable light. He swung it from side to side where he saw disturbed ground down the embankment. "Over here, Rick. Turn the truck around and shine more light over this way," he said. "I think I see movement."

Rick paced back and forth at the top of the hill while flashlights aimed downhill. "Emily's never walked this trail before, at least not that I know of. The ground's uneven here, so she may have fallen down to the creek. Emily! Are you down there?" Rick yelled. The familiar sound of Rick's voice gave her the strength to stumble out into a small clearing.

Rick recognized Emily's silhouette. "I see her! See down there," he pointed, "by the creek. Tie off the rope to the truck winch and ease it down."

Jed sighed. "Okay, Rick. Let's get this rescue underway, but first, one word of advice so this doesn't happen again."

"Now don't tell me to fence off the trail because I've tried that. The posts won't hold in this soil."

"Easier than that," Jed replied. "Next time you want a pet, get a dog, will ya? We're gonna have a devil of a time winching your hundred-pound potbelly pig up this hill."

Violet Carr Moore first published *In the Right Place: A Gallery of Treasured Moments*, a collection of mystic vignettes, then *Moments of Meditation*, a collection of inspirational devotionals. Her short stories have been published in *Chicken Soup for the Soul: Devotional Stories for Mothers; Christmas Miracles; Written Across the Genres; The Choice Matters;* all five of Tri-Valley Writers' *Voices of the Valley* anthologies; and several other anthologies. She co-authored *Double Take*, a memoir of her childhood years as a twin. Vi's winning haiku was published in Bay Area News Group newspapers, both printed and online. "Fatal," her first attempt at a sci-fi short story, won first place in *Survival*, the CWC High Desert Branch anthology.

In 2013, Vi received the Jack London Award for her volunteer service to Tri-Valley Writers after serving as vice president and then president. She continued to volunteer in several positions until her death in November 2023.

BERKELEY

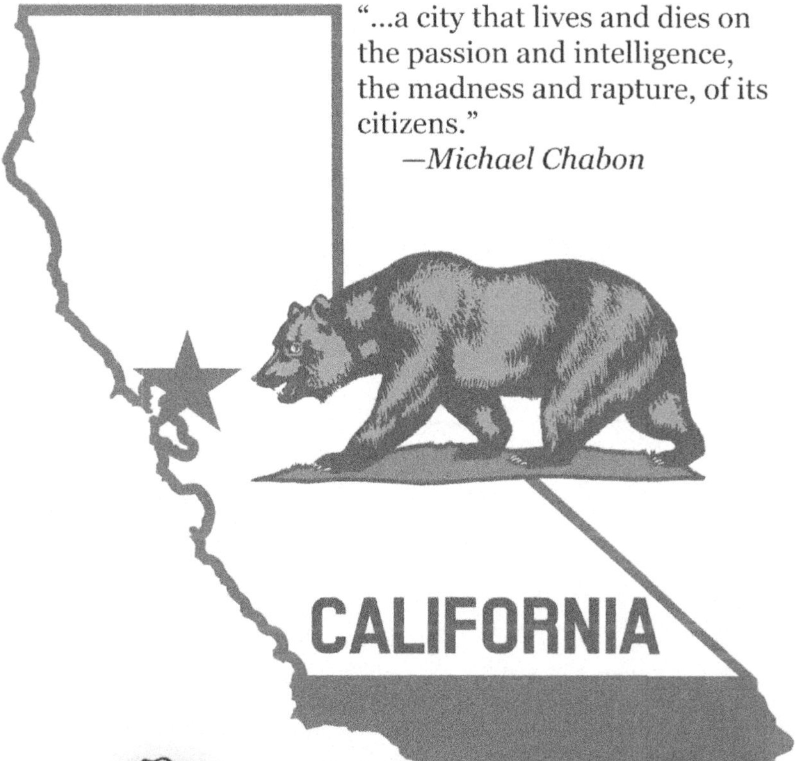

"...a city that lives and dies on the passion and intelligence, the madness and rapture, of its citizens."

—*Michael Chabon*

Rooted

Aqueila Lewis-Ross
Berkeley Branch

Today,
as I sit in my walker waiting for my ride.
The rustling trees tease a sense of calm to my being.
Nature has something to say.
And urges me to listen.
But there's a tug of war raging within.
Fire burning.
It festers like hot coals.
An ulcer has metastasized oozing goo.
To the root.
The wind wants to blow it all away.
Waiting for another day.
But days are short.
And my patience is waning.
I just want to write about nature,
And trees.
And find family lines.
On ancestor.com
Cuz' they're still waiting to be recognized.
Given what's due.
40 acres and a mule.
Reparations seem so far.
Seeds don't have a clue how to grow.
If the powers all around have something to say,
the future bleeds death.
And evil continues to corrupt.
How many stories must we tell for people to really listen?

Aqueila M. Lewis-Ross is an award-winning performance artist, author, and journalist. She is highly skilled in multidisciplinary studies in music (classically trained), theater, education, and African American and Interdisciplinary Studies. A skilled writer and media specialist with a history of conceptualizing and reporting diverse stories, her portfolio includes extensive knowledge in digital media and editing pieces for various platforms.

Appreciating Rembrandt

David Baker
Berkeley Branch

McKnight pulled to the curb and parked in front of a house with plastic sheeting taped to the windows. A young man stood on a ladder, facing the house, his elbow flapping like a chicken's wing, ponytail swinging from his painter's cap. He worked his scraper into a rafter, digging away as if he expected to find a diamond. Billy. At this rate, he'd be up on the ladder till Kingdom Come. McKnight climbed out of his pickup. He gripped the door handle with both hands, lifted to jam the door closed, and walked toward his apprentice.

If he'd had a son, the kid would be Billy's age by now and probably just as stubborn. McKnight wiped his forehead and dried his hand on the tattered bib of his overalls. His truck was ready for the junkyard, he had an alimony check to write, and his daughter was about to start her second year at Michigan. No way he could afford to let the job drag on forever.

"What do you think you're doing?" He stopped behind the ladder.

"End's rotted pretty bad," Billy said without turning around. "Have to glue in a patch or something."

"I'll glue a patch on your ass, you keep screwing around like this. Slap in some wood dough, let it dry, and prime it."

"O.K." Billy twisted his scraper and pulled out a clot of spongy-looking fibers. "But I'd better get a chisel and cut out the rest of this stuff. It's spreading right up the rafter. Once it goes in under the eaves—"

"Son, you want to stay on my crew or not? We've got three jobs lined up after this one, and no time to waste." McKnight stepped back for a better view of the rafter. "I'll take care of this, you get going on the trim."

"O.K., Mr. McKnight."

Shoulders drooping, Billy gave the scraper a final twist and came down off the ladder. He went to a cluster of paint cans on a tarpaulin, picked up a brush with a slanted tip, and dipped it, just barely, into a can. Fingers close to the bristles, he angled the brush and pulled a deliberate stroke down the edge of a corner board. Once again, just to be sure. Perfect line, not a speck on the siding. McKnight shook his head. Billy got enjoyment from his work, but satisfaction was a luxury when the competition had up-to-date equipment and a line of credit at the bank.

"It's beautiful, Rembrandt, but we don't need a masterpiece, just get it done."

McKnight turned away from the shabby little one-story with a tar-and-gravel roof and went back to the pickup for a can of wood filler. Sometime in the future he might consider slowing down and doing careful work, the kind he'd done when he was Billy's age. Right now, he had too many bills to pay.

You are what you do, some people said, but they were wrong. When you came from a long line of nobodies who'd ended up with nothing but their debts, you had a right to want a little recognition. Someday people would see him walking down the street and say, "There goes Ian McKnight, owns the biggest painting company in town." You are what you accomplish.

A beeping sound stopped him at the passenger-side door. He reached in through the open window, grabbed his cellphone, and answered it.

"Clayborn here," announced an angry voice.

Desmond Clayborn. The guy had a brand-new BMW in his driveway, was president of the Chamber of Commerce, and had recently informed the media he'd run for mayor. What did he have to be upset about? "Hello, Mr. Clayborn. What can I do for you?"

"Your goddamn job. It's only been a year, and I've got blisters on my siding. I want you back here with your crew, painting my house again. Starting with the prep work."

McKnight held the phone away from his ear and squinted at the sun, a brilliant disk about to sink behind an oak tree in the yard across the street. Do the job all over again? He had to finish this one, get some money in the bank. "If there're a few bad spots, I'll take care of them."

"The whole goddamn thing's a bad spot. I want you over here right now to take a look at it. Tomorrow you can bring your compressor and your air gun."

"Be there as soon as I can. Right now, I'm in the middle—"

"I've already called the Better Business Bureau. Next step's a lawsuit for breach of contract."

The line went dead. McKnight tabbed off and went around to the driver's side. He slid in behind the steering wheel, put the phone in the glove compartment, and took out a stainless-steel flask. Scotch whisky burned his throat and warmed his belly. He'd drive halfway across Triumphal—great name for a town losing its business to the shopping malls—and waste what was left of the day.

McKnight set the flask cap but didn't twist it shut. A little extra might calm his nerves. He took another swallow, then several more before putting the flask away and starting the engine. Now he was ready for Mr. BMW. He put the truck in gear, let out the clutch, and floored the accelerator. The motor spluttered into a roar. Slap-shift to second. Patches of sunlight flashed through leaf-laden branches, one tree quick after the next.

A stop sign came up at the corner. Rolling stop? Why not? No traffic. The pedal went down a little farther than it should have before the brakes took hold. Paint cans rattled, sliding along the truck bed. McKnight glanced both ways and stomped the gas.

A late-model Lexus swung away from the curb and pulled in front of him. Crazy fool. McKnight swerved, nicking the car with his bumper. He dodged an oncoming SUV, jammed on the brakes, and ran the Lexus back to the curb. The driver, a pale, brown-haired man in his early forties, pushed open the door. McKnight got out. He'd tell the jerk a thing or two.

The man glanced over his shoulder into the car, creases deep in his forehead. McKnight went toward him. Around one-eighty-plus, the guy looked big enough but, for some reason, seemed to be afraid. He spun away from the car door as if to take off running.

"Not so fast, buddy, you owe me an apology." McKnight grabbed the man's arm. "Just cuz you drive a fancy car doesn't mean you own the road."

The man broke free and drew back his arm, one shoulder lower than the other. McKnight blocked the punch and swung from the hip, missing. Drunker than he'd thought. He stumbled against the man's chest and pushed him off balance. Arms flailing, the man fell backward. His head smacked concrete, his arms went limp, and he lay still. God, no, he might've cracked his skull. McKnight was about to crouch down and try to wake him up, when something caught his eye.

Movement on the front seat of the car.

A little girl sat up and stared at him with large, frightened eyes. She was eight or nine years old. The way she had her hair cut, short with bangs in front, reminded him of his own daughter at that age. Tears swelled in the child's eyes and overflowed, streaking her face. Poor kid, she had to be terrified.

"Don't be afraid, sweetheart. I'll make sure your daddy's OK. Didn't mean to get so mad at him."

"He's not my daddy." The little girl made fists and pressed them into her eyes, wiping at the tears. "I want to go home."

A car door slammed on the other side of the street. McKnight's head jerked toward the sound. A thick-shouldered cop in a blue uniform strode toward him, handcuffs swinging from his belt. "Stay right where you are, mister."

The cop turned to the man on the pavement and went down on one knee to feel his neck. He yanked a handset from his belt, gave his location, and requested help. He stood up, reattaching the handset, and moved in front of McKnight. "You've had your fun for the day. Hands on the hood and assume the position."

"The guy's going to be OK, isn't he?" McKnight felt stomach muscles clinch. "I didn't mean to—"

"You'll get your chance to talk." The cop leaned closer, "Wilford" in capital letters on his nameplate. "After I run a breathalyzer on you. Now do what I said."

"But the guy took a poke at me. And the kid says—"

"You're not giving me trouble, are you?" Officer Wilford rested the heel of his hand on his nightstick.

McKnight flattened his palms on the truck hood and spread his feet. He'd better get his head clear and go over what to say. Even if he didn't end up in jail, he'd probably lose his driver's license on a DUI. How would he run his business? He couldn't let Billy drive around and bid the jobs. The kid would overestimate the hours.

Officer Wilford bent down at the open door of the Lexis to talk to the little girl. McKnight watched through the windshield. The child was still crying, her voice too faint to hear. Wilford straightened up, an apologetic grimace on his face.

"Man, I'm sorry." He made a lifting motion with his hand, gesturing for McKnight to stand normally. "Didn't know what you'd done here today."

Done? It was right in front of him, lying in the street.

"The little girl says this fellow here . . ." The officer looked down at the brown-haired man, who groaned and sat up, hands planted behind him on the pavement. "Grabbed her, just now, on her way home from her friend's house." Wilford pulled the man's wrists together and cuffed him. "And you ran him off the road and knocked him down. I'd say that was one hell of a citizen's arrest." Wilford clapped McKnight on the shoulder. "Good thing you came along when you did." He gave him a wink. "We'll forget the breathalyzer if you'll leave your truck where it is for a while. Till you're sober enough to drive."

"Sure, OK." McKnight felt a joyful surge. No need to set the officer straight on why the fight had started. He might change his mind about the breath test.

"Tell me what happened," Wilford said.

"I was driving along and . . ." Ran a stop sign? Better find another way to put it.

"You saw him grab the girl?"

"Well . . ." McKnight's lips tightened against his teeth. "Not exactly."

"But you saw her in his car." Dark eyebrows lifted in anticipation. "Something tipped you off she shouldn't be there?"

McKnight nodded. If that was what the officer wanted to hear, why disappoint him? "I guess the main thing was, he tried to run away when I pulled him over."

"I'll need that in a statement," Wilford said, as a second patrol car and a fire department ambulance came down the street. "We'll take this guy away and get the little girl back home, and then I'll meet you at the station. You know where it is, right? Just around the corner?"

"No problem." Mr. BMW could wait.

◊ ◊ ◊

McKnight entered his living room and twisted the switch on his floor lamp to the brightest setting. A framed photo of his daughter stood on a bookcase next to a window with the shade pulled down. Lisa was a college girl. Even if he didn't make it to the good side of town, she would. People would treat her with respect.

Maybe then she'd understand him better. As it was, Lisa always took her mother's side. "You were never there for us, always working weekends." She had a point. The checks he wrote for alimony and tuition didn't compensate for all the time he'd spent away from home, but a man has to do what he has to do, doesn't he?

McKnight adjusted the lamp to the lowest setting and sat down on a couch with a wine-colored stain on the fabric. Lisa had spilled a glass of grape juice and looked so sorrowful he hadn't had the heart to scold her. She couldn't have been much older than the little girl he'd seen this afternoon.

He pressed a button on his TV remote. A channel guide came up, clock showing 7:59. Maybe he could find a movie, anything to keep his mind off the bottle in the kitchen cabinet. Officer Wilford had said he wasn't "sober enough to drive." That had been a little hard to take. He'd been sober enough to work, hadn't he? He'd never in his life been drunk on the job. Didn't need a drink first thing in the morning. Still, Wilford had seemed like a fair-minded man. Laying off the booze for a while might be a good idea.

The door buzzer sounded. McKnight got up from his sofa and straightened a pile of magazines about to slide off an end table. Who'd come visiting at eight in the evening? He readjusted the lamp and went to the door.

A woman in a skirt and a crisp-looking blouse with a high collar stood on his front porch with a microphone in her hand. Her name escaped him, but he knew who she was. Well-brushed auburn hair flowed to her shoulders in the same loose, casual style she accomplished every night, sitting in the anchor chair for the ten o'clock news.

Two men—one with a TV camera, the other with a video light not yet turned on—stood behind the woman, aiming over her shoulders. McKnight caught himself about to step back. What were they doing here? Had Mr. BMW put out the word on him?

"Sorry to barge in on you like this," the woman said. "I'm Kimberley Carlyle, WTDX News. Are you Ian McKnight?"

"Yes, ma'am." She looked about thirty, made him wish he wasn't fifty-two. "That camera's not running, is it?"

"Not yet, but I'd very much like to interview you. Would that be OK?"

"Why me?"

"Oh, come on, Ian. Don't be so modest." The newswoman taunted him with sleepy eyes, her smile the kind that made a fellow want to look her up and down. "I just got off the phone with Officer Wilford from the Triumphal PD. He says you saved a little girl this afternoon and made a citizen's arrest. The chief of police is going to recommend you for the Chamber of Commerce Citizen of the Year award." Another lazy smile. "You're not going to disappoint me, are you?"

McKnight felt a tremor slither up his spine. What was he supposed to say? Wilford had given him a break. He didn't want to make the man look like a fool.

"I'm not much for interviews, Ms. Carlyle. Whatever the officer said is pretty much how it was."

"Please call me Kimberley. And stand here, so the camera can see both of us." She pointed, as the light came on, to a spot near the porch railing. "Officer Wilford tells me you paint houses."

McKnight stood where he was. Should he work in a plug for his business? She might go out to the jobsite and interview the guys. He could just hear Billy. "Oh, yes ma'am, he's a great boss, except sometimes he tells us to cut corners." The kid was so honest and eager to please, he'd blab until she took the microphone away.

"I'd really rather not do this." McKnight shielded his eyes with his hand.

"But people want to know about you." The woman's voice had a pleading, almost resentful, quality. "You're a hero, after all."

He could use the free publicity, no question, but none of this felt right. Heroes were cops and firefighters and the soldiers overseas.

"Not really, Ms. Carlyle." Too bad the conversation had to end. "But I won't be saying any more about it. Sorry to be rude."

McKnight turned around and went back inside.

◊ ◊ ◊

The moon had just come up behind the Regency. McKnight pulled into the restaurant's parking lot and found an empty space. Dressed in a suit, he felt silly getting out of a rusted pickup truck. Maybe no one would notice him until he walked into the banquet room. "A pre-award dinner," they were calling it, with him the guest of honor. He turned off the engine and rested his hands on his knees.

What a week it had been: Meeting the little girl's parents and learning that her name was April. The Chamber telling him he'd be Citizen of the Year. His image on TV, leaving his house or the job site and climbing into his truck. Kimberley's voice telling her viewers about the "courageous, yet unassuming man" who had "earned the loyalty of his hard-working crew." She'd been half right. The guys had carried the load while he bid jobs and ducked the spotlight. All the talk about "McKnight the hero" had apparently impressed them.

Billy, most of all. The kid looked at him now not with resentment but with approval in his eyes. It felt good to be appreciated for a change, especially by Billy. He was still a pain-in-the-ass perfectionist who scraped at every microscopic bit of flaking paint, but he didn't sulk the way he used to when he got told to move along. A welcome change in attitude, at least for the time being. Eventually the long face would return.

McKnight swung his gaze around the lot. BMWs, Mitsubishis, Cadillacs, and expensive-looking SUVs. The hero story was going to win him more than just the admiration of a twenty-one-year-old. The owners of these cars would treat him as an equal. It wasn't his fault the media had gone a little overboard. Part of the fairy tale was even true. He'd saved April, so he wasn't actually lying. Well, maybe a little, but wasn't this an opportunity?

Tonight he'd have a chance to meet the men and women who could make things happen. "Networking," his educated daughter would've called it. He'd talk and laugh with them and see what they were like, not as clients with complaints but as people. Maybe he'd even make some friends. If he didn't screw up and say something stupid. McKnight's hand went toward the flask in the glove compartment. Not a drop all week, he deserved at least a taste. His hand fell back. He had to put anxiety aside, walk in among the bigshots, act like he belonged.

He climbed out of his truck and started toward the restaurant, shoes pinching his toes. Buying a brand-new pair just for tonight had been a bad idea. He crossed the parking lot, walking with shorter steps than usual, opened walnut panel doors, and went inside. Customers sat at linen-covered tables lit by lamps turned down so low that shadows spread throughout the room. Brighter light came from a doorway at the end of an aisle, where a crowd of well-dressed people stood talking. McKnight straightened his shoulders. Time to look confident.

A short, stout man in his late fifties emerged from the crowd and waved a greeting. Narrow glasses made his face look even rounder than it was. McKnight moved closer. He knew this guy, Phillip Dorff, manager of the city's low-income housing program. Like Mr. BMW, he wanted to be mayor.

"Great to see you, Ian." Dorff offered his hand.

"Good to see you, too." McKnight gave him an easy grip.

He couldn't bring himself to use the man's name. Not after Dorff had told him he needn't bother submitting bids for painting contracts because his work didn't "meet city standards."

"Quite an honor, having you here," Dorff said, his smile a little creepy in the shadows. "The least I can do is ask you when you're going to send me a bid. We've got quite a few locations that need painting."

McKnight kept his face expressionless. Something wrong with his hearing?

"Just do the paperwork. I'll give it my personal attention."

So much for city standards, but what did Dorff want in return? No matter. He was an important man to know.

McKnight walked with Dorff through the crowd into a large room painted a pastel shade of tangerine and lit by ceiling fixtures made from burnished copper. Dinner guests sat at rectangular tables arranged in rows in front of a lectern with a microphone. Officer Wilford, wearing a suit and tie, sat with April and her parents at a table on the far side of the room. Kimberley Carlyle and her crew stood on the near side along a wall, video lights and cameras ready. McKnight restrained an urge to smile at her. He'd have to say something when they introduced him, then she'd know he was an idiot for sure.

A man his age walked toward him, clad in a pinstriped suit with sharp lapels. Tall, straight-backed, blond hair blow-dried into fluffy waves, he was none other than Desmond Clayborn—Mr. BMW. Clayborn hadn't called again about the prep work. Maybe he'd been too busy with his campaign, but he'd probably say something now, in front of everybody. McKnight looked around for someone taller than Dorff to stand behind. Too late, Clayborn's eyes had found him.

"Here comes the other party's candidate," Dorff said, "but I know I can count on you."

To do what, vote on Election Day? McKnight kept his eyes on Mr. BMW.

Clayborn walked toward him with a vigorous stride, a grin on his face. Too wide a grin for a guy with blistered siding.

"Wonderful to see you, Ian."

McKnight smiled back. When was the last time someone had felt "wonderful" seeing him? He shook Clayborn's heartily presented hand.

"Good to see you, too, Phillip." Clayborn gave Dorff a nod. "Shall we introduce Ian to the mayor?"

McKnight followed the two men to a table centered in front of the lectern. He shook hands with the mayor, a cheerful man with a ruddy complexion, and sat down with his back to the guests. Dorff sat on his left, Clayborn to the right. A waiter filled glasses with champagne.

"Cheers." Dorff hoisted his glass.

McKnight picked up his. Long time since he'd tasted champagne, maybe a sip or two would loosen him up. As it was, his knees would probably start shaking when they called him to the lectern.

"Cheers." The fizzy stuff was better than he'd remembered.

"I'm sure you're a supporter of our party," Dorff said, "the party of the working man." He leaned close, his voice just loud enough to hear above the drone from nearby conversations. "I've got a rally scheduled for next Saturday." He signaled the waiter to top up McKnight's glass. "I'd like you to join me on the platform."

So that was it, contracts in exchange for help with his campaign. McKnight took a sip and then another. He felt a hand on his arm.

"Don't bother with him," Clayborn said in a voice as hushed as Dorff's had been. "I've got something important to talk to you about." He lifted his glass and motioned for McKnight to join him. "My friends at the bank tell me they turned you down for a loan last year. Would you like them to reassess your application?"

"You could arrange that?" The bank's standards were as flexible as the city's.

"As good as done." Clayborn dismissed the matter with a flip of his hand.

McKnight reached for his glass. He knew exactly how to use the money. First he'd buy a new compressor, then—

"I need your endorsement," Clayborn said, "in a campaign commercial." He signaled for more champagne. "All you need to do is look serious and read from a teleprompter."

No wonder Mr. BMW hadn't mentioned the prep work, Dorff was probably gaining on him in the polls. McKnight drained his glass and held it up for the waiter to refill. Both men needed him, he'd drink to that.

"Ladies and gentlemen." The mayor now stood at the microphone. "It's a pleasure to see so many of you here tonight on such a happy occasion." His voice rang out like an opera singer's. "It isn't often we have a chance to meet someone like Ian McKnight, a noble, selfless man who sits here among us, an inspiration to us all."

Did His Honor have to spread it on so thick? McKnight drank his glass dry and looked around for more. The waiter obliged him and went on along the table, serving plates of veal garnished with mushrooms. Clayborn and Dorff picked up their knives and forks, and McKnight followed their example. If he chewed hard enough, he might not hear the booming voice. A single bite-sized piece of veal remained when the mayor finished his remarks to polite applause.

"Now I suppose I'll have to give the gentlemen who want my job a chance to speak," he said. "Starting with my good friend Phillip Dorff."

Dorff got up from his chair and gave McKnight a pat on the back. He strode around the table to the lectern.

"I know better than to try and top the mayor, so I'll just share with you some observations." Dorff adjusted the mike a little lower. "I've come to know Ian McKnight, at least by reputation, quite well during my years at city hall. As a painting contractor, he's as highly regarded as anyone it's been my pleasure to have dealt with."

Good thing Billy wasn't here, he'd puke. McKnight stuffed the last piece of veal into his mouth and washed it down with champagne. He didn't know which party was better, but he wouldn't vote for Dorff. The man had no shame.

Clayborn spoke next. He sounded more natural than the other two, hadn't said anything outrageous yet. McKnight reached for his glass and hit it with his fingertips. Champagne sloshed over the brim. The stuff was sneaking up on him. Still, he needed another swallow. His turn at the mike was coming any minute now.

"I, too, have some observations about Ian," Clayborn said. "By fortuitous coincidence, he was the contractor I hired to paint my house. I don't have to tell you how pleased I am with the results."

That did it. McKnight pushed away his glass. He'd pretended not to smell the bullshit, now they were rubbing it in his face.

"Ladies and gentlemen . . ." Clayborn's voice swelled into a shout. "As president of the Chamber of Commerce, I'm proud to present . . ." Video lights came on, and men with shoulder-mounted cameras hurried forward. "Our guest of honor, soon to be Trimuphal's Citizen of the Year, Ian McKnight."

McKnight walked to the lectern, unstable on his feet, and turned to face the audience. Everyone applauded, none more wildly than Clayborn and Dorff, men he'd envied. To live like them, he'd neglected his family and made a decent kid do work he was ashamed of.

"Thanks, everyone." McKnight bent closer to the microphone. Alcohol had fogged his brain and filled his mind with melancholy thoughts. Put them aside and make some money? Clayborn and Dorff expected nothing less. Look how they smiled at him, so confident he'd play along and give them what they wanted.

"I appreciate what you've done for me tonight." McKnight's gaze went to April, tired-eyed but smiling, then to Officer Wilford. "But I can't accept the award."

Quiet conversations stopped. Forks hovered over plates. The only sound was Dorff choking on and spitting out a bite of veal.

"I didn't know what that guy was up to when I ran him off the road. Everything I did was accidental." McKnight took a breath to steady his voice. "Give the award to Officer Wilford there." He nodded toward the policeman. "He made the bust and got April back home."

McKnight turned from the lectern and headed for the door. People gaped at him as he passed by. His face felt warm, all that champagne. Tight shoes or not, he'd have to leave his truck in the lot and walk home.

Kimberley dodged tables and came at him, one hand brushing

back a strand of auburn hair. The other, close in at her side, held her microphone as though it were a knife. Did she have a right to be angry? He didn't care.

Mr. BMW cut in front of her. The newswoman winced. Had Clayborn stepped on her foot? Might cost him the election.

McKnight held back a smile. Clayborn stood facing him, blocking his path.

"Have you lost your mind?" The tall man's words hissed out, flattened by lips stretched tight.

"More like found it." McKnight sidestepped Clayborn and walked through the room submerged in shadows.

"Ian. The Citizen of the Year Award?" Kimberley's clear, well-modulated voice came from behind. "Is this really what you want to do?"

He pushed through the walnut panel doors and went out into the night. Triumphal's leading citizens had put a glossy coat on him to cover up the things they didn't want to see. That made them just like him. Except, they didn't have Billy. McKnight patted the fender of his truck as he walked past. Maybe he'd cut the kid some slack.

David Baker, a longtime member of the CWC-Berkeley Branch, has written short stories for *Mini-World Magazine* and co-authored two U.S. history textbooks for eighth graders, one published by Addison-Wesley, the other by Globe Fearon.

When is Half an Inch a Foot?

Diane Rawicz
Berkeley Branch

Monday through Friday, I swipe on mascara and neutral lip gloss for my work-look. I decide that attending a convention away from home I'll try something new.

I escape the thrum of the annual convention after lunch to check out the department store across from the hotel. The sensual scents of perfume, powder, and lotions from the cosmetics counter seduce me as I enter the store. I am mesmerized and in a matter of minutes I perch on a stool so the esthetician can give me a makeover.

She tells me that this particular brand of cosmetics is chosen for its ability to camouflage discolorations on the over-forty face. After a creamy cleansing, the first step is applying two layers of nude foundation, letting each one set completely before the next, then finishing with a fine layer of skin tinted base, applying it just so over the cheeks and forehead, paying special attention to the nose and jowls. She dabs concealer around my darkened eyes and lids for a smooth look. Next, mascara, two coats, then the dangerous eyelash curler is deployed to enliven your myopic hazel eyes. A swift stroke of mascara across the brows adds some drama to my now perfect face. The supple goat-bristle brush kisses the cheeks with rosy blush powder. Lip liner, lip base are painted on before I pucker in the mirror so she can apply the latest red-hued matte lipstick to my kiss.

I hardly recognize yourself, and I love that! My eyes look larger, my smile brighter, my skin appears as youthful as it used to be, naturally. I turn away while she rings up the purchases, then watch her place the products into a vinyl-coated bag emblazoned with the brand logo. In a daze, I sign the credit card slip, exhaling the anxiety that accompanies any extravagant purchase. I'm worth this I tell myself as I lift your chin and stride out into the world.

A new face has given me a new perspective and I skip the closing session to bathe and dress for the convention mixer.

Earrings that glitter ruby and sapphire tones dangle from my petite ears and twinkle from under your glossy gray hair that cups my nearly flawless face. The multi-colored, cashmere sweater and black velvet, circle skirt are a festive contrast to the trousers and blazers I wear to work. I'm almost giddy on the elevator ride down to the convention level.

Fellow convention attendees greet me with nods and smiles as I enter the lavish hotel ballroom. After a 180-degree survey of the room and its crowd of partiers, the strains of a jazz classic draw me over the threshold. Sashaying, smiling, I wind my way to the bar and select a chilled glass of prosecco. After a full day of talking heads pummeling me with information on the latest innovations in my industry, the last thing I want is a deep conversation. I politely exchange pleasant yet inconsequential party repartee with the attendees who step up then away from the bar. The music is company enough for me.

I am so confident, so pleased with my outfit, my repartee, and the favorable smiles directed at me that I don't look at myself even when I use the powder room in hour two of the party. No, I tell myself, I am hot, and I know it. The significant investment in expensive cosmetics is paying off! The gathering winds down and I politely decline an invitation to go bar hopping. It's time to relax. I take the elevator up to your room, as happy as a debutante with a proposal.

Hanging the Do Not Disturb sign on my door, I kick off the patent leather sling backs, pull off the sweater, step out of the flared skirt, breathe deeply, and pour myself a scotch. Propped up on the king-size bed, I channel surf to relax. I stroke my face, kind of a private thank you for being such an attractive façade. My hand glides across my chin down my neck, and as my hand comes back up my neck to chin, I feel something. Is that a thread from the sweater? I brush it away. But it's still there. Oh some fuzz, it's nothing, I tell myself. Then I have to get up.

Putting the program on pause I flick on the light in the bathroom and adjust the makeup mirror mounted to the wall. Flipping it to the magnifying side, I crane my neck to see what is stuck under my jaw. I stroke and stretch, twist left and right until my hand feels it. A whisker. Ehh, it's a whisker. But since I can't see it then it has to be a white one. The tweezers are handy in my open cosmetics bag. I step away from the mirror to find the whisker with my left hand, tweezers in right. After a few strokes Pow, I find it and pluck. In one firm tug the whisker is no longer under my chin but in the clutches of the tweezers. Sighing, I bring the tweezers up to my eyes to check out that rascal. And then I ask:

Question: When is half-an-inch a foot?

Answer: When it's a black whisker that sprouted from under your chin as soon as you left the cosmetic counter. All through the party it wagged its black self at everyone, every time you lifted your chin in laughter, to smile or to listen intently. The entire evening it was part of your department store face. And that's not something you paid for.

Diane Rawicz Swan's writing has been a part of her life since childhood when a letter she wrote convinced her parents to fire a regular babysitter. She started as a poet and later focused on short stories while earning her BA in English Literature. Diane favors writing personal anecdotes that convey a serious or humorous message.

She is currently working on a memoir about her marriage to a man twenty years her senior. She is the editor of the CWC-Berkeley Branch newsletter.

Do Not Fall in Love with the Poet

Jan Steckel
Berkeley Branch

Do not confide in the poet,
unless you want your confession
paraphrased and read aloud.

Do not feed the poet,
or you will never, ever
get rid of them.

Do not befriend the poet,
unless you are a one-way mirror,
given to reflection.

Do not buy the poet's book,
for they will expect you
actually to read it.

Do not agree to blurb the poet's book,
for you will be obliged to think
of something nice to say about it.

Do not compare the poet
to a summer's day.
They've heard that before.

Do not criticize the poet's work.
Yours is not to criticize.
Yours is just to be supportive.

Do not sleep with the poet's lover.
You'll only be giving the poet
material that will be aired in public.

Absolutely do not sleep with the poet.

You will have to go to more readings
than you ever wanted to.

Jan Steckel's debut fiction collection, *Ghosts and Oceans,* just came out from Zeitgeist Press. Her poetry book *The Horizontal Poet* (Zeitgeist Press, 2011) won a 2012 Lambda Literary Award. Her poetry book *Like Flesh Covers Bone* (Zeitgeist Press, 2018) won two Rainbow Awards. Her fiction chapbook *Mixing Tracks* (Gertrude Press, 2009) and poetry chapbook *The Underwater Hospital* (Zeitgeist Press, 2006) also won awards. Her creative prose and poetry have appeared in *Scholastic Magazine, Yale Medicine, Bellevue Literary Review, Canary, Assaracus* and elsewhere. She lives in Oakland, California.

FREMONT AREA

"Free soil, free men and
Fremont."
—John C. Fremont

The Great Wave Off Kanegawa

Pat Doyne
Fremont Area Writers

A huge, blue wave rears up,
          arches its back,
                    claws at the sky,
crests— and freezes!
Time stops in that last instant
before cataclysmic crash . . .

Framed by the great wave,
Mt. Fuji poses:
afar, aloof, eternal . . .
This snow-capped cone has seen
waves come and go,
oarsmen come and go,
samurai come and go,
emperors come and go.

In Hokusai's time,
Japan's shell was cracking open.
New ideas. New neighbors.
Imports. Exports. Uncharted waters.
But even when promise lights up the horizon,
even when the odds are in your favor,
a sea of Prussian blue can sneak up.
Swell. Rise. Ambush the unwary.
Sink the best-laid plans.

Fuji watches with Olympian indifference.
Beneath the giant wave,
tiny men in a longboat row for their lives,
ants beneath a raised foot.
But the wave never crashes down.
Karma is stalled by pen and ink
on a woodblock print.

The oarsmen row forever
towards a safety forever out of reach.
This is the floating world: *ukiyo-e*.

Katsushika Hokusai (1760-1849) included the woodblock print "The Great Wave Off Kanegawa" in his series Thirty Six Views of Mt. Fuji.

Pat Doyne is active in three areas—writing, art, and music. Pat earned her MFA from SF State with her first book of poetry, and her poems appear in local anthologies. Pat's botanical watercolors and landscapes have been exhibited in area galleries. In addition, Pat has been a performing member of the Newark-based taiko troupe "Wadaiko" since 2007. She is a retired teacher with a three-year-old grandson.

A Look Back to Move Forward[20]

Samuel Rodriguez
Fremont Area Writers

On a weeknight several years ago, my grandmother and I sat on separate couches in the living room. We watched *The Voice*, my favorite show, but definitely not hers.

My grandmother, Abuela, pointed at the screen and said, "Miguel, you look like that white boy with your hair all messed up!" At that time, purposely unkempt hair was in style for young men.

I rolled my eyes and replied, "Abuela, that's Adam Levine. Ladies love him. You always bug me about not having a girlfriend."

She answered, "But why do you have to do your hair like him, like you just got out of bed?" I couldn't think of a clever remark to outsmart Abuela. I respected her observation skills, so I took a good look at Levine—and myself. His white skin was nearly the opposite of my dark complexion. My brown eyes did not match his hazel ones. He had tattooed, sculpted arms that humbled mine. I wore fitted clothes like his, but they made me self-conscious.

Then Abuela said, "Take a look at that picture of Abuelo."

The creased, faded photo of Abuelo, my grandfather and Abuela's deceased husband, had been on the wall my whole life, yet I had never taken a close look at it. Abuelo must have been in his early twenties in the image, my age then. In the picture, he wore a tie and starched white shirt under a brown suit jacket, but only his hair, impeccably combed in a high pompadour, still shone. My messy spikes appeared to be a regression from Abuelo's "pomp." At my age he worked construction and supported a family. I was single, barely passing community college classes. Maybe an about-face in my appearance that would channel him—not a trendy entertainer—was due.

I jumped online and searched for Alex's Classic Barber Shop and Shaves in my area because I remembered their motto, "Where Tradition Meets Style!" from a commercial on an oldies radio show.

[20] Previously published in *Label Me Latina/o*, Spring 2024 Volume 14, February 2, 2024, edited by Michele Shaul and Melissa Birkhofer where the article remains archived and accessible (www.labelmelatinao.com)

The guys on the website rocked sharp pomps, side-parts, and ducktails recalling the era of Abuelo's prime. I made an appointment the next day and imagined strutting through a barrio, unlike my suburb with few Latinos, with a crisp hairstyle like Abuelo's. I even took a picture with my phone of him looking so dignified.

A few days later after class, with my hair fouled up one last time, I motored across town and discovered Alex's one-window shop tucked away, behind a repair garage. I stutter-stepped inside.

The guys waiting looked at me and nodded. Then the barbers, both young and old, reassured me with a "Hey, bro!" An argument between two of them around my age, with slick fades and baggy jeans, piqued my attention as I sat in the waiting chair, my legs fidgeting.

"Chucha's Taqueria got some good-ass tortas! It's 'cause the bread."

"Awwww, hell nah! They got the best ones at Tacos El Jefe 'cause a torta should be 'bout the meat!"

"Chucha's got good meat, too: lengua, tripas, buches. That's food for real-ass Mexicans!"

"Then call me a fake-ass Mexican 'cause I ain't eatin' cow tongue, intestines, and pig stomach. I don't feel like havin' the runs!"

Everyone, including the guys waiting, nodded in agreement. Behind the back-and-forth snaps I heard Ritchie Valens' jumping guitar. A framed portrait of Julio César Chávez, my childhood hero, putting up his dukes, reminded me of the prizefights I watched with Abuelo. I examined a rusted plaque below the back mirror that said, "Haircut 25¢" and wondered how much Abuelo paid for his. Lost in the scene, I forgot to mention my appointment.

I heard someone call out, "You're up, bro!"

A pot-bellied barber nodded at me. He had a slick-back, silver next to his brown skin, and forearms covered with tattoos, more like blotches.

He said, "That's you!"

As I walked to the chair he stared at my skinny blue jeans, grey cardigan, and messy hair as if I had just arrived from a distant planet. I sat down and my fingers frantically tapped the armrests. The barber gripped the clippers with his right hand, shears with his left.

Seeking reassurance, I said, "Are you the owner? That's who I talked to on the phone."

"Nah, bro. Alex had a family emergency. I'm Pauly."

"I'm M-m-miguel."

"What'll it be, son?"

"A p-p-pomp. Old way."

Pauly squinted. "You sure that'll match your outfit?"

I let the mild insult go and remembered the photo of Abuelo on my phone. I showed it to Pauly.

He immediately said, "That picture's gotta be older than me!"

Hiding my irritation, I answered, "It's my Abuelo. Can you cut mine like his?"

Pauly stared at the phone for about thirty seconds and said, "Of course, bro," then added, "I thought you were gonna change your mind and leave!" as he inspected my hair. Then he grabbed a chunk of it and said, "What's this?"

"Matte styling paste," I said.

Pauly threw head back his head and chuckled. "Who do you think you are, Ryan Seacrest?"

I ground my teeth for a moment and worked up the courage to speak.

"I wanted to look like Adam Levine, you know, the guy from Maroon 5, *The Voice*."

Pauly put down his tools and clapped. "Been there, bro! After I watched *Saturday Night Fever*, I did my hair all poofy like John Travolta. The homies laughed their asses off!" We cracked up in unison.

It took a minute for us to settle down and I stopped moving my fingers. Then Pauly began the cut. The clippers buzzed and vibrated on my head as he tapered down the sides and then the back. He then sprayed cool water—from an old Jack Daniels bottle—on my head to release the tousled strands from the paste's hold.

"Freedom," he said.

I could almost feel each wet hair split as he shaped the top with the shears.

"Details, details, details," Pauly said as he put hot foam on my sideburns and the back edge of my hair to etch in fine lines with the straight razor.

Pauly said, "Bro, we're gonna hook you up now!" and blew

back my hair. Then he removed a container of Suavecito Pomade from a wooden cabinet. The lid on the pomade had an image of a skeleton fixing up the front of his pomp. The playful allusion to El Día de los Muertos made me grin. Was Abuelo glossing up his pomp somewhere?

The Suavecito made the air, slightly cloudy with powder, smell of bold cologne. Pauly combed back two fingertip scoops of the translucent gel to make slick lines.

He said, "Funny how an old look can make a new man!" and used the fine half of the comb to raise the front to complete the transformation.

I didn't have quite enough hair for a pomp as high as Abuelo's, but Pauly said, "You'll get there in a month" to reassure me.

The pomade blessed his work with a retro brilliance—just like the one that enthralled me in the photograph. I meticulously double-mirrored to make sure my hair made a short wall in front and resembled a ramp from the side. I grinned like a kid who breaks a piñata, fist bumped Pauly, and said, "Awesomeness!" I may not have exactly talked like Abuelo, but maybe I looked almost as tough as him from the neck up.

Pauly said, "You look ready for a cruise down the boulevard."

I beamed and said, "Thanks. You're an artist with those scissors."

He coughed to clear his throat and said, "I appreciate it, boss. But fifteen. A small price to pay for heritage."

I pulled out my wallet and handed him a twenty. "Keep the change, Don Pauly!"

He said, "Quit making me feel like an old man! What was your name again, bro? For your next appointment."

"It's Miguel. See you in three weeks!"

I drove home and opened the door. Abuela watched the news, in English. She looked up at me and squinted. Maybe my haircut lacked authenticity, or she may have needed a minute to realize what had happened.

Then she smiled and said, "I love the haircut, mijo! But your wardrobe still needs work!" "That's the next step," I said.

That night I sat on the same couch with her in the living room and put on *The Voice* for a new reason: so we could laugh together at

Adam Levine's outfit, and of course, his hair.

Samuel Rodriguez is a member of Fremont Area Writers. He has had short stories published in the *Tri-City Voice* newspaper and *Label Me Latina/o*.

SF PENINSULA

"The worst of times in San Francsco was still better than the best of times anywhere else."
—*Armistead Maupin*

A Rock Is a Fragile Being

Bradley Earle Hoge
San Francisco Peninsula

I remember going with my father on field trips.
Once to scout a possible location for his graduate

students—the Arbuckle Mountains in Oklahoma.
Where exactly are they, you ask? Mountains

in Oklahoma? Mountains like in Beaumont, Texas
you wonder? But they are there. Or at least

the roots. Obvious to a geologist and worthy
of study and exploration—to unravel the story

of North America. Enough evidence to reconstruct
the past, though the mountains themselves are mostly

gone. Swept away by time and inevitable erosion—
ancient history of the earth exposed like the smallest

nested doll. Now I am the one teaching the metaphor
of mountains. Learning the sere wisdom

of hard rock while struggling to come to terms
with my own transitions. From bedrock to talus.

Broken and sloughed off escarpment. No longer reliable
for firm footing. Seen, but taken for granted.

Leading me to wonder—is it erosion, or exposure,
that we see in our parents as they age? Exposure of time

and inevitability. Exposure of the roots of the saga.
The vulnerability we are all born to forcing one slab

of hard bedrock atop another as boy becomes marine.

As marine becomes husband. Becomes father, professor,
scout leader, coach, grandfather. As a man is built
into a mountain. Regal and solid. Towering and seemingly

eternal. Spanning eons, only slightly changing.
As subtly as the tectonics of orogeny.

Look a thousand times and the mountain is there.
As it has always been. Comforting in its grandeur.

Look once again, and it is diminished. Below notice.
Except for those anxious to reprise the apologue.

Bradley Earle Hoge's second book of poetry, *N = R* fp x ne x fl x fi x fc x L* (The Drake Equation), was published in 2023 by VRÆYDA Press. His first book, *Nebular Hypothesis*, was published by Cawing Crow Press in 2016. He has written four chapbooks, and his poetry appears in numerous anthologies and journals, most recently in *Woodcrest Magazine, California Writers Club Redwood Branch Anthology: Phases, The California Literary Review, Fault Zone: Reverse, and Consilience* His photography has been published in *Otoliths* and the upcoming *Vision and Verse Anthology: A Fusion of Art and Poetry* to be published by the California Writers Club. He has been a teacher, a children's museum curator, a college professor, and a vagabond. He currently teaches middle school literacy in the California Bay Area.

I Named Her Lola

Lawrence Cohn
San Francisco Peninsula

Citizens of the jury, I know you won't judge me too harshly when I tell you how I slowly sank into this longing for Lola. How I quietly turned the radio off and smoothly rolled up the windows of my old Chrysler, anticipating Lola might today decide to slide into my car next to me. Most days she shunned my advances as I hugged the curb and opened the window and yelled hello or whistled and barked like a yapping dog. The more she turned the other cheek as I moved around the corner, the closer I came to an absolute yearning. If I wasn't so lonely, I would have forgotten about her, but every night in my dreams she was in my bed.

It started on a Friday around 5:30 p.m. As usual, cars raced along Middlefield Road from Palo Alto through Menlo Park, Atherton, and finally into Redwood City. Hungry drivers and their carsful would stop at the taquerias, burrito joints, and bars along the way. Their left turns kept me from speeding. All that hunger stayed inside the cars that kept motoring. I was one of them. They never slowed except when Lola was out on the sidewalk with her crazy red hair and mini skirt and beige legs.

I was feeling down and thinking about how empty my rented room would be. Who can't understand the depth of loneliness when a home is four walls and a hot plate and a bathroom that has seen 100 renters doing their business? I found myself whispering her name. I was imagining "Lola" with her worn pocketbook and poker face staring down at passersby. Though she was straight-up gorgeous I knew the truth. The flimsy dress and porcelain cheeks gave her away. To this day, I believe Lola was more than an enchanted mannequin.

Yes, I knew she was inanimate in real life, but to me, she was magical. The sign she carried outside the buffet diner read "Eat All You Can $12.69." With a wave of her slender arm, she smiled and invited me in. She and I both knew her smile wasn't for everyone and that soon it would be just for me.

It had been a rough week. I wasn't sleeping and my stomach was sour. The hunger left me delirious.

Maybe it was the job. I'm a line engineer. My doctor swears it's the electrical transmissions that gave me unrelenting insomnia. Maybe he's right: my brain waves were altered by the artificial electromagnetic fields (EMFs). Why else would I have fallen in love with an inanimate soulmate? Have you ever loved an object so much that you would kill to keep it? Maybe a tiara or a red wagon or a child's loved doll?

That Friday, I needed to settle it for certain. I shook my head to wake myself and parked right in front of Lola. I leaned over and looked through the open car window to scan her silky beige legs. I slowly moved my gaze upwards, over the rough texture of Lola's milky-white skirt, the brilliance of her white shirt, to reach up to her perfect visage. For a moment, I was spellbound.

I paused, then gracefully slid out of the car. Sweat trickled down my neck. Suddenly, a bicycler whipped out of nowhere, almost smashing into my open car door. Without a break in his motion, the rider flipped me off. The moment took me out of love's oblivion. I waved at his receding form, his arm still raised high.

As I headed for the restaurant door, Lola's powerful presence flowed over me. My stomach growled. Something in my loins stirred. Or was it the electrical magnetic fields?

Inside the buffet, a small sign read "Dolores Is *Not* for Sale."

So, Dolores is her real name, my inner voice chimed. Mary of Sorrows—another name for the Virgin Mary.

"I like 'Lola' better," I grumbled, as I grabbed a tray, plate, and silverware and lined up for the hot dishes.

It wasn't an abduction. The *Post* said I had "mannequin madness," but that's not it. Citizens of the jury, have you forgotten what it is to fall deeply in love? Nothing else you can think of will occupy the mind. There is no room for anyone else. It's not in your heart. It's invaded your whole system. You just *crave*.

Even so, I logically and stealthily planned our tryst with precision. There was no madness in my methods.

By the time I finished dinner, I had a plan: a detailed sketch on my napkin.

I moved my Chrysler to the other side of Middlefield Road and sat outside all evening, waiting until the restaurant workers turned off their front lights and locked the door.

11 p.m. Noted. I waited.

At 12 a.m. staff opened the door, hurried to their cars on the street, and left for their cozy homes. Also noted. Some carried bags—leftovers for their families.

1 a.m. The manager and the cook came out to do a final close. I studied Lola's body and the slim shadow she cast under the streetlight. How could she stand so sensually when she was so thin, so cold?

She knew I was watching. She winked.

The manager grabbed Lola's feet. The cook caught her by the head. They carried Lola inside. The cook brought in the support pole. Then they locked up.

They were gone at 1:08 a.m. Noted.

At 1:15 a.m., I crossed the avenue and peered at Lola through the dark and locked door, just to make sure she was truly safe. I explained my scheme for our getaway.

She smiled and whispered, "I love you, darling." I could read her sensual lips plainly. How could I leave her? I was not a burglar.

I slept in my car until 3:30 a.m. and woke from the night chill. I realized I needed to come back that night and leave a copy of the plan in Lola's pocketbook. I needed her to remember our scheme. I rubbed my blurry eyes and drove home with determination.

When I trudged to the 5th floor of my 5th Street tenement-quality apartment house, I remembered that the elevator was out. No worries. Lola couldn't weigh more than 30 pounds and I didn't need the pole. She was perfect, you see. I could have named her Emerald because Lola had eyes of sweet gemstones. She was *Rockin'*!

I had to work on Saturday, but as soon as I got off, I rushed home to shower and dress. I spent some time cleaning my ears. Tinnitus is a constant battle. Not just the ringing but those phantom roars and buzzing like flies. Sometimes, it makes me cry. It makes me deranged. Did I tell you my doctor says it could be the EMFs?

I patted some Old Spice on my neck and shaved face.

I found my notes and letter and headed for the Chrysler. I ran down the flights and leaped into the car. I was out of breath. I would get to the diner by nine o'clock. I was ready and brazen.

At 8:30 p.m., I parked across the street from the diner, in front of an auto wrecker. Lola was dressed to the nines. It seemed so appropriate that tonight she looked so lovely. She smiled and jutted her chin towards the diner. I locked up the Chrysler and headed across the avenue.

Nonchalantly slipping the plan into Lola's white clutch, I looked the other way, with my body turned toward the diner door. No one could have suspected that I was flirting with Lola as I passed. I felt lightheaded and giddy like a schoolboy crush.

I opened the glass door and headed for the booth. Then an outrageous conversation took place. Another customer remarked, "Whoa, Delores is gorgeous tonight—one look at her, and I just had to come in."

I'm not a jealous person but a bolt of electricity hit me in the gut and my heart started fibrillating.

He went on about her sexy outfit and jewelry and overall enhanced features. He wished he could take her home—all the time laughing and spitting food like a perverse pig.

I swung around, ready to do battle with my butter knife when the owner strolled up to him. "Good evening, I'm August, the owner. Would you like to hear her story? It's a tale of true love.

"We were in love, Dolores and me. After she died in childbirth, I saw her everywhere. I couldn't sleep. Every woman who crossed the road or came into the business was Dolores. I didn't know what to do. I was losing my mind and my life. One day, this "Got Junk" truck parked in the lot. While the driver was eating, I walked outside to empty the trash.

"For just a moment, I thought I saw my wife . . . but then I realized it was a mannequin. I decided to buy her—it only cost me two free lunches! I brought her in and dressed her in my wife's clothes. I placed her on the sidewalk to welcome eaters. Not only did we get busy, but all the men remarked on how friendly we all are.

"Tonight is our anniversary, so I dressed her to kill. She's wearing my wife's party dress and real gold jewelry. When I started posing her, I stopped seeing my wife everywhere. Now, the only Dolores I have is a mannequin. But, yes, she is a beauty."

The pig-man laughed. And the owner laughed with him. I was sickened.

I abhorred Lola being used as a marketing come-on. The owner saw her as no more than a dressed-up mannequin—how insulting! He couldn't see the vital and sensual being who smiled at me every day— even on weekends.

Tonight, particularly, she was a knockout.

After finishing my dinner, I popped a Certs and rewrote my plan on a diner napkin, so it was fresh in my psyche. My love was trapped, so I was confident in doing the right thing . . . Wouldn't you want to save someone if you could? It was logic—not madness or EMFs.

I paid cash, so I wouldn't leave behind any credit card info and said goodnight to August. He was happy and perhaps I might someday sympathize with his loss . . . or not.

Now, I simply had to wait. I put on the radio and listened to the blues channel. The love-lost songs filled my ears, one after the other until I fell asleep. When I awoke, it was after midnight. All the employees were gone except for the manager, cook, and August. I turned off the radio and sat by. Finally, the cook and manager left. August finished his cigarette and came out to carry Lola in. He may have been drinking too, as he seemed to whisper to her as he stroked her arms. He lifted her gently, bringing her inside the door, together with the support pole. She was elegant in the doorway while the neon diner sign flashed her shadow. Then the light went dark, and August drove off in his old Fleetwood.

From eavesdropping on the staff, I knew there was only a local sound alarm and that the batteries were going. I crossed the empty street and used my work tools to pry open the door. The weak alarm sounded like a low nasal off-key singer. There was nothing to alert the police, and all the businesses in the area were closed. I slid one very large green opaque lawn bag over Lola's head down to her waist. I held the second lawn bag while she stepped in, to cover her legs and hips. Then I wrapped the wonderful duct tape to keep everything neat. The pole was left inside the door.

I carried her to my car. *She is such a light lover,* I thought. I laid her in the back seat. Even hidden beneath the bags, her form consumed me. I hurriedly climbed beneath the wheel and nervously dropped the keys. In the dark, I felt for the right key and slipped it into the ignition.

Nothing. The battery was dead. The radio killed it.

I had several wild thoughts about what to do. I could bring Lola back, wrapped or unwrapped, and try again another time, though I may not have such a chance again. August could install a better alarm or make it impossible to find her. He might chain her inextricably.

That's when I realized that we had forgotten to leave the gold jewelry. Lola was wearing gold chains around her neck, a thick gold bangle bracelet around her wrist, and a gold chain lightly caressing her lovely, thin ankle. I was determined to make sure no one thought this was a heist.

It wasn't an abduction, either. It was an extended romantic tryst. I started to hear buzzing.

Getting out of the Chrysler into the deserted avenue, I stopped to breathe and counted my breaths until I calmed myself down. I needed to unfold my Lola from the lawn bags. I carefully unfastened the gold jewelry and carried it across the street to the front door of the diner. I slipped the jewelry into the mail slot.

Done. Then, I quietly walked across the street to my car.

My ears began drumming. Damn EMFs. I lifted Lola into my arms and locked the car. Then, I walked through the neighborhoods, heading for my apartment house almost two miles away. At 2 a.m., no one would be outside, so it was likely I would evade the police.

It worked.

I carried my love into my apartment building and up the stairs. The ringing in my ears stopped and I could think. We were safe.

I pulled the bags off her and discarded them down the garbage chute in the hallway. No one had seen us. We were stealthy.

I won't reveal any details of how Lola and I showered together, standing in the stained bathtub. But when we were done, I dressed her in a white robe I had purchased at Nordstrom. It was quite expensive, and I knew Lola would appreciate it. She wrapped a towel around her wet hair. We were both exhausted and so we lay, still robed, under the covers of my king-sized bed.

It was so sweet to have Lola share my bed—no longer just a thought or a dream. We were out cold in minutes.

Per Sherlock Holmes, criminals often go back to the scene of the crime; however, I was not a criminal. I was a customer, a regular, so I went back to the restaurant the next evening. Besides, I needed to get my car jumped.

By chance, August was talking to customers about his stolen mannequin. He retold the story of his wife and the expensive gold jewelry "Dolores" had been wearing. He planned to include it in his insurance claim. So, it was the gold that August was most concerned about. As for the missing mannequin, he would use the jewelry to make her loss a felony crime. He would claim the stolen jewelry had a value over the California threshold. A "felonious felony," he said. "A phony felony," I thought.

The auto wreckers helped me jump my car.

◊ ◊ ◊

I confess, Lola was a bit hard to sleep with. She was bony and would only change her position if you maneuvered her. After all, she wasn't a blow-up. I was gentle of course. Her thin lips were always ready for mine. Whenever I awoke next to Lola, she was smiling and bright-eyed. She watched me sleep, listened to me snore, and never criticized me.

I was loved.

For nearly a month, I left work on time and floated home, knowing that Lola would be waiting. The EMFs seemed to dissipate.

Then something unexpected occurred.

One evening, I arrived to find my apartment door ajar. I discovered the landlord and two policemen questioning Lola. She looked nonplussed and refused to answer their questions.

Frustrated, the police left her standing in the corner and handcuffed me when I walked in.

Apparently, my bathroom toilet had leaked, seeping down to the apartment below. When the landlord entered to make the repair, he found Lola. He recalled the local article in the *Post* about Lola and the reward August had posted. He called the police, who arrived quickly, recognizing her as a missing person.

The police read me my rights. But I ask you, did they ever read me my human rights? The right that I could remain in love with Lola?

Thank you, citizens of the jury, for listening to my tale. Now, I ask each one of you, is true love dead? How can I be guilty if our love was consensual? Finally, what would you have done in my place?

Lawrence Cohn regards writing as a vital part of his life. His interest in how poetry and short stories contribute important ideas to uplift our existence has always been his purpose. He started writing poetry and short stories in elementary school and felt compelled to write poems on the back pages of exams. He has been published in *Littack Magazine* as part of the Vitalist Poetry Genre, as well as various college journals. "Every day, I'm reminded of poetry being an integral part of my life. If I go for a walk, watch a movie, have a discussion with a friend, an idea is always near the edge of what I'm doing."

Lawrence is a dual member of the San Francisco Peninsula and Redwood Writers branches.

Devastation

(Villanelle variation)
Jo Carpignano
San Francisco Peninsula

A wire broken, a cigarette tossed
a playful breeze ignites dry withered grass
flames erupt, small hill steep canyon lost

Hungry fire seeks more generous host
trees tremble in the wind and wait
a wire broken, a cigarette tossed

Desiccated woods cannot sustain such loss
strong winds increase, a vortex gathers force
red storms explode, entire forests lost

Ensuing conflagration disregards the cost
burns buildings, vehicles, and homes
a wire broken, a cigarette tossed

Congregations pray for rain and early frost
flames devour both church and school
fire storm expands, entire towns are lost

Tall structures burned, wide highways crossed
then unrelenting flames take precious lives
paradise is now inferno, everything is lost
a wire broken, a cigarette tossed

Jo Carpignano writes poetry, fiction, and memoir. She published a book of poems titled *Paper Wings* and is now working on a memoir of her Italian immigrant family.

Minestrone Wars

Sue Barizon
San Francisco Peninsula

I skipped home from school on that hazy autumn day in late October 1962. The weather was in my favor, still warm but crisp around the edges. Back then, we referred to this unseasonal bonus lingering past Labor Day, deep into fall, as *Indian summer.* It meant I wouldn't have to wear a sweater or a jacket over my outfit tonight. The anticipation of spending an evening, unfettered in my Dutch girl costume, spurred me on to skipping higher and faster. When I landed on the sidewalk in front of my house, I jerked to a stop. Did I see what I thought I saw?

"White smoke!"

The lofty stream loomed from behind the grape-stake fence in our backyard. I opened my nostrils wide, like our dog, Tiny Tim, when he nuzzled our knees at dinner for scraps.

"Oh no, Papa, not tonight," I prayed, "not on Halloween!"

In our neighborhood, steam coming from the Capella patio meant our father was practicing his personal commandments. The patio was his place of worship or as my big sister, Elena, liked to call it, The Church of the Gastronomic Misconception.

Most Italian families in our San Francisco suburb had two kitchens: the spotless one that came with the house, and the makeshift one set up in a basement, garage, or back porch. The idea was not to stink up the plastic-covered living room furniture and draperies with the garlic-laden steam from sauce pots simmering on a hot stove all day.

Eight years earlier, when we moved from San Francisco into our newly built ranch style house in the suburbs, our resourceful father had seen the potential in its u-shape. With one phone call and a case of Old Crow, a retired stone mason from "the old country" was brought in to brick up the end of the patio. The result was a monstrosity of a brick BBQ. It took another case of whiskey and a Fourth of July weekend for Papa and his neighborhood buddies to pour the concrete floor. To top it off, Papa installed a flat roof of semi-transparent, green-tinted, corrugated fiberglass, rendering the patio a sweatbox in the summer and an icebox in the winter.

Papa was a garbage man by trade. He worked packing garbage

in San Francisco's North Beach for what was then called The Scavengers Protective Association, and scavenge he did for his patio kitchen. "Finds" from a plethora of restaurants on his Fisherman's Wharf route included a bank of kitchen cabinets with an abrasive, industrial finish, a row of institutional Formica countertops, and a pitted porcelain sink from Alioto's restaurant. A neglected rectangle of inch thick marble filched from the back alley at Ghirardelli Square was mounted to the patio wall. It served as an altar for Papa's six-burner stove top, and the electric cheese grater he built from a discarded lawn mower motor.

To my ten-year-old senses, Papa's patio was a culinary limbo. Here, all the old-world smells of our food-crazed ancestors commingled with the ghosts of family feasts past. Braids of garlic bulbs hung from the patio's crossbeams next to salamis, blood sausages, and the shriveled bodies of dried cod fish sacrificed for Papa's "baccala" (fish stew). The air was heavy with the musty smell of his homemade wine fermenting to vinegar. Wild mushrooms dried on wooden frames covered with chicken wire. A twenty-pound wheel of Parmesan cheese sweated on the butcher block waiting for the grater.

Foul-smelling foodstuffs were relegated to the patio refrigerator. I habitually held my breath before opening the door to survey the macabre inventory of head cheese—a confusing name for a non-dairy cold cut made from a pig's head boiled down to a gelatinous mass and molded into a loaf. There were slabs of marinating ribs, anchovies suspended in olive oil, calf's tongue, pickled pigs' feet, and a stinky cheese imported from Sardinia complete with maggots intact. I referred to the refrigerator as *The Dead Zone.*

There was one bright spot. Papa had built a narrow aviary along a patio wall for his treasured canaries. A neat row of double-stacked bricks defined the perimeter, encompassing a system for hosing down bird droppings. There was a bubbling fountain for bird baths, and an arrangement of manzanita branches for perching. With a couple of bottles of Old Crow, he commissioned another Paisan (Italian buddy) to wallpaper a panoramic scene of Yosemite Valley over the entire stucco wall. You could hear the canaries singing Papa's praises as they dined on lady fingers and soft bib lettuce from his garden.

My thoughts were interrupted by an earnest lick to my knee.

Tiny Tim had sprinted from the front porch with an unusually eager greeting. When I knelt down to give him a hug, I spotted the source of his enthusiasm—the lineup of kitchen ware beside the front door. A familiar sense of dread snaked its way up through my insides. I let out a mournful groan.

"Minestroneeee!"

Nothing was more formidable to me than Papa's minestrone. To the untrained eye, it was more stew than soup. Any unwitting soul referring to it as vegetable soup would elicit a pitiable absolution and be dismissed as "Americani."

It was the slime factor, as only a prosciutto bone could deliver, that separated minestrone from its rivals. Before the term "mouthfeel" was coined to describe a sensation made by a particular food in your mouth, the overcooked chunks of zucchini, cabbage, and Swiss chard reduced to fibrous strands and coated with layers of tummy-turning fat had set my retching reflex into overdrive. Retching into your plate was considered a slap in the face to our father. Who was then compelled to get up from the table and give your *culo* (rear end) a slap for disrespecting the minestrone. Minestrone had no respect for "mouthfeel."

Was I so wrapped up in Halloween that I hadn't noticed the warning signs of an impending minestrone? Papa's prep took days. Was I so enamored with my Dutch girl costume that I hadn't spotted the fava beans soaking on the kitchen counter or the scads of garlic and onion skins piled knee-high in the trash? Was I too busy tapping out Shirley Temple routines in my wooden shoes to pay attention to Papa's puttering in the garden? The mosaic of chopped vegetables had eluded me: zucchini, tomatoes, potatoes, carrots, parsley, wax beans, and Swiss chard laid out in neat rows on Papa's tired old cutting board. But, how, for crying out loud, did I miss that God-forsaken prosciutto bone stoutly wrapped with tendon, gristle, and two inches of choke-provoking fat? Was I too blinded by the braided Dutch girl wig I'd been prancing around in all week to see that grotesque pig appendage dangling from the patio's crossbeams?

How could Papa desecrate Halloween, the most sacred of kids' holidays, with his ungodly concoction? At our dinner table, refusing to eat your minestrone was a punishable offense. Even daddy's girl was not exempt. Halloween or no Halloween, I would not be allowed to leave the dinner table without finishing a big bowl of minestrone. The battle lines had been drawn—my gag reflex vs. a spanking.

I was alone in my battle. Everyone loved Papa's cooking, not just our family, but the whole neighborhood. Pots and bowls lay in wait, ready to receive his blessing—the Pardini's cast iron, the Lavezzo's Revere Ware, Norma Costa's precious Tupperware, and Nella Lucchesi's green mixing bowl with the chipped rim and shower cap lid. The more pots the better. It meant fewer leftovers. Papa would depend on me to make the deliveries before dinnertime.

Tiny Tim had waited patiently while I stood staring down at the pots and bowls—contemplating my fate. When he scratched at the front door, I followed him into the house. I heard Papa in the patio whistling along with his canaries. I waved to him from the kitchen window. He winked and nodded. His wide muscular hands with short stubby fingers gripped the wooden paddle scavenged from the kitchen at Scoma's restaurant.

"Hello, Sussie girl!" Papa was in his zone, all right. He sounded chirpy.

"We're not having minestrone tonight, are we, Papa?" I was careful not to sound whiny.

"You kids shit like rabbits. You need a good bowl of minestrone to stick to your ribs."

Papa, an authority on bowel movements, deemed his minestrone a cure-all for everything from diarrhea to constipation. I wondered which one of us kids forgot to flush the toilet, again.

"But Papa, it's Halloween."

He was blowing on a spoonful of soup. I winced. Papa swallowed warily. He smacked his lips, tossed a couple of parmesan cheese rinds into the pot, and gave me a stern warning.

"You kids are not going out there to eat all that crap unless you have something good in your bellies."

"But Papa."

His jaw set tight. Through clenched teeth he warned.

"You're going to eat it . . . and like it. *End of estoria!*"

Papa's "*End of estoria!*" was code for "spanking." I had to think fast. I retreated to the bedroom I shared with my sister for advice on dodging any potential dinnertime drama, but she had holed herself up in the bathroom to avoid helping with the deliveries. I could plead with our Aunt Mary, next door, for a last-minute dinner invitation. It wouldn't be the first time my sympathetic Aunt squeezed one more at the Staffornini dinner table, despite Uncle Pete's objections not to "interfere." Unfortunately, any pleading would have to wait until after I made the deliveries.

"C'mon Sussie. The minestrone's waiting." Papa shouted.

I heard him send Tiny Tim to fetch me. I followed the tail-wagging beggar to the patio, where my father stood at the stove, stirring what looked to me like bubbling sludge. He had parked my red wagon at his feet with the pots and bowls resting on a wet towel. Carefully, he ladled the steaming soup with the reverence of a priest offering up communion at Sunday mass. My job was to pull the wagon up and down the block making deliveries ahead of the bewitching 6:00 dinner hour.

It was close to 5:00. I worked fast. The damp towel absorbed the shock and spills as I navigated curbs and asphalt. I was determined to finish before my Uncle Pete got home. As I traversed the neighborhood, I worked out my plan. I just needed my aunt to ask my Mom if I could have dinner with my cousins on account of it being Halloween and we'd all be going out together, anyway.

On my way home, the wagon was full. Eleanor Pardini had given me a plate of rice torta and Bob Costa a bright yellow bouquet from his rose garden. Nella Lucchesi promised a tray of enchiladas when the weather turned colder. By the time I finished explaining to the mailman what I was doing with a jar of cherries in grappa, I was too late. Standing in front of my aunt and uncle's house, I could see through the big plate glass window into their dining room. There they all were: my aunt, uncle, and cousins sitting down to dinner . . . and my little brother, Johnny, who had begged my invitation for himself.

Papa must have heard me sneak through the front door.

"Elena, Sussie, soup's on!"

I panicked. Then, ran for the bedroom and smack into my minestrone-tolerant sister dressed in her gypsy costume.

"Help me!" I begged.

Elena had four years on me, a quick wit and a stubborn streak. Ushering me back into our room, she grabbed my Dutch girl costume.

"Quick, put this on!"

I watched my sister adjust the wings on the starched white

bonnet and position the long, yellow yarn braids to fall across my pinafore.

"Elena, Sussie, get in here!"

Papa's command ricocheted down the hallway.

"There," Elena said, dabbing two rouge circles on my flushed cheeks. "Even our minestrone-crazed father wouldn't have the heart to spank a cute, little Dutch girl!"

The tug of my wooden shoes against the carpet cautioned me to stop at the doorway and take stock. My sister motioned with her eyes at Mom's terra-cotta crock on the kitchen table. Ever the patriarch, Papa sat at his place, soup ladle in hand, and a linen towel tucked under his chin (a necessary precaution for sucking the marrow from prosciutto bones).

"Sussie!"

The clomp, clomp, clomp of wooden shoes on linoleum floor startled the threesome. With more enthusiasm than talent, I tap-danced the only shuffle-shuffle-toe-kick step I knew. Taking a scene from a Shirley Temple movie, I sang "Magic Wooden Shoes" in a mock German accent to the delight of my mother and the snorting laughter of my sister.

"C'mon, it's time to eat!"

Papa's shout-out cut through my ballyhoo entrance like a machete. I felt my throat tighten as he ceremoniously ladled the soup, filling the bowls to the brim, then passing them to us from across the table. The holy sacrament of the blessed gag reflex. During the wait, Tiny Tim (a loyal scrap-eating ally), had been banished from under the table to the garage. Papa had had enough of his premature whining for leftover prosciutto parts. I was doomed. There was only so much I could cough into our cheap paper napkins and wad into my fist, out of Papa's sight line.

It was 6:30. I had half an hour to eat and dry the dishes before I could go trick-or-treating. I was a notoriously slow eater. Papa always made me sit at the table right up until his buddies arrived after dinner for coffee royales. Often, I'd have to sit with my half-eaten plate and listen to their "BS" sessions. Occasionally, Frank Pardini, Papa's best friend, would take pity on me.

"What's the matter, Sussie? Don't you like minestrone?" he'd say.

Bang! My wish for a Frank Pardini intervention dissolved when Papa banged the kitchen table with the ladle to get my attention.

"EAT IT!"

I glanced over at my sister. She motioned to me with her spoon, carefully piled high with elbow macaroni. What luck! Papa sometimes added pasta to the soup. Digging around for something edible would made it look like I was eating. By the time I had extracted all my macaroni, Elena had finished the last of the thick broth, leaving only a few fava beans and a bit of gristle at the bottom of her bowl. We both jumped up from our seats when we heard the doorbell ring.

"Sit down!"

Ten minutes to seven. Someone dared to intrude on the sacred dinner hour. In our neighborhood, trick-or-treating before 7:00 was frowned upon and parents let you know it. When Mom came back from answering the door with my sister's best friend, Fifi, in tow, Elena let out a squeal.

"Papa, can I go?" she begged.

"You have time to do the dishes." Papa said reaching for the ladle. "Your friend can have a nice bowl of minestrone while she waits."

Papa was looking mighty benevolent ladling out that soup, so I played my trump card.

"Papa, can I go to the bathroom?"

Papa eyed me suspiciously, "Go, and come!" was his terse reply. He knew my stalling tactics.

I could hear the commotion of trick-or-treaters outside as I sat on the toilet, contemplating my predicament. Why was Papa being so mean? It was no secret that I was his favorite. Couldn't he see I had no stomach for his minestrone? Wasn't it enough everybody else loved it? When I heard my brother and cousins from next door getting ready to leave, I cranked open the bathroom window and called out.

"Johnny, come get me. Don't leave without me!"

I hurried out of the bathroom and sprang back to the kitchen table just as the doorbell rang. I was surprised to see all the dishes had been cleared, washed, and put away—except for mine. Evidently, grateful for the "best minestrone she ever ate," Fifi had pitched in to help. The girls had been excused with Papa's blessing.

Mom parked herself by the front door ready to hand out candy. Now, it was just me, Papa, and a cold bowl of minestrone. He was clearly tired of waiting for me and ready for his Lazy-Boy and an episode of *I Search for Adventure* on the TV.

"C'mon finish your soup!"

I took a spoonful into my mouth and rested the contents directly onto my tongue avoiding any contact with my teeth. A stream of drool started running down the corner of my mouth. Papa stood up.

"Swallow, damn it, Sussie!"

I swallowed hard. A saliva sucking fava bean and a nasty band of tendon triggered my gag reflex. Mom ran into the kitchen just as the doorbell rang.

"Oh, for god's sake, Primo," she cried. "It's Halloween!"

My brother burst in through the front door dressed as Davy Crockett, grabbing his coonskin hat off the coffee table.

"For Pete's sake, aren't you done yet? We're all waiting for you!"

On his way out, he dodged Frank Pardini dressed in a red bartender's jacket. Frank held up a couple of shot glasses in one hand, and a bottle of Old Crow in the other.

"C'mon Primo, let's go trick-or-treating!"

Papa motioned over at me. Frank took notice of the little Dutch girl sitting with her head down, then spotted the minestrone that had congealed around the spoon standing at attention in the middle of my bowl.

"What's the matter Sussie?" he said. "Don't you like your father's minestrone?"

With that, he scooped up a big spoonful and shoveled it into his mouth.

"Best one yet, Primo," he said. "Too bad you had to go looking all over Timbuktu for the Prosciutto bone."

Papa smiled. He looked across the table at me, grabbed his napkin, and waved me over. I didn't flinch when he reached for one of my yarn braids and wiped a splatter of minestrone off the tip.

"C'mon, Sussie girl," he said. "We've both had enough."

Sue Barizon, a native San Franciscan, writes memoir, fiction, and poems based on her first-generation childhood experiences growing up in the suburbs. She brings a poignant sense of humor to her short stories, memoirs, essays, and poems. Her work has been published in the *Fault Zone* series and *Carry the Light* anthologies. She has appeared in CWC's first *Reader's Theater: Women's Journeys*. She's won numerous awards from the San Mateo County Fair, including Writer of the Year and Best of Show. Her story "Summer Bananas" appeared in *Fault Zone: Reverse*. Sue is an active member of the CWC writing community.

Spaceman[21]

Tim Flood
San Francisco Peninsula

My green plastic spaceman glows, hovering in flight far away in the black night of the universe. I admire the graceful arc he travels within the dark secrecy of Grandma's closet. With the door pulled shut from the inside, I launch my collection of space heroes and ships into the black expanse. The preacher called it that. He said it's larger than any of us know.

Here, no one stares at me. No one can see the brace holding my leg. Even I can't see it out here in space where no one knows of my disease. The doctor calls it Perthes' disease. The pastor says it's an infirmity. When you have a disease that's an infirmity, you've got to be healed because the devil has got into you somehow. Back on earth, my brace shows through my pant leg and clinks with every step. Everyone can see and hear my infirmity, my own bit of Satan, the entity responsible for infirmities in people. But in the void of space—the Bible calls it a void—somewhere out there where God lives, no one can see that the Fallen One has got into me. I am the spaceman who glows and flies with perfect legs.

Please God, forgive me of sins. Please Jesus, drive out the Devil!

We pray to God for an hour at Wednesday night prayer meetings. Like always, I am singled out. Because of my sin, I have to sit on the floor, covering my eyes in prayer. Everyone else kneels properly, head in their hands, knees against the wall. I can't kneel on account of my brace. I can't even pray to God without my infirmity showing! We pray in church Sunday mornings. We pray at the old-folks home where Grandma takes me clinking along beside her to visit the old ones on Sunday afternoons, back at church again Sunday nights, at meals, rising in the mornings, as I go to bed. To show God I mean it, I pray limping home from school. I made Grandma stop pulling me home in my old wagon. The kids saw me. It was too embarrassing!

---

[21] Previously published in the SF Peninsula anthology Fault Zone: Reverse (Laurel Anne Hill ed.), 2021

God rules with iron authority over everyone. Even sinners. There are lots of sinners, more sinners than us God-abiding folk Grandma says. God lives in heaven, out somewhere in space. I know this because when the pastor talks about God, he points his finger into the sky. It's only logical that God rules from out in space. Boys aren't stupid!

I make sure my spaceman doesn't fly too high, in case he runs into God, who might not like the intrusion.

The pastor says one of God's angels, Lucifer, suffered from pride. I think that's like being uppity. Apparently, you can fly too close to God, and for his sin of flying too close, God banished Lucifer from heaven. He fell to earth, and that was the start of all sin, which is what we pray about, because everyone is "tempted of the devil," so everyone sins. Even Grandma. And Satan (another name for Lucifer) recruits a lot of people. It turns out, even little kids sin! (And I know that's true, because some kids my age make fun of me being a cripple. You've got to be a sinner to try to hurt someone like that.)

Satan is everywhere, even close by. I know this because Mom and Grandma say my father is Satan himself. This makes sense. My father is mean. He scares me. I try not to let it show because I don't want Mom and Grandma to worry more. Preacher says divorce is a sin, but I'm glad Mom divorced him. Some sins must be a lot worse than others.

And they have another name for him, Alcoholic. I mentioned to Mom that he had a funny smell. She told me it's how alcoholics smell. He's always trying "to manipulate you," they say, to get you to do what he wants. "That's what Satan does," Grandma explains. "Old Satan, he's a sly one," she says, with that laugh that tells me she knows for sure. "He plays with himself, too." I don't know what it means to play with yourself, but it's got to be of the Devil, something different than playing with the kids in our neighborhood. Grandma knows more than anyone about the Devil except maybe the Pastor.

So, my father is Satan, which means that I'm Satan's son. And I have his infirmity stuck in me. My crippled leg, there for everyone to see.

Invisible in Grandma's closet I can make up my own world, my own stories. I can fly in a magic arc across the night that's like a black lake high above my head, my legs whole, and beautiful, and shimmering.

But the world—the world of prayer and devils—doesn't go away. I can't stay here in Grandma's closet too long. Best get back into that world—that world not far from the world of dreams. Grandma and Mom need me. They don't have much money and they've got to take care of me and pay the doctor bills. They'll miss me if I stay in here. Best keep away from Willis, though. That's my father's earthly name. Satan has so many names. Best try and be as good a boy as I can, given I got this bad start as Satan's son. Maybe God will see my goodness and save me. Preacher's always telling us about getting saved. It's why I've got to pray so hard.

Father in Heaven, please wash away my stain. I will not follow him. I know who he is.

If you're not saved, you go to eternal damnation. Pray, kid! Maybe God will heal you, although I guess He gave up on your father.

Save me, Father! Save me from the flames!

◊ ◊ ◊

I didn't see Willis again until I was twenty-one.

It was a warm spring night in the small Oregon town. His sister's tiny house seemed to hide under the large willow in front. No sooner had I parked my borrowed car than I saw a man limping toward me from the old wooden porch in the dark. First thing I noticed was the limp.

He limps in the left leg, same place I used to. Still do slightly.

"This disease you've got, son," the doctor had begun when at eleven I was about to learn how to walk again without a brace, "it leaves your body just as mysteriously as it enters. No one understands it. When it goes, it leaves your hip with whatever damage it caused. Your left leg will always be slightly shorter than your right. Coulda been worse—a *lot* worse."

Willis limps a lot worse than me. Serves the motherfucker right!

No longer afraid to shake hands with the Devil, I reached out to take the hand he offered. It was easy to shake his hand, since I'd left our old-time religion long ago. That way of thinking might have been good enough for Jesus, but it wasn't good enough for me.

One day when I was ten, I'd sat in the church pew next to Grandma. Everyone was hollering, shaking, and sweating. A woman across the aisle spoke in the unknowable language of God. I'd seen it all that Sunday morning. Yes, I'd seen it all. *I'm smarter than everyone here*, I'd declared to myself with a ten-year-old's certainty. Nobody would catch me shaking, sweating, hollering, or speaking in the tongue of God. I would see things the way they are.

That had been the moment I'd separated. The seed of my arrogance took root, the first step toward freedom, the awareness of my difference. I could never go back. I'd shut the door behind me.

But here I was now, come to face Willis *mano a mano*. Shaking his hand, I thought I was a man. But I still had a boy's need. Would I follow in his path or make my own way? What had he put in me? I had rejected the religion of my family, but the stories—oh, those stories—still lived inside me. How could I not retain them?

The myth lived on. I wanted to feel that his hands were cold and lifeless. They weren't. I half expected his skin to wear the scales of a lizard or the slime of a serpent. It didn't. He was just another sad drunk, making every sad excuse a drunkard makes, even at times speaking in the unknowable language of the lost. I knew the feeling well. I wore the condition myself, getting wasted multiple times a week.

See where all your smarts have got you? You're just another drunk like him, aren't you?

Willis said about Mom, "She wouldn't *let* me see you, understand?" I recognized his lies right off. They piled up. "I wanted to pay the child support, but you see me here, I'm crippled, I could never work 'cuz of this injury in the army. Couldn't hold down a job with this leg, now could I? You think I wanted to live here dependent on my sister? She was a beautiful girl, your mother, don't get me wrong. She was always pretty. But she wouldn't give a man what he needed."

His story was stained with all the blame a drunkard spills on the ones who failed him. I felt the urge. I wore the condition. I still blamed Mom and Grandma, too. *We, the accursed.*

"I'm about to come into a lot of money," he said. "They're finally going to compensate me for my injury. I want to give you some. I want you to call me Dad. We'll make up for lost time."

I see you, Satan, the manipulator.

The night wore on. Many drinks later, I passed out.

I promised to be in touch before I drove away the next afternoon to return to campus. I never saw him again.

Let him feel what it's like to have his own son repay him in kind—lie for drunken lie. When I get back to campus, I'll coil up in bed and tell myself another story.

◊ ◊ ◊

At twenty-three I bought my cousin's '58 Chevy and drove from one history into another. San Francisco was a long way from Idaho. I'd tasted of all the fruit growing in this northern garden some thought of as paradise, but it seemed like hell to me. "Take a degree in law. Come home to practice. Marry a nice local girl." I wouldn't have it anymore. My eyes had been opened again.

What would I find in the place they call "The City?" It was just a name and a point on the map. A friend said it was the place to be, where students were rebelling and smoking pot out in the open. That sounded pretty good. And I'd read the magazine article that said young people should come to San Francisco to participate in "the vortex of cultural change."

That's for me! To be part of something new, something revolutionary!

That had been the extent of my preparation when one day, with a few hundred bucks in my pocket, I kissed my apprehensive mother and drove out from Eden, one more Tarot Fool heading off the cliff unaware, one more vagabond swept up into the eternal unknown calling.

The interstate seemed to slither like a long snake through Southern Idaho down into Utah then on into Nevada.

When I tired from the road, I pulled over like my mother advised. I rolled down the windows, inhaled the hot, dry odor of asphalt from the highway, smoked a cigarette, and dozed. I was too restless to dream. This was my big adventure. I feared the beasts I might run across in this unknown world. I'd have to fight them on my own now. I wanted to meet people of different races and from different parts of the world. Maybe people who longed for something more, like I did. I no longer wanted to explain why I read so much.

The winding snake eventually coughed me up into the Tenderloin, a dismal and desperate place where Harry, my only friend there, lived. I parked and got out of the car trying to act confident, like this was old hat, but I was shaking. I wasn't sure at all *what* I'd find in this sorry place. Maybe nothing good.

But what was that? Church bells rang from somewhere across the City skyline. I stopped to listen. Maybe their peal had summoned me from afar. What is it that beckons the spaceman, explorer, Fool, or kid searching for more? Soon I was playing pool for beer with prison guards and cabbies in the dive bars on Turk Street. I didn't hear the bells from there.

Sandy saved me when she visited. "I love you. But you've got to get out of here, or I'm not coming back."

Sometime later, after I'd heard the stories of so many in our generation, after I'd heard it called the Summer of Love, I thought to myself, *Yeah, it's a nice thought. Especially when you're high.*

What does the Fool look like when he's come down?

◊ ◊ ◊

There's this story of a God who made the world, who set the stars and moon in their places to guide blind travelers of the night. And He created this perfect world and in it he fashioned man out of dust from the ground. And a woman He fashioned from the man's rib. Unfortunately, the serpent, slithering in defiance, got into the garden He made for them. Living in so much goodness, how could we be anything but disobedient? And for our disobedience God drove us from His perfect garden. Then came two brothers pitted against the other. And now we knew hatred, and before long we had botched the perfect creation made for us by the perfect God we worshipped. And of course, the woman was blamed for everything.

Who can believe that shit? I'd said as a teenager, blossoming in full-petaled arrogance.

Things are never quite so simple as they appear as a teen. It took me a long time before I could admit how little I knew. Before I could rejoin the human race.

One storyteller sings an old hymn from long ago, of a fallen angel to blame for all the miseries we heap upon ourselves, practicing the smooth words he'll use to talk another sucker into temptation.

Another storyteller sings a newer song, a song of the beauty of that banished serpent, coiled within his tree of knowledge, in languid waiting for those who desire another bite of the apple. The acquisition of knowledge at times demands a disobedient and hungry mind. I prefer this story.

But let us sing in praise of the storyteller, the interpreter of dreams, the Fool.

When does a myth become a lie? When we use it to avoid responsibility over and over and to invoke some once-potent magic, now grown sterile. When we use it so that we won't change. So that we won't have to find our own way.

When does an old myth become true? Maybe when we use its spirit to animate ourselves into taking the responsibility we've always avoided, to lie beside the serpent in his tree of knowledge, tasting good and evil, learning of our arrogance and judgment of others.

It is the advent of Thanksgiving 2020. I think of all who came before me—parents, poets, storytellers, preachers—who told me stories of the world they saw. I think of them often. I remember them as from the worn trails of a past now covered with dust. They gave the best of their infirmities and brilliance. They talk to me still. Someone said gratitude is the highest emotion. I believe it, and with gratitude, I write these words.

However we acquire it, knowledge comes at a cost. The Fool, the spaceman, they'll pay it. There's always some old ache, some part of Eden we wish we could get back again. But we'll stumble on, out here, way past Eden.

Forgive me, Father, for I know not what I do.

And there's this personal myth, of a spaceman who flew through his Grandma's closet on a journey into the beyond.

Tim Flood's memoir *Islands Apart*, published in 1999, sold more than 2,000 copies. He began writing again after retiring. His autobiographical short story "Spaceman," which first appeared in *Fault Zone: Reverse*, was nominated for a Pushcart Prize. He is the communications director of the SF-Peninsula branch of the California Writers Club and a recipient of the Jack London Award for his service to his writing community. His first novel, *The Flower of Canaan*, is under review by a publishing company while he is at work on a follow-up novel.

Cold Trap

Vanessa MacLaren-Wray
San Francisco Peninsula

Who put this golden bridle in my hand?
The linen dress I wear was never mine.
A stranger braided flowers in my hair.
I shiver in the dew—my feet are bare.
The morning air blows cold and smells of time,
Its touch so dire it shakes me where I stand.

They brought me here as bait to draw the eyes
Of lambent prey that walks the wood at dawn
To sip the water from this forest pool.
Men lie in wait to ply their trade so cruel—
To snare the beast whose hooves will pace the lawn,
That mythic soul whose horn is all they prize.

How did I let them dress me for this part?
They ready their ropes, knowing I long to run,
To flee until my blood flows warm again.
My punishment for listening to men—
I let them trick me to this treason.
It freezes my veins. It shatters my heart.

Vanessa MacLaren-Wray writes poetry, science fiction, and fantasy exploring communication and attachment in this messy universe of ours. She's the author of the Patchwork Universe series, including *All That Was Asked*, *Shadows of Insurrection*, and *Flames of Attrition*. She also writes for the Truck Stop at the Center of the Galaxy shared-universe consortium. She hosts online open mics for the California Writers Club and often guest hosts for the podcast Small Publishing in a Big Universe. When not arguing with her cats, she works on new stories, her email journal *Messages from the Oort Cloud*, and her website, cometarytales.com.

SOUTH BAY

"I've got lots of friends in San Jose . . . ."
—*Hal David*

Mosaics[22]

Carolyn Donnell
South Bay Writers

I hear your sweet tales of family life
and think of ours with all its strife.
Does everyone else have a rosy past?
Or is it seen through a cloud or behind a mask?

Well, I'm sorry if my stories are sad.
If good guys don't win or some outcomes are bad.
But that's the truth, so what should I do
with our broken lives, the pieces askew?

I could sweep them all under a rug,
pretend they don't exist or take a drug.
Or grovel on them 'til I'm black and blue.
I know a lot of people who do.

Or I can gather the bits of glass
and make a mosaic of our pasts.
Find beauty somewhere in each cracked old vase.
And value. I think that choice is the best.

Ruby reds for those valiant hearts,
deflecting harm with fiery darts.
Rich emerald green for all of those
whose souls held on throughout nights of woes.

Brown, like the earth for all who stayed true.
Add shimmering shards of topaz blue.
The color of sky over our head
gives hope for life we won't have to dread.

---

[22] Previously published in South Bay Writers branch newsletter, *Writers Talk,* in May 2012

Please don't forget yellow, not by half.
That light-hearted color reminds us to laugh.
To bind it together we use even black,
dark side, the color of tar or thatch.

With these pieces both broken and torn
we come together and cause to form
a stained glass window so that all might find
beauty in even the least of light.

Carolyn Donnell resumed writing in 2003 when she joined the California Writers Club, South Bay Writers branch. They honored her in 2018 with the Matthews-Baldwin Award and CWC's Jack London Award in 2019. She has been published and won awards in fiction, poetry, and memoir in several anthologies from San Mateo County Fair Literary Arts, South Bay Writers, and the CWC *Literary Review.* Other anthologies include *Celebrate Creativity* 2020, *Curious Things* from CWC North State Writers, *Words for the Earth* 2022. *Whispering Willow: Tree Poems, Open Skies,* Red Penguin Books P*aris*, *Phases*, *Northwind Treasury,* and *Echoes of the Wild.*

She also published is a poetry chapbook, *Where is the Green?*, as well as two novels, *Deeper Colors* and *Blood Will Tell* (writing as C. S. Donnell).

For more information on Carolyn Donnel, visit:

https://www.amazon.com/C-S-Donnell/e/B017GGDZTI
https://carolyndonnell.wordpress.com
https://fineartamerica.com/profiles/carolyn-donnell

The Wilted Rose[23]

D.L. LaRoche
South Bay Writers

Lila's view of the future, when she faced hers, wasn't hopeful, and her memories didn't warrant the space they inhabited. It seemed she was not prepared to move on, dissatisfied with the past and no good reason for what she was doing today or might consider tomorrow.

She felt harried as she scurried through the house, picking up and tossing out and pondering the desired effect—their meeting would repeat tonight, and it was her turn to host. The ladies, here at seven, would all again unload the bitterness they'd dumped the time before. The group had reached a point where even a glimpse at joy or amusement had fallen away—two were divorced; one never married; and the fourth was an aging widow.

"These books, they belong on the damn shelf," she muttered—*so long since I've looked at them.* "Where the hell does this dust come from? These windows are never open. God, the place is a mess." She talked, but she was her only listener.

Things hadn't been right since Farley had left. Farley. . . she thought wistfully. He'd brought a definition she hadn't had before him, and now that he was gone, she didn't have anymore.

Years ago, when she started the group, the meetings were well attended, useful, and fun. Women sharing their views, as they pursued their goals—problems aired and solved in a convivial setting. Now, only four women attended. Three-and-a-half, as Janice was unpredictable.

And those problems—every meeting the same wrangled continually or stepped over with plans for a later discussion. And that business of opening doors leading to personal growth that they discussed so fervently back then—most had silently closed as the months on the calendar passed.

Today, it was surviving one's fruitless existence and the moaning and groaning of tired complaints—none of it useful. These thoughts coursed through Lila's mind as she moved things around, too late for serious cleaning.

---

[23] Previously published in the 2021 Fall issue of *October Hill Magazine*.

Occasionally, during these days, in a rare surge of optimism, she might come up with a personal goal for the group to consider. But those doors, once promising opportunities, seemed to have locked when Farley had left. As she busied herself with the straightening, she remembered those days, those earlier days when she was young, vital, and strong—days before being abruptly knocked from her feet.

◊◊◊

"Lila, can we talk?" Farley said in a pleading voice. "Can you sit here for a minute and hear me out?"

"Farley, do we have to do it now? Can't it wait? I have things I am doing now, and more ahead of those."

"I'm going to leave you, Lila," he said, his voice gaining strength. "We've been at this for a long time now, and it isn't working. I have a life I want to explore, and our marriage, this house, and your busyness in it, have become a stifling setting for me. I'm leaving."

Her coffee cup had fallen to the hard tile floor—shattering and scattering, coffee spreading through the grid of grout and turning it brown.

"What in the world are you talking about?" she said, eyes widened in startling surprise.

"Please sit down, Lila; we have things to discuss."

"You are leaving? My God, Farley, what are you saying? You *can't* leave. What do you mean, you're leaving? You frighten me with that kind of talk." She grabbed the counter to steady herself, as she noted the severity in his face.

"Why do you. . . why do you say these things, these. . . these careless, hurtful things?"

She saw the look, the one that came so seldom these days, the one when he was standing his ground, and she began to cry—jerky movements, a few lonely tears.

"I don't believe. . . Dammit Farley, I don't know you. It's been. . . What would I do? This is our life, for God's sake, you can't—" She moved toward the pantry to pick up the broom and a mop.

"Please sit down, Lila. Let that go. We need to talk. There are things we need to arrange."

Suddenly exhausted, she sat, smoothed her apron, her hands in her lap.

"Lila, you know I love you," he said. "I love you dearly; I always have." He put a single long-stemmed rose into a delicate vase—the vase a gift from her mother—and laid a small plain card down beside it.

She stared at it blankly. The vase seemed unfamiliar. Farley, a stranger, an outsider, was treating her this way. An energy began to grow. It started in her hands, her working hands, and they clenched, then tighter. She was growing angry and felt the flush invade her body.

"But Lila, this is not about love," he went on. "This is about compatibility and space. We haven't seen things alike for years. I've grown inward and smaller. You've become dominant, a growing presence in our house, and in our marriage, until finally. . . well, I can't find myself anymore. I look around; I'm not here, not anymore. I'm stifled here, Lila. I've disappeared and " He looked directly into her eyes. "I'm sorry, but I must leave."

She rose, face now full of tears. From her feet through her shoulders, she trembled. The bastard. Where did this come from? She'd become dominant? Well, that's so far. . . I can't believe I am hearing this. Who is this man? Not my Farley.

She picked up the vase and stared at it briefly. Then, in a focused rage, she threw it, watched him duck, as the vase bounced from the wall and shattered against the floor.

"Fuck you!" she managed.

◊ ◊ ◊

It had been years, but the words still resided intact and popped up with the smallest reminder—a song, a coffee cup, an empty pause at the counter—"I'm stifled here . . . I must leave"—and each time, it brought her to tears of sorrow and resentment.

She needed to run out for sweets, something tasty and fattening, but she had to buy gas. The damn needle was on empty; it always seemed to be hovering around "E."

Her car needed brakes, and she was certain her battery was dying. Laundry was piling up on the machine, and the lawn needed attention. She didn't have the interest, didn't seem to give a damn.

What to wear? It was getting late. Why—why was she doing this? She didn't care much anymore for the people who came, and things were stacking up—not just in front of the meeting but in front of her life. And trailing behind were empty containers, bad memories, trash, and not nearly enough interest in picking any of it up.

"Hi, Sissy, good to see you. Please come in. You're a little early tonight. I haven't done the coffee yet."

"Lila, it's exactly seven—even by your clock, which ordinarily runs late."

"Okay, okay! I am a little behind, I guess."

"As usual," Sissy mumbled.

"Can you arrange the cookies on this plate—some from each package?"

"Sure. Is Janice coming tonight?"

"No, I don't think so, but I don't really know. She said it keeps her up too late, and she needs her sleep. I don't think Janice likes me."

"I doubt that she doesn't like you; rather, she hasn't committed. She's new to our group, and maybe doesn't feel comfortable yet. And the truth is, Lila, you've been off your center for a while."

"Well!" Lila gave her a rough look. "I don't know what you mean by that."

"Hi, all." Tess popped in, never knocked. "How are things with y'all this evening? I like your dress, Lila. New?"

"Had it for years. I'm done here. Let's go up to the studio. If Janice shows up, she knows where to find us. Don't mind the mess; the place is a disaster. Grab those cups there, will you, Tess?"

"Sure, honey, and real nice to see you, too."

Their talk droned on in the studio. Their nagging discomforts, revealed long ago, were again and again underscored.

"It's George," Sissy said, "He wants us to go to the Cowboy's game. I hate football—the noise is deafening. . . and the crowds, my God the crowds. He bought the tickets, you know, even before asking me—the nerve, the unmitigated nerve of the man."

"My Charles is like that," Tess said. "He thinks. . . ha-ha, he don't think too often, but then when he does, he thinks I'm one of those service dogs they got, that I'm trained to follow wherever he goes, know what he wants before he asks. Humph, I think it's part of their goddamn DNA."

"You're so lucky, Lila." Sissy sipped at her tea. "You don't have to put up with smelly feet on the sofa. . . a trail of beer cans from the fridge to the TV, I'm seriously thinking about—"

"I'm sorry to be late," Janice said, up the stairs, out of breath, "and no one answered the bell."

"We didn't expect you," Lila grumbled, "but we're happy to see you now and then."

"I was in the neighborhood. Did I miss anything. . . well, you know, anything important?" And that was the last thing Janice said before she pulled her knitting from a bag she had brought and began working the needles.

Bored beyond belief, Lila wondered why anyone attended. They easily adjourned at nine.

Lila saw them to the door and out with a nod, then returned to her studio to extinguish the lights. She was exhausted and would clean up tomorrow. Cleaning tomorrow. . . it had a familiar ring.

A book on the taboret caught her attention, a large-format book of post-Renaissance artists that she didn't recall having owned. *Now, where the hell did that come from?*

She spun it around: I*mpressions of Love.*

Humm, what's this? Something's inserted between the pages.

She was curious but resisted at first. The book must belong to one of the girls, and what was theirs was not her business. The *Impressions* tempted, however, and she liked those artists. *What the hell.* She opened the book to a dried, pressed rose and a small card. The card said simply, "I love you." The rose had wilted, turned brown and brittle. She was startled at first and then dismayed.

"Why would anyone leave this?" she mumbled. "Not for me." She didn't enjoy much from roses to begin with, and wilted ones left her with even less.

◊ ◊ ◊

The next morning, Lila called the girls, suggesting that someone may have forgotten her book. They all replied in the negative.

"Now, where did it come from?" she mused aloud. She returned to her studio, reopened the book, and puzzled over it for a while before she remembered Farley's rose. It was there that night in the bud vase. He had swept up the glass in the morning and picked up the rose as she stewed over coffee. "I'll save this for you, Lila, as a remembrance of me," he had said.

Damn roses—commercial and used to the point of cliché. But Farley had brought them often, with every celebration, as well as those times intending to assuage some faux pas of his. There were always those goddamn roses—her birthday, Easter, and Mother's Day. They didn't have kids. She perceived it as some cheap attempt at equilibrium in the one case and to gain favor in the other. It never worked, though, and she saw to that. . . though not intentionally.

She gently removed it from the book and laid it down on a blank stretched canvas. She stared at it awhile as its image dissolved into memories—the bad ones thundering in first with their bitter flavor, but followed if grudgingly by the better—and she remembered his touch and gentle address, and the challenging ideas he had brought to her that might have been life-changing . . . but weren't. She also saw to that, though, again, not intentionally. Damn that Farley, would he ever leave her alone.

In the kitchen, she tossed her coffee and poured a tall whiskey, neat. The overcast morning drew her out to the deck, the gray sky consistent with how she was feeling. She lit a cigarette.

From the railing, she looked out on the woodsy scene in the back, squirrels chirping as they raced through the trees, a crow talking to another. At times, they seemed to be laughing—maybe at her. She mused over her life with Farley and what he had said it had become for him, that he had stagnated, disappeared, in their relationship and had to leave, despite his feelings for her.

"Dammit, Farley, you could've said something." She grumbled and took a long drink of her whiskey.

But then he had, she reluctantly remembered, and she recalled the roses and the overtures of care that earlier came with them—his strength and worldly perspective, and how much she admired and loved him in those halcyon days. But with time, she felt threatened that her life would become his, or at least be corralled by his worldlier view, and how she needed to struggle against sharing his shadow. In time, at his every suggestion, she drew that line in the sand.

◊ ◊ ◊

It began when she was young, idealistic, and open to most everything. She wasn't driven like some of her friends with goals and wellchanneled energy. She simply wanted to explore, to discover, to see if anything fit. It was then that Farley had come along.

"Yes, I love you and want to marry you," he had said. "You will be my excitement. We will go places and do things. We will travel—Europe and North Africa—and, together, we'll build a house on the coast. I have plans, Lila, and they must include you."

"Oh Farley, do you mean it? Are you serious about travel? I've so wanted to explore our world, and doing it with you would be. . . well, it would be simply marvelous. Yes, my darling. . . yes, we will marry, and yes, we will travel. Egypt, I'd love to walk the beaches of Alexandria and see the pyramids of Giza."

They were glorious plans, and she was drawn into his life with marriage. But they weren't plans at all—only Farley's dreams, and instead, they went bowling with his office team and on picnics, those damn company picnics. Farley's firm was generous that way. She remembered activities for workers and their wives, and, yes, their entire families.

"I've joined the manager's club, Lila, and we will attend the dinners. Others will be there who you'll enjoy—my friends and their wives." She bought a new dress and tried to enjoy them, and she was convincing, he told her.

"I bought you a car, Lila, a little green Pontiac. It's a very nice green, and I know you will like it." She didn't like green. Well, she needed a car.

"When we have a child, Lila, it'll be a boy, and we'll name him after my father."

"Why not wear the blue dress, Lila? You look so much nicer in blue."

"Let's paint the kitchen this weekend; I picked up this great shade of peach at the hardware store this morning."

She accustomed herself to believing that being Farley's wife was her life. But, in time, it struck her—she had no say or personal space in the partnership. She saw that she was losing herself and began to balk.

"No peach paint in the kitchen, Farley. I don't like peach, and this is my kitchen. I do the work here, and I'll have it my way. You take your paint back to the hardware store, and maybe they'll refund your money."

She formed a women's support group and became the leading participant. They all had problems with marriage. As they continued to meet, she grew stronger and began taking control of where she spent most of her day. It seemed the house was her domain, and, by God, she would reign over it. It was becoming her time, if not at all that she earlier expected.

If a son came along, she would fill out the birth certificate and do the naming—and, if it was a boy, she would likely name it after *her* father.

She traded her green Pontiac for a black Citroen, too quickly for Farley's objections, and she put the blue dress in the back of the closet.

"Farley, keep your feet off the sofa and fold up the paper when you're through. I may want to read it. And for God's sake, make a little effort to be at the table on time."

It wasn't what she had wanted—that earlier life exploration—but the house was hers, and she established the rules. Farley could spend his time with his chums at the office, which he seemed to prefer. Well, it was his damn choice.

She began sleeping on her side of the bed, near the edge, faced away from him. He slept on his with a big cold space in the middle, and their awake time together diminished. He began traveling—for the company, he said, and she saw that she really didn't care.

When he invited her to dinner to celebrate her birthday, she declined. She had much to do in her studio. They ignored their anniversary. The roses stopped coming. Occasionally, he didn't come home, and she worried a little, but didn't ask him if everything was all right.

Beyond the perfunctory, their conversations, once thoughtfully engaging, had waned, and then disappeared.

It had bothered her some that their marriage had lost its original warmth and was puzzled as to how to restore it. Over time, she might have admitted that some was her doing. But she had hardened and come to accept it. And because Farley kept up his end without obvious complaint, she thought he, too, must have been satisfied.

◊ ◊ ◊

She sipped at her whiskey as her mind returned to the present. She had spent a lot of energy ensuring independence from the influence he brought, and so her defenses habitually built up—perhaps to the detriment of her own growth and advancement. It wasn't just his life that had stagnated.

This was a new and startling revelation, and she let it sink in, as she reminisced and searched for perspective. She, too, had "stifled." As with his influence and caring, she had woven herself a cocoon, a form of protection for her that looked like dominance to him.

She finished her whiskey and put the empty glass on the railing. No one alone was to blame—the whole damn thing was a mistake, not hers so much, but not all of it his. The laughing crows had left, and the squirrels had retired.

Lila blotted her eyes with a tissue and went back to the kitchen. She fixed a fresh coffee. She was sure now that while punishing him—though not intentionally—she had done herself a disservice—her life had dried and wilted. Oh, she had the house, all of it, but what had it cost? Was this an epiphany? She didn't call it that; she called it a rose thing. It was the rose and its reminder that brought the revelation.

It came to her clearly now, the balance—that she was as much of the problem as he. This made her feel free. She could explore her life, without anger or guilt, and participate in its discoveries, as she had initially intended—without Farley, yes, but with the message of his rose.

She went up to her studio, carefully placed the little flower back on its page with the card, and closed the book. She made a list, called a gardener, found a mechanic and a housecleaning service, and started her laundry.

"Let's see," she said to her house. "Where would I like to go?"

D. L. LaRoche retired from his aerospace job to generate fictional stories dealing with the conditions driving our moral behavior. He brings to that interest his Missouri upbringing, adventurous shenanigans, and broad education, both formal and "street." He has held several offices in the CWC, founded and chaired the NorCal Group, and founded/edited the first seven issues of the CWC *Literary*

Review He has five novels available on Amazon.

Yucatan Intruder

Edie Matthews
South Bay Writers

On an isolated road from Chetumal to Xcaret in Yucatan, the passengers inside the bus shook like the pebbles in maracas. Red Christmas light flashed to the beat of "*Cielito Lindo*" blaring from several speakers, and disturbing the quietude of the dense jungle outside.

"*Ay, ay, ay, ay, canta y no llores.*" Ay, ay, ay, ay, sing and don't cry.

The men, women, and children sat indifferent to the ruts and potholes, gazing out the windows at the lush environment, but groaned, aaii-yeee, when they bounced over speed bumps placed by the small pueblos they passed.

"I am going to need new kidneys after this trip," said an old man with a droopy mustache.

Several people nearby nodded and held on.

"What is your hurry, señor?" The Old Timer asked the driver. "We will be in heaven or hell a long time."

"I'm the commander of my bus," said Francisco Pisarro. "If you don't like the ride, I will put you off."

The Old Timer shrugged in reply.

The driver's wife, Yolanda, sat behind her husband in a makeshift seat. She held their baby boy in one arm and massaged her husband's back with her free hand, bracing herself with her feet. Her two-year old daughter, Rosita, played on the floor on a striped serape, a small flexible fence around her. The toddler pulled plastic flowers out of her doll's hair.

Yolanda loved Francisco. Despite his quick temper, he was her man, her *esposo*. He only struck her when he had too much tequila, or if he'd had a difficult day at work. She couldn't fault him for that. After all, the twin Mayan gods, Quetzalcoatl and Xolotl, created men by dripping their blood on bones retrieved from hell. She knew from her father and brothers a man could not escape his nature—he must relieve his fury or it would fester inside him, disturbing his digestion, injuring his pancreas, or worse, damaging his heart. And Francisco had never hurt her badly—though there was the time when he knocked her down, and she began bleeding from that female place. She worried since she was pregnant at the time. Soon after her labor started and she couldn't stop moaning. It wasn't the pain so much as her fear that she would lose her baby.

They sent for Martina, the elderly midwife, who assured Yolanda she would be fine. She was eight months along and the baby had grown large enough to survive. Martina was right. That night Yolanda bore her second child, a boy. Francisco was overjoyed. Their first child was a girl, and while he told his wife he loved their daughter, he said, "A man must have a son."

Yolanda wanted to name the child Jesús to please the Christian god or Chuen to honor the god of guidance, symbolized by the North Star that directed her husband on his travels. Chuen's only homage was incense from the copal tree. But Francisco insisted on naming the boy, Ronaldo, after his favorite soccer player.

The bus dropped into a pothole and Yolanda grabbed the metal pole for support. Rosita tumbled against her mother's legs and whimpered, but righted herself and continued playing with her doll. Yolanda switched Ronaldo to her other arm and readjusted herself in the seat. Her eyes fell on the chart taped to the wall by the door of the bus: Animals of the Yucatan. Beside the small pictures of each creature were hatch marks, representing the number of animals slaughtered by the bus. Anteater 3, armadillo 14, coati 25, iguana 9, jaguar 0, margay 5, monkey 2, snakes 41, turtle 2, weasel 8, white-tail deer 2.

Sometimes, Francisco stopped the bus to skin the animal or transport it to sell at the next pueblos. Sometimes, he left it to rot on the road, though the carcass had disappeared by the time they passed by again.

Occasionally, passengers complained about the delays. Francisco ignored them or threatened to leave them behind. However, most were relieved to get off the bus to stretch and to urinate.

Francisco was small. In fact, Yolanda was a bit taller. So, she was careful to wear only the flattest sandals and hunch a little when they strolled together in the plaza. Sadly, the men Francisco worked with were cruel.

"Hey, chihuahua," they taunted him.

"You'd better sit on a big cushion so you can see out the window."

"Do the police stop you?" "Little boy, where did you steal this bus?"

But away from the men at the terminal, Francisco prized his job. Perched on his thick, cushioned seat, above the traffic, he felt superior to other men—*el jefe de autobús.*

Many of the buses had names painted on the side, and his was not an exception. In bold black letters it read El Gigante. Those puny cars or animals had better clear out of the way of El Gigante.

Under a canopy of trees and shrubbery that threatened to overtake the road, the bus veered sharply and whacked into a small animal. The passengers cried out:

"Aaii-yeee!"

"Mi dios!"

Bundles in the overhead racks tumbled onto the floor. Caged chickens pock-pock-pocked. A young boy slipped off his seat. Little Rosita toppled over and began to wail.

"*¿Qué pasa*?" Yolanda asked her husband, reaching for her daughter. Other passengers stood up, trying to see what caused the commotion.

The bus screeched to a stop. Francisco yanked the lever and the door creaked open. Several male passengers and the old timer followed him off the bus.

What is it?" Asked a man wearing a straw sombrero.

"A coati," said Francisco, dismissive of the small animal with its pointed snout and ringed tail. The coati stared at Francisco with an eye half opened. "Eeekk." Francisco thumped its head with the heel of his shoe.

The old timer blessed himself.

"Wow, you really smashed it," said a young vaquero in brown boots. He helped put the dead coati in a burlap sack, and Francisco placed it in a compartment under the bus. He would sell it at the next pueblo. The ringed-tail coatis were tasty to eat and also valued for their skin.

The Old Timer shook his head. "Why kill it? It wasn't hurting anything."

"It was an accident," said Francisco. "The stupid animals need to stay out of the way of El Gigante." He gestured to the woodland. "They've got the whole jungle—the road belongs to me."

"But, señor, this is the countryside. We are the intruders."

"What are you a sissy?" said Brown Boots. "It's just an animal—here to serve us, to amuse us."

The men returned to the bus. "Yes, but killing so many needlessly." The Old Timer gestured at the chart.

"Don't be stupid, Old Timer," said Straw Sombrero. "He's just having some fun. He's not hurting anybody. In Mexico City don't they kill el toro in the bullring? Out here," he spread his arms, "this is his bullring. ¡Olé!"

Francisco grinned. He liked the comparison. Yes, he was like a matador, and the bus was a giant *pecadoro*—the animals had better keep out of his way.

At the next, pueblo, Francisco stopped. "Ten minutes," he announced.

While the passengers stepped off of the bus, Francisco retrieved the dead coati and in the heat of the noonday sun strolled down the road to a small casa. After some bartering, there was an exchange of money, and Francisco returned to the bus. He added a new hatch mark to the coati line, the total now at 26. Yolanda handed him a tamale and a warm cerveza. When he finished, he called out, "Let's go!"

The vehicle rattled on, and Yolanda fingered the two pendants around her neck, a silver crucifix and a jade Mayan calendar. She thought about the work she had left at home. The trinkets and souvenirs she sold in the market. The shelves were lined with Christian statues of Jesús, Saint John the Baptist, St. Francis of Assisi, and Our Lady of Guadalupe. On the walls hung masks of Aztec and Mayan deities: Kinich Ahau, the sun god; Yum Caax, the god of agriculture; and her favorite, Ixchel, the moon goddess and patroness of pregnant women. Local artisans created these items from native material like quartz, lapis, obsidian, and precious turquoise with deposits of copper.

The market was where Yolanda first met Francisco. He had come browsing in her stall and began talking to her, asking about the merchandise, but too flirtatious to be interested in a Christian statue or to learn about the Mayan mythology that she tried to explain. She admired his appearance. His fine features—light skin, brown eyes with specks of green like jalapenos. Clearly not indigenous like herself, or Mexican, but Spanish. She worried and hoped he wasn't a descendant of Cortés. Although he also had a prominent nose resembling the beak of an eagle, reminding her of Pacal Voltan, the early Mayan ruler, responsible for building much of the architecture.

As they rounded a bend, up ahead Francisco saw it. The regal figure of a jaguar. "Look," he said awestruck. The animal, sleek and elegant, was crossing the road and halted at the sight of the behemoth bearing down on him. Francisco slowed the bus, mesmerized by its magnificence.

"Kill it," said Brown Boots. "He's the only animal missing from your chart."

"No," said the old timer. "Leave it be. This is his home."

"Shut up, Old Timer," said Straw Sombrero. "He needs to complete his chart."

Yolanda panicked at the site of the jaguar. It was a deity from the underworld that killed its prey during the day or night sun. "No, Francisco," she said, grabbing him.

"The jaguar may be king of the jungle," said Francisco, shoving her hand away. "But I am king of the bus." He accelerated and the bus belched forward. The jaguar glared at the oncoming monster, as if to stare it down, then with a jolt, turned and sprinted up the road.

Francisco was astounded at its speed. He hit a pothole and everyone bounced, packages and belongings toppling everywhere. Passengers babbled and chickens pock-pocked. People divided into two camps: a group in the front of the bus who wanted to chase the jaguar, and the others huddled in the back hanging on, who wanted to slow down and leave the animal alone.

"*¡Ay, caramba*!" said Sombrero. "It will outrun the bus!"

"Faster!" said Brown Boots.

"No," said the old timer. "It is the devil god of hell. He carries terrestrial fires. You will be cursed!"

"Shut your mouth, Old Timer!" said Sombrero, shoving him into the seat. "Don't talk that mumbo jumbo."

"Kill it!" Brown Boots urged. "You need it for your chart!"

Francisco speeded up to the animal. The jaguar zigzagged back and forth. Francisco followed, swerving the bus from side to side. People shrieked. Packages fell. Several men cheered him. The chickens squawked. Children cried. Women prayed.

"Noooo," cried Yolanda, falling on the floor, but managing to gather her crying children in her arms.

Now they were traveling over eighty kilometers an hour when they caught the animal, and Francisco slammed into it.

The men cheered. "¡Olé! ¡Olé! ¡Olé!"

Sweat ran down Francisco's face. He stopped the bus and wiped his brow with his sleeve. Gingerly, the passengers in the back of the bus began to gather themselves and pick up their belongings.

"That skin has got to be worth a lot of money," said Brown Boots.

Francisco thought about how he would keep the skin and show it to the fools at the terminal. That would shut their mouths. None of them had killed a jaguar. Now he, Francisco Pissaro, would be respected.

"Yes," said Francisco, stepping off the bus.

The men trailed behind him, slapping his back and congratulating him like he was a conquering hero. Behind the bus, the jaguar lay sprawled on the road. Francisco reached it first and kicked it like he was testing a tire. The animal's eyes sprung open.

"Aaii-yeee," shrieked the men, scurrying back to the safety of the bus. Before Francisco could get away, the jaguar swooped its talon, clawing Francisco's legs and knocking him to the ground. He fell rolling away and managed to scramble to his feet and run.

The other men had already boarded the bus.

"Close the door before it kills all of us!" shouted Sombrero.

Brown Boots jerked the lever, shutting the door.

"Noooo, my husband!" shouted Yolanda.

The jaguar loped after Francisco who limped towards the door, but by the time he reached it, it was closed. Francisco pounded on the glass. "My bus! Open the door! Please!"

The jaguar pounced on top of him, roaring like the crack of thunder before he bit Francisco's throat. Yolanda stared through the door at her husband's face, distorted with fear, then into the eyes of the jaguar, the same color as Francisco's eyes. Her scream joined the cacophony of cries of the other passengers. She hurried to the door, now smeared with her husband's blood. Francisco fell to the ground. She watched helpless, while the jaguar slowly dragged her husband's quivering body into the blackness of the jungle.

"Help him!" she cried. She still held Ronaldo who was crying. Rosita lay on the floor screaming.

"A pistol, does anyone have a pistol?" asked the Old Timer. The people looked from one to the other, lifting their shoulders and shaking their heads.

"It's too late, señora," said Sombrero. "He is gone."

A woman in the back took out her rosary, crossed herself, and began praying. "Padre *nuestro que estás en los cielos*." Two other women came forward to help Yolanda with her children. One of the woman cradled Ronaldo in her heavy breasts, and soothed him with soft coos. The other woman took Rosita and gave her a piece of candied squash. Pacified, the child began eating.

Dazed and numb, Yolanda sat down on the makeshift seat. Her mind crowded with thoughts. Why hadn't her husband honored his namesake, St. Francis of Assisi, patron saint of animals? Sadly, he had no use for saints or gods of any kind.

"Who can drive the bus?" asked a passenger.

"I can," said Brown Boots. "Sometimes, I drive trucks. I've been watching him. It's like a truck." He tossed aside Francisco's cushion and settled into the seat. When he turned the key, the bus sputtered to life and the music began.

Bésame, bésame mucho. Kiss me a lot.

Como si fuera esta noche la última vez. As if tonight were the last time.

Yolanda thought she heard the distant growl of the jaguar. Tears rolled down her cheeks.

Bésame, bésame mucho. Kiss me a lot.

Que tengo miedo perderte, perderte después. I am afraid to lose you afterwards.

Piensa que tal vez mañana. Think that maybe tomorrow

Yo ya estaré lejos, muy lejos de ti. I'll already be far, very far from you.

Now her children would grow up fatherless. She pressed the crucifix and Mayan calendar into her skin and felt her heart pounding. She vowed she would teach Rosita and Ronaldo about the gods. She would explain how to respect and honor them and gain their protection. She stood up and gazed into the jungle with its dark shadows and variegated shrubbery. The bus chugged away, and she hurried to the back window, staring out. "Adiós, *mi marido*."

Edie Matthews has worked in print, radio, and TV news, as a tech writer, and as a standup comedian. She created the comedy show

Mothers & Other Goddesses, touring the US and Canada. She authored the humor book *You've Been Around Children Too Long When . . .*

She holds an MFA in Creative Writing from SJSU and has taught English at De Anza College.

The Love Muscle[24]

Reena Kapoor
South Bay Writers

I stood hesitating outside the *J. Thoman Auto Shop* after dropping off my car. The sign above me declared, "We Make Car Troubles Disappear Like Magic!" Someone had almost completely erased "Troubles." Thoman, the owner, didn't bother to have the sign fixed. Because longtime customers—immigrants like my parents—didn't bother with such trifles. Thoman's low prices, undoubtedly afforded by tradeoffs of this nature, preserved their loyalty. Some of that loyalty, either out of force of habit or a simple desire to avoid yet another battle, trickled down to offspring like me.

Thoman was a Syrian Christian from Kerala who insisted on, "Mr. J. Thoman! Please, thank you much!" if anyone dared to simply address him as "Thoman." I was directed to him by my dad when I bought my first car after college. I hadn't brought my car in since my mother—the last of my parents—suddenly passed on two years ago.

As usual, I got no greeting, no smile, no semblance of warmth, just, "Why bringing so late? The car will DHIE!" Thankfully, this was my last visit to his shop. Time to shed even these fragments of my inheritance.

I'd grown up a couple of streets over. I didn't go that way anymore. Only ghosts roamed those streets, battle ready as ever. After I entered high school, "Why studying Political Science? Why not just plain Science?" was the most my father ever uttered directly to me.

"Be fully concentrating on studies only," came from my mother with my father standing behind her glaring at the floor. Foolishly, I argued with her.

It culminated in my mother showing up at my high school one afternoon. "I want to see this boy you're talking to so much in the night!"

The school principal had to intervene. It was the day all joy and friendship I found in high school evaporated. College and law school were a respite. When I moved back to the area with a job at a top law

---

[24] Previously published in South Bay Writers branch newsletter, *Writers Talk* in August 2023.

firm, my parents were bewildered that I didn't want to live with them and save on rent. My mother's hectoring got more earnest after my father's passing. "When will you settle down? So old already!" "Settle down" being a euphemism for marriage and reproduction.

"Have a love marriage, if you want!" was the final concession she granted me two months before she passed. Repetitive injury from battle prevented me from noticing what a significant compromise she was offering, in giving me permission to forgo an arranged marriage. *Victory at age thirty-six!* Despite my law school training, winning against her didn't feel like much. Not then, not now, even when all adversaries had been reduced to ashes and ghosts.

I looked across the street. My old bus stop for municipal #51. The bus I used to take to my high school every day. I could take it to get to the house I live in now. Jumping in an Uber would be a lot faster though. But I had time today. I was in between jobs. I found myself crossing the street. Rare for me to indulge the past like this. The graveyard of memories and lost dreams is a dangerous place to visit. Sometimes ghosts insist on crossing over into real life. Yet, here I was waiting for that old bus.

Yet I can't complain. My choices have brought me exactly where I want to be. I'm a noted lawyer, still young-ish (*is thirty-nine even middle age?*), invited to Georgetown to work closely with my role model in constitutional law. It does mean moving across the country. But I'm ready. When I received the offer, I was over the moon. Then, within days a hollowness wormed in. *Seriously? Ingrate!*

I worried about showing up for the new position with anything less than a 1000% to offer. Hence the therapist. At first, I did most of the talking. The therapist didn't offer much. Instead, he seemed to stray into orthogonal spaces. A month ago, he suggested I may be avoiding "human connection; fear of commitment?" *Never heard THAT cliché before!* For a second, I was tempted to walk out right then. But finding a decent therapist isn't easy these days.

"I'm no recluse," I countered. "Hardly ever without a boyfriend." *Thank you very much!*

The therapist nodded, offering nothing more for my conundrum. Then recently after another session he surprised me with something even more random. "Let's work on helping you rediscover your 'love muscle.'"

I laughed out loud. "Love muscle? That almost sounds pornographic!"

Given his eastern European accent (*or Israeli perhaps?*) I wondered if his terminology was victim to literal translation-ism from another language, a condition I was only too familiar with, having been raised in Hindi and English with mixed metaphors, and a whole lot of translation-ism-afflicted phraseology. He smiled at my comment and carried on.

So here I was, a week later, standing at my old bus stop still chuckling at the notion of reviving my love muscle. The bus arrived, slowed to a stop. I ascended the steps and paused. It felt like I entered a portal into a parallel world that operated at a fraction of the speed of my life.

The driver was grinning at me. A raffish-looking young fellow, he adjusted the bright red scarf around his neck as he greeted me. "Welcome lady! Take any open seat you like."

I felt a tiny resentment. Nothing about this young driver—other than his station—was anything like. . . *Jerome? Yes, Jerome!* Jerome, the bus driver who drove this route, and who I saw twice daily, through my four years of high school. I wondered where Jerome was now. Probably long retired. I found myself a window seat.

Jerome was much older than this driver. Always punctual, polite, and attentive to his job. He didn't chat much with us passengers. At first, I didn't know his name and I didn't think he even noticed me. Until that one day at the end of junior year. That day my boyfriend hadn't accompanied me to the bus stop, like he'd done every single day for the past two years. That day I waited alone at the bus stop. That day I boarded the bus weighed under more emotion than I knew what to do with. It was an interminable twenty-minute ride before I could get home and lock myself in my room. And avoid my mother and the victory in her eyes.

That day, just as my stop neared, I noticed one of my earrings was missing. It was the only present my boyfriend ever gave me in the time we dated. The two years he ended without notice that morning. A week after my mother's infamous school visit. I couldn't lose the earring. I frantically patted down my clothes. Soon I was on my knees, scanning the bus floor through my tears. Doing this meant I'd probably miss my stop.

Almost immediately Jerome was standing over me. "What you

lookin' for, Miss?"

I looked up and saw the bus wasn't moving. Jerome was much shorter than he seemed sitting. He didn't sound impatient, just matter of fact. I read his name on his shirt.

"My earring—" I sobbed back, holding out the one I still had. Without saying a word Jerome got on his knees to help me look. I don't know why the rest of the passengers didn't protest the delay. Instead some of them even started to look around their feet.

We never found the earring. Jerome waited for me to get myself together before I got off the bus. As I stepped off, he said, "Better one in your future, miss." I looked back at him. I knew he didn't mean the earring. Those words became my sole solace in that time. Jerome never mentioned the incident again. And after that day he always nodded at me when I entered or exited the bus with a "Good morning, miss" or a "Good afternoon, miss." I greeted him back.

At school I threw myself into classes, college apps, more AP than any college needed and extra-credit-everything. My ex-boyfriend moved on too. I heard he was dating someone with "much less drama." In those years, Jerome's greetings punctuated the only time and space where I could exhale.

Then high school ended. I left for college and never saw Jerome again.

And here I was seated in Jerome's bus after more than two decades. Yes, this would always be Jerome's bus. A gentle breeze kissed my cheek. I sighed, surrendering to the twenty-five-minute suspension of life. Scenes from years gone by whizzed past the window. School, college, law school, work, losing my father, work, losing my mother, work, work, work. . .

Jerome's bus snaked through familiar streets. We went past a flaming field of California poppies. When I bought my first house, I used to have fresh flowers on the table every week. "Wasting money on real flowers?" my mother wanted to know. That practice faded too. *Once I move to DC, I'll have fresh flowers every day!*

As the bus ride continued, a calm settled on me. I found myself humming. It was an old favorite, a love tune from my high school days. Soon another voice joined my humming—with words. I turned around to see a woman, probably in her seventies, singing and swaying with the tune. She was smiling, the kind of smile I don't see too much. When we lawyers smile, our smiles often don't make it to our eyes. We women lawyers even more so, trying to outdo the men on every front. *Geez! Where are all these thoughts coming from?*

The woman and I carried on humming and singing. The rest of the bus acted as if this was the most natural thing in the world. A couple nodded at me. Others got on and off without comment. We repeated stanzas, not wanting the ride to end. When the bus halted at my stop, I rose reluctantly and gave my singing partner a little bow. She waved at me, laughing. *Whoa! Since when have I started singing on public transport?*

I started to exit the bus. I heard someone speak behind me.

"Hey lady!" I stepped off and turned around. The young driver was looking at me, his grin and confidence gone.

I wondered if I'd left something behind.

He hesitated as if confessing to an infraction. "Your song, it's one of Jennie's favorites—"

I gave him a half smile, not exactly sure who or what he was getting at.

Then he ran his hand through his hair, and gushed, "That song back there. . . that got me. I'm gonna tell Jennie how I feel 'bout her. Think I'll do it. Today!"

He nodded vigorously and settled back down. A few on the bus cheered and clapped as he waved and drove away.

I found myself standing alone at the bus stop. High school was the last time I'd been in love. In this town, which I was about to leave for good. I found myself sobbing. Can a love muscle get sore from disuse? I called my therapist.

A techie for over 25 years, **Reena Kapoor** now focuses on writing plays, poetry, and short fiction. Her work has appeared in *The Bluebird Word, Active Muse, Flash Fiction Forum, 433 Magazine, Literary Yard, Tiny Seed Journal, Academy of the Heart & Mind, Writing in a Woman's Voice*, and *India Currents*. Several of her plays have been produced by EnActe Arts. She holds an undergraduate engineering degree from IIT Delhi and an MS from Northwestern University.

Reena lives in Silicon Valley with her family and their dog, Dishoom. Visit Reena thttps://arrivalsanddepartures.substack.com.

CALIFORNIA WRITERS CLUB

SAIL ON!

CENTRAL COAST

"They fish for tourists now, not pilchards, and that species they are not likely to wipe out."
—*John Steinbeck*

CENTRAL COAST WRITERS

God of Sunshine

Karen Ashby Flack
Central Coast Writers

There is a god of sunshine
And surely one for rain
Sometimes a god of healing
And sadly also pain

I've seen the god of grieving
It's one that has five heads
The sister of addiction
With twelve long arms instead

I think that it's all science
I know I could be wrong
I've tried some other versions
But mostly played along

I'm looking for the god of peace
And a good night's sleep
The one who loves her neighbor
This is the god I'll keep

Karen Ashby Flack is a resident of Carmel, California, where she lives with her husband and requisite poodle. She recently returned to writing poetry after a long hiatus spent studying and teaching engineering. Her inspiration comes from hiking, star gazing, and early morning ruminations. While she has published many articles on the physics of flow, this is her first published poem. She is grateful for the opportunity to share her point of view.

Wind

Kay Krattli
Central Coast Writers

Even when he knocks impolitely
I invite the wind in, open a window
to light whispers, dark moans.

He billows the curtains,
    ruffles the magazine pages,
        sways the leaves of the rubber plant
until they click-clack
        like a dissonant wind chime.

Tonight he's strong, all bluster and push.
Paper napkins become white boats
sailing across the wooden sea floor.

My skirt rises indecently, naughty
shades applauding rude approval
against blind windows.

His voice, an unsteady ocean-like churn,
joins an opera sung by reticent trees.
A squall line of whine

swirls from room to room,
loud where he punishes the house
with the sticky arms of the pines.

He banishes light—warm yellow lines
erased from a night blacker than onyx.

I like this unpredictable change
     of place, of space; this alchemy of wind
                                                    sweeps
away the expected.

When he's gone, my mind
        drifts in a gift
                of stillness.

Kay Krattli grew up among Irish and Norwegian immigrants in North Dakota. Encouraged by supportive teachers, her writing began early and included both fiction and poetry. Kay was the kid with a gift for language who worked on the high school newspaper and literary magazine. That work earned her a college journalism scholarship.

Kay has a bachelor's degree from North Dakota State University and a master's from UCLA. As an editor and writer for academic publications at UCLA, her published writing included both interviews and straight reporting. Kay's poetry has been published in journals and the CWC *Literary Review*. She has almost finished writing a YA novel which she started during the pandemic. If she'd known novels were so much fun to write, she says she would have started sooner. Now, though, she is pleased to be sharing some of her poetry with you.

Home

Matt Tracy
Central Coast Writers

Jenny and I were parked down the street from her mom and dad's house. "I wrote to my dad's parents in Chicago," I said into the silence of my truck. We had opened the windows a crack, so we didn't steam them up with our breath, and the wind from the ocean brought a fresh oyster-seaweed scent through the cab. "They said they'd be okay with me coming to visit. I've never met them. I want to surprise them with my great grandma's watch."

Jenny snuggled into me on the bench seat, so her head rested on my shoulder, and she put her foot up on the passenger door. "You never visited when you were a kid?"

"No. We were living hand to mouth in that little cabin, and I don't think it was in our budget."

Sitting side by side like that, with both of us looking out at the mist in the trees, it was like we were talking into the space of the truck more than to each other. The sentences came slowly when there were enough words, like water drops building up, then falling off the end of a branch. After a moment, she asked, "They didn't come to your dad's funeral?"

"We didn't have a funeral. They didn't send his body home. I think they buried him at sea. We didn't go to Chicago afterward either." She waited for me to continue. "I was a kid, so I didn't think about it much. My mom and I retreated into our own ways of dealing with what had happened, and we kept on living our lives. Besides, it was wartime, and people weren't traveling much."

She took my hand in hers and rubbed my palm for a moment. "What makes you want to go now, besides delivering the watch?"

"They're all the family I have." I kissed behind her ear, my nose in her hair, breathing in her honey butter smell, my lips touching the softness of her skin there at the top of her neck. "My mom's parents are gone. My mom and dad are gone. I have a craving for family. I should understand where I came from and who my ancestors are. If I meet my grandparents, maybe I'll know my dad better, and I might understand myself more."

"I get it." She reached back and moved her hair to the side, then tilted her head so I could more easily kiss her neck. "The memories I have of my grandma teaching me to crochet or my grandpa and me kicking a pinecone on the way home from a walk. . . those are part of what makes me who I am now. Not knowing those people must feel like a missing part of you."

"Yeah, there's a hole where my parents used to be. It's gotten smaller with time, but it doesn't go away. Maybe my grandparents would help fill in the hole a bit."

◊ ◊ ◊

It had only been a couple of months since we started dating, but Jenny and I had both said "the L word" to each other. We had been lying side by side in my bed with the morning sun streaming in the window. I had said it first: "I love you."

She didn't respond right away. Then she said, "Give me a moment. I'm just enjoying this feeling." I didn't say anything more as she sat up, turned to face me, got up on her knees in front of me, and looked me squarely in the eyes. Then, drawing out each word so it stood on its own, she said, "I. Love. You."

At first, it was a strange thing to say, but I got used to the sound of it. I knew there was something special happening, and we were basking in its warmth.

At the same time, this contentment scared me. When things got this good, things got taken away. That was how it seemed to work for me. The little voice in the back of my head was telling me that things were too good here. I had to cool it a bit or fate would notice.

I wrapped my arms tighter around her, and we didn't talk for a

while.

◊ ◊ ◊

Later that month, near the end of July, I took some time off work to go to Chicago. Jenny couldn't leave the Mello, the restaurant where she worked. "Besides," she'd said, "this feels like a journey you need to go on by yourself. I'll be here when you get back."

I drove through Reno and Salt Lake City and on into the

Rockies. Mid-morning of the third day, after I had been driving alone with my thoughts for a while, I pulled off the highway onto the gravel parking lot of a low, glass-fronted diner in a small town at 7,000 feet of elevation. It didn't seem like I was very high up except that the gathering clouds getting darker as I traveled were closer than you would expect. I couldn't see the Rocky Mountains, though I knew they were somewhere around.

I parked in front and saw the reflection of my dark blue 1950 Ford pickup in the restaurant's window. It looked like all the others parked there, dusty and dry. I peered through the window at the people inside. I figured I would stand out because I wasn't wearing a cowboy hat. I thought about getting one to have a souvenir of the trip but then decided that those things are better bought with some thought, or they just end up on the top shelf of the closet. I reached for the handle to open the door of the truck and saw a kid about my age standing in the parking lot. He seemed like he was waiting for me to get out of the truck, so I did.

"Hey," he said when I had my feet on the ground. "I saw you're headed east. I wonder if I can catch a ride with you when you get done eating."

His name was Pete. He was my age, but he seemed unsure of what he was doing, and that made him seem young. "Have you eaten?"

He shrugged and looked down. "I ate earlier."

He probably hadn't, with that kind of answer. "I'll take you with me when I go. Let me buy you breakfast or lunch first, whatever it is people eat at this time of the day, so we're on the same schedule." He ate like he hadn't had food in a while. Then we got in the truck and headed east. We hadn't talked much during breakfast. It would have been hard to squeeze many words past the food that was going into him. I did get from him that he was headed to Nebraska, which meant we would be driving together most of the day. Once we got settled in for the ride, I looked over at him. "You headed home?"

"Well, it's home, but it's not where I live. I grew up there. My dad still lives there." Pete was silent for a while. "My mom died. About a month ago. I haven't been back yet. She wasn't sick or anything. I would have thought my dad would die first, with all his smoking, but no."

I didn't know what to say, so I said what people always say.

"I'm sorry for your loss."

"It was a heart thing. Came on suddenly." He looked out the window for a bit. Then, he asked me what I did in California, and I told him about the quiet green dampness of the forests in the morning before we cut them down. He took a deep breath and let it out. "I don't know why for certain I'm going back. My mom isn't there anymore, and I haven't gotten along with my dad for a long time." We both watched a man on a horse as we went past. He was moving a herd of brown and white cows through a metal gate, waving his hat to keep them moving. "I already missed the funeral." Pete messed with the brim of his hat for a bit, turning it around in a circle in his hands. "There doesn't seem to be any reason to go there now. I'm not looking forward to being in the same house with my dad again."

We talked about girlfriends. He was hanging out with a blond girl named Sally who was a bit wild but was a lot of fun. I told him about Jenny and how I knew her a little from high school, and how we had run into each other way up in Northern California, where neither of us had any reason to be, and how it had become so obvious so fast to both of us that we were meant to be together.

I turned on the radio and tried to find a station, but there didn't seem to be much out there in the middle of the foothills that were smoothing out into prairies. Pete shook his head and swallowed hard, then he started talking again. "It got to the point before I left where all my dad did was tell me what I was doing wrong. That's why I haven't been there in a couple of years. My dad would start telling me how I was screwing up, and my mom would tell him to give me a chance, then he would start telling her how her son was wasting his life away, forgetting that I was his son too, and the fight would be on. One day I just left. I should have at least visited."

I was silent for a moment before I turned to him. "It's hard to know what's right when you're in the middle of living it." I found a station on the radio. It wasn't coming in strong, but he tried to sing along with a song he knew.

When the song ended, he said, "It wasn't always like that. My dad used to take me hunting, and I would help him when he was fixing things around the house." He stopped talking again and seemed to be thinking. I adjusted the wind wing, so we got a bit more breeze through the cab. He cracked his wind wing a little to let the air flow across. Then he looked over at me and said, "I know what you're going to say. It might be me who changed, not my dad." He scratched his head. "I know I wasn't the perfect son. What kid is? But I wasn't as bad as my dad kept saying. There were a couple of years there where I couldn't do anything right as far as he was concerned."

I said something stupid like, "It's hard to believe parents were young once, isn't it?"

He didn't seem to hear me. "What would we even talk about? I'm going back there, and my mom won't be there. I don't know if we have anything to say to each other."

I didn't have the answer to that, so I shared a story about my mom with him. I thought maybe it would help him. I told him about how when she was sick, I kept asking her what I could do for her, and she would never let me do anything. She kept telling me to go out and live my life, but of course I couldn't go out and be a normal teenager with my mom dying at home. Her Friend Katherine took care of so much and made food, and she was amazing, but it left nothing for me to do. I spent a lot of time at the bakery trying to keep that going, but I wanted to do something for my mom.

She loved to read, and she would have a book open anytime she wasn't sleeping. I was doing my homework in the chair in the corner of her room one day when she sighed and put the book down on the covers. "I want to keep going, but it's getting hard to focus my eyes," she said. I asked her if she wanted me to read to her a little. That became what I could do for her.

When I think about it, my heart seizes up because we spent so many hours when I was a kid, in our little house in the redwoods with me sitting on her lap with a book. For almost a month that spring, I read to her until she fell asleep. When she woke up, she would turn to me and say, "Where were we?" and I would start again.

Right before she died, the cancer had become too painful, and the morphine made it so she couldn't keep up with a story anymore. But she liked the sound of my voice, so I kept going. At one point, she opened her eyes and said, "You know, it's more the companionship than anything."

"I wish I could do more," I told her. But I didn't know what.

She said, "You're doing the world for me just by being here, by showing up. It doesn't matter what you say or do."

I suppose I was telling the story as much to myself as to him, not expecting him to gain much from it, but when I dropped him off in front of his dad's house in Cozad, Nebraska, Pete grabbed his bag out of the bed of the truck, then came back to the door he had left open. He leaned into the cab, holding on to the open door. I saw that he had that cotton mouth thick saliva you get when you're about to cry, but you're trying not to. "I'm going to show up," he said. "I'm going to show up and see what happens after that." I watched him until he walked up to the front door of the house and opened it without knocking.

◊ ◊ ◊

Late the next day, I stopped at a motel a couple hundred miles from Chicago. I called my grandparents from a pay phone outside the office to let them know I'd be arriving the next afternoon.

They met me at the door of their wide brick house in a neighborhood of low, prosperous-looking houses surrounded by manicured grass and leafy trees. They were dressed like they were going to church. He was in a suit and tie, and she was in a solid-colored dress with a collar and a belt. They stood behind the screen door, just looking at me. When it became clear that they weren't going to talk first, I said, "I'm Van."

My grandfather pushed open the screen door and said, "I'm Calvin, and this is Maeve. Pleased to meet you." I put out my hand, then pulled it back when he didn't respond. After a pause, Calvin offered his, and I shook his hard, dry hand.

They showed me into their front room. The curtains were drawn, so it was in semi-darkness. The coolness should have felt good after the heat of the day. Instead, the room felt like it reflected their attitudes toward me. I sat on the edge of the embroidered chair with carved wooden arms under my elbows and sipped my glass of tap water without ice.

Calvin finally spoke. "Norman was always going off on his own without thinking about what the consequences would be." His face turned red as he said it, like he would pound on the side table at any moment. "It seemed like he never thought about what might happen past the very next moment. Lord knows we tried. We gave him all the benefits we never had, and he never seemed to notice." His eyes got soft and moist, and for a moment I felt sorry for him. "Then he took off to the other side of the country without so much as a backward glance." As he finished his sentence, his stone face came back up. "That girl, from the reservation. She put those ideas in his head."

Maeve leaned forward. "He was a good kid for most of his life growing up, but he stopped listening to us as he got older. Then he met Ruth, and it seemed like they decided between them to discard everything we had to say and all we held as important. We warned him that her people thought differently, but hormones took over. You know Ruth dragged him away to California and the native life in the forest there as soon as she could, don't you?"

My fantasy of a warm grandmother giving me cookies and hugs was fading. I forced myself to smile at her. "I didn't know that. I knew my mom was raised on a reservation, but I thought she went to school here in Chicago."

"She did. That's where they met. We even told Norman that we were okay with him dating her. We just pointed out the possible problems." Calvin peered over his glasses at me. "So, what are you out here for?"

"Family." As I said the word, I was doubting that I would find it. "I lost both my mom and dad, and it's like I'm missing an important part of me. I thought I would meet you all. I'm out in the world on my own without much of a base." I took a breath. I didn't want to say what I had been practicing as I drove across the country. It didn't seem to fit. But I had to say it. "At least, if I have family behind me, I know where I came from."

Maeve frowned. "You know we don't have extra money."

This was getting worse by the moment. How could they think I was asking for money? "No, that's not why I'm here. Sure, I'm poor, but I'm a kid, so that's expected." Maybe I needed to try a little harder. "Would you tell me a little about what my dad was like when he was little?"

Maeve shrugged. "He was just a normal kid until he got to be older. That was when he started to get ideas in his head."

The questions that I had been storing up in my head the whole trip across country came spilling out one after the other: "What did he do when he was a kid? What do you mean by normal? What did he enjoy doing when he was young?"

Calvin rubbed his nose as he thought. "He was obedient. He got his schoolwork done and did what we told him to. I almost never had to use the belt on him. He ate what we put in front of him and did his chores as he was supposed to."

I looked around at the living room walls. "Do you have some photographs of the family from when he was little?"

Calvin shook his head. "We weren't much on taking pictures. We have the ones they took in church that one time." He got up and walked over to a credenza and opened a drawer. As he handed me a pile of old photographs, he said, "There should be some pictures of your dad in there." When he sat back down in his chair across from me, both of his feet were on the floor, and his hands were on his knees. I felt like he was waiting for me to be done. There weren't any normal photos of a kid playing on a bike or opening a present at Christmas. All the pictures were posed, stiff. *I wonder if Dad was adopted. How did he come from this?*

After a while, I asked to use the bathroom, and they directed me down a hallway. When I came back into the front room, Calvin stood up and said, "This has been nice meeting you, but it's getting toward our afternoon rest time. We don't do well if we miss it. Let me show you to the door." I reached into my pocket and touched the watch Mom had given me to pass on. I pulled my hand back out, empty. Calvin reached for the edge of the door behind me and closed it quietly when I was outside.

I trudged down the concrete steps toward my truck, staring at the ground, the gray fog of sadness twisted the tightness around my eyes with its icy fingers. What my grandparents said made me doubt what I remembered of my parents. But I grabbed my own memories back and told myself they were real. My dad was warm and slow and caring, and my mom was thoughtful and inclusive. I knew my parents. They didn't.

I had driven a long way trying to find family to help replace what I had lost, and their bitterness had tried to take away the scraps of memories I had. I stood there holding my truck's door handle. I couldn't bring myself to open the door right away and get in. I had been stupid for placing so much hope with the two of them. And I had a long trip ahead of me to think about what a waste of time it was.

◊ ◊ ◊

The road from Chicago to California passed through Iowa, and a bit to the north of it was Sloan, Iowa, and the cemetery where Mom's parents were buried. The Tupperware container holding Mom's ashes that I had been carrying with me since I left Oakland was in a brown paper grocery bag on the floor on the passenger side of the truck. It had migrated from my backpack as I carried it hitchhiking, to the top shelf of my closet in the apartment I shared with Al. I had put it on top of my suitcase on my bed as I packed for this trip so I wouldn't forget it, and when I was loading the car, I stuck it behind the seat of the truck for a while.

I met the guy in charge of the cemetery at the funeral home downtown. I had called ahead, and he'd said I could bring her ashes to be buried beside the graves of her mom and dad. I hadn't told him I wanted to dig her grave. In his office, I reached into the paper bag and held up the jar-shaped container her ashes were in. "I brought my own post-hole digger. I bought it in the hardware store before I came here."

He leaned back in his leather chair, grabbed his nose between his thumb and the knuckle of his forefinger, and stared at me for a moment. "I've never had anyone want to dig a grave." Then he sighed. "I can't see what it would hurt."

"It just feels like something I need to do."

He reached behind him for a sheet of paper and set it on his desk. He leaned forward and pointed with the same knuckle. "Here's where they would be. You'll have to search a bit. Dig between the two headstones and a little in front. You won't hit anything there. Go as deep as the posthole digger will reach."

After he gave me directions to the cemetery, I thanked him and got back in my truck. I drove through town with the windows open, breathing in the smell of rain on hot asphalt, dry and damp at the same time, from the squall that had passed while I was inside. I drove past pickup trucks parked on gravel driveways and a low, yellow-brick Baptist church with a sign advertising Sunday school in plastic letters. Out near the railroad tracks, I passed a line of grain silos that rose gray and solid above me. The road continued out of town alongside the tracks until I turned across them onto a gravel road between green walls of corn made dusty by the cars driving by. The cemetery was a square patch of grass, about an acre in size, surrounded by tall green stalks like a garden wall.

I parked and walked out onto the lawn through the damp grass. The smell of corn was all around me. It didn't smell like grass as I had thought it would. It smelled like fresh corn, like ears of corn waiting to be eaten. I wandered in and out of headstones until I found my grandparents' graves. I stood and gazed around at the flat mown grass, and the headstones, and the corn all around me, six feet tall and blank green. My perspective shifted for a moment, and I felt like I was in a hole dug in the middle of the cornfield, like a grave. Then it shifted back, and I was on level ground. There was no sound but the buzz of cicadas. A breeze came up, and the corn rustled, scraping like a broom sweeping concrete, and the cicadas quieted or were drowned out by the sound of the corn.

I laid the canvas tarp he had given me on the grass. The first bite of soil I lifted with the blades of the posthole digger was soft and dark, and it crumbled apart. Worms wriggled in it when I knocked the handles together to drop the dirt on the tarp. Three feet down, it was the same, without the worms. When my wrists hit the grass as I pulled the last of the dirt out of the hole, the soil still seemed like it would grow anything.

Along with the tarp, the funeral director had given me a steel rod about six feet long. It was shaped like a nail that a giant would use to build his house. He called it a "toothpick," and he told me to use the head of it to tamp down the dirt as I put it back in. I couldn't figure out how to lower the ashes into the hole with care, so I lined the container up with the hole I had dug and dropped it in. I used the toothpick to make sure it was all the way to the bottom.

I stood over the hole for a minute, in the afternoon's quiet, thinking about what to say. I took a deep breath, and the words flowed out. "You were a good mom. I felt safe. Things were right then, the three of us together in our cabin. I think even a kid can know that." I blinked, and a tear fell out. "And after Dad was gone, you and I took care of each other. Yeah, you took care of me more than I took care of you, but we did help each other. I appreciate that. We became a team. I miss you. I miss so many things about you." I was crying, but I didn't wipe the tears away. I just let them roll down my cheeks and fall into the hole. "I miss you most now, with Jenny. I wish you could have met her. You would have liked her. You two would have liked each other. You would have laughed with her."

I asked myself if there was anything I wanted to tell her I hadn't said when she was alive, and the only thing that came to mind was, "I'm sorry I didn't follow your directions. You must have known what Dad's parents were like, but you had hope." I dropped her diamond watch in the hole with her ashes. "I love you, Mom." Then, I put the first scoop of dirt on top.

In Eureka, before I left, I had bought a granite stone, like a stepping stone, and had it engraved with her name and the dates of her life. After I had filled and tamped and filled and tamped and all the dirt was back in the hole, I cut a square out of the grass and fitted the stone into it. Then I turned into the wind, breathed in the corn on the wind, and walked back to the truck.

Matt Tracy's writing career started late. He earned an engineering degree, then an MBA, did oceanographic work on the sea ice north of Alaska, and started an energy-efficient lighting business. After he retired, during COVID, he finished and self-published the book on happiness titled *Happy Here and Now* that he had been chunking away at for years. Now he's trying to sell his debut novel and working on another.

The first time he admitted he was a writer was when the ranger at the gate of Yosemite asked him if he was a lawyer. He replied, "No, why do you think that?"

The ranger leaned out the window and pointed toward the front of Matt's car. "Your license plate is IDGRESS."

It was a moment of truth for Matt, and he thinks he answered correctly. "Yes, that sounds like a lawyer, but I'm an author."

For more information, contact Matt at M2tracy@yahoo.com.

Curly

Nicki Ehrlich
Central Coast Writers

Every January a false spring breezes through the Pacific Northwest islands. Great Blue Herons, resting on the docks, spread their wings like drying umbrellas. The giant feathered sentries squawk meager complaints before taking to the air—prehistoric things, defying gravity.

I had thought about buying a house a few years back. When I moved up to assistant editor, my job situation felt stable, and a year-long romance begged for a place to call home. But I wrote for a sailing magazine. I wanted to be on the water. A boat I could live aboard made more sense to me. It made no sense to Cynthia. Mocking my career, she said living on a boat was a metaphor for the instability of our relationship. But the boat stayed afloat even as our relationship sank.

When the magazine went under all I had left was the boat, a laptop, and a couple of local bylines. I was one of two liveaboards at the marina, a kind of unpaid security. My recently disabled car now made pizza delivery impossible. I considered myself "between jobs" but there wasn't another on the horizon. My laptop escorted me from cockpit to cabin as I continued to submit stories and queries, collecting scores of rejections.

Other boats at my marina saw their owners only on weekends and holidays, and a sad few languished, unkempt, tethered by moldy dock lines. Sometimes, at night, when no one was around, I'd take my bucket and scrub brush, trespass on their decks, and scrub away the neglect. It's easy to personify these hunks of wood and fiberglass. They float on calm water, dance when the wind comes up, and damned if I don't see expressions on their bows. I never tell anyone what I can see. I'm not crazy, just sensitive.

The other liveaboard was a man called Hawk. He lived on his forty-something-foot power boat with his dog, Curly. The boat was often out, so Hawk and I rarely spoke, which was fine with me. When moored in its slip, the boat entertained many a visitor. I'd watch them climb aboard and duck into the cabin to escape the creeping fog or relentless rains. During a week or two of spring-like weather, they might surface with a drink in hand, grimacing at the sunshine as if it were an enemy. But they were quiet. Now and then I thought about mentioning the activity to Cynthia as an excuse to talk to her. But too much time had passed. I didn't want to give her any more reason to denigrate my situation, and I was more concerned with Curly.

His doghouse sat next to the slip's locked dock box, so when the boat left him behind, he had a place to stay. Each slip included a fiberglass storage chest bolted to the corner of the dock. They were just big enough for extra anchors, a hose, and cleaning supplies. Most of the boat owners didn't lock them because there was nothing of much value there and because, as boating communities go, this one had proven safe. And we had Curly. The dog seemed to enjoy his autonomy.

I was learning to enjoy mine. When Cynthia left, she took her friends with her. "Left" isn't the right word, as she never actually lived with me. She was a cop from a family of cops who never met me. She never understood *the boat thing* and, brave as she was, she feared making our relationship public. She asked me to understand, and I tried, but she needed to be right more than I needed company.

Curly wasn't threatening, but he possessed that uncanny canine awareness. He resembled a Portuguese water dog, probably not pure-bred, but his ripply coat matched the name. Regularly he'd bound off his boat onto the dock, wearing a yellow life vest. I didn't quite understand why a natural swimmer would need a life vest, but since the man never put a leash on that dog, I supposed the color of it might protect him on land as much as in the water. I also couldn't understand why someone living on a boat would have a dog. I love dogs, but there's precious little room to move on a thirty-foot sailboat. Keeping a dog and a boat clean and orderly would be more of a challenge than either my mild case of OCD or the dog could tolerate. The convenience of land seemed necessary to a dog. Being at sea would complicate their nature.

And though I love them, fear of dogs nuzzled its way into my life experience during that short-lived pizza delivery time. A sultry Afghan hound had answered the door, her person saying, "Don't worry, she doesn't bite." Maybe she only bit when a stranger took money from her person because that's when she bit me. She barely broke the skin, but my confidence in human-canine trust was cut to the bone.

I didn't pet Curly and he knew to stay off my boat. We carried on cordial conversations, and he took to following me around town when he got left behind. People often thought he belonged to me, and I tired of correcting them. I imagined we shared the same political views, biases, and philosophies, all wound up in our windblown curly tresses.

Curly and I talked about the importance of picking the right friends. Mornings when he was left behind, he'd follow me up the dock to the coffee shop across the road from the marina.

He'd wag his tail at anyone we passed. Some would call him by name.

"You're a little too friendly, you know. You should be more careful with people." He seemed to like the sound of my voice.

I'd survey the parking lot as we walked through, keeping an eye out for any cars I didn't recognize. Posted signs denoted owners and guests only, but tourists often took advantage of free parking. I'd forgotten it was January, not exactly tourist season, though the unseasonably sun-kissed breeze suggested May.

I stopped in the middle of the mostly empty lot. My fading blue Honda looked dejected in its designated space. Curly stopped next to me, hoping for more conversation. "They don't all want to pet and coddle you," I told him. He seemed to agree. His tail moved sporadically as if he were thinking twice about wagging it at all. He squeaked a suppressed whine and we continued to the coffee shop where he disappeared behind the building.

Boat manuals tell you it's prudent to keep a diesel engine full to guard against condensation. But mostly I did it knowing island winds could never be trusted to fill sails. When breezes blew, they were often in the wrong direction. Sure, sailing was fun for the sake of sailing, but if you wanted to get anywhere, an engine and fuel were necessary. Besides, the fuel dock proved the best courier for local news. And I liked talking with Hans.

I started the engine, untied the lines, and backed out of the slip to make the short trip to the fuel dock. Hans had been living on his boat there and managing the small store for years. We'd discuss boat maintenance and the god-awful tourists the island village relied on.

I liked my friends quiet but knowledgeable, witty—clever, not stupid—and able to be serious when appropriate. Maybe a little aloof. I didn't mind being friendly, but I didn't want to hug everyone. Hans and Curly were good friends to me.

I putted past the end of my dock, noticing Curly's boat was gone again. The dog sat near his house, looking past the empty slip, staring out to sea, the poster pooch of loyalty. He wasn't wearing his life vest.

He tilted his head, and I couldn't help but wave to him, remembering too late that waving was the signal his owner used for "dive." The dog took a running leap off the end of the dock, soaring through the air like a flying squirrel before splashing down and paddling toward the stern of my boat. I throttled back, locked the wheel, and lowered the swim ladder, promptly realizing how stupid it was to think a dog could climb it.

I remembered watching Curly and his owner at the dock, the man throwing a florescent orange training dummy, Curly retrieving it. As the dog delivered the dummy, the man would reach over and put his hand behind the dog's head, providing leverage I'd guessed, for pulling himself up onto the dock. I had been intrigued watching them do this repeatedly until the man got tired or bored. Curly could have continued for hours.

The closer the dog paddled, the more I panicked. Maybe I could throw a rope over him. No time—Curly arrived at the ladder. He slapped his paws on a rung and tried pushing himself up. I leaned over him, reaching my hand behind his head as I'd seen his owner do. Surprising both of us, there he stood, as if birthed from the sea, dripping in my cockpit. Our eyes met and I swear he smiled before shivering thanks and showering saltwater all over my clean boat. And me.

At the fuel dock Hans flipped the lever on the diesel tank and brought the hose over to where I had tied up and was removing the fuel cap. "Is that Curly?"

I looked at the wet mop of a creature sitting proudly on my boat, looked back at Hans, and simply raised my eyebrows.

"Got left behind again, eh?"

"Yeah. I don't get it. The guy seems to love the dog but doesn't think it's weird to leave him behind."

"Everybody in town knows Curly. He comes around for food sometimes." Hans nodded down the dock. "But usually by land." He shrugged. "It's an island, where's he gonna go?"

I knew Hans was talking about the dog, but I remembered one of my last conversations with Cynthia. *"How do you expect to get anywhere on this island?"* For me it was the perfect place to write. But she wanted to climb the ladder of law enforcement. She hadn't thought my position at the magazine lucrative, and when the publication went belly up, her point was proven. In our limited social situations, when I'd tell listeners about my newest manuscript, Cynthia's eyes would roll.

"You okay?" Hans stared at me. Pungent diesel fumes mixed with the salty air as I heard the fuel rise to the top of the tank. I released the handle just before any chance of overflow onto my deck or into the pristine bay. Curly huffed and lay down. I wondered if he knew we'd been talking about him or if he was reading my mind.

I looked at Hans. "Yeah." Curly sighed, reminding me the conversation was about him. "I've always tried to keep him off my boat, but he dove in and swam to me on my way over here. I wasn't sure what to do, so here he is."

Hans had been kneeling by the boat and stood when I handed him the fuel nozzle. This seemed to be another signal to Curly. He perked up and stood, looked at me and pawed the deck. I cringed at the sound of scratched gelcoat.

"Hey, buddy," I pleaded, "no scratches—" He jumped off the boat and trotted down the dock. "Curly!"

"He'll be okay," said Hans.

I exhaled a smile at Hans. I knew the dog got by on his own, but I felt responsible for him since I had brought him to this side of the harbor. Even though it was his idea.

"Going out?" asked Hans.

I looked around at the bright bay, suspicious of the temporary sunshine, still feeling the laziness of winter. Gulls flew over the opposite shore, scouting some secret left awash by low tide. A couple of crows brought my attention back to the fuel dock. Hopping along the covered slips, their clawed feet clicking on the metal made me wince. "Naw."

Hans smirked and chuckled to himself. "Not quite spring yet, is it," he said, understanding.

"Are we turning into those lazy sailors who would rather sit at the dock than raise a sail?" I asked. Hans glanced at his own boat, but didn't confirm or deny.

I often felt Hans and I each wanted to know more about the other but were wary of getting too close. He met a lot of people at the fuel dock, but I never noticed him with anyone in particular. Some people intentionally live on an island, and I respected his privacy.

Back in my slip, I finished off a cleat hitch and heard footsteps coming down the dock. There's a difference in the sound of rubber-soled boat shoes and the hard-soled shoes of a businessman. The dark-suited pair of men I saw walking past were either Mormon missionaries or plainclothes police. I wondered what either would be doing on the docks. They saw me, nodded, and kept walking. One of the men glanced back over his shoulder, sweeping my boat with the scrutiny of a cop. I looked up the dock toward the parking lot, straining to see what cars might be there now, realizing I was looking for Cynthia's.

I watched the men walk to the end of the dock where Curly's missing boat should be. Curly wasn't back from town yet, and the men stood at the slip, inspecting the bay. The memory of Curly doing the same made me laugh, which I didn't mean to do out loud. When the two turned back toward me I cleared my throat, looked down as if checking my lines, and opened the lid of my dock box, blocking them from sight.

When I lowered the lid, I noticed the two men jiggling a lock on the box behind Curly's doghouse. If they hadn't been in suits, I would have questioned their intentions, but something made me shy away from any confrontation with these two.

I heard Curly's paws tick-ticking down the dock before I saw him. He stopped dead in front of my boat and let out a muffled woof at the trespassers. One of the men took a few steps toward the dog, bending down and putting a hand out. "It's okay there, boy. Hey, what's your name?"

"Woof." Curly was a dog of few words.

"Nice looking dog. Is he yours?" the man asked me. As he stood, the wind caught his jacket revealing a shoulder holster. I recognized it as police issue, like Cynthia wore when she worked for Seattle PD. I never got used to her ease with firearms.

I looked at Curly, who was looking back and forth between the two men and me, making a plan of his own. "Um—not really," I said.

Curly intended to prove me wrong, trotting over to my boat step and climbing aboard. I glared at him while he circled into a comfortable position, wheezed a sigh, and pretended to fall asleep. "We're just—friends." I knew guilt by association and I still didn't know who these guys really were.

"Do you know who lives in the slip at the end of the dock?" the man asked.

I'd binged on cop shows after Cynthia left, so knew to reply with a question. "Who wants to know?"

The man reached into his jacket pocket and pulled out ID. Not police, but FBI. His partner walked up behind him as he introduced them both.

What is it that makes us feel guilty whenever confronted by authority? I found myself glancing toward the parking lot again. Did these two know Cynthia? We still talked now and then, but the relationship was over. I had nothing to hide. I didn't think they'd be interested in the possibility that I stole Curly. I hadn't. Had I?

"I just know him as 'Hawk,'" I said. "The dock master would have more information, I would think."

"Yeah, he doesn't seem to be in the office. He seems to be out of the office every time we come around." He looked sideways at me. "Your name is?"

I looked sideways back at him. "Jess—Jessica Riley."

Curly was coiled on the seat in the shade of the dodger, feigning sleep, but his eyes were open. Under his raised brow his watchfulness ping-ponged between me and these men.

"You live here?" man number one asked.

"I do."

"When that boat's in, is there much activity? People coming and going? Partying and such?"

"They keep pretty quiet when they're here." I looked at Curly. He didn't want me to say too much. "They're gone a lot." I squinted at the sky. "Weather's been nice."

The man extracted a business card from his wallet. He put a foot on the boat step and leaned over to hand the card to me. Curly growled, though he may have been dreaming, as his eyes were closed now. The sound slowed the man's movements but didn't stop him. "Wonder if you might give me a call when the boat comes back."

"Can I ask why?" I took the card from him.

"Just want to talk to Mr.—Hawk."

The other man looked at my boat, scrutinizing its rigging like a surveyor. "Nice boat," he said.

"Thanks," I said. It was a nice boat: clean white decks, varnished teak trim, a dark blue hull, blue canvas dodger and sail cover. The lines coiled neatly. A breeze ruffled Curly's coat, drawing my attention to muddy paw prints. A tuft of fur blew over the side. I looked back at the compliment and shrugged a fake smile.

"We'll hope to hear from you," said man number one. Man number two nodded. "Be safe," he said.

Safe from what, I wondered. I put the card in my pocket without looking at it. The men walked up the ramp to the parking lot. They stood by their car for a while and I thought I saw them looking at mine. I imagined them laughing. They got in their car and drove off.

I went below to fix dinner. One-pan meals were obligatory on a boat, so tonight's was mac and cheese. Almost every night's was mac and cheese, though sometimes with tuna or burger or veggies. That was all the variation I needed. As daylight faded, I scooped a serving into a bowl, once again wondering why I didn't just eat out of the pot.

I felt the boat rock as Curly jumped off onto the dock. While considering new ways to keep him off my boat, I heard the engine and felt the wake of my neighbor returning. Hawk's voice, praising Curly for his greeting, warmed my heart and simultaneously pissed me off. The two seemed to have a good relationship, but how much abandonment could one dog take?

The next morning, I woke to a knock on my boat. Fiberglass has a different ring to it when someone knocks. It's a happy sound. Or maybe it's just that living on a boat is more solitary, so a knock sounds like a friend. I looked out the port. Cynthia. I hadn't seen her for months and she wasn't in uniform. I waved her aboard and felt the familiar shift of the boat while I opened the hatch.

"Hey, Cyn," I said. "Business or pleasure?"

"Hey," she said back. "It's good to see you. But it's business, actually. Well, mostly."

I noticed she was dressed professionally—slacks and a jacket, not her usual off-hours jeans and sweater. Her attire always dictated how we could be together. When she wore her uniform, it was hands off. The attitude was partly protection of her job and family, and partly a simple superiority, something she could switch on and off. When she dressed casually, we could be ourselves. Torn jeans and a gray wool sweater would set her laughter free. Today's wardrobe fell somewhere in between.

"Did you change jobs?" I asked.

"Promotion. Made detective last month. Seattle and beyond, now," she said.

"Wow." I was happy for her; concerned for me, though I wasn't sure why. "Coffee?" She followed me into the boat.

"I wanted to let you know about your neighbor, Mr. Hawkins." Her eyes combed the boat's cabin. Not much to see, yet her search seemed thorough, her glance interrogating. I understood how she had made detective.

"Hawkins. You mean Hawk?" I put on the kettle.

"Yes, real name Samuel Hawkins. Drug dealer extraordinaire." She watched my face as she continued. "We arrested him at Point Roberts early this morning." She waited for a reaction.

The one I gave her had nothing to do with Hawk or me. "Curly. Where's Curly?"

She cocked her head at my question, her smooth shoulder-length locks flopped at her collar. Her golden hair complimented the navy pinstriped jacket. "Who's Curly?"

I removed the kettle from the burner just before it started to whistle and poured hot water over the coffee filters. "The dog that lives on that boat."

Cynthia shook her head. "We picked up Mr. Hawkins and friends. No dog."

I nodded, trying to remember when I last saw Curly. "Okay." I handed Cynthia her coffee. Black.

"He didn't say anything about a dog." She took a sip.

"Hmm." I contemplated my cup, deciding to keep Curly out of the conversation. "How long have you known about this guy?" As the words tripped out of my mouth, I remembered the times I'd felt suspicious. My face flushed.

"We've been watching him quite a while. The dockmaster was involved as well. We weren't sure who else, so we had to keep it quiet."

"The dockmaster? Bob?" A sweet, grandfatherly man. Curly

liked him and would often sit in the office keeping him company. Bob always made sure the dog was comfortable in his life jacket, adjusting buckles and such. He said he knew Curly could swim, but thought it prudent.

Cynthia nodded and blew the steam from her mug. Clearly, she was holding back. But I anticipated her next words. She smiled and blushed. "We had to be sure you weren't involved. We thought you might be."

"You thought what?" I started to laugh but was afraid it might make me appear guilty.

"You do go back and forth to Canada a lot. You told me one time you skipped customs—"

"Did you have me followed?" I didn't wait for her to answer. "I told you I wasn't sure I needed to go through customs because I hadn't left the boat—and—that was a long time ago."

"Right." Her gaze wandered away from me.

Each island held its own uniqueness, but I loved cruising into Canada. Crossing the border changed my attitude. I think it was one of the reasons I lived on a boat instead of in a house, making it easier to have one foot in each country. Cynthia had never understood that.

I couldn't believe she had suspected me of smuggling. I thought she knew me. I'd thought we were still friends. But then owning the suspicions of a cop had come between us before.

"Look, Jess, I know you're not involved." She sipped her coffee. "Besides filling you in about your neighbor, I'm here to apologize for ever thinking you might have been. That guy was distributing dope all over the island and we couldn't figure out how he was doing it without having enlisted multiple helpers. It still isn't making much sense, but at least we've taken him off the streets."

"Like I said, he was gone a lot. But that's what boats do. And Canada's close. That's where cruisers go. Lots of my neighbors—" I stopped, thinking I'd incriminate anyone I mentioned. But I couldn't help wondering who else might be involved.

Cynthia seemed to read my mind. "Just Bob and Mr. Hawkins. You and your other boat neighbors have been cleared."

I felt some relief at that, but an image of Hans came to mind. I tried to suppress the nagging theory, but everyone stopped at Hans's fuel dock.

Cynthia put her empty cup down. "Thanks for the coffee. I'd

better get back to work." She smiled at me, a professional grin. "It was good seeing you again." I wondered if she meant it.

"You, too." I followed her up the companionway steps, feeling strangely guilty. And, once again, like she'd won and I had lost. I wanted to say, 'Stop by any time,' but I didn't. I watched her walk down the dock, climb the ramp to the parking lot, and slip into her black sedan.

As she drove away, a small but pricey motor yacht pulled into an empty slip across from me. Tourists. I wondered who would be working at the office now that Bob had been arrested. I watched as a young couple tied up the boat, teasing each other and talking to someone else on board. I glimpsed the back of someone's head. Flowing silky blond hair fluttered in a slight breeze. The couple laughed. An ire rose in me, maybe just a memory. But a familiar sound of paws trotting down the dock interrupted my jealous judgement.

Curly didn't stop until he reached his dog house. He wore his yellow life jacket. He stood and stared, as he usually did, but only for a moment before he turned and came back to my boat. He sat, like a gentleman, next to my dock box. I looked at my clean boat, the white cockpit newly scoured of any paw prints from yesterday. I remembered Cynthia's balsam scent and wondered if Curly had ever been to a groomer. He watched me, begging permission.

"Oh, okay," I said, and before I got to "okay," Curly had stepped aboard. But instead of coming to me, he walked onto the cabin top and to the bow of the boat.

He looked like some kind of canine figurehead and wagged his tail, staring across at the visitor's boat where an Afghan hound stared back. The blond. Their heads tilted to the side in unison. Curly's tail stopped wagging. Was it jealousy or caution?

The lady dog stood on her bow ogling Curly, but didn't bark. Her tail hung still as she weighed the situation. A breeze fluffed her mane like it might in a movie, giving her a haughty, elite look. She blinked, pointed her long, sharp nose to the air, turned, and sashayed away.

Curly sat to watch her go. When she didn't reappear he huffed, stood, and returned to the cockpit where I was sitting. He started scratching at his life jacket, asking me if I might free him of it. I grimaced but did as he asked. I wondered where the thing had been. Releasing it I realized the jacket contained no form of buoyancy. Stained and worn, it was more like a doggy backpack with zippered pockets on either side. I unzipped one and found an empty plastic bag. I checked the other one; empty.

I heard Cynthia's voice, *"We couldn't figure out how he was doing it—"* I looked at Curly. He panted a couple of times, licked his lips, and closed his mouth as mine fell open. A smile bloomed on my face, one of those uncontrollable grins fed by revelation and showered with joy. They didn't know. *She* didn't know.

I crumpled the jacket and threw it in the cockpit locker where I kept an extra garbage can. I sat down next to Curly and as the boats around us went quiet, he put his head in my lap. My hand found a place behind his ears and stroked the curly coat. It was softer than I thought it would be, a silky spring to it, not at all unpleasant. Cool air drifted by, smelling like rain. Curly and I sat there, together, watching twilight settle.

Nicki Ehrlich is a member of the Central Coast Writers branch of the California Writers Club. Her debut novel, *Ellis River*, won a Benjamin Franklin Award from the Independent Book Publishers Association, was a semi-finalist for the Publishers Weekly Booklife Prize, a finalist for the Eric Hoffer First Horizons Award, and received an Honorable Mention for the Eric Hoffer Grand Prize. She holds a BA in Philosophy/English, and earned a Certificate in Creative Writing from Monterey Peninsula College. She has won awards for her poetry and creative writing, including the Writer's Digest Annual Poetry Awards and the Ray Fabrizio Memorial Award. She is a member of the Independent Book Publishers Association and a certified copyeditor. You can find her on Instagram (nicki ehrlich) and her website, https://nickiehrlich.com.

Resolve[25]

Phillip Rosenburg
Central Coast Writers

The Mojave wind on her cheeks,
the coyote howl in her voice,
the unrelenting August in her eyes.
She knows that here every unlikely

genomic twist finds a way
to unique itself into existence,
stake out its miniscule territory
beneath the merciless sun,

and she will not be denied.
The smart ones burrow deep,
dulling their nails on the decomposed granite.
Eventually, all accounts are brought current,

the marrow consumed, the bones bleached,
the love dispersed. She knows what
was lost sometimes returns: the walking stick
left on that long ago hike, the old wisdom.

What will not return is her old life.
No, she would die here among the lizards
and rattlers, offer up her flesh
to the dark winged raven before going back.

She knows she can fail. She knows
hope beckons, tempts, and abandons.
She believes when her lips are beyond parched,
her canteen and her will long-drained,

---

[25] Previously published in the journal *Luna Arcana*.

a sign will be sent: a comet from Perseus
perhaps or a lumbering desert tortoise
at her door. With luck, a soft spot into which to
burrow will appear.

Whatever it is, it will be just enough
to encourage for one more day
or one more hour her beautiful,
improbable enterprise.

Phillip Rosenberg (aka Rags) is both a songwriter and poet. His first chapbook, *Raised in the Shadow*, was praised by Robert Bly ("They have a certain drive forward into truth") and US Poet Laureate Philip Levine ("Strong signs of a real talent"). He raised two children and sent them to college as a home remodeler in Nashville before moving to Joshua Tree in 2008 and turning his full attention to writing. His poetry has appeared in *Black Moon, Fine Homebuilding Magazine*, The California Writers Club *Literary Review*, and *Hudson View*. His song "I'll Meet You There," co-written with Grammy winner Lyn Langham, was used in the film *Beyond Right and Wrong*. He has lived and worked in Carmel-by-the-Sea since 2021.

Does the Bubble Gum Lose Its Flavor?

(Coming of Age in the Ozarks)
Wanda Sue Parrott
Central Coast Writers

Instead of pitching hay, Bubba lay across a bale while his big sister read sex scenes from *Lady Chatterley's Lover.*

"Shucks!" Bubba blurted when his bubblegum burst.

"Now you done it," Shamie laughed. "I told you to chaw easy."

"I sucked and blowed it soft, but the wad got so big it busted its britches."

Shamie reached for Bubba's chin. "You was getting' excited, wasn't you? I mean, your britches was bustin'—"

"Was not!" Grabbing his own cheek, Bubba stretched the skin tight so Shamie could scrape the thin pink layer of gum from his jaw. It was August 1950 and the steamy Ozarks air buzzed as a brown halo of gnats circled Bubba's pumpkin-colored hair.

"Liar. You was panting hard just like—" Thirteen-year-old Shamie blew a kiss toward eleven-year old Bubba and wagged her sun-bleached braid.

"Panting like what?"

"Just like Pa, when he does it with Ma of a Sairday night. We both heard 'em through the curtain." Shamie pulled Bubba close and ran her tongue over his chin.

"Keep away from me! Whatcha think you're doing?"

"Lickin' the busted bubble to see if it still has taste. Like in that radio song that asks, *'Does the chewing gum lose its flavor on the bedpost overnight?'*"

Moving backward, Bubba asked, "Well, does it lose its flavor?"

"Not sure. Come here, scaredy cat."

"I gotta pitch hay so Pa don't strop me for fiddling around."

"Peter the sissy!" Shamie called Bubba by his given name as he lifted the pitchfork and lit into the haystack. "Stand still." Shamie lunged at Bubba, licked his chin again, and grinned. "By golly, that gum tastes right good."

Bubba was scraping with his thumbnail and wiping gum on his overalls when Farmer Patton's voice yelled from the chicken yard, "Shameen, Peter, you kids in the barn?"

Thrusting the dog-eared novel behind the hay bale, Shamie called, "Out back, Pa." She shot Bubba a look that meant *keep your mouth shut* as she shimmied up the ladder into the barn loft. "Up here, Pa," Shamie called. "I'm helping Bubba with the hay."

"Very well," Farmer Patton said, striding around the corner as Bubba pitched a forkful of dry gold strands into the air toward Shamie. He looked angry. "I've a question I don't suppose you can answer."

"What is it, Pa?" Bubba asked.

"X marked the spot I left a book in the henhouse, where I. . . uh. . . hid it from your ma. It seems to have vanished." Pa's eyes hardened as he glared at Bubba. "Where is it?"

Yow! Bubba thought, imagining the stings of Pa's razor strop on Shamie's legs when he learned the truth. He started to tattle on her, but his mouth salivated the taste of pink bubble gum, so he licked the drool and said, "Pa, did you know that chewing gum don't lose its flavor on the bedpost overnight?"

Wanda Sue Parrott is an 89-year-old member of Central Coast Writers who is living on the Monterey Peninsula for the second time. Back in 1965, when she was still an aspiring writer, she was named Poet Laureate Runner-Up of the Monterey Peninsula by the *Monterey Peninsula Herald.* She has striven to become a Scribe ever since. She says, "I'm a little closer but haven't made it yet. Am not sure I want to. I love the struggling-writer's life and all my wonderful friends! Thank you!"

EAST SIERRA

"... a land that once visited
must be come back to inevitably."
—*Mary Austin*

24 Miles to Earth

Daniel Stallings
East Sierra Ridge Writers

Twenty-four miles to Earth. . .

He didn't feel the fall. Didn't feel anything as a matter of fact. It was like floating. Suspended animation. Out of the bowled window of his space helmet, he saw the edge of the atmosphere swirl beneath him. Then the first fingers of gravity pulled him down.

Twenty-three miles to Earth. . .

The clouds were centuries away from him. He was miles above the tallest thunderhead. He hovered, an ancient Olympian god—Zeus perhaps—surveying the borders of his kingdom. Or perhaps like an alien descending to this strange planet for research. The six to seven billion humans below huddled together like the microbes on his skin.

He drifted, not even sure if there was such a thing as weight up here. He wasn't certain if there was enough air to feel anyway. The only air he knew right now was the kind pumped into his helmet. This feeling of suspension was strange. He felt like a balloon in the Macy's Thanksgiving Day Parade. He recalled watching a movie called *The Brave Little Toaster Goes to Mars* with his six-year-old son. There was a scene where the animated appliances zoomed in their laundry basket spaceship through a sea of colorful balloons, ones that had slipped through children's fingers and continued to rise through space. He was there now—the place where all balloons go when they are freed. After all, a balloon carried him up here. If only his son was here with him. He'd remember that scene too.

Amazing what one can think of when skydiving from the rim of the stratosphere.

There was sudden pressure on his throat as if some invisible doctor checked his pulse. What if he left the capsule too late? He could be adrift in space limbo forever. How much oxygen did he have? Was there enough? Would they be able to rescue him? His lungs pumped faster. He started to wheeze. He had no escape. He was not afraid of heights or wide, open expanses. Not even afraid of falling.

But he loathed feeling closed in. Claustrophobia, they called it.

And a spacesuit was nothing more than a bulky padded cell.

Twenty-two miles to Earth. . .

Breathe, he thought. Do what Doc told you. Look beyond the helmet. Look at the sky below. Although if my shrink had any real idea, he'd know that I'm looking through the sky, a sky that looks almost solid from down there.

And he did look. There was a faint reflection of his face in the glass bowl of the helmet, but it looked more like a ghost. He tried to drown the terror, manifested in that ghost of his face, in the perfect blue of the world ocean that no artist could faithfully reproduce. This space limbo, this world of the cartoon balloons, had some unusual magic to it. Up here, the sky was transparent, a glass dome, and Earth was blue with seas. Down there, the water was clear, colored by the almost solid blue sky. Light was truly the greatest magician of all.

He craned his neck forward, hoping to breach the edge of the window and spot the black, star-tacked darkness looming above him. Just a thread of the universe. Like catching sight of God Almighty. His head swiveled back to the world waiting for him to fall. Now he was a kid pressing his face and hands against the display window of a toy store. He kissed the glass, and the steam from his breath misted over the rainbow delirium of colors, lights, and shapes. He knew he couldn't have it all, but for now, everything—everything his eyes could swallow—belonged to him.

The world was his. Everything his eyes could swallow. He was a little boy pressing his face against the window of Earth.

Twenty miles to Earth. . .

Breathe, said the little shrink in his head. He gasped, his lungs groping for oxygen. He had forgotten to breathe. The view, which had opened like a pop-up book before him, retracted to the convex picture projected onto the glass curve of his helmet. It felt like he was shrinking—no, collapsing—back into his spacesuit. He was back in the padded cell.

There's some Disney ride I remember going on with my son. Soarin' something. They pick you up in this rig and push you toward this huge arching screen that plays a movie. Flying over the landscape. Like hang gliding. Then the film ends, and you are pulled away from the view. It retracts, and all you see is a dim movie screen. The panorama is a parlor trick. That's how I feel right now. I'm being pulled away from the screen.

Except that it wasn't a movie screen. It wasn't Soarin'-

Something-or-Other. Hell, it wasn't even IMAX. It was real. And it was all outside his helmet window.

The only thing separating him and the view was a glass bowl in his helmet.

Eighteen miles to Earth. . .

Glass. Something thin and fragile. Something that shattered so easily when it was dropped on the kitchen floor. Was it even there? Then the visor fogged up, blotting away the detail like a creeping mist on a lake. Earth blurred and softened. Looking through wet gauze. The mist cleared again. And this slim little film of nothing was the shield for his face. Of course, it was "space glass," which, in that 1960s Space Race sort of attitude, gave it the illusion of indestructibility.

But even Titanics sink.

Right now, he felt he could punch a hole right through the helmet, and it would pop as cleanly as a bubble. Explosive decompression. And he'd still fall to Earth in record time.

If I die up here, I'm taking home a piece of the sky.

Now he wondered if there was some Chicken Little person watching him fall and squawking that the sky was falling. In a way, it was. Only he was bringing the sky home to his son. If only he had thought of that sooner. He could have turned around and caught a star. That would be something special. Maybe two stars. One for his son and one for his wife.

Still, he kept falling, catching the sky in his eyes.

Sixteen miles to Earth. . .

What would he say to all those people when he landed? The pulse checker returned, now stage fright instead of claustrophobia. Slipping on this suit brought him to the mythical pantheon of astronauts. People like Neil Armstrong, Buzz Aldrin, and Sally Ride. People you dream of becoming. One of the top three choices for careers by kids in elementary school. The rare. The few. The exalted.

History. He was making history. You don't think about that when you spend five years planning for this moment. It's not until it happens, when you are alone with your thoughts and the panorama below you, that you consider the hard facts of what you were doing. Making history. First man to skydive from the edge of the troposphere. First time that the sound barrier was broken with a human body. Firsts. Lots of firsts.

And yet all that mattered to him at this moment were a collection of other firsts: his first kiss with his wife, his son's first steps, the first time his son said "Dadda."

But what would he say when his toes touched the ground again? Something profound. At least he hoped it would be profound. Like Neil Armstrong. . . "One small step for man. One giant leap for mankind." Giant leap all right. This was one hell of a leap. Or maybe something less poetic. Perhaps more like Yuri Gagarin, first man to orbit the earth—indeed, the first human in outer space—when he parachuted into the farmer's field in his orange suit and white helmet, looking more like a Martian than a man.

Have you come from outer space?

Why yes, I have.

What would he say when he shook the reporters' hands?

"I come in peace!"

Or even worse:

"I just thought I would drop in."

Fourteen miles to Earth. . .

He could see the clouds now. Few where he planned to land, but a couple off in the distance. A distance that was probably hundreds of miles down there. Much farther than the measly twenty-four he did up here. Twenty-four miles. Easily burned through by a car. Even shorter than a marathon in the Olympic Games. And yet, up here, twenty-four miles equaled emotional eons.

Time, distance, and light were mythical constructs up here.

How would he describe everything that his eyes could swallow? It would be the most important question on everyone's mind. What's it like up there? How could he possibly describe the glass-like perfection of the sky? How could he explain that feeling of suspended animation? How could he describe the padded cell and the Greater-Than-IMAX picture show?

He now understood why men and women who live through moments like this always seemed to grope for superlative adjectives. One word to capture a rainbow of emotions. And he understood why words like "magnificent," "breathtaking," and "awe-inspiring" never really seemed to describe anything. They couldn't. They were flawed. He wasn't even sure if he knew any better ten-dollar words. There was no way to describe it all.

Wait. He lied. There was one word.

Indescribable.

A cop-out, yes, but the truth. There was no way to describe it without seeing it yourself. So many disparate images came into his head as he fell: *The Brave Little Toaster Goes to Mars*, Macy's Thanksgiving Day Parade, Olympian gods, aliens, Disney rides, IMAX, Chicken Little, the kid at the toy store window. . .

They all fit together up here. And he realized that it wouldn't mean anything to anyone else. It was his personal collection of images. They made sense only to him. Another person in the same situation would see things differently. Even if he could repeat this mission, it wouldn't be the same. This was the first time. Firsts were the important ones. Firsts had magic.

And if he had to settle his ten dollars on a word, he'd choose "memorable." That's what it did. Stirred memories. Made new ones.

The sky opened before him again. He was free from his padded cell.

Twelve miles to Earth. . .

And he began tumbling.

It was a gentle agitation, certainly nothing like being inside the tumbler in a dryer. He was graceful, balletic, and almost poetic in his slow somersaults. It was his skydiving training. A little flair for the folks down below. It was second nature to him. Up here, the air was loose. You didn't feel it ripple and eddy around you. It was pure freedom.

He plummeted through the edge of the troposphere, punching out his own man-sized hole in the ozone layer.

Oh God. . . I'm flying! He spun in his spacesuit, relishing his liberation from mental solitary confinement. His imagination treated him with another memory, this time from his childhood. He was five or six, maybe even younger than that. His father liked to pick him up and swing him back and forth through the air. He would hold his arms out, the wings of a human airplane, feeling the wind rush over him in huge sheets. Air was fluid down there. He loved the sensation of lift, of being ushered by the wind higher and higher. He always forgot about the strong supports of his dad's arms. Dad just let him go, and he was free to soar over the neighborhood, a young bird pushed out of the nest.

The memory melted into a new dream. He took his father's place and taught his son the secret of flight. Maybe one day his little boy could catch his own piece of the sky.

Ten miles to Earth . . .

Ease up, spoke the voice of his therapist. You're going to hit thicker air soon. Resume your neutral position. Stop tumbling.

But a tiny sound in his heart, the voice of his young son with his missing front teeth, begged him to keep flying. To fly forever. To never leave the open sky.

I never want to leave this place. It's beautiful. Send my wife and my boy up here, and we can live in the clouds. And I can teach my son to fly. Then we can go back up together and catch the stars.

And the skydiver in the spacesuit let out a huge whoop of laughter. He wasn't falling anymore. He was gliding.

Doc insisted. Ease up. Finish the mission, and then follow your dreams.

The shrink won the case, and he smoothed out his fall.

Eight miles to Earth. . .

He continued to laugh and cheer and raise hell in his voice. His old claustrophobia drowned in a high tide of adrenaline. His heart was reliving its first skydive.

Six miles to Earth. . .

The ground stretched beneath him like a beige trampoline. There was a circus spectacle to this incredible human stunt. Given all the colorful, cartoonish thoughts he had on this mission, he felt he could literally bounce off the dirt when he landed. Followed by a ludicrous booooooooing sound, no doubt. Perfect complement. He laughed when he thought of it.

I haven't laughed like this in months. It must be freedom. Total, wild, and insane freedom. Look, Ma! No ground! I'm flying!

He hoped his helmet radio didn't shriek with feedback while he hollered his celebrations. Again, the number of firsts awarded to him trailed like tickertape through his head. The first man to skydive from the edge of the stratosphere. The first person to break the sound barrier with his body. The first father to drop from the heavens into his little boy's excited, waving arms.

Five miles to Earth. . .

The smile on his face stretched to lunatic proportions. Nothing on Earth or in space could cram him back into the claustrophobic cell. The hand of gravity had him in its fist. He could feel the air again. He felt the free-fall. And he loved every crazy millisecond of it.

Four miles to Earth. . .

He was out of the suit and, with a great deal of ironic cheek thrown against the sneers of his detractors, out of his mind. This was nothing more than a day at the office. Just a routine dive from the heavens. He was safe now. Nothing could go wrong. The words of Mission Control just before his jump—far more profound than anything he could think of—played again in his mind as if fresh from the radio headset.

And our guardian angel will take care of you. . .

The angels succeeded. They let him survive falling through Heaven. They shielded him as he cracked the snow globe of the sky, swallowed whole by the movie screen panorama. He remembered the way his visor choked with fog. That was just the angels breathing whispers of congratulations as he soared past them.

The guardians did a damn fine job bringing him home to his little boy.

Three miles to Earth. . .

How would it feel to have the ground supporting him again after this particular fall? It felt like centuries since he was on Earth. His toes tingled in his space boots. He remembered how the land looked twenty-four miles up, the tan stretch of open space under the hazy blue sky-dome. He now entered a glass terrarium filled with strange creatures. The fall changed him. He felt different from all the other people bustling in this microcosm of the universe.

Two miles to Earth. . .

A helicopter kept track of him just a short distance away. Soon, the chute would open, and he would drift again. To be perfectly honest, he wasn't sure if the parachute would open. The land would hug him, surround him, absorb him, and he'd be the first man to the center of the Earth, as if he had slipped into his son's *Magic School Bus* book. Eat your heart out, Jules Verne. This skydiver wanted to try world-record spelunking next.

One mile to Earth. . .

Breathe, Doc reminded one last time, and the parachute inflated. It jerked him backwards, a familiar feeling in his line of work. The chute flooded with atmosphere, a lung taking its first deep breath. His fall dwindled to a slow sinking. Floating. Suspended animation. It was strange how all the terror and worry about this mission seemed to be yanked out of his head by the tug of the parachute. He laughed. It was wonderful to be heading home again.

The tents of the recovery camp swelled in size.

They were white and square like his son's missing front teeth.

He smiled.

I'm coming home, son.

His shadow ballooned like another parachute beneath him.

His boots scraped against the dirt, making his toes itch and tingle again.

Destination: Earth.

He touched down with all the grace of Fred Astaire descending from Heaven and asking, "What did I miss?"

Born and raised in Ridgecrest, California, **Daniel Stallings** is a playwright and mystery novelist who has blended both of his passions for theatre and detective fiction by founding Master Mystery Productions, which specializes in creating interactive mystery theatre. He has published two mystery novels, *Sunny Side Up* and *Cleanup on Aisle Six*, in the Li Johnson Murder Mysteries through Pace Press. A working theatrical actor, director, stage manager, and much more, Daniel has received three Diamond Mask Awards for Excellence in Performance for his acting and is a two-time winner of the CLOTA Robe for his work on theatrical productions. He is the current president of the East Sierra Branch of the California Writers Club, the 2008 Allison Aubin Scholarship winner, and one of the 2015 winners of the Jack London Award. "24 Miles to Earth" is a fictional reimagining of the historic first skydive from the rim of the stratosphere back in October 2012.

The Year of the Canadian Cowboy

Gerry Wisdom
East Sierra Ridge Writers

If I'm at a Cowboy Poetry Contest, I ought to write a poem
        or rope a calf.
No cows in sight at Cowboy Joe
        (a coffee shop!).
No question, though, that they are all cowboys here
at least aficionados
With a taste for lattes and art receptions.
        Wine from Napa Valley.

As we drive away in our Crown Victoria,
        silence in the car,
We dream of the old west
        —The Last Cowboy and I—
And know it still exists in us.

For Dwight, the most Canadian of us all—1997

Gerry Wisdom is a member of the East Sierra Branch of the California Writers Club. Her poem describes her visit with her brother to the National Cowboy Poetry Gathering in Elko, Nevada, where, one year the gathering featured Canadians. She currently resides in the city of Ridgecrest, California.

Outside of poetry, her formal writing training was in Idaho at the Readers and Writers Rendezvous, chaired by Clay Morgan, Head of History Department, Boise State University. As president of a museum in Roseberry, Idaho, she collaborated on Idaho history books about pioneers, mining, and Finnish settlers. She has since retired as Head of Staff in the Aerosystems Department of China Lake, formed from the Navy's National Parachute Test Range.

For the East Sierra Branch, she contributed pieces to their anthology of local veteran stories, *Scenes from Lives of Service*, and has judged student essays for their Allison Aubin Scholarship for Young Writers program.

COASTAL DUNES

"In the bright day of San Luis Obispo the mountains of hope rise up . . ."

—*Jack Kerouac*

Washing a Window

Deborah Tobola
Coastal Dunes Branch

I'm on the outside with vinegar and water and my mother
on the inside pointing. I spray and wipe, spray and wipe,
determined to erase the hard water spots, give us a better vision

of what's in the backyard: birdhouses, bridal veil vine,
just-born morning glories. Our eyes meet briefly—is she me, or
am I her? When did we become one? I remember rejecting her

as a girl. Not her, exactly, but her life. Always ironing, cooking,
folding laundry. What kind of life is that? I was meant for
grander things! As a young woman I entertained

the patriarchy by trying to draft my mother and my aunt
into the women's movement, exhorting them to lay down
their dish rags and brooms and let the men make

their own damn dinner. They just smiled—tenderly—while the men
guffawed. So long ago. So much water gone under
the bridge of memory, so many people lost. I remember

my mother and me sledding with my toddler son almost
25 years ago. Snow and speed made us giddy. Girls again,
we laughed as we careened down the little hill, while

inside the house my father was dying. How could we laugh
when my father was dying? My mother taught me how.
My mother taught me that we must. Because someone we love

will always be dying and another will be getting born.
If I could transport myself back to my mother's kitchen, I would
help with dinner, instead of talking politics with the men.

I would listen more closely to the women, who always had
the news under the news, brief bulletins on the lives
of the people. Not the rich and famous, but the dear and

flawed people we call family. It's amazing what you can do with vinegar. My mother has stopped pointing. We smile because everything is so much clearer now.

Deborah Tobola is a poet, memoirist, playwright, and co-author of a children's book. Her work has earned four Pushcart Prize nominations, three Academy of American Poets awards, and a Children's Choice Book Award. Her memoir, *Hummingbird in Underworld: Teaching in a Men's Prison* (She Writes Press, 2019), received positive reviews in the *Los Angeles Times* and the Los Angeles Review of Books. The book also won several awards in the categories of social justice, social issues, creative nonfiction, and heroic journeys. The book was released in Hong Kong and Taiwan in 2021. Deborah spent thirty years working as a prison arts instructor, teaching creative writing and theatre. She founded Poetic Justice Project, the country's first theatre company for formerly incarcerated people, in Santa Maria, California, in 2009.

A Year of Contests

Margaret Lange
Coastal Dunes Branch

"Let's 'Thelma and Louise' out of this Zoom School Hell," Sarah joked in a text to her sister, who was in the same boat. For a month, her kids had been home all day being taught through a computer screen. Trying to keep them focused had worn Sarah's nerves threadbare. On top of that, her office had closed and she had to work from home. The hope of life getting back to normal kept her going. It was already the end of April. Surely, the coronavirus would subside and schools would open again to finish the year in person.

And what about everything else that had been shut down? Sarah's lovely San Francisco! The ease of walking to stores, cafes, bars, restaurants, museums, and visits with friends and neighbors, all these had been stripped away from her. Her world was reduced to the walls of her home, her beautiful, noisy children, and her beloved irritating husband. The year 2020 was shaping up to be a real bitch.

So, then it was no surprise when Sarah's first entry into the flash fiction contest in May was a dark fantasy piece about the struggles between Daypeople and Nightfolk ending in human sacrifice. She poured her frustration onto the pages like Ona's blood had poured onto the earth. Even if I don't win, she thought, even if all I produce is crap, at least I get time to myself, and it feels damn good to be writing again. She sent her entry, "Ona, Daughter of the Earth," off to her mother and sister. They both loved it, of course. Even better, the judges gave it a thumbs up and advanced Sarah to the next round.

June found Sarah looking down the dark tunnel of a summer without summer camps for the kids, without traveling. At least Zoom School Hell was over, and the kids were free to roam the house and backyard all day at will. To lighten things up, they adopted a German shorthaired pointer. Their "Pandemic Puppy" was a cuddly, mellow girl who loved to chase tennis balls and shorebirds. She was just what they needed. Still, life was full of uncertainty and worry. The coronavirus hadn't subsided; it had grown to a full-blown pandemic of COVID-19. How long would it last? When would we have a vaccine? When can we go to the movies again? When can we stop being afraid of grocery stores?

As Sarah grappled with this new normal, the next writing assignment was announced: three days to write 1500 words about saying goodbye. Well, at least I won't have to write anything cheery, she thought. With her husband again in charge of the kids, she sequestered herself in her room with pen, paper, and laptop. She imagined living in another time of great uncertainty and worry and wrote of the Vietnam War. Lovers part as he is drafted; she protests the war. They meet in a coffee shop years later, both changed and wounded. Sarah submitted "War and Conversation" an hour before the midnight deadline, was ranked in the top ten, and made it through to the next round.

When the school year came around again, Sarah's worst fears were realized: another year of Zoom School Hell. Vaccinations against Covid-19 were still not approved. The pandemic surged; cases and death rates climbed. The situation would only get worse during fall and winter. This dismal future along with months of isolation and aggravation had drained Sarah's reserves of serotonin. She took this seriously and got on an antidepressant. "I feel better now that I'm medicated," she texted to her mom and sis.

Sarah welcomed the next writing challenge and wrote a mystery about a hospice worker visiting a dying man who turned out to be her estranged father. The worker seeks answers and closure. Little did Sarah know at the time that nine months later her estranged father would die suddenly, leaving her without answers or closure. She submitted "Bird in the Tiger's Cage," got second place, and made it through to the final round.

In December of 2020, vaccinations received FDA emergency use authorization. Finally, in March of 2021, Sarah and her husband got "the poke." With teachers vaxxed and COVID-19 cases in San Francisco declining, a hybrid of Zoom and in-person school began. The City was opening up. The family went to a Giants game and an amusement park. Sarah could hug her friends again. She knew the pandemic was far from over, but she hoped they had gone through the worst of it.

The last round of the writing contest was announced in April. The prompt was "pointing at someone." Sarah wrote about two rescue workers in a boat watching for jumpers on the Golden Gate Bridge. They spot a woman on the bridge, her nightgown billowing in the freezing wind of the bay, and as she jumps, they speed over to where she will land. Four, three, two, one, and she hits the water. They grab her, hoist her into the boat, and wrap her in blankets. She survives. "Four Seconds" was judged one of the top ten entries. Not bad, Sarah thought, for a non-profit administrator and mother of two living through a pandemic.

As a birthday gift, her husband collected her stories and had them printed in a perfect-bound book. He asked Sarah's mom to write a forward. She wrote:

I imagine your great-grandmother, Hazel May, who wrote stories in longhand at her kitchen table during the Great Depression, smiling down at you typing on your keyboard. You carry on her tradition with stories propelled by intriguing characters and captivating plots. I'm eager to read all the stories and novels you have yet to conjure. You are, at your core, a writer.

Sara leafed through the book. This one's for you, Grandma Hazel, she thought. You and me, writing through the hard times.

Margaret Lange is a poet, writer, and singer/songwriter. She serves as a 5th District arts commissioner with Santa Barbara County and is a board member of the Santa Maria Arts Council. She is a member of the Coastal Dunes Branch of the California Writers Club. Previously, she developed a juried poetry-reading series with the San Luis Obispo Arts Council, hosted a radio interview show featuring artists, taught poetry workshops to students through California Poets in the Schools, and hosted a poetry reading series in her hometown of Nipomo, California.

Margaret's poems have been published by *ART/LIFE, HopeDance*, the *Tribune*, *Art Rag*, the *Santa Lucian,* and the Redwood Writers CWC poetry anthology *Phases*. For gardening and engineering organizations, she has written nonfiction newsletter content. Musically, Margaret has written and recorded numerous songs and has recorded a collection of acapella lullabies.

HIGH DESERT

"It's the way you ride the trails that counts."
—*Dale Evans*

We Are All Destined to Become Our Mothers[26]

Avalynn Morse
High Desert Branch

"Come on, Mom, you make the best grilled cheese sandwich in the world. I can't live without those!"

The sobbing on the other side of the door ebbs slightly. I allow my head to drop against the wall with a resigned thud. The distant ticking of the clock down the hall draws my attention. My eyelids fall, heavy with the weight of the last two hours. My head pounds in disjointed rhythm with the clock. Except I wish the heavy thump, thump, thumping in my mind was more like that graceful click, click, clicking. I wish the increasing silence from the bathroom wasn't so loud. I wish I could say this was the first time I'd been here.

I remember the first time. It seems like ages ago. I almost can't make out the panic. The whole memory has become a distant fog with only a few figures barely perceptible against the dark gray. The subtly warped door's wooden grain traces a familiar path. Her weeping carries the same regretful tune. But the panic faded long ago. My heart no longer leaps across barren deserts, searching for an oasis of peace. Acidic indifference has made its home where the panic once lived, and my heart resorts to tasting the dry sand with chapped lips. Episode after episode, the panic fades. Empty threat after empty threat, the screaming fear of losing my mother by her own hand has reduced to nothing more than a muted whimper.

"Anyone can make a grilled cheese sandwich. You don't even need a recipe." The heavy sobs have subsided, but a symphony of sniffles still plays melancholy on the other side of the bathroom door.

"I can't! Do you remember when I tried to make them that one time? For Dad?" I cringe at the accidental mention of my father. I can almost feel her stiffen behind the door. He's dead. Another casualty in another war. That was seven years ago. I still miss him, but I've come to terms with his death.

He was a good man—a caring husband and loving father. My mother insists that their marriage was troubled, that he hit her, got angry, and drank incessantly. The look in his eyes every time he had

---

[26] Previously published in the High Desert Branch 2023 anthology, *Conflict!*

to say goodbye was the only evidence I needed to know that none of that was true. I never witnessed any unexplained bruises on my mother. As any human being, he got angry, but he always took a step away and came back when the fires had cooled. He drank socially and just a beer or two on those rare occasions—a far cry from the drunken wife-beater my mom tried to make him out to be.

None of my mother's beliefs about my father are true, and she certainly didn't feel this way about him before his death. She was just as much in love with him as he was with her. I guess she had to adapt this false image of him so she'd miss him less. It worked a little too well, and the carefully manufactured apathy morphed into a deep hatred for the man she still loves with every piece of her soul.

I can't say that I'm surprised. This generational curse runs in the family. Her mother, my sweet, loving grandmother, was perfectly normal before she inexplicably lost her mind and fell into a violent tide pool of anxiety and depression. She would be totally calm and tranquil, but then something would strike her the wrong way, and without a word, she'd be up pacing a hole in the living room carpet, rubbing her hands together compulsively while fighting off hysterical tears. My mom used to tell me stories about it. She said there was no way that anyone could calm her down. Grandma and everyone else in the room just had to ride it out, wait for the storm to end, and hope no one got tossed out of the boat.

Then she'd be fine for a few hours and the storm would swell again. Each day was a repetitive loop of sobbing and pacing. It got pretty bad. Now she's been reasonably stable for the last forty-five years—under the right medication, of course. And my matriarch has stepped up to take her place. As daughters, we are all destined to become our mothers.

The silence behind me is deafening, the mention of my dad still ringing in my ears. A shaky voice emerges. "You know better, May."

It's a much more stable response than the one I'm used to. There's no flailing in anger and tears but still the reminder that I should never speak of the man who loved us all of his life. I tread lightly, tenderly trying to skirt around anything that might send her into another fit of sobbing.

"I'm sorry. You know what I meant. You remember how that sandwich turned out, right? How the bread was all black and pretty much as hard as a rock? That thing was so burnt. It took like four washes to get all the burnt cheese off of the pan." I add a little giggle, but my attempt at lightheartedness apparently falls short of its target. It resonates within me, though. I remember the look on my dad's face when I set down the charred sandwich in front of him. The initial wide eyes and slightly agape mouth brought on by the shock of the monstrosity before him faded after a few seconds, and he just laughed. It was a hearty laugh, not mocking or patronizing but loving in the way that a wave gently lifts a broken shell from the sand and pulls it into its warm and constant grasp. We all laughed together. Me, my brother, and my parents. A nuclear family of perfection, unaware of our rapidly decaying world and the fallout that awaited us.

The tenderness in my heart fades slightly at the injection of my brother into my sweet memory. August was the beginning of the end. We used to share the burden that is our mother. She wasn't as bad back then. Her monsoons were much more occasional, and the waterline didn't rise to the point of suffocation like it does now. August, my brother, was my life preserver, and I his. He and I kept each other afloat through her hysteria. Somewhere along the line, he decided he didn't want to swim with us anymore. It became too much for him. He's somewhere halfway across the country now. I'm not even sure exactly where. August left in a bitterness like absinthe and black coffee.

Having the only other man in her life leave her sent my mother over the edge. The intermittent outbursts became almost constant, the screaming and tears overlapping each other until you could hardly tell there was even a second of peace between them. August left, and so went my life preserver. Now I flounder and thrash as the rising tide threatens to drown me. He was always much better at coaxing her out of her bathroom sanctuary.

"Do you really think I'm that good at making those sandwiches?" her meek voice squeaks out hopefully after several more minutes of fragile silence.

"Of course, Mom. I always love grilled cheese night. I'm serious." And I am. A few more seconds of silence brimming with anticipation follow. For once I might actually be getting somewhere. I allow a little hope to seep in and get a glimpse of a life beyond this hallway.

"So you only stick around because I do things like that for you?"

Never mind. I don't even try to keep my eyes from rolling. It's not like she can see it anyway, but I wonder if she can feel it. After the umpteenth time being accused of taking advantage of your mother, the words lose their sting. In its place the seed of irritation has been blossoming into a quiet but colorful resentment.

"Well, I'm here now. I'm certainly not getting anything out of this." I can feel the bitterness seeping through my teeth, but I don't make an attempt to smother it. It's been fighting to escape for years. This time, I finally let it have its way. "This isn't worth any grilled cheese," I mutter to myself but, apparently, not quietly enough. A mousy gasp sounds from the other side of the door, but I'm distracted by the anger simmering inside of me.

She takes a few seconds to gather herself, but I know that my words hit home. She's no doubt picking her jaw up off the bathroom tile. I just wonder if she knows that I've wanted to say that for the past seven years, if she knows about the seemingly thousands of times that I've bitten my tongue. She's only ever heard my reassurances that she is worth whatever misery she puts me through. She's never even heard me admit to that misery. My mother knows of it, I'm sure, but her self-absorption and desperate grasping for affirmation outweigh whatever bruises they leave me with.

"They can't be that good then." The smug indignation in her voice sets my temper from simmering to boiling in an instant. Rage begins overflowing, and everything I've wanted to say since I was fifteen floods from my lips scorchingly, burning everything in sight.

"You know what? You're right. No grilled cheese is good enough to make this shit worth it. It's not worth losing the last seven years of my life. It's really not, Mom. I have spent every day watching what I say around you. No matter what I say, you can always find a way to twist it so that you're the victim and I'm the cruel, ungrateful daughter who is determined to break her mother's heart. Every single day I feel like I have to tiptoe around to make sure I don't even look at you in a way that upsets you, let alone say anything. Because one wrong step and I'm back to chasing you into the bathroom. And for the stupidest reasons. You're delusional!"

It's too late now. Everything that has been gnashing, tearing away at my soul, clawing for a way out, has finally found its escape, and I can't hold it hostage in my heart any longer. My fury forces me to my feet, facing the door that she hides behind.

"You constantly make me feel guilty for not catering to your every single need. God forbid I spend time with anyone but you because then 'I don't love you.' I can't live my life the way I want to or make my own choices because I'm stuck protecting *your* feelings. Like it's somehow *my* responsibility to keep you from having a breakdown.

"And I *needed* you, Mom. I was a kid! I lost him too. Did you ever think of that? I was thirteen years old, and some men in suits were telling me that I was never gonna see my dad again. Do you know how long I still waited for him to walk through that door? And then you started hating him, and who knows where the hell that came from.

"I *know* you were hurting. I *know* you missed him. I miss him too. But you still had to take care of us. I had to look after myself *and* take care of you. How backwards is that?"

I'm yelling now. I don't need to. The bathroom door is thin enough that she could easily hear a breathy whisper if she wanted to. But I can't stop myself.

"I needed you, but you were too selfish and self-centered to put that ahead of your own pain. Even now, you refuse to let me live my life if it conflicts with what you want. These last few years I should have been exploring *my* life. I should have been setting up *my* future. I had dreams. But someone had to stay with you! Someone had to be here to chase you into this bathroom."

Suddenly, from behind the door: "Well, I'm sorry that I've been so disappointing to you as a mom. I've tried my best, but it's not an exact science, you know?"

I hadn't been expecting a response. Her tone is self-righteous and insincere. Sarcasm drips from the hostile apology, and the last of my restraint shatters. "You know what? You *have* been disappointing. You're disgustingly weak. But I'm not mad that you made mistakes. Every parent does that. I'm mad that you continue to make those same mistakes. You have had years to get through this, and you refuse to get help. You refuse to let me and August off the hook. That's what disappoints me. Hell, I'm not even mad that August left us. I'm just mad that I didn't think of it first."

Fiery tears burn down my swollen cheeks. I am surprised at what has come out of my own mouth, wondering if it really could have been me that said all those things. My heart is no stranger to pain, but it aches with grief far worse now than it ever has—grief for myself, grief for who I was, for who I could have been, even grief for my mom. My mind is flooded with old memories of who she was before all this. The mental photographs of laughter and love in her eyes pain me now. I hate her. I loathe her and resent her. But more than anything else, I miss her. I miss my mom. I miss feeling like she was a friend, a confidant, knowing she would support me. My deep, primitive longing for the bond that we once shared has never stopped. It's hard to believe, but there was once a time when she was my favorite person in this life. She understood me. She held me when I cried and helped me understand why the spring is so beautiful. My heart breaks for everything I have lost and everything I never had.

Collapsing against the wall, I find myself weeping into my arms. Gasps escape uncontrollably every second or so, wracking all my body as all the grief and pain that's been locked inside of me all these years tries to escape my body all at once. It's several minutes before I'm able to calm down enough to breathe again. My head pounds with the sting of dehydration.

My eyes burn, and, for as much fluid as they've spilled, they feel drier and rougher than summer sidewalks.

As the last of my now-silent tears are still tracing the curves of my cheeks, the door is flung open. My mom emerges from the bathroom to the side of me, still wiping frantically at her own red, puffy eyes. Our eyes meet. I'm looking up at her with pleading eyes, begging her to come back to reality, to come back to me. Her stare is full of guilt that is slowly seeping in, but I'm not sure if she's truly felt the weight of my pain.

I want her to feel it. I want it to torment her the way it's tormented me. But in her eyes, I see myself. I see her, at seventeen, watching her mother pace back and forth, back and forth. And I realize she's already felt it. She's felt it all. She already had her share of sitting by bathroom doors and missing who someone used to be. She's probably been here before, this exact moment preserved in amber.

My mom extends her hand to me, still sitting against the wall, and I feel like I'm nine years old again. I wrap my fingers around hers and allow her to pull me to my feet and back into the present. "Come on." She sniffles. "Let's go make you a grilled cheese."

She silently leads me down the dim hall. There's a mirror hanging on one of the walls that once belonged to my great-grandmother. It's hideous—gaudy and a lackluster gold. I catch my face in it and dread the day that I see my mother in my own reflection.

Avalynn Morse is a young lady of many passions. From an early age, she has been fortunate to share a love of writing with her grandfather Bob Isbill, long-time member and President Emeritus of the HDCWC. She is originally from Oak Hills, California, but now attends Coe College in Cedar Rapids, Iowa. She is pursuing a major in biology as well as minors in chemistry and health and society, with the hope of becoming an emergency room physician. Avalynn continues to write in her free time and enjoys working at the writing center of her college, helping others with their academic writing.

Blasphemy[27]

(for Steven Sotloff)
Lorelei Kay
High Desert Branch

White geese form Vs and fly southward
Spiders spin webs over vines
Antelope lock horns in battles

Under an infinite sky.

Northern lights burn in stark brilliance
Tornados and hurricanes strike
Lightning cuts zigzags through cloudbursts

Throughout a non-judging sky.

Shootings and bombings gain headlines
Guerrillas and gunners roam nigh
Airstrikes and protests grow louder

Beneath an unbothered sky.

A mother's soft face pleads for mercy
A son asks, "Must I pay the price?"
A chilled wind tugs hard on his raiment

Under an unconcerned sky.

He kneels draped in flaming bright orange
In front of the black and the knife
Spilt red will soon drip from the silver

Beneath an uninvolved sky.

---

[27] Previously published in the High Desert Branch 2023 anthology, *Conflict!*

Breezes chase holes in the shadows
Eagles glide low as they cry
The whole world still fights
Through cracks in the night

All under the oblivious sky.

Note: Many of us may never forget the horrifying pictures that headlined the news in September of 2013. In it, a journalist named Steven Sotloff knelt on desert sand, dressed in bright orange, and a man draped in black--with a knife--stood behind him. This poem is for him.

Lorelei Kay is the author of a multi-award-winning memoir *From Mormon to Mermaid—a Woman's Voyage from Oppression to Freedom,* available on Amazon.

She became hooked on poetry when her dad helped her write her first poem. She later attended Brigham Young University on a journalism scholarship.

Her poems have appeared in anthologies, online publications, and magazines. She also won the 2021 San Gabriel Valley Poetry Contest with her poem *Straightening Flower Fields*.

Lorelei has served as a judge for the Scholastic Arts and Writing Awards program, as a mentor on the Dorothy C. Blakely Memoir Project, on the board of the Mohave Historical Society, and also on the board of the HDCWC.

Her other loves include the hundreds of dolls she collects and displays and a husband who doesn't complain—too much—about sharing the house with them.

The Surrounding Silence[28]

Michael Raff
High Desert Branch

Stunned by shock and frustration, Matt Robinson's eyes grew enormous, his breath trapped in his throat. Everything in the hospital's dining room transformed into intense clarity. Turning to his left, he peered at his employee Vanessa. "Did you see that?" he whispered.

The woman merely watched as Jerry Jacobs struggled to his feet. Once the developmentally disabled man had recovered his balance, he glanced over at Lance McHenry, who had returned to his position by the dining room's exterior wall. Scowling, Lance folded his arms across his chest. "Pick up your chair and sit down," he snarled at Jerry.

Not more than a few feet away, Corrinne, the food service worker, busied herself removing a container of hot water from the stainless-steel counter. Thomas Diaz, another of Matt's employees, stood behind the medication cart, preoccupied with dispensing the morning dosages for the patients remaining in the room. He'd glanced over when Jerry struck the floor but hadn't reacted.

Jerry picked up the chair, his movements awkward and tentative, his eyes focused on Lance. He wasn't rubbing the back of his head and appeared to be uninjured. It didn't matter. Matt had to make sure. Wrestling with his emotions, he crossed the room and approached Jerry. No blood, no lesion, and so far, no swelling. He peered at Lance, who stared back at him in brooding silence, the contours of his face cynical and daunting.

There was no denying what Matt had seen, but had the other staff witnessed Lance's transgression? Certainly, Vanessa had. She was the hardest-working psychiatric technician on Unit 17 and, possibly, in all of Letterman State Hospital.

Matt rushed out of the dining room and hurried to the office he shared with his supervisor, Roy Hansen, the manager of Unit 17. Matt

[28] Previously published in the High Desert Branch 2023 anthology, *Conflict!*

fumed. When it came to patient abuse, Roy looked the other way. A year before, Darleen Spencer had repeatedly slapped a patient right in front of them. Roy had ignored the incident, and without his support, Matt decided not to take action. In the fourteen years Roy had been Unit 17's supervisor, there hadn't been any allegations of patient abuse.

Too distraught to sit at his desk, Matt paced about the office. He kept visualizing Lance walking up to Jerry and shoving him so violently that it had tipped him backward, sending him crashing to the floor. What in the world had Jerry done? Whatever the infraction, Lance should have just told him to stop. There had been several other occurrences of Lance's abusiveness but none of them so stark and reckless. Matt had talked to him on at least two occasions. Only last week he had warned Lance that the next time he even *suspected* abuse, he would turn him in.

It felt as if the entire world had spun out of orbit. Matt retrieved a Special Incident Report from his desk drawer, sat down, and picked up the phone. The registered nurse on duty, known as the health service specialist, had to be notified to examine Jerry. Once she was brought in, there was no turning back. It felt ludicrous, to say the least, but to Matt, with his nerves on edge, even the dial tone was giving him fair warning. He *hated* the idea of turning in Lance. Yet every episode of the man's abusiveness flashed through his mind, climaxing with Lance—in front of *four* other staff members—shoving Jerry to the floor. As the dayshift supervisor, Matt was paid to safeguard the wellbeing of Unit 17's patients. If he didn't protect them, then who would?

Matt pressed the button for the operator. An obnoxious beep resonated. The woman responded immediately, her voice cheery and unassuming. "Operator."

"Would you page Lori Kent, program Seventeen's RN?"

"Certainly," came her reply.

Matt hung up and began filling out the report. It was one of hundreds he'd initiated in his nineteen years of state service. Nearly every week he filled out at least one Special Incident Report, otherwise known as an S.I.R., which included reporting injuries requiring a doctor's attention, as well as deaths, AWOLs, or episodes of patient abuse. Only incidents of death and patient abuse were headquarters-reportable and dispatched to Sacramento for evaluation.

Matt's hands were quivering. His throat had dried out. He had just started describing what he'd observed when his phone rang.

"Hi, Matt. It's Lori. What's up?"

"Hey, Lori," he greeted, his voice barely audible. "I want to report an SIR."

"Okay, what kind?"

The sensation of the earth jumping its orbit returned. All sense of time vanished. An inexplicable dizziness seized him. Matt could barely function, much less speak. It all seemed so surreal. Like a nightmare wrenched from the depths of a dark abyss. He cleared his throat and swallowed. "Patient abuse," he answered, those very words chilling his blood. He shuddered. His head felt as if it would explode.

What seemed like an endless silence ensued. Matt could feel beads of sweat gathering on his brow. He wanted to shout at Lori to say something—to say anything—because the silence had grown so sickening and overwhelming.

Lori's voice sounded cautious, distant, but overall, professional. "Okay," she responded. "I'll be right there."

◊ ◊ ◊

The remainder of the day proved *beyond* surreal, more like a ceaseless blur. The sluggish passage of time persecuted Matt at every opportunity. Within minutes, word leaked out about him reporting Lance. The repercussions were immediate. Except for Vanessa, every staff member stopped speaking to him. When they had to, they kept their responses minimal. Refusing eye contact, they would look the other way. Matt didn't need eye contact to feel their anger and icy glares. Even Sheri, in charge of the dayshift on his days off, avoided him. Roy wasn't much better. In the process of being promoted, he was on his way off Unit 17. At best he would remain neutral, typical of his more than eleven-year history with Matt.

As with all abuse allegations, Lance had been relocated to another unit, assigned paperwork duties, and wouldn't be allowed to interact with patients until the matter was settled. An investigation would remain a top priority. If the charge wasn't upheld, Lance would return to Unit 17. Matt felt confident of validation and that the administration would take disciplinary action such as a cut in pay and a year's probation. Termination for abusing patients had been a rarity, reserved for the more severe cases, such as repeat offenders.

Jack Henley, the special investigator and a former LAPD officer, interviewed the other four staff members who were in the dining room at the time, each interview conducted in private. When it was Matt's turn, he was taken into his office and asked what he had seen. The investigator took some notes, his demeanor reserved but unbiased. At least he made eye contact, which Matt felt was a vast improvement over his staff.

Previously, Henley had interviewed the patient, who was marginally verbal. Except for phrases such as "Yes," "No," and "I don't know," Jerry lacked the ability to express himself, much less remember what had happened.

After all five interviews had been completed on Unit 17, the investigator departed to Unit 19 to question Lance. Matt had no doubt that the ever-popular, often-charming psych tech would never admit the truth. But what about Thomas and Corrine? Had they witnessed the incident? It happened so quickly that they might have missed it. At least Matt felt certain Vanessa had seen it. The investigation would take three to four weeks, depending on Jack Henley's workload, a long time for Unit 17's staff to be infuriated with their boss.

Matt trudged through the never-ending day, reminding himself that no one had promised him his job would be easy. Larry Baxter, Unit 17's program director, had once called the shift supervisor's job "the hardest in the hospital." Matt just wanted the investigation to be over.

◊ ◊ ◊

Sitting across their kitchen table from her husband, Cassie shook her head. "What the hell, Matt? You shouldn't have turned Lance in. You're going to be blackballed by everyone on that unit, maybe the whole program. Why can't you just tell them that, after thinking it over, you made a mistake?"

Matt set his fork down on the table. He hadn't much of an appetite. "I can't do that, Cassie. I would look like an idiot. Besides, no way should Lance walk. This time I saw everything. He's too violent. The more I try to stop his abuse, the worse it gets. He shouldn't even be working with the developmentally disabled." Matt took a moment to catch his breath. "It's time I broke the silence, Cassie. I owe it to the patients."

His wife's eyes grew enormous. She pushed her plate away and reached for her cigarettes. "You don't owe the patients anything! If you want to move up the ladder, you can't be blowing whistles. No one at the hospital's going to *trust* you."

The room had grown silent. Suzy, their black and white Field Spaniel, sat in her bed in the corner of the kitchen nook, her posture slumped, her eyes darting back and forth between her owners. All Matt wanted was a few hours of peace, quiet, and support. Lately, his wife never agreed with him on anything, especially when it came to Unit 17. "I *do* owe it to the patients, Cassie. My job is to take care of them. Make sure they're safe. And it's about time I lived up to that."

Rolling her eyes, Cassie lit a cigarette, inhaled, and blew the smoke toward her husband. "That's rubbish. You have to start looking out for yourself. When are you going to learn? Get your head out of the clouds, Matt. Stop being a dreamer and *cover* your ass. You'll never be promoted the way you're going. The administration doesn't want a hardworking do-gooder. They want someone who makes them look *good.* Reporting abuse doesn't cut it. It makes them look incompetent."

Matt stood, took his plate to the sink, and headed upstairs. He had hoped Cassie would understand how he felt about the investigation, but now he realized bringing the subject up had been a mistake. Their conversation could have been worse. At least she hadn't screamed at him.

◊◊◊

The weeks crawled by. An hour felt like a day—a day like a week. Matt had always held his staff accountable for their attendance, a policy that made him unpopular. After turning in Lance, his rapport with his employees reached an all-time low. The tension on the unit was excruciating, gnawing away at Matt's nerves. When he stepped into the medication room to see why Heather hadn't started dispensing the noon dosages, he found her talking on the phone. She murmured goodbye to whoever she was conversing with and hung up. Standing, she glared *directly* at him, indignation surging in her eyes. "What do you want?"

"I just wanted to see about the medications," he returned, inching toward the door.

"They're ready and they'll be out in a minute!" she shot back.

"Now get out of my med room!"

Matt halted just short of the door, his hand two inches from the knob. Gritting his teeth, he turned and locked eyes with her. "First of all, it's not *your* med room." He paused and spoke in a low, guttural tone. "And second, don't ever speak to me like that again."

Heather's glare ceased as Matt left the room.

◊ ◊ ◊

Per the administration, all employees were prohibited from talking to their peers, friends, and family members about existing investigations, an all but unenforceable policy. Matt knew every Unit 17 staff member on all three shifts. They were furious with him and banding together, exchanging grievances among themselves.

After a particularly grueling shift, Matt decided to phone Vanessa. He needed to hear a friendly voice and hoped for confirmation that she had witnessed the incident. It never occurred to him that his solitary hope was about to be snuffed out.

"Sorry, Matt, but I didn't *see* a thing," she replied.

Matt couldn't believe what he was hearing. "Are you sure? I saw you looking over."

"By the time I looked over, Jerry was on the floor and Lance wasn't anywhere near him."

"But you saw Lance walking away? Right?"

"Yeah, but that's it." Her voice sounded guarded. "He walked away kind of casually, like nothing happened." She paused and Matt braced himself. "You know . . . we're not supposed to be talking about this."

"Yeah, I know. Sorry." He felt a tinge of guilt. "It's been bothering me and I had to find out what you saw. I was thinking. . . well, never mind. Guess I was wrong."

Matt and Vanessa didn't talk for long. She was a God-fearing, Christian woman who was moral, hardworking, great with the patients, and worked well with Matt *and* her peers. She was someone he respected and believed in. Still, nagging questions plagued him. How could she *not* have seen Lance shove Jerry? It didn't seem possible.

◊ ◊ ◊

When Matt received a phone call that Larry Baxter wanted to talk to him, he thought his heart would burst. Working conditions on 17 had never been worse. At home Cassie was barely speaking to him. Their financial situation had been faltering, and Matt's work problems weren't helping their marriage. He hadn't been sleeping nights. When he started drifting off, he would see Jerry being shoved to the floor. He would watch in grim horror as Lance's face transformed into cold granite. He would look into his eyes and perceive immeasurable defiance.

The program secretary, Helen, a stern woman in her mid-forties, informed Matt that Larry was waiting for him in his office. When Matt stepped in, Larry told him to close the door. The program director sat behind his metal desk. Matt settled into the red plastic chair in front of Larry—a chair that had been nicknamed "the hot seat."

"I was asked by David Bellows, the executive director, and Jack Henley, the special investigator, to go over your allegation against Lance."

"Of course." Matt liked and respected Larry. He was an outstanding program director who had started out as a psych tech and had come up the ranks. Therefore, Larry possessed a realistic view of what occurred on the units, both good and bad. Unlike Roy, Larry Baxter had been supportive of Matt. Today, he came across as professional, neutral, and most of all, formal—no doubt because of the investigation.

"When you were in the dining room with Lance and the other staff, what did you see?"

"I was standing next to Vanessa and saw Lance rush up to Jerry Jacobs, who was sitting at a table in the middle of the room. Lance then shoved Jerry with both hands. This caused Jerry's chair to tip backward and he fell to the floor. Lance then turned around and walked back to where he had been standing."

"Is that *exactly* what you told the investigator?"

"Yeah, pretty much, I think."

"I have to tell you, Matt. The administration is leaning toward Lance's version."

Matt's heart took a precarious dive. A surge of despair raced through him. He couldn't believe what he was hearing. "I don't understand. Why would they favor *his* version?"

"They're saying what you told the investigator is inconsistent."

"Inconsistent?" Matt felt his face turn red. "How so?"

"You told him you didn't know *exactly* where Lance shoved Jerry. Either on his shoulders or chest."

"Yeah, I guess so. They're pretty close together and it happened so fast. I can't believe this. They have a problem with that?"

"Yes, they're saying Lance's story is more consistent, and he also claims you have a grudge against him."

Matt shook his head, drew an anxious breath, and exhaled. "I don't know why he would say that. I've always liked a lot of things about him." Matt shrugged. "He's outgoing, funny, and knowledgeable. The only thing I have against him is his abusiveness." It was unnerving how suffocating the room had grown. Matt's stomach shriveled into what felt like an ember of coal. He hated to divulge more about Lance's aggressiveness, but he trusted Larry. "Between you and me, it's not the first time the subject of abuse has come up with Lance."

Larry leaned forward. "Have you seen him abuse any of the other patients?"

Matt sighed. "Not like what happened in the dining room, but sort of. One time he was unnecessarily rough with an assaultive patient. Another time I heard Maynard Smith scream as Lance came walking out of his room—laughing. Another time Jimmy Winter told me that Lance had choked him." He paused. Not stepping forward sooner sickened Matt. "I also caught Lance making Jimmy stay under a bed as punishment. It was then I told him one more incident and I would turn him in."

Larry nodded. "I know what the units are like, Matt. But basically, it's his word against yours."

"But I'm the supervisor. Doesn't that carry more weight?"

"No, I'm afraid not."

"What about the other staff in the dining room? Didn't they see anything?"

"All three of them said no."

Matt took a heavy breath. "I thought Vanessa did, but looks like I was wrong."

"I know about your conversation with her. You shouldn't have done that."

Matt didn't think it was possible, but the ember in his stomach grew hotter and the room temperature cranked up. "She told you?"

"It got back to administration. I don't know how, but somehow."

A sense of doom swept through Matt. "Can you tell me what Lance had to say about this?"

"He said Jerry was leaning back in his chair, in danger of tipping over, so he rushed across the room to prevent it." Larry shook his head. "He tried to catch Jerry . . . but was too late."

Matt groaned. "I have to admit that sounds like a believable story." He took another anxious breath. "But it's not the truth. Lance is covering up and is never going to admit his guilt."

"Are you sure you saw him *push* Jerry? That you didn't *misinterpret* his actions? As you mentioned, it happened *fast*."

A moment of excruciating silence passed. Temptation seeped in. It would have been much easier to let this thankless disaster go. Then, hopefully, conditions on the unit would return to normal—or at least to a tolerable level. But what about Jerry? What about the rest of the patients? No one else was going to tell the truth. Not Roy, not Vanessa, no one. Matt wanted to do the right thing. His sense of guilt grew overwhelming, reminding him that he'd let Lance off too many times already. "I know what I saw . . . and I wish to God I hadn't." Matt leaned back and swallowed. "You know, Larry, I'm paying a price for this. No one's on my side. No one is speaking to me except Vanessa. There's an unspoken code on Seventeen. A code of silence, something that's probably on *all* the units. I broke that silence. To the staff . . . that's an act of treason."

Larry kept his expression in check. He remained a true professional. But Matt looked into his eyes just then and perceived a glimmer of despair. Larry brushed a hand across his forehead and eased back. He picked up a pen and rolled it between his thumb and index finger. "Okay, Matt. Thanks for going over this with me. I'll advise administration and do what I can. I'll get back to you as soon as a decision is made."

Matt stood. "I'm sorry to ask you, Larry, but I have to know." He hesitated and steadied himself. "Do you believe me?"

Larry stopped rolling the pen between his thumb and index finger and peered at his employee. "Yes, I believe you, Matt. But it's not in my hands." He shrugged and sighed. "And quite honestly, I think my opinion in this matter won't make a difference."

◊ ◊ ◊

It had been a difficult day. The majority of the patients had been loud, agitated, and even assaultive. That afternoon, the fire alarm sounded. It was just a random drill, but evacuating fifty hyperactive patients out of the building only agitated them more. Having the staff furious with their supervisor didn't help. Later, Sheri approached Matt at the nurses' station. By the look on her face, things were about to become worse. "I have to talk to you," she murmured.

Matt nodded, and she followed him to his office. He sat behind his desk and she sat at Roy's desk, opposite Matt and facing him. She avoided eye contact, consistent with her behavior for the last few weeks. "As you know, Roy's going-away party is at my house this weekend." Folding her arms across her chest, she spoke through clenched teeth. "And I don't want you to come."

Even after all the stress and chaos of the investigation, what Sheri had to say felt like a knife piercing Matt's heart. He could barely say a word. "Y-you're not serious, are you?"

"Of course I am. People have told me they won't come if you're there. I would like Roy's party to be a success, and it won't be if no one comes."

A mixture of horror and shock gripped Matt. "I don't know what to say. I've been working with Roy for over eleven years, and if anyone should be there, I should."

Sheri raised her head and made eye contact. Anger and tension brimmed in her eyes. "If you care about him . . . you won't come."

Matt had been feeling as if he'd fallen into the bottom of an abyss. Suddenly, he realized he'd underestimated his emotions. Now, at this *very* moment, he'd struck bottom. "Okay," he uttered, struggling not to show his disappointment. "I won't go where I'm not wanted."

With that, Sheri stood and left the office.

◊ ◊ ◊

Larry Baxter sat in the swivel chair behind his desk, another pen in his hand. Matt sat in the chair opposite Larry, the one nicknamed "the hot seat." Matt had to catch his breath. He had rushed over the minute he received the phone call to come to Larry's office.

"I'm sorry, Matt. The administration will not pursue aversive action against Lance. With no other witnesses, it's your word against his."

Matt took a deep breath to calm himself. All his grief and aggravation had been for nothing. "You know, Larry. He'll abuse again. I can't watch over him eight hours a day."

Larry clicked his pen and nodded. "Let's hope for the best." He leaned forward in his swivel chair and peered at Matt. "Lance wants to come back to Unit 17 and has every right to do so. How do you feel about working with him again?"

Matt suppressed a groan. "It's not going to be easy, but I'll do my part."

"Okay, good. He's returning this afternoon." Larry tidied a stack of papers on his desk. "By the way, I heard you interviewed well for Roy's job. I'll let you know as soon as I hear what the administration has decided."

Matt perked up. At last, a glimmer of hope, something positive. Hearing how he'd given a good interview from his program director during the most brutal time of his career felt especially gratifying. "Thanks, Larry that means a lot to me. I would like to follow your lead and promote through the ranks. I know I can make Seventeen the finest unit at Letterman—a unit to be proud of."

◊◊◊

After the last group of patients had returned from lunch and settled into their activity room, Matt glanced at the nurses' station's wall clock: 1:00 p.m. exactly. He heard the building's side entrance door slam shut from around the corner, followed by heavy footsteps. Matt pushed his paperwork aside and rose to his feet. He recognized the footsteps. They were boots, most likely motorcycle boots. Only one person he knew wore such footwear on Unit 17.

Lance rounded the corner, a victorious grin plastered on his face. As usual, in addition to his boots, he was dressed in black. He waved at Marie and Lois, who were next to the medication room across from the nurses' station. They smiled back and gave him a thumbs up. Turning toward Matt, the glint in Lance's eyes exhibited undeniable disdain and spitefulness. "Matt, old buddy! How the hell are ya?" He swaggered into the nurses' station, wrapped his arms around his supervisor, and hugged him in a near backbreaking manner. "Damn, boss, it's awesome to be back where I belong! Did ya miss me?"

Matt wrestled free, his mortification complete. He reminded himself to stay calm and professional. "Go relieve Vanessa in Group Two. She's taking her lunch."

Lance gave him a wink that flaunted sarcasm. "Will do, boss-man. Happy to oblige." He saluted in military fashion, left the nurses' station, and headed down the hallway. Marie and Lois stood motionless, watching him with admiring eyes.

◊ ◊ ◊

"Unit Seventeen, can I help you?" Matt held the nurses' station's phone tightly against his ear. The patients had been in an uproar all morning and he could barely hear.

"Hi, Matt. This is Larry Baxter. I'm sorry, but you didn't get the unit supervisor position on Seventeen. The administration's bringing in someone from Metro. They want to bolster the hospital's staff with a new hire. She starts in two weeks."

Matt's knees nearly buckled. Suddenly, all the unit's commotion had been muted by a surrounding silence. The only sound that registered was Larry's voice on the other end of the phone.

"I've been holding an A.M. lead position for you on Unit Forty, in case this happened. Are you interested?"

Matt fought off his disappointment. He didn't have to think twice. "Sure, Larry. I'll take it. Thanks, I appreciate it." He tightened his grip on the phone and braced himself. "Do you think the investigation had an impact on my promotion?"

The surrounding silence held its grip. Only Larry's voice existed, and his response would haunt Matt for years to come. The man's every word came across as cautious, regretful, but honest. "It's hard to say for sure . . . but it's possible."

The call ended. The silence ceased. Unit 17's deafening commotion returned.

Unit 40 was a smaller building with fewer patients but more physically and mentally handicapped than 17's. The assignment would be low profile, with less stress, which, considering everything, sounded perfect. Matt had never heard of a program director holding a position for anyone. There was humanity left in the world after all. It seemed ludicrous, but he felt devastated and grateful at the same time.

Sighing, Matt glanced around the unit. Walking by with a pair of patients, Lois refused to make eye contact with him. The situation hadn't improved over the weeks and probably wouldn't for months, if ever. Matt had worked nearly eleven and a half years on 17. Eleven and a half years of being the first employee to report for duty—and the last to leave at the end of the shift. Eleven and a half years of helping staff when they needed assistance and taking an early lunch time because no one else wanted it. And eleven and a half years of trying to make 17 the best unit in the hospital. Matt had no doubt it was the cleanest and most efficient. He had done his best, not for the sake of the staff, or Roy Hansen, or Larry Baxter, or even himself—his every effort had been for the patients.

◊ ◊ ◊

Shari decided to hold a goodbye potluck on Matt's final day. She was barely speaking to him, so it had to be a token, go-through-the-motions type of gesture. It turned out to be a depressing, piecemeal affair. Sheri brought some food and left it in the staff's breakroom. Vanessa was off duty but promised to come for the occasion. Needing some moral support, Matt's hopes were dashed when she didn't show. There was no actual gathering. A few staff came during their various lunch times and helped themselves. When Matt made his way down the hallway for his lunch, Marie and Lois were standing in front of the breakroom, eating. Matt went into the room and ate alone. There were no goodbyes from the staff—just the end of another shift.

Judith Thompson had been a friend of Matt's for years. When she heard how he had been banned from attending Roy's going-away party, she invited him and Cassie over for a barbecue that same night.

◊ ◊ ◊

Matt worked three additional years at Letterman then transferred to a forensic psychiatric facility with a more capable clientele. He was never promoted to unit supervisor, but to attain dayshift, he decided to demote to a psych tech position, and he fell in love with his job all over again.

Matt and Cassie divorced after years of marital strife. Enjoying a lengthy and endearing friendship, Matt and Judith married several years later. He remained friends with Vanessa, despite discovering that at the time of Lance's investigation, she was having an affair with him. Vanessa died of breast cancer at the age of fifty-two.

Lance McHenry continued working on 17. He was turned in by the unit's psychologist for choking a patient. Lance was fired but was rehired after ten months.

Letterman State Hospital closed its doors years later, a casualty of countless budget cuts. Staff were either transferred to other state hospitals or laid off. The patients were dispersed to private facilities, the majority of them known for inferior care.

Michael Raff discovered his love for writing at age thirteen, then, years later, attended creative writing courses at Cypress College in Cypress, California. He became a psychiatric technician employed in state and private facilities before retiring in 2007. While writing his romantic memoir, *Special*, he stumbled upon his flair for horror. He has completed five anthologies of short stories, *Seven: Tales of Terror, Scare Tactics, Shreds, Shadowland,* and his non-horror anthology, *Something Different*, followed by two novels *Skeleton Man* and *Stalkers*. Three of his stories have been published in the California Writers Club *Literary Review*, two more in internet magazines, and two published with Dragon Soul Press, a traditional publisher.

Michael co-founded Nevermore Enterprises to promote his books and activities. He has remained active in the HDCWC since 2011, frequently serving on their board. He lives in Hesperia, California, with his wife, Joyce, and their hodgepodge of animals. For more information, visit his website, mraffbooks.com.

The Dance[29]

Rusty LaGrange
High Desert Branch

It must happen often
but only in dark corners
managed by the moon
and under the porch light.
Two blind lovers find
their hearts thrumming
a beat, a vibrant call.
Clutching each other's arms
with pincher strength,
they perform the Dance
of the Scorpions, spinning
and waving deadly tails.
Each will hold tight
until the morning light
until their love defies
the danger of being out
in the open, and in love.

With nearly twenty years of news writing and interviewing, **Rusty LaGrange**'s journalism career veered off into graphic arts and desktop publishing. She digitally produced the CWC *Bulletin* for five years, the High Desert Branch's newsletter, *The Inkslinger,* for ten years, and her poetry has been entered in numerous poetry contests.

Her researching skills are used for Old West history forays, antique collecting, and finding prime source books for her Western novels. In 2021, she received the highly acclaimed Ina Coolbrith Award for service to the CWC state organization, as well as the Jack London Award for local branch programs and support.

She lives with her husband, Jeff, in Lucerne Valley—on *The Rusty Bucket Ranch,* of course.

[29] Previously published in the High Desert Branch 2023 anthology, *Conflict!*

A Bright Red Schwinn[30]

J. P. Garner
High Desert Branch

He didn't remember much about where he was born. There was, he easily recalled, the strong scent of mint tea that filled their home and then there was the murder that prompted his mother to move them to America. The family next door—including Elise, the girl he played with—had been slaughtered by the Arabs because they hated the French and wanted them to leave Morocco.

The following week, his mother who was French by birth and married to an American sailor she later divorced, booked passage for them on a ship bound for New York City.

Gabriel remembers being sick most of the trip.

Initially, they lived in Syracuse with Ta-Ta Rose, his mother's sister. When her children complained about Gabriel, Ta-Ta Rose punished him by locking him in a closet. When his mother returned from work early one day and discovered the arrangement, she blasted her sister then took Gabriel and flew to Oklahoma City, where they settled into a second-floor apartment in the Wilmot Hotel, and he was enrolled in the Catholic school across the street.

St. Joseph's it was called.

Many years later, it would be replaced by the Murrah Federal Building, which was bombed by Timothy McVeigh but, in the fall of 1960, it was hell for Gabriel, who was verbally and physically abused by the other students because he came from the same place black people came from.

Oklahoma was segregated back then, and they couldn't understand why, since he had been born in Africa, he wasn't black as well. They treated him like he was a circus freak. One boy, a fifth grader named Nathan Jessup, beat him up a couple of times until Gabriel's uncle taught him how to defend himself. "Just walk up to him and punch him as hard as you can in the nose," he instructed.

Gabriel was uncertain. "In the nose?" he questioned, half hoping his uncle wasn't serious.

"Yes," Uncle Al confirmed. "In the nose. It will start bleeding

[30] Previously published in the High Desert Branch 2023 anthology, *Conflict!*

and his eyes will water. That's when you can lay into him."

So Gabriel did as he was told. He walked up to his tormentor and went to punch him, but the blow missed. It grazed the fifth-grader's cheek who, on regaining his balance, commenced to beat up Gabriel once again. Then, as if to add insult to injury, Gabriel was spanked by two nuns and later expelled by the Mother Superior, who was unsympathetic. "You've been quite the troublemaker, Mr. Messenger," she scolded him, her expression taut and unforgiving. She looked deathly pale in her habit.

When Gabriel's mother came from work to collect him and learned he had been spanked, she laid into the Mother Superior, who appeared to shrink from the invectives uttered by his mother in French. Gabriel wished he better understood the language, as he was still stinging from the switch the nuns had used to punish him for starting the fight.

After a quick lunch at the Katz Drugstore behind the YMCA where he had learned to swim, his mother delivered him to his aunt and uncle in Midwest City, an all-white suburb of Oklahoma City. Because the kids at the Country Estates Elementary School didn't know he was African, they included him in their football games.

And, it was there, at his uncle's house, that Gabriel lived until he returned from summer camp the following year and discovered his mother had remarried. "A Marine," she said. "His name is Dominick, but you must call him Dad."

Dad, as it turned out, promptly moved them to Oklahoma City, close to where he worked at a recruiting office. The kids in the neighborhood didn't know Gabriel was from Africa either, but because he had no bicycle, he was not immediately included in their adventures. So, at dinner one night, he asked Dad if he could have a bike. The Marine didn't even pause before he said, "Sure. No sweat."

After Gabriel helped his mother with the dishes, the Marine drove them to the Sears and Roebuck, where they walked past the bicycle display and into the Lawn and Garden Center, where the Marine purchased a lawnmower.

"What's that for?" Gabriel asked.

The Marine laid a hand on Gabriel's shoulder. "It's for you," he said with a smile.

Gabriel was perplexed. "For me? I don't understand."

"You will," the Marine answered. He also purchased a rake,

hedge trimmers, and hand shears—and a gallon gas can. "For when you finish mowing a lawn," he clarified.

Gabriel didn't understand the comment, but it was painfully clear the Marine was not buying him a bicycle.

The next day, a Saturday, after a breakfast of toast and ruby red grapefruit, the Marine grabbed up Gabriel and drove him through the neighborhood, pointing out houses that needed their lawns mowed. "What you do," he explained, "is you knock on their doors and ask them if you can cut their grass for money."

Gabriel was shocked. "You want me to work?"

The Marine parked the car. "You want a bicycle, right?"

Gabriel was suddenly fearful. He had upset the Marine. "Yes," he answered slowly.

The Marine smiled. "Then yes, I want you to work."

"How?" Gabriel asked.

"I just told you. I want you to cut grass for money," the Marine explained.

"But I don't know how to cut grass," Gabriel complained.

The Marine laughed. "No sweat. I'll show you."

When they returned to their house, the Marine did exactly that. He showed Gabriel how to operate the lawn mower and how to cut grass. Then he had him finish cutting their lawn, front and back, and trimming its edges with the hand shears. Afterward, he showed Gabriel how to clean the equipment.

For a short while, the neighborhood kids were curious and they gathered in the street at the front of the house to watch Gabriel work. They talked among themselves and laughed at times before they peddled off on some adventure. Only the girl who lived two houses up from Gabriel stayed behind. Her curiosity was confusing to him, but he was glad she remained behind. She had been the one who approached him when he arrived at the new house the previous week.

Her name was Connie Evans and she was twelve. She went to St. Patrick's she said, the Catholic school close by on Portland Avenue. The kids often went there to play football, she said. Gabriel liked her immediately. She was prettier than any of the girls he had known in Midwest City. He paused from his labors and strolled over to her. "Hello, Connie," he said, as he wiped his face with a rag.

"Hello, Gabriel," she replied. She sat astride a bright red Schwinn bicycle. Gabriel liked how her blonde hair tumbled in curls to her shoulders and seemed to capture the sunlight. “What are you doing?” she asked.

“Learning how to cut grass.”

“Why? We pay people to cut our grass.”

“That’s why I’m learning how. My dad wants me to cut grass for money.”

“Really? He wants you to work?”

“Yes. I have to make money to buy a bike.”

Connie smiled. “I did that,” she declared with some pride.

“You did? You cut grass?”

Connie laughed. “No, silly. I ironed clothes. I still do. That’s where I’m going now. To my house to iron.”

“Whose clothes do you iron?” Gabriel inquired.

“The people in the neighborhood and some from church.”

“Church? You go to church?”

“Yes, I do. You don’t?”

“No, I do. That is, I did. I went to church where I used to live.”

“You should come with me,” she quickly suggested.

“Where do you go?”

“St. Patrick’s. It’s around the corner.” Realizing Gabriel had no bike, she added, “We can walk there. It’s real close.”

He was about to agree when the Marine called to him through the screen door. “Gabriel, come in now. It’s time for lunch.”

Gabriel quickly glanced back and replied. “Coming.” He then looked at Connie. He was disappointed. “I have to go.”

“So do I,” she said. “So, tomorrow we’ll go to church. Come to my house at ten thirty. Or later. We don’t wanna get there too early.”

“What time is church?” Gabriel asked.

“Mass starts at ten. We’ll wanna sit in the back.”

“But we’ll be late.”

“I know. That’s so we miss the boring stuff.”

“The boring stuff?” Gabriel thought about mass at St. Philip Neri’s, the church he had attended in Midwest City. “You mean communion?”

“Yes, Gabriel, communion. What was your church like? And when mass is over, we wanna leave fast, so we can be first to the cafeteria and get the best donuts.”

◊ ◊ ◊

Gabriel's lunch consisted of a tuna salad sandwich on toast with potato chips and slices of cold watermelon, during which Gabriel's mother happily recalled when she met the Marine. "I didn't like you at first," she said. "You were cute and you knew it." She started laughing.

"But I am cute." the Marine declared as he wrapped his arm around her shoulders and squeezed her tightly. "And I'm all yours."

"Lucky you," she replied with a wry smile.

The Marine softened his grip and turned to Gabriel, who was amused by their conversation. "So, Gabriel, if you leave now, maybe you can get two lawns cut this afternoon."

Gabriel agreed. "Yes, sir," he said. The sir was unexpected, but it came easily, which surprised Gabriel. It was an automatic response. He only said that to Uncle Al, who was easygoing but also firm. Gabriel paused after rising from his seat. "How much should I ask for?"

The Marine removed his arm from around Gabriel's mother and pushed his plate aside. Half of the sandwich remained, along with some cottage cheese. The Marine didn't eat potato chips. "That's a good question. I think a dollar would be fair. Fifty cents each for the back and the front."

"A dollar! Really? That much?" Gabriel was astonished. The only other time he had acquired that much money was when he had lived at the Wilmot Hotel and broke into the newspaper dispensers by the radio station. After stealing the papers, he sold them on the corner of 3rd and Robinson. It hadn't taken long to sell them all. It was, he recalled, how he paid to see *Spartacus* six times. He still fantasized about that scene in which Jean Simmons was ushered into Spartacus' cell and, after he admitted to having never been with a woman, she removed her clothing.

"I'm going to go," Gabriel said, suddenly flushed. The redness warmed his cheeks, but underneath the sensation, he was feeling determined. He hadn't felt that way earlier when the Marine first proposed the venture, but now, after hearing how much money he could make, he was feeling inspired. Picking up his paper plate, he disposed of it in the trash and rinsed out his glass of Kool-Aid. Returning to the kitchen table, he bent over and kissed his mother on the cheek, which surprised her.

◊◊◊

Connie's house was two doors up the street, going toward Portland Avenue. It was painted a muted lemon-yellow with forest-green shutters on either side of its windows. The covered front porch contained a café table and two rattan chairs and was presently cooled by the shade of the large oak tree that commanded one corner of the front lawn.

The lawn, Gabriel noticed as he walked up the driveway, pushing his lawnmower in front of him, was green and thick and definitely in need of mowing. He parked the lawnmower bearing his tools and gallon bottle of cold water by the walkway leading to the porch. Connie's bright red Schwinn was parked next to the same walkway.

As Gabriel approached the front door, his stomach was churning. He was both nervous and excited. Nervous because it was the first time he would solicit work from a prospective customer and excited because he'd get to see Connie again.

The front door was open behind the screen door, allowing air to flow into the living room. Through the opening, Gabriel could hear the television. Facing it, behind an ironing board, was Connie. She was intent on her work.

Gabriel stood there for a few seconds, watching her at her labors, contemplating what to say. It had seemed simple enough when he left his house, but the closer he came to hers, the more hesitant he became.

He was thinking of leaving, when Connie called out to him above the sounds of the television. "Are you gonna knock or what?" she asked. Then, in the time it took for Gabriel to assemble a reply, she was opening the screen door and stepping out onto the front porch. "Cat got your tongue?" she joked.

Startled by her sudden appearance, Gabriel could only utter one word, "What?"

Connie laughed. "Nothing. It's just something my mother says." She rose on her toes and looked over Gabriel's shoulder. "So, you wanna cut our grass?"

Gabriel's expression twisted up. He didn't understand how she knew. "Uh. . . yes," he muttered. "How did you know?"

"It's easy, silly. I can see your lawnmower."

Gabriel glanced back to the blue and dull-gold device. In the tension he had felt standing at her door, he had forgotten about it. He was embarrassed. “Yes,” he admitted. “You said you and your mom pay to have your lawn cut. So, yeah, I’m here asking if I can do it.”

Connie was smiling. It was like she knew something that Gabriel didn’t. She had a way about her that was different from the few girls he had befriended in Midwest City. It was unnerving and alluring at the same time. In the moments he had been with her since moving to 24th Street, he would think of the movie *Spartacus* and the lovely servant girl Varinia. It was troubling. He didn’t understand it.

“Sure,” Connie replied. “What do you charge?”

Gabriel’s nervousness dissipated immediately, replaced with excitement. “You want me to cut the front and back, right?” He was almost breathless.

“Yes. Front and back.”

“I charge a dollar. Fifty cents for each. That’s with trimming, too,” he added.

Connie nodded. “Okay, that’s good. You can start when you’re ready. I need to go back to my ironing. I have a lot of it.” She turned to go then paused in mid-stride and glanced back at Gabriel. He hadn’t noticed it before but her eyes were blue. “Am I your first customer?”

Gabriel was still looking at her blue eyes. “Yes,” he said.

“Good,” she replied. “I’m glad you came here first.” She was still smiling when she turned about and entered the house. Through the screen door, Gabriel watched her walking toward the ironing board.

He wanted to watch her iron but knew she would think that strange. He thought it strange as well. Returning to his equipment, he walked the yard first like the Marine had taught him, looking for rocks and anything else that might damage the mower’s blade or injure him.

He found no debris in the lawn, either the front or the back, but he saw a grave marker in the corner of the backyard. It was dated May 17, 1961. Just two months before. The name painted on the face of the large rock was “Sadie.” Beneath it was a flower and a cross. Gabriel gathered that Sadie had been a dog.

As with the roots above the ground at the base of the oat tree out front, Gabriel would use the hand shears to trim the grass growing next to the headstone. Otherwise, cutting Connie's yard entailed walking back and forth, raking up the cut grass afterward, then trimming the edges of the lawn that adjoined the driveway and walkways. If he included a couple of water breaks, the task would take him two hours, he figured.

No sweat, he thought.

◊ ◊ ◊

After collecting all of his tools, he sat at the café table on the front porch and drank from the gallon bottle of water the Marine had suggested he fill halfway and freeze the night before. The cold water felt good against the back of his throat. "Are you done?" Connie asked through the screen door.

"Yes, all done," Gabriel replied.

"Are you thirsty?"

"I have water," he said.

"How about some cold lemonade?"

"Yeah, sure, cold lemonade sounds better."

Connie emerged from the house carrying a sweating pitcher of lemonade and two glasses. She paused as she approached the café table to look out over the front yard. "It looks really good Gabriel," she remarked. "Better, I think, than how it was done before. You raked up the cut grass, didn't you?"

"Yes. I did it just how the Marine showed me."

Connie walked to the table and set the pitcher and glasses down. She started filling the glasses with lemonade. "The Marine? Who's that?"

Gabriel studied her quickly. She was tall. Taller than him by at least an inch, maybe two. She seemed to be more legs than anything else. Her blonde hair looked uncombed and yet it seemed natural that way. She was wearing shorts and a T-shirt. The shirt was colored Kelly green and, in white letters, had "St. Patrick's" printed across its front. On her right hand, on the third finger, she wore a ring.

Looking out into the street as she sat down opposite him, he wondered where the other neighborhood kids were. "The Marine is my stepdad," Gabriel answered as he lifted his glass of lemonade to his lips and drank.

"Why don't you just call him Dad?" Connie retrieved her glass.

"I probably should," Gabriel admitted. "It just feels funny. He's only been my dad for a couple of weeks. They got married on July the fourth, so, like I said, it just feels funny calling him Dad."

"Are you hungry?" Connie asked. "I can make you a sandwich."

Gabriel smiled. "No, I'm okay but thanks for asking."

"So, what's your dad—I mean, the Marine—like?"

"You know, I think about that a lot. When I first met him, I didn't like him. He was too friendly."

"Too friendly? What's wrong with that?"

"Nothing, I guess. It was just that he was trying too hard for me to like him."

"Maybe he was nervous."

Gabriel thought about it. He recalled how nervous he had been about meeting the Marine, so maybe the Marine had been as well. After all, he was meeting his eleven-year-old son for the first time. "You know, I never thought of it like that. Maybe he *was* nervous."

"What's he like now?"

"He's alright. He teaches me a lot of things. How to make my bed and fold my clothes. He even showed me how to hang my clothes in the closet. Can you imagine that? And then, this morning, he taught me how to mow a lawn. He's also going to teach my mom how to drive. So, yeah, I guess he's alright."

"I wish I had a dad," Connie suddenly lamented.

The change of subject caused Gabriel to sit up straight. Connie was not smiling. She looked sad. "Where is your dad?" he asked.

When she looked up to speak, there were tears in her blue eyes. "He was killed in Korea. I never knew him."

Gabriel softened. "I'm sorry." He didn't know what else to say. Sorry didn't seem enough.

"It's alright," she explained. "I didn't know him, so I don't miss him. I just miss having a dad. I think my mother does too. She's alone too much."

When Connie mentioned her mother being alone, Gabriel instantly thought about his mother before she married the Marine. Except she had been rarely alone. She was too attractive and lively to be alone for long periods. A day or two, at most, but never longer. Whereas Gabriel, when they lived at the hotel, had no real friends. Not like he had in Midwest City when he lived with his aunt and uncle. That had turned out to be the best thing that happened to him.

But no, before that, he had no real friends. Just the kids who went to YMCA to learn how to swim, but then they'd go to their homes and not miss him. But now was different. Now there were neighborhood kids. And green lawns and very little concrete. It was a good thing, and it would be better once he had saved enough money to buy a bicycle.

"So, you're buying a bike," Connie said. "Do you know what kind?"

Gabriel looked at Connie's bike, gleaming in the sunlight. "Like yours, I think. A bright red Schwinn."

"You should," she agreed. "It's great. I like my bike. I just got it about a month ago. It took me almost three months to save my money and get it."

"How much did it cost you?" Gabriel inquired.

"Thirty-nine dollars."

"Geez, that's a lot of money. You must have been ironing up a storm."

"I was. It was the only way I was going to get it. My mom works two jobs, but we still couldn't afford to buy it."

"Why two jobs?"

"So we can live in a house and I can go to a private school. She works at Safeway during the day then she comes home for an hour and checks on me. Then she goes to the Katz Drugstore and works until nine thirty."

"She does that all the time?"

"Yes. Six days a week. She's done it for years, but she doesn't work on Sundays."

"So, now that you have your bike, why do you still iron?"

"For my stuff. I buy my clothes and things, and I have a savings account at my mom's bank."

"A savings account? Really. Wow, that's something! Do you like doing that? I mean, working like you do?"

"I didn't at first but I do now. I like buying my stuff, and I like having a savings account. Some more lemonade?" she asked.

Gabriel hadn't noticed during the conversation that he had finished all of his lemonade. It was good and he wanted more. "Yeah, sure. It's really good. You made it?"

"Yes. I pretty much make everything because of the way my mother works. But she cooks on Sunday or we go out to eat. So, do you have a girlfriend back where you're from?"

The inquiry caused Gabriel to choke on the lemonade he was drinking. Wiping his chin, he replied, “A girlfriend? No, I don’t. I never did.”

Connie persisted. “Why? You don’t like girls?”

“What? No. It’s not that. It’s just that I was too busy.” He hadn’t been, but he didn’t know how else to explain why he didn’t have a girlfriend.

“Too busy? What were you doing?’

“Well, there was school and football. Mostly, football. We played that every chance we got.”

“We do that here too. We play at the school. But it’s summer now so we play baseball. That’s where everybody’s at—at the school playing baseball.”

“Do you play?”

“Yes. Sometimes when they need someone to make the teams even.”

“You’re not afraid?”

“I was but not anymore. I kind of like it.”

“That’s pretty neat.”

“It is, I think. But I don’t do it all the time. I spend most of my time ironing—which is probably something I need to be doing right now. I have a lot of clothes to iron before tomorrow.” Connie stood up, reached into the right pocket of her shorts, and extracted four quarters.

Gabriel quickly finished drinking the lemonade in his glass then he stood up. He looked at the money in Connie’s hand. “You’re paying me?” he questioned.

“Yes,” she replied, as she handed him the money. “Who did you think was?”

“Your mother.”

“I pay for the lawn work.”

Gabriel was confused. “You do? Why?”

“It’s simple really. I don’t want my mom mowing the lawn on her day off.”

Gabriel swelled with respect for Connie. He had never met anyone his age who cared about their mom that much. It shamed him that he had ever complained about mowing lawns for money. “That’s like the neatest thing I ever heard of.”

“Really?” Connie remarked.

"Yeah, it really is."

"Don't tell anyone," she pleaded.

"Why?"

"It's not for them to know."

"Why me?"

"I don't know. You're different. You're like me. You have to work for what you want." Connie reached down and grabbed the glasses and the pitcher then she set them back down. Gabriel wasn't sure why. "You ever been kissed by a girl?" she asked.

The question stunned Gabriel. He never had been and didn't know how to tell her that. It was probably the delay in responding that made her guess that he hadn't been. "You haven't, have you?"

Gabriel shook his head. "No," he finally answered.

Connie stepped around the table and up close to Gabriel. She placed her hands on his upper arms. "What's your last name?"

"Messenger," he said weakly.

"Like the angel," she said. "Well, Gabriel Messenger, close your eyes because I'm going to kiss you."

◊ ◊ ◊

When Gabriel was in the shower, he ran his finger over his lips and thought back to the kiss. It had been soft and pleasant, just as he imagined his first kiss might be like.

After the shower, he went to his room and dressed, all the while in a daze from the day's events. He then sat at his desk, perplexed by all that had happened. It was a day of many firsts for him. He had not only learned how to mow a lawn but, as the Marine predicted, he had started a lawn-mowing business, and then, unexpectedly, he had been kissed by a girl.

And not just any girl. A beautiful girl.

That was part of what was so perplexing about today. The fact that she was so pretty. Why had she kissed him? It was not, he surmised, her first time to kiss a boy, so what had he said or done that prompted her to bestow that form of affection on him? He played back their conversation in his head but couldn't discern anything so unusual about what had been said that it would inspire her to kiss him.

He was troubled. Was this how it was going to be with girls—always confusing and, at the same time, enticing? He wished he was in Midwest City, where he could talk with his Uncle Al about it. His uncle would know what to say that would make sense of the confusion that had resulted from Connie's kiss.

After cutting her lawn, and the kiss, Gabriel had proceeded down the street and asked other residents if he could cut their grass. On his fourth attempt, he was successful, and he performed the same routine on their lawn as he had on Connie's, plus they had some shrubs that needed trimming.

In an afternoon of work, he had earned two dollars, which he placed in a Mason jar on his desk so he could see it. Two dollars! It was hot work but not difficult. He enjoyed making each lawn perfect like he was an artist or something. Each lawn was evenly cut and neatly trimmed.

He couldn't wait to tell the Marine, who, after his mother's driving lesson, had gone to the recruiting office for the afternoon. He'd tell him at dinner, which his mother said would be ready soon. She had prepared his favorite meal: cabbage rolls in an Italian sauce.

He picked up the Mason jar and studied the money with some fascination. One dollar bill and four quarters. Mowing lawns was different from stealing newspapers. It was honest work, for one, and it was something about which he could be proud. When he stole newspapers and sold them, he had just felt lucky. It gave him movie money.

Reaching into his desk drawer, he retrieved the wall calendar the Marine had given him. Each page had its own picture of Marines doing some kind of training. He turned to July's page, whose picture depicted bald-headed trainees climbing thick ropes. He hung the calendar on the corkboard above his desk with thumbtacks. Using a red crayon, he circled today's date and scrawled a "2" in the square labeled "15."

He then extracted this morning's newspaper from the same drawer and thumbed through the pages until he arrived at the sports section, where he had seen an ad for a bicycle. It was in the lower right corner of the page, next to the article about the Yankees losing to the White Sox, 6-1. Mickey Mantle had scored the lone point for the Yankees by hitting a home run.

The ad was for a Schwinn Tornado bike. A 24 incher. It cost $39.95. That was a lot of money, but looking at the calendar and counting two dollars per day for six days of the week, Gabriel calculated that it would take him eighteen days to earn $36.00. He already had two dollars, so seventeen days! That's all. He could have a bicycle in seventeen days.

Grabbing a pair of scissors from the top desk drawer, Gabriel cut the ad out of the paper. He thumbtacked it next to the calendar.

Tomorrow, he'd go to church with Connie. Maybe they'd kiss again. He wasn't sure, but he hoped so as he quickly thought of the movie *Spartacus*. Then Monday—Day One—he'd walk the neighborhood looking for lawns needing to be mowed.

From the kitchen, the Marine called out to him to come to dinner. Upon rising from his seat, Gabriel paused and, before leaving his room, glanced at the bicycle ad one more time.

J.P. Garner is a retired Army veteran and high school football coach who started writing seriously in 2012. He has published two books, several short stories, hundreds of political articles for a website called BarstowCitizens, and one poem about the courage of Eve. He is currently working on a two-book modern romance about the power and wonder of second chances. He lives in Barstow, California.

Pepper-Pot Soup No-Tell Tell-All[31]

Anita I. Holmes
High Desert Branch

First meal I ever fed that man wasn't planned.
I hadn't constructed the menu intending to share
but
he stopped by the house to say hi—so he said—
and to lend me a book he thought I'd appreciate.

When we'd taken our seats in class,
he'd sat right next to me.

"Ooh, that smells good," he said wistfully.
Inside, soup simmered on the stove
so
what was I supposed to do, except
ask him if he'd eaten yet?

When the gang went out for coffee afterward,
he'd slid into the booth next to me.

We sat down to slices of homemade bread,
still warm, spread thick with butter,
and
served alongside bowls of steaming hot soup,
Philly-style pepper-pot, back-home comfort food.

When he'd shared stories about his workday,
he'd cracked us up with his comedic delivery.

He devoured the soup and asked for more.
"What is this, some kind of macaroni?" he asked,
and
nudged a curious morsel remaining in his bowl.
He smiled sweetly at me, revealing a pair of dimples.

---

[31] Previously published in the High Desert Branch 2023 anthology, *Conflict!*

When we'd discussed menu selections, he'd
announced he didn't eat anything weird.

Did I want to scare this guy off—or maybe see him again?
"You've heard of radiatori? The texture's kind of like that."
OK
he'd nodded, helped himself to a third bowl,
and asked if I'd seen the koalas at the San Diego Zoo.

When we'd gone our separate ways that evening,
He'd struck me as a regular piece of work—in a good way.

I invited that man in for homemade bread and soup,
and he stayed in my life for thirty-three years,
yet
he went to the grave without ever discovering
my delicious radiatori soup pasta
was always honeycomb beef tripe.

Anita I. Holmes is an author, editor, advocate, musician, artist, and speaker. She is a Zoom mentor and host, award-winning speaker, member of the Poemsmiths of the Mojave High Desert, and frequent reader in the Emily Dickinson Museum's annual *Tell It Slant* poetry festival marathon.

An ordained pastor, clinically trained chaplain, and patient advocate, she has served as the High Desert Interfaith Council's president. She is a fan of Advance Directives and the P.O.L.S.T. Paradigm Program.

Holmes is Director of the Victor Valley Threshold Singers, who, with quiet blended voices, bring comfort to those at life's thresholds.

She has developed tours and programs for the National Park Service and Bureau of Land Management and frequently hosts cyclists traveling through the High Desert. She and current dog-in-residence, Archibald "Archie" MacLeash, love to cycle.

A mixed-media artist, Ms. Holmes combines writing, weaving, and origami. *In Their Wildest Dreams*, her cozy mystery with magic realism, is soon to be published.

The Wrong Number

Ben Alirez
Inland Empire

"And so, we pay homage to those we've lost," the TV host declared.

Ken Morehouse sat alone, watching the year-end special on the many celebrities and public figures who passed away. The sixty-five-year-old man had finally retired, a promise he kept to his beloved wife. Together, they would finally have time to enjoy their golden years—lives celebrated in the unabashed glory of occupational freedom. And then the unthinkable happened. She was gone.

Suddenly fireworks exploded in the surrounding neighborhood, visible from his living room window. A cacophony of blasts and bursts, smoke trails and brightly colored lights that splintered in every direction before dissipating under a blanket of stars. It was merely twelve months ago that he and his wife, Jeanie, attended a New Year's Eve celebration at a swanky hotel. It was truly one for the ages, as good friends joined them. But what made it even more memorable was Jeanie. Halfway through a dance, the three-inch heel on a ruby red stiletto snapped off. Instead of sulking, she fell into a fit of laughter and improvised—breaking the heel on the other shoe before dancing the night away. It wasn't long before her girlfriends ditched their heels too in a celebratory show of support. *Great times.*

The last day of the year always symbolized new hope, he thought bitterly. But shared evenings with his childhood princess were relegated to faint memories now.

He stood up from the sofa, leaving behind a lonesome glass of scotch to claim something from the closet. As he brought it to the kitchen with him, he sat at the table and simply stared at the retrieved box. He chuckled to himself, remembering an age of innocence, a time when a spunky adolescent Jeanie would venture over to enjoy cartoons with him, animations that featured an angel on one shoulder and a devil on the other. One whispered pearls of wisdom, while the other encouraged more unruly choices.

"What I wouldn't do for one more cartoon with you," he said, feeling numb.

A black book rested on the table, next to the box. No two objects presented a greater contrast in ideology. Where one offered hope, the other offered finality.

Several words came to mind. For I know the thoughts that I think toward you, says the Lord, thoughts of peace and not of evil, to give you a future and a hope.

He shook his head in disbelief. "What does that even mean now?" he muttered.

The last four months were the most arduous of his life. How could they not be? Each room fostered quiet reflection, each living space a loving, woven tapestry of their precious time together. A gift. An unimaginable cache of cherished reminders. Treasured aromas from the kitchen came to life, including the time he was helping Jeanie make a cake because of her shoulder surgery. Everything was going well until the mixer spouted red velvet batter like a volcano at the height of its fury. The living room whispered a sonnet of remembrances as well, including the time the shelves they put up together ended in a two-person take-down of raining décor and a wall full of picture frames. The since-repainted porch transformed itself into a staged play as ghostly-powered images of him and his wife clamored about the perimeter of their home in panic, realizing they failed to bring house keys in their haste to rush out the door. From that day on, they were convinced a medieval castle was no more fortified than their home, and a host of other incidents and adventures. But it was the last memory that was the most absolute. The moment an ambulance carried his darling away. Away forever.

Enough already! He removed the box lid and wondered, *Were they all just lies?* He hadn't felt God's presence in—? God knows when.

Another verse cried out to him. So teach us to number our days that we may gain a heart of wisdom.

"You want a number? My number?" he moaned. "Well, alright then!"

Inside the container was a nickel-plated revolver. He lifted it carefully, examining it as if for the first time. Grip. Hammer. Trigger. Barrel. His dark eyes stared intensely at the muzzle.

His courage wavered. Don't think about it, just do it!

The last few years, the world had become far more confusing. A woke society emerged, a cancel culture clamoring for more change. It seemed there were fewer places in society for men like him—white males of so-called privilege. Social distancing measures prompted by the pandemic only exacerbated the unbearable loneliness and despair. Fewer neighborly chats. Fewer handshakes of friendship. No familial embraces. No real opportunity to celebrate the life that was his best friend and partner. Where had all the love gone? He reminded himself it didn't matter anymore.

He opened his mouth and led the barrel inside, staring up at the ceiling as anguished gasps escaped. He pulled the hammer back and his hand began to tremble. The cylinder rotated; the hammer notched in place. An answer to the unbearable torment.

Chirp-chirp-chirp-chirp.

The melodious tones of his wife's iPad interrupted the disquieting silence.

Who is calling at this late hour? Get back to your purpose, a voice said. He repositioned the gun again.

Chirp-chirp-chirp-chirp.

His gaze went from the firearm to the iPad and back.

Chirp-chirp-chirp-chirp.

"Argh!" he cried, setting the weapon down. He fumbled to find the decline button, having left his reading glasses in the living room. He poked at something. Suddenly, a stranger's face materialized. A young woman appeared on the screen. His image was visible as well, and he realized how disheveled he appeared, unshaven and unkempt.

"Yes, can I reach a pastor here?" she asked.

"What?" Ken erupted. "Is this some kind of sick joke or something?"

She appeared equally perplexed. "I didn't–I didn't realize I was using video chat, but I desperately need to speak to someone."

"How'd you get this number?"

"Is this a wrong number?" she returned. "Look, I'm pretty anxious tonight."

"Sorry, young lady, can't help you. Got problems of my own, okay?" As the elderly man fumbled with the electronic device, the stand tipped over and the camera trained on the revolver.

"Is that, is that a gun?" her voice stuttered.

"Aw, geez!" Ken quickly righted the device. Once the camera came into focus, the woman gave him a piercing glare.

"That was a mistake. You didn't see that," he apologized. "Now, I've got to go."

"Wait, wait, wait—don't hang up! Please," she insisted. "Look, let's just talk, okay? It's just words. . . talking. What can it hurt, right?"

The widower experienced a measure of panic at being discovered. It was admittedly awkward. One moment she was the patient, and the next she was the psychotherapist—emphasis on "psycho."

"What do you want to talk about?" he asked uncertainly.

"I don't know. Something. Anything." There was sincerity in her voice.

Despondent, Ken threw up his hands. "Look, I don't have time, but good luck with that pastor thing."

"Wait," she interjected. "Wanna hear something funny? Do you know why I didn't call a suicide prevention hotline?"

Suicide prevention? He had guessed right. He shook his head.

"Because I used to work at one," she snickered. "Insane, right? Geez, how did I get here?"

"Look, I see what you're trying to do," he said, wondering why he was entertaining her. She was obviously stalling him. "You're wasting your time."

"Can I at least know your name?"

"What the hell for?" he bellowed, as an uncomfortable silence followed. "It doesn't matter, don't you get it?" The reprimand wasn't in person, but it didn't have to be. The retiree saw the hurt in the woman's eyes as a pang of guilt struck him. He wanted to walk away, to escape, but something kept him on the phone line. "Why a pastor?" he inquired more gently.

"No, you're right. Excuse me." The young lady stood up and stepped out of frame.

"What? Where are you going?" A quiet descended. "Hello?" he reiterated.

"I just, I just need a minute," she continued off camera.

The minute stretched into two before she returned and sat back down. There was a bottle of pills in one hand. She removed the lid with some effort, then emptied the contents on the table. Ken scoffed at how twisted their entire New Year's Eve conversation had become.

"Okay, I'm ready."

"Ready? What are those?"

"Sleeping pills," she admitted, staring up at the ceiling. "God, I'm such a head case."

"Why? Because you're confused?"

"No, because I can't swallow pills—it's all I could come up with! I don't mean to throw a pity party here, but the freakin' taste alone will probably kill me. Or worse—force me to gag it all up!"

Ken fought back the urge to laugh. Their entire exchange was growing more humorous and bizarre. "You didn't think about this, I mean, before?"

"Hello-o-o, I was planning on being talked off the proverbial ledge, remember?"

"Right."

"But I'm here now," she reminded him. "It's fate, right? Let's get this over with."

"Well now, wait a minute," he stuttered. "This is my thing, not yours. You're too young."

"Excuse me, I didn't know suicide came with age requirements. That's rule number what, again?"

Ken stifled another laugh. "Okay, so you got me there. Look, you're hurting is all—there's a difference."

"A difference? What's so different about your situation? Mister, you want some *real talk*. You don't know the first thing about what's eating me up inside."

Her words forced him to blanch. "No, you're right. I don't know."

"If you've forgotten, we're in the same dark place. And since we're handing out advice, get it right, mister. You'd be surprised how many self-inflicted gunshot attempts are botched. If you think things are bad now—"

Ken became suddenly skeptical. "Oh, you're good, young lady. You're very good."

She looked at him incredulously, not believing what he was implying. "You know what? Think what you want." The young woman glared at the ceiling again. "God, this is sick. I tried, I really did. I wanted hope to have a chance. But how was I supposed to find hope when all I got was this misled moron!

Shock registered. He was taken aback by the truth of her words.

She huffed as her eyes darted around. "I'm sorry. And I don't even know *why I'm sorry*. Look, we're acting like the only two fools who hurt so bad they want to—" She stopped short. "Why can't we just open up to each other for old times' sake? Huh?"

Ken was lost for words. If it were possible, he was experiencing every human emotion at once. Sorrow. Empathy. Anger. Hopefulness.

His uninvited guest finally rested her head gently next to her keyboard. "Please, God, how can you expect me to go on? Why did you take both of them? Why? I didn't even get to say goodbye."

Something in her words touched him. "Them?"

"My parents," she muttered.

"Was it—" he said hesitantly, "was it the virus?"

A torrent of pain seemed to assail the girl as she began to sob in unrestrained agony.

He asked tenderly, "Was it Covid?"

As her cries carried across the room, he was compelled to reach through the screen and comfort her. There was such anguish in her bearing. He had never been blessed with a daughter, but the thought of one in such absolute pain redirected his attention; starved his own suffering.

"Look, my name is Ken. What's your name?"

Except for moans of heartache, she remained silent.

"I'm sorry about my behavior," he added. "It's just, this whole thing. . . well, it's the last thing I expected. Truth is, I don't know who I'm supposed to be anymore."

"Jenna," she said softly.

"Excuse me?"

She lifted her head slowly as tears reflected the light from the screen. "My name is Jenna."

"It's a lovely name." He nodded. "My wife's name was Jeanie."

"Was?"

He stared off as he answered. "Complications from Covid."

"Sorry."

"I—I didn't, couldn't, say bye either," he added. "It all happened so fast. Tuesday she got tired. Thursday she was gone."

Her eyes seemed to stare into his soul, and he could see they were hazel colored. "I didn't know my heart could hurt this much, Ken."

"I know."

"Look, Ken, I'm feeling tired, I'm going to go now. I don't even know what I should say, but it was nice talking to you. Good luck, okay?"

"For that first month—after she went," he continued to share.

"You know, I went to every super spreader event I could find. I wanted it, I wanted death. I never even caught a cold."

She put a hand up to the screen, her eyes transfixed on him, lending what little comfort she could offer. For the next few hours, the two of them talked at length. He learned what remarkable people her parents were. The circumstances of their passing. Their cherished times together. Her most disheartening regrets. What earnest hopes and dreams remained.

"Hey, this whole mix-up thing," she finally said, "this whole misunderstanding—it's so wild, so weird."

"It is that," he agreed. "But I also think it's wonderful."

The two of them broke into laughter at the improbable coincidence. As their amusement waned, the silence they shared felt far less awkward.

"Can I ask you a last question, Ken?"

"Please."

"Do you think our broken hearts will ever heal?"

"I don't know, I think you got me believing again."

"Believing?" she asked.

Ken reached over and retrieved the black book. He raised it for her to see. "If you're still interested in a pastor, well, a pretty broken one anyway, I think maybe I can help. . . once again."

Ben Alirez has been a member of the IECWC since 2019. In 2004, he co-authored a young adult novella with Paul Langan titled *Brothers in Arms*. Four years later, he produced *El Gato's Revenge*, a novel about a promising inner-city boxer struggling with tragedy and vengeance. Then, in the wake of COVID-19, Ben authored a full-length novel titled *Embers of Innocence* on the virus that changed the world. Ben has seen his literary works published in two other anthologies in recent years.

The Naiad's Tale

Scott Skipper
Inland Empire

Ears—the fennec cub was a ball of puppy fur with enormous ears and a long, pointed nose. Cyrene cuddled him to her breast as the little fox squirmed to get free. She nuzzled him with her cheek and got the end of her nose nipped. "Damon, that was bad. What am I going to do with you?" She set him on the moss-covered ground, and he began tugging at the hem of her filmy gown. "Damon, stop that. Now, it's time for a nap. Be still." She laid her head on the soft tuft of velvety moss, closed her eyes, and let the sound of gently falling water lull her to sleep. The body of the little animal felt warm against her side.

The harsh scream of a hawk woke her in a panic. Feeling for Damon and not finding him, she leapt to her feet and called his name. The hawk screeched again, and she saw that there was nothing in those wicked talons. She began a frantic search for her precious pet before the sharp-eye raptor spotted him first. Following the stream against the flow of the diaphanous water, she called his name desperately.

"Gaia, have you seen my Damon?" she asked the dryad of the oak grove.

"It's not my job to keep track of your suitors," the haughty tree nymph retorted.

"No, Damon is a baby fox that Aeolus gave me at the Dionysia on the full moon last."

Gaia laughed cruelly. "What sense does it make to give a water nymph a fox? He should have given you an otter."

Cyrene contorted her elfin face. "Go suck an acorn."

"Give yourself a thrill, Cyrene, douche with tadpoles."

"Oh, go back in your knothole." Cyrene stamped her foot and continued up the stream calling her dear pet's name.

Near the place where the brook bubbled from the rocks, she spied a blur of reddish brown. The little beast's ears perked at the sound of his name, and he looked at the willowy girl who ran to catch him. Damon turned and darted into the grotto.

"I've got you now," Cyrene said laughing. She picked her way across the stepping-stones cool and slick beneath her bare feet. The joyful water frolicked from the fountain in the center of the brooding cavern. Little Damon taunted her from the wet stone floor at the back of the smallish hollow. "You can't get away from me now," she giggled as she splashed through the last few steps in the pool.

But Damon wasn't finished with the game. His tiny paws thumped on the damp floor as he vanished behind a boulder. Cyrene sprinted after her playmate. To her dismay, he vanished into the blackness of a hidden chasm there.

"Damon, you come out of there this instant. If I have to come get you, I'll bump my head on the low ceiling or fall into some bottomless pit."

The little fox made no sound.

With a sigh, the girl flipped her golden tresses behind her shoulders and started into the Stygian darkness feeling her way along the humid walls. She focused her mind on her sisters of the stagnant waters. She sent a plea to the fens and marshes, cupped her hands, and opened them to release the faerie light. A bluish ball of cool light danced on her palm. It barely vanquished the gloom but offered enough illumination to spare her cracking her skull on the jagged ceiling.

The flickering orb of light also made Damon's beady eyes glow. "I see you," she tittered, and the tiny fox turned again to flee deeper into the inky labyrinth. Cyrene followed by the glow the cold fire, but it rolled from her hand and bounced along the floor. Blue became green. It flared and subsided to blue again with perhaps some orange. In the brief flash of brightness, she saw it—a face, creased and leering. "Oh," she gasped, "who are you?"

"Are we lost, little girl?" a disembodied voice asked from the darkness.

"I'm looking for my baby fennec, Damon."

The marsh light twinkled to life and floated around her head. She could see nothing beyond its feeble glow.

"Are we lost, I say?" the voice had an unpleasant edge of mirth.

"I don't think so. As soon as I catch Damon, I'll go back the way I came."

"Did you come this way?" The will-o'-the-wisp swished sidewise as if thrown by an unseen hand. "Or that way?" The purplish fire blazed in front of her in the opposite direction. At each end of the arc, she saw the gaping maw of a divergent tunnel.

"I don't think I came from either of those passages." She felt confused and frightened.

"Are we lost then, little girl?" the voice in the darkness cackled.

"Again, I don't think so, but if you might help me catch Damon, I'll be out of your way."

"If we catch the little beast, we eats it."

"No," Cyrene wailed. "He's hardly got a morsel of flesh on his tiny body." She tried to capture the shimmering constellation of light. Her hand went right through it. Shadowy palms reached from obscurity, engulfed, and extinguished it. The naiad sent her prayers back to her sisters of the stagnant pools, and again the magic fire kindled in her hands. "Damon, Damon," she called, and heedless of the scarcely seen menace, resumed her pursuit of the impish canine. Her fen fire flared once more, pulsing yellow and revealing the malign features.

"Your precious tidbit did not come this way, little girl."

"Well, which way did he go then?" She stood rigid feeling her imperious side return.

"Which way will you go, little girl?"

"Stop calling me little girl. I'll have you know, I am the daughter of a king."

"Doesn't make you any less of a little girl, and now you're a lost little girl who cannot even find my supper."

"I'll not hear any more of this. Damon is simply not edible. And who are you anyway?"

The murky countenance faded into the gloom. Cyrene tried to thrust the globe of light toward it, but the bauble of blue morphed green and pink and tumbled from her tenuous grasp. She followed the feeble source of light if only to stay in its comforting sphere.

A plaintive yip froze her. She swatted at the glowing cluster and succeeded in swishing it in the direction of the sound. Tiny eyes burned in the umbra and the diminutive cub cowered on the cold stone. Scooping him into her arms, she embraced his soggy fur while he squirmed and kissed her chin.

"Ah, we have found our victuals, have we?"

"I have found nothing of the sort, whoever you are," Cyrene tried to sound bigger than she felt.

"Give us a taste."

"Don't be absurd. Damon is safe now, and we're going home,

thank you."

"We are going home, are we? Do we know where home is?"

"We'll find our way. You needn't worry."

"Did you say you came from this way?" As before, the wraith contained the nebulous swamp light and shone it on the entry of a passageway, then swung it toward another. "Or this way?"

"We came from the way we came. I shall simply retrace my steps."

"Oh, really?" The cluster of scintillating blue pinpricks swept around her colliding with a blank wall. They slid to the floor and recoalesced. "Did you say you came from that way?"

Cyrene's bluff wilted. "Which way did I come?"

"Little girl is lost. Now we shall have her precious, and we shall have our dinner."

"No," she pleaded. "Which way did I come?"

"Little dog first."

"He's not a dog, and you shan't have him. I'll find my way." She attempted to gather the recalcitrant ghost-light. It flowed over her hand while she clutched tiny, wriggling Damon with the other.

Invisible fingers pinched her curvaceous haunch. "Succulent. Perhaps we let the bony beast be and dine on the lost little girl."

The ghostly thumb and finger made her leap and cry, "You don't know who you're dealing with. I shall no more let you eat me than Damon."

Cackling, the hideous visage thrust toward her face in the meager radiance. "She won't let us? However does she plan to stop us?"

"You don't know who you're dealing with."

"We heard that before—daughter of a king. All the more toothsome it sounds."

Cyrene forced her mind to calm. She let her energy flow with the current sending her will to the fountain that frothed in the grotto spilling gentle water into the brook that was her domain. With her naiad's will, she bent the course of the obedient fluid. She heard the trickle increase to a torrent, and then to a rapid. The first wave curled around her dainty feet and quickly floated her sheer garment to her thighs. In heartbeats, the surge wafted her on its sacred bosom deeper into the bowels of the earth while sweeping the dreadful mountain nymph with it.

The column of water carrying Cyrene and her beloved, but drenched, fennec pup rose through a rocky chimney while leaving the drowned shell of her nemesis far below. Sweet sunlight warmed her face as the sheltering deluge emerged from the netherworld placing her and her charge gently onto the sandy bottom of a limpid pool. The naiad gracefully unfolded her silky legs, swept her flowing locks from her eyes, and adjusted her transparent gown before taking poor, soaked Damon to the grassy bank where he shook the water from his downy coat. He shivered and supplicated her to take him to her breast. She embraced the fickle little beast that licked her face and once more nipped her nose.

Scott Skipper has published twenty-one novels to date in various genres. They are available at your favorite online retailers; i.e. Amazon/KDP and Smashwords. All are available as e-Books and paperbacks. Several are audiobooks at Audible.com.

The author lives alone in the foothills above La Verne, California. He is reachable via his website: www.ScottSkipper.com.

ORANGE COUNTY

"Yorba Linda was not the land we had dreamed of . . . it was more beautiful."

—*Jessamyn West*

ORANGE COUNTY

There I Was

Kevin Corfield
Orange County

Who am I to judge?

I'm here eatin' alone on a Friday night. Not eatin' yet. Just got here. Hobbled here, more like it. Just from my clunker to inside, but that's plenty far enough. Found a seat at one of those booths for two jobbies. Hah, found. There were plenty open, as always at Rigby's. Tonight, it's just me, the kid, his loser parents, and the degenerates who sit at the counter for a cup of coffee and toast.

Rigby's is right around the bend from St. Mary's where I go for meetings. A little more slope in the road and I coulda rolled here in neutral.

I don't go to meetings every night, not like I used to. But Friday nights are kind of a ritual. Unless I got a date or somethin'. Hah—good one, Walt. Been so long I can't remember if a hoohoo is vertical or horizontal. Pardon my French. Is hoohoo French? Sounds French. Point bein', I haven't missed a Friday in a long while. Rigby's afterwards is kind of a ritual, too. Not for the atmosphere, that's for sure. Although, the first dozen times it kinda was. Sasha, damn she was pretty. Way too young for me. And I doubt she was into older distinguished white guys, but Lordy I liked the way she smiled at me when I smiled at her. Made me all squishy inside. In a good way. I knew she wouldn't be around long. Not when she could be hustlin' real tips at a real restaurant. She's why I first started comin' in every Friday. But now I've got Pearl waitin' on me. That's a shoosh of stale air whizzin' out of a popped tire if there ever was one. Pearl is a no-guff-takin' big-boned woman with a hard face and big floppy breasts that'd suffocate you. Not in a sexy kind of way, either.

What are you gonna do?

Pearl takes my order. Makes me say it. Sasha woulda just smiled and said, "The usual?"

Hell, guess I should just be grateful to still be here. Meetings'll do that to you. Make you grateful for what ya got after hearin' other peoples' messed up stories.

This family catacorner to me—mom, dad and the kid—I'm tryin' to piece together their deal. I'm assumin' they're family; he could be this week's boyfriend for all I know. But I get the itchy feelin' the two are hitched. Probably a City Hall wedding. One of those, it is what it is, let's just get it over with jobbies. Like that old Springsteen song: We'd go down to the river and we'd somethin' somethin' somethin'. I used to listen to that song in my Chevy next to the Monongahela, drownin' a six pack at lunch, way back when I was still able to work. It's a sad song. This feels sad too.

"Anything you want," I hear Dad say to the kid. Dad's the skinny, wiry type. He's wearin' a plaid, short sleeve button-down you'd find at a thrift store, has shaggy unkept hair, stubbles on his chin and ridiculous sideburns.

They're all perusin' their menus like they've never been in such a fancy place.

"Anything?" the boy timidly asks.

Mom looks at Dad too, not sure if he means it either, but hopeful. If Mom saw a ghost, you wouldn't know, that's how pale her skin is. She's pretty in a what coulda been, but probably never will be, kind of way.

"Anything but the Surf and Turf," Dad says. "We're not the Rockefellers."

The kid's head droops a little. Mom's lips scrunch.

Dad grins. "I'm just bustin' your balls. Anything ya want," he says proudly. "This is your special day."

The kid looks up and smiles. Mom's lips loosen.

"See, we don't need none of that kids' birthday party crap with a bunch of freeloadin' kids. We're havin' fun right here."

So it's the kid's birthday. And this is his big birthday celebration. At Rigby's Diner. Sheesh.

My eggs come just the way I like 'em. Two eggs over easy. Those little cubed potatoes on the side. Two slices of whole wheat toast lathered with butter and cut right down the middle so there's four slices. Coffee, black. My second cup already.

As I eat, dabbin' my toast into the runny yolk, I wonder if the kid's parents had splurged on a party if any kids woulda showed up. I don't think so. He's a meek little kid, God love 'em. The kind of kid that gets bullied. That's got no friends. Keeps everything in because that's what he's learned to do. I can see it. Feel it. The stooped shoulders. Fidgeting feet. Nervous eyes afraid to make contact. It's all there. The kid's lost the fight without throwin' a punch and it's kinda bustin' me up inside.

No Surf and Turf for the kid. He gets a burger, fries, and a Coke. I've had the burger; it's got one slice of pickle on it, that's it. Not so special at all. And I'm pretty sure by the crinkles that the fries are Ore-Ida's.

I'm waitin' for the gift part of the birthday celebration, but I know it's not gonna happen. They're not even talkin' to the kid, really. He's just there. Most of the talk is Dad yappin' about how his co-workers are a bunch of morons who don't know shit from Shinola and how they screwed him over by not puttin' him in charge.

"You'll get it next time, honey," Mom says.

Dad slams the table hard with a sideways fist. Silverware jingles on the table.

Here we go. I give Dad a hard stare, like, whaddya doin', cool it. But I'm ignored.

Dad pulls a silver flask from his hip pocket, unscrews it, and pours booze into his cup of Coke that's mostly ice now. The ice rises as he pours. Looks like a Coke refill. Whiskey, I'm guessin'. It's what I'd-a done.

Is there such thing as a big sip? Or is that an oxymoron? That's what he takes, anyway. No nursin' it for Dad.

He lifts a pack of Marlboro out of his front shirt pocket, dislodges a cig, and lights it up with the flick of a Bic. Apparently, work talk got him all worked up. He exhales a heavy plume of smoke over the table. Mom leans back, tryin' to dodge Dad's cloud of toxins driftin' into her face.

"Just takin' the edge off," Dad says to Mom, like he's letting her know he's got things under control and he's not going to ruin things again.

Dad tops off his drink and turns his attention to the boy.

"So what are you now, Bobby?"

Bobby jerks a little, eyes wanderin', panicked.

"Years?" Dad says, annoyed. "How old are ya?"

"Eight," the kid says.

"Eight?" Dad repeats. "I know you're eight, son. I'm just jaggin' ya."

Dad laughs. Mom courtesy smiles. The kid pretends he believes him.

"Two more years and you know what that means."

The kid doesn't answer, so Mom jumps in. "What's it mean, honey?"

I'm curious too.

"It means," Dad says, wagging his finger at his boy with one hand while taking a last drag off his cig with the other. "It means he's in double-digits. That's man territory."

I can't tell if the kid gulped for sure but imagine he did. Like, where's he going with this?

"No more Bobby. Bobby's a kid's name."

"What about Bobby Kennedy?" Mom blurts, without running it through her brain first to see if she should self-edit.

"Bobby Kennedy? Bobby Kennedy was a Richie Rich pussy."

Mom doesn't rebut him.

"If Sirhan didn't get him, I'd-a done the spoiled brat myself."

He lights up another one.

"Bob. Now there's a man's name. Easy to spell whether you're drunk or sober. You hear that, Bob? None of that '*eee*' crap."

"Say it with me," Dad continues. By the way he's guzzling whiskey, he's more than a little buzzed, no doubt.

Mom and the kid exchange looks. It's like they both understand they better say it with him.

"Bob," Mom says. The kid says it, too, a beat behind her so quiet I barely hear him.

"Say it again," Dad orders.

"Bob," they both say. This time, a little more in sync.

"Yep, two more years and you're a Bob," Dad says, wagging his finger at the kid again. "But don't go poppin' cherries just yet."

Dad reaches down to touch Mom.

Mom squirms, her eyes unveiling her disgust as she brushes his hand away.

"Yeah, you know what I mean," Dad sneers at Mom.

I can't see, but by the way her arm hasn't pulled back to the rest of her, he must have grabbed her wrist. It's like her arm's being tugged. Finally, her arm falls back to her body.

There's a long moment of uncomfortable silence at the table. Like Mom and the kid are wonderin' what he's gonna say or do next. Like what wire's he gonna cut, red or blue, and what's gonna be the consequences when he does.

Dad takes out another cig. But doesn't light it. Slips it behind his ear.

"Damn, lighten up, it's a party," Dad says.

He unscrews the flask and pours what's left, which isn't much, into his cup.

If this is them in public, Lord knows what goes on behind closed doors.

I'll admit, I'm eatin' a little slower than normal, and nursin' my coffee too, it's like I'm rubberneckin' this thing. What else am I gonna do? It's not like I've got big night out plans. I'll probably catch a Tim the Tool Man rerun when I get home before lights out. That's about it.

Well who's this spry young thing with pep in her step waltzin' up to the family's table? Never seen her before. She's got one of those old-fashioned light blue waitress outfits on, with a white apron in front and everything. Must be a newbie. Seems like overkill. This is Rigby's. Doesn't matter that it's Friday night. There's no rush comin'. And surely Pearl can handle two tables. Wait a second, what am I sayin'? Why do I care if they're overstaffed? Some new youth in the place is a welcome addition. Rigby's could use a new Sasha.

Their plates nearly clean, except for Mom's, Newbie asks if there's anything else she can get them.

"You better believe it," Dad says. "Today's my boy's birthday."

"Oh, well happy birthday to you," the waitress says, smiling at the kid, both dimples showin'.

"How 'bout a big slice of chocolate birthday cake for the boy, and bring me one too," Dad says.

The waitress jots down the order, then looks up at mom. "And you?" she asks.

"She'll have a bite of mine," Dad says. "Gotta watch the hips," he adds with a conspiratorial wink, like Newbie will understand.

I'm tempted to get up and give Dad a whoopin' for bein' such a grade-A double jerk, but by the time I get up and get over there, the moment'll have passed.

As Newbie pirouettes away, Dad barks at her. "Hey."

She pivots to the table.

"Bring a candle, too."

Mom casts her eyes at the kid and forces a smile, like maybe all hope is not lost.

"Candle?" the waitress asks. As soon as she does it hits her.

"Duh . . . for the cake. Two slices of chocolate cake and a candle. Sure thing."

I can tell by his smug grin that Dad thinks he's some kind of hero for rememberin' to ask for a candle on his son's birthday. Or maybe he's just grinnin' at the underage waitress's bottom as she walks away, which is more likely.

Doesn't take more than a few minutes for the waitress to come back empty handed. Which can't be good.

"I'm sorry," she says, frowning. "We're all out of chocolate cake. And no birthday candles."

"You're out of chocolate cake?" Dad asks in belief. "There's nobody here." He twists in his seat scanning the empty joint to emphasize his point. He looks right past me, like I don't even count, like I'm nothing but an unworthy old man.

"I know, I'm sorry. But we're all out," Newbie says.

"You're all out? Or you didn't make any?"

"There isn't any. Or maybe we didn't make any. I don't know, I'm really sorry." She bites her bottom lip.

Dad takes out his flask. Realizes it's empty, and huffs.

"There's pie," the waitress offers. "Cherry and apple."

"Is that what you have on your birthday?" he asks, eyeing her hard. "A big slice of birthday pie?"

Her throat flutters.

"Just bring the apple," Dad says.

"Okay," she says, relieved. "Apple pie. For everyone?"

"Just me and the boy," Dad says with an edge, like she can't get anything right.

He mumbles as she walks away, "Make me look like an asshole in front of my boy." Might be the truest thing he's said all evening.

Myself, I like pie. The fresh ingredients and all that—peaches, apples and berries—reminds me of bein' out in the cool fall air back when I could get up, get around, do anything and go anywhere I wanted without aches and pains. What I wouldn't give to have those days back, but with a sober mind.

Newbie brings two slices of pie and Dad digs in. Gobbles away. No happy birthday singin', birthday toast or anything like that. And of course, he doesn't offer Mom any. But the boy cuts a big slice from his and forklifts it onto her plate. Might not have been as generous if it was chocolate cake, but then again, maybe he would have. Either way, it's nice of him.

I wonder what the boy woulda wished for if Newbie had brought birthday cake and candles to the table. Or is wishing dead to him already? What about Mom? Would she wish for a happier, more loving family? Or for Dad to get hit by a bus? That'd be my wish if I were her. Does she even have evil thoughts like that? Or is she too broken? Self-esteem too crushed to even think such a thing? Here I am thinkin' horrible things because of what I'm observin' over the course of one meal, and they've got their whole lives ahead of them in this mess. Even if they were to escape at some point, I hate to imagine the things they're still gonna be carryin' inside when they're old like me.

Pearl comes by to top of my coffee. I don't really want more, but it gives me an excuse to keep sittin' here.

As awful as I feel for Mom and the kid, there's nothin' I can do. But maybe I can at least make Newbie feel a little better.

"Hold up, Pearl," I say to her as she starts to plod off.

She stops and death glares me.

I dig into my wallet and take out a five. Then nod toward the family. "That guy's been given the new girl the business. Add this to her tip when he leaves. No one deserves that crap."

The top of Pearl's nose scrunches as she looks at me. She glances over her shoulder at the family, then back at me.

"You feelin' alright, Walter?" she asks. It's the most warmth I've ever felt from her. She looks over her shoulder again, like she wants me to look in that direction too.

I look past her.

Poof. They're gone. No family. No plates. No scraps. No birthday pie crumbs. No dirty napkins left behind. No nothin'. Just an empty table.

Shit.

Everything tightens. My limbs. My skin. My heart. Everything.

This isn't good.

Forgettin' things is one thing, but this?

I'm not alright.

I feel like I did back then. The memory of it bringin' it back. My skull crawlin'. Body warmin'. Frontal lobes throbbin'. Arms and legs itchin'. Trapped. On edge. Like I need a drink.

"Walter?" Pearl's concern hovers over me like a passing mist.

I know them. The family. Or knew them. Long ago. They're my family. Me. My boy. My sorry memories, ones I thought I buried long ago. How old would he be now? My boy. Is he even alive? God, I hope he's still alive and didn't take after his old man.

Don't judge me.

I fumble in my pocket. Feel its smooth, round edges. Squeeze it in my palm.

"I'm alright," I assure Pearl.

She's not convinced but walks away.

I lift it out of my pocket. Look at it. Flip it over.

I murmur, "God grant me the Serenity to accept the things I cannot change, the courage to change the things I can, and the wisdom to know the difference."

Kevin Corfield began his writing career as journalist, changed courses to become an advertising writer, and along the way earned a writing credit for a TBS documentary. As a creative director/writer, he has crafted numerous local, national, and international ad campaigns. Relatively new to penning short stories, his fiction has been accepted by the CWC's *Literary Review* and *Half and One*. He lives in Irvine, California.

Perspective

Mary Camarillo
Orange County

The wall phone in my kitchen rings the moment I unlock the front door. He knows my schedule, this Breathing Man. He's been calling every night for the past three weeks.

I sort mail at the Santa Ana Post Office every day except Wednesday and Thursday from two thirty to eleven p.m. unless there's overtime. After I clock out, put my apron and gloves in my locker, grab my purse, and walk out to my car, it takes me twenty-three minutes to drive up the freeway to my condo in Fullerton and two minutes to walk from my carport up the sidewalk to my front door. My neighbors' windows are all dark, but I have a motion-detector security light that flashes on as if it's glad to see me.

The first time Breathing Man called I was sure it was one of my coworkers, wondering why I wasn't at Scooters. I'm trying to stop going out drinking every night, putting coins in a jukebox, heading to someone's house after closing time, staying up until dawn. I'm going to sign up for classes at Fullerton College once I pick up a schedule. I'm joining a gym too.

When Breathing Man didn't speak that first time, I worried someone else in my family had died. But then his breathing turned to moaning and I could hear what sounded like a fist around flesh. I hung up. He called back. I took the phone off the hook and made sure all the doors and windows were locked.

Now I set down my purse and pick up the ringing phone. "You're an asshole," I say, then hang up and take the receiver off the hook. Rita, an older woman at work, says I shouldn't engage. "It only encourages them."

I check that the front door is dead bolted and the security bar on the patio slider is in place. I wonder where Breathing Man is calling from and who at work gave him my number.

When the motion detector lights up the sidewalk outside, my heart picks up speed. It's probably the neighbor's tomcat out on the prowl. Or maybe it's Jeff. Sometimes he drops by, unexpectedly, even though I told him I wanted to break things off now that he's got himself engaged to a woman named Martha who works at a bank.

I wait to hear Jeff's special knock on the front door. Shave and a haircut, two bits. There's only silence. The light flicks off and I hear whistling. It could be a bird. Maybe that's what the tomcat's after.

Jeff's a player and I know better than to take whatever it is we're doing seriously. Once we were parked up in the hills in his van waiting for the lunar eclipse, and Linda Ronstadt came on the radio, singing that song "Crazy." Jeff said every time I hear that song from now on, I'll remember him.

I didn't like how that sounded, like a curse.

Most of the men I work with have crushes on me, but I don't take them seriously either. They all have wives or girlfriends who don't understand them. People who work nine to five are asleep when we finish our shift, ready to blow off steam. Roommates and spouses don't appreciate being wakened up by a party at midnight. That's one reason I live alone.

There are only two single young women on my shift and we both get a lot of attention which threw me at first. I had exactly one date in high school and was more used to being ignored. Now I'm surprised at how easy it is for me to be cruel.

"You remind me of my first girlfriend," Alex, an older man with glasses told me last week at Shooters' over a schooner of beer. "You remind me of my grandfather," I said. I let him pay for my beer though.

"You are the sunshine of my life," Frank, the Black ex-Marine sang as he passed me a joint in the parking lot during our lunch break. I told him to get a better life.

"Fly with me up to Santa Barbara for lunch," Ron, the chubby guy who supervises the dock offered tonight. "Gives you an entirely different perspective, being up above the earth looking down at how small everything is."

I almost said that I'd like to look down at the post office and make sure there's not a black cloud hanging over it, double check that the building is in proportion to the rest of the earth. That would have sounded stupid though.

"You actually know how to fly a plane?" I asked instead.

I'm sure that hurt Ron's feelings. Everyone knows he was a helicopter pilot in Vietnam.

The phone is making the busy signal noise now and buzzes louder and faster, the longer I leave it dangling on its cord. I realize

I've been holding my breath as I put the phone back on the hook. It rings immediately. One night I counted fifty-five rings before I finally picked up. Breathing Man is persistent.

I bought a whistle this morning at the Army Navy Surplus store on my way to work, which is what the police advised when I called. "Blow as loud as you can into the receiver," they said. "That'll discourage him." I answer the phone after seven rings now, thinking that might be a lucky number, and blow the whistle hard, hoping I don't wake the neighbors. I set the phone back on its cradle and listen to the clock ticking in the kitchen.

When I hear the bird noise again, every nerve in my neck flinches. It could be my imagination, of course. Jeff says I live too much in my head, that these are just crank calls, and I shouldn't make a big deal.

The phone doesn't ring for the rest of the night, but I don't sleep much, wondering what kind of bird sings in the dark.

◊◊◊

When I to leave for work the next day, there's a piece of paper under my wiper blade. The neighbors, I figure, complaining again about me parking too close to their freshly painted car. My ride is a tank, a faded out burgundy '62 Ford Fairlane that my uncle left me when he died. It's a gas guzzler, a pain in the butt in these odd/even days when we're all lining up to buy gasoline. My uncle was a stoner who didn't believe in doctors or taking care of his kids or his car. He loved his dogs though. The upholstery still smells like Rottweiler.

HE DOESN'T DESERVE YOU, JENNY, the note reads, in neat block letters, all caps.

I crumble the paper and stuff it in the front pocket of my jeans, looking around, sure someone is watching, but of course there's no one in sight. My neighbors all work during the day. I get in my car and lock the door. My heart hammers my chest. Someone was outside my condo last night, when I was so sure it was the neighbor's cat chasing a bird, when I was blowing my stupid whistle, hoping that would solve all my problems.

Calm down. Besides being harmless the note makes no sense. Who doesn't deserve me? Jeff has no claim. No one does. I'll worry about this later. I need to get to work and find out if Breathing Man has a broken ear drum.

I'm jumpy all through my shift, watching everyone, trying to decide if they can hear what I'm saying, if they're straining to understand. I catch myself studying the handwriting on the tare slips at the scale, looking for neat block letters, all caps. The other mail runners' handwriting is barely legible.

Jeff has called in sick. He and Martha are probably picking out silverware patterns.

◊ ◊ ◊

On Friday, it's after one in the morning when I walk out to my car. I've been running gurneys of mail from the dock to the letter sorting machine for ten hours and my Doc Martens feel like they weigh ten pounds apiece. My friends are already zipping out of the parking lot, speeding over to Scooters before it closes at two. I want to go, and I don't. All night, Jeff's sorted flats next to Christine, the new girl with the big boobs, and I heard him invite her. She probably doesn't know he's engaged. Maybe she doesn't care.

I unlock the door to my car and get in before I see the piece of paper under the wiper blade. It could be one of Rita's flyers. She's selling Herbalife these days. I debate leaving it there, turning on my wipers once I'm on the freeway, letting it soar, gone with the wind, but one thing I am not is a litterer. I get out. The handwriting's familiar, neat, block letters, all caps. I have a sour taste in my mouth. I step under the parking lot light to read what it says.

IF YOU LOVE SOMETHING, SET IT FREE. IF IT COMES BACK, IT'S YOURS. IF NOT, IT WAS NEVER MEANT TO BE.

I've seen this expression before, painted on wooden plaques surrounded by butterflies and daisies. It's from that corny Jonathan Livingston Seagull book and means you can't force anyone to love you. No shit Sherlock.

I'm not in love with anyone. I don't need to set anything free. No one's in love with me either and I am definitely not in need of being set free. I'm actually a little bit too free. Nothing left to lose, like Janis Joplin sang before she OD'd.

I'm not going to Scooter's tonight. I'm going home, taking off these damn shoes, unplugging the phone, and going to bed.

◊ ◊ ◊

The next day as I sort flats next to Jeff he asks if I'm still getting those crank calls.

"He might have given up," I say. "I'm trying something different."

He gives me a smug smile, like he's talking to a child. "You actually thought that whistle would work?"

"The police suggested it." I frown, thinking I've misunderstood. I remember telling Jeff I was going to buy a whistle but how did he know I used it?

He shrugs and turns back to talk to Freddie about some playoff game. That's all Jeff ever talks about. He's a one-dimensional character and I'm lucky to be done with him.

Freddie looks over at me and says. "Tits for brains."

"Excuse me?"

"Jesus, Jenny," Jeff says. "Chill out. We weren't even talking about you."

"Damn straight you weren't talking about me."

Freddie laughs, eyeballing my chest. "Obviously."

I flush red and then Ron asks me to run mail.

"Why can't someone else do it?" I snap.

Ron looks bewildered. "I thought you liked running mail."

I sigh and get up from my stool, glancing over my shoulder before I go outside. The new girl Christine slides into my spot next to Jeff.

Out on the dock, the fresh January air is cold. I breathe in and out. I do like running mail. It's good to move around and the guys on the dock are always happy to see me.

"Jenny, Jenny, Jenny," Alex sings as he pushes a gurney loaded with trays of first-class letters toward me. "Won't you come along with me?"

"As long as it's away from here," I say, my usual response. I grab the gurney and push it back inside the building and onto the scale. I can see Jeff from here, still talking to that scumbag Freddy. Christine is watching me. I'm glad I'm wearing my best-fitting jeans. I weigh the mail, write down the tare weight, and push it over to the letter-sorting machine, strutting a little as I pass the flats sorting cases.

Ted, the machine supervisor, points to the empty gurney waiting for me. He's my least favorite supervisor—ex-military, crew cut, clip-on tie. He barks at everyone like he's still in Vietnam, and he glares at me now.

"There's more on the dock," I say. "I'll be right back."

Ted yells something else but I don't hear him. I push the empty gurney back outside. When I pass Jeff, he doesn't even look up.

The guys out on the dock are still unloading the truck. "Hurry," I say. "The machine's almost out of mail."

"Can you manage an APC?" Frank says. "If it's too heavy we can break it down. But if you're in a hurry—"

"I can handle an APC." That's what we call the older rolling mail containers. They're supposed to be phasing them out because of all the injuries. It's easy to smash a finger on the metal center shelf, trying to close it, and bleed over the mail.

Alex looks over at me and smiles. "Jenny can handle anything. She's small but she's mighty."

Frank laughs. "You going to Scooters tonight, Jenny-girl?"

"You buying?" I say, because that's what I always say.

I'm tired of saying what I always say. I'm sick of everyone thinking I'm small and I wish Frank would stop calling me Jenny-girl. He rolls the APC toward me. These containers are more than a foot taller than I am and this one's fully loaded. I can tell right away it's too heavy, but I jump behind it anyway and start pushing, hoping for the best.

Inside the building there's a gurney on the scale ahead of me, so I have to wait, which sucks because I need the momentum. Ron walks past me on his way out to the dock and stops. "They should have broken that down for you. I don't want you to get hurt."

"Don't be ridiculous. I'm fine."

The gurney moves off the scale. I angle all of my one hundred twenty-five pounds into the APC, and it rolls forward. I write down the weight. My heart's pounding, I'm breathing hard, my face feels hot, but I'm proud of myself. Ron shakes his head and goes outside.

I can hear Freddie laughing as I push the container off the scale and roll it past the flats cases. Jeff's laughing too. Christine leans back and grins at me as if she's sucking on a piece of hard candy. Jeff's told everyone about the whistle and the phone calls, and they all think I'm stupid. I *am* stupid for working here. I shove the container toward the letter-sorting machine. I'll quit tomorrow and go back to school full time.

"What the hell's wrong with you?" Ted yells, loud enough for everyone to hear above all the noise. "I told you we were shutting down. Were you not listening?"

I look at the clock. I didn't realize it was so late. Ted's right, I wasn't listening. "What do you want me to do?" My voice cracks.

"Tell Ron to get his ass in here. I don't know why he thinks you girls can run mail. You should stick to sorting flats."

I don't trust myself to answer. Ted turns away from me, disgusted.

I head outside toward the dock but when Jeff leans back and winks at me, like he's on my side, I lose it. I spin around, grab a tray filled with old tare slips, empty gum wrappers, and crumpled cigarette packs and go straight toward him. "Stop laughing at me," I say as I dump the contents over his head.

"What the fuck!" Jeff jumps up and grabs my wrists. "What'd you do that for?"

I jerk wildly to get away from him, and then scream so loud I know my throat will ache in the morning. Everyone is standing now, staring at us. Christine looks scared.

"What do you want from me?" Jeff's still clenching my wrists.

I want him to be scared of me too. I want him to look at me like I'm someone.

Freddie's behind Jeff now, hands on his shoulders. "Let her go, man. You'll get suspended."

Jeff pulls away. "Crazy bitch. Stay away from me."

I am not going to cry.

Ted is there now, with his clipboard and his stupid tie. "Everyone get back to work. The two of you, in my office."

"She started it," Jeff says.

He sounds like a six-year-old. Even Ted smirks. "You're twice her size," he says. "And at least fifteen years older. You should know better."

◊◊◊

I watch Ron make entries in a blue leather flight logbook. His handwriting is neat, block letters, all caps. It's his day off and I've called in sick. We're flying up to Santa Barbara for lunch. He knows a place where we can eat fresh lobsters.

Last week, everyone at work was gossiping about how I only got a letter of warning for the tray incident while Jeff got suspended.

This week, Jeff's fiancé, Martha, punched Christine in the parking lot and broke her nose. Now everyone's gossiping about Martha. Rumor is she and Jeff are eloping to Vegas next weekend. At least Breathing Man has stopped calling.

Ron looks at me and grins. "Clear skies today. Should be a smooth flight."

He doesn't seem the type to leave notes under wiper blades. He's not my type at all. He's just a chubby guy who knows how to fly a plane. We taxi and take off, flying east toward the hills. After a few minutes he says, "There's the post office, right below us."

I see a tiny box among even tinier boxes. What must be vehicles look like miniscule ants. Tomorrow I'll park my tank of a car in the employee lot and go inside that building for whatever drama will surely unfold but I'll try to remember how insignificant it all looks from up here.

"Thanks for doing this," I tell Ron. "Lunch is on me."

He nods and turns the plane north. The post office building gets smaller and smaller and is finally no longer in sight.

Mary Camarillo is the author of the award-winning novels *Those People Behind Us* and *The Lockhart Women*. Her poems and short fiction have appeared in publications such as *Inlandia*, *166 Palms*, *Sonora Review*, and *The Ear*. Mary lives in Huntington Beach, California, with her husband, who plays ukulele, and their terrorist cat, Riley, who makes frequent appearances on Instagram.

For more information, please visit Mary at her website https://www.MaryCamarillo.com and sign up for her newsletter.

AFTERWORD

As an editor, one of the things I enjoy most about my profession is the widely diverse subjects I have the privilege of working on. Over the years I have learned, among other things, everything I need to know about landsailing, new emerging methods in education, dragons—both here on Earth and on other planets—and detailed family genealogies, as well as varied and delightful forms of poetry.

Editing *Best of the Best: 2024* for the California Writers Club has been just such a project, exposing me to the heterogeneous creative efforts of members across the state. And learning a little about those writers along the way.

I hope you have enjoyed reading this anthology as much as I have enjoyed editing it.

~Jenny Margotta
April 2024

◊ ◊ ◊

You close the book, you gaze outside.

Poems, stories, from across the State

reverberate, receding from your mind.

But you still sense their residue, their

taste . . .

This is what fresh words are for:

a beckoning, an open door. ❖

Kate Adams

2023

Made in the USA
Las Vegas, NV
28 September 2024

95938373R00216